NO LONGER PROPERTY OF
SEATTLE PUBLIC LIBRARY

INSIDE JOB

I reached out to touch his face with my imaginary hand.

He froze.

"That's what you were afraid of," I told him. "You never dreamed I could reach through a phone screen to do *this*." I reached into his head, felt smooth muscle and grainy bone and sinus cavities like bubbles. He tossed his head, but my hand went with it. I ran imaginary fingertips along the smooth inner surface of his skull.

Then he screamed.

D0099425

By Larry Niven
Published by Ballantine Books:

The Known Space series:
PROTECTOR
RINGWORLD
THE RINGWORLD ENGINEERS
THE RINGWORLD THRONE
THREE BOOKS OF KNOWN SPACE:
  World of Ptavvs, A Gift of Earth, Tales of Known Space

Other titles:
CRASHLANDER
FLATLANDER
THE INTEGRAL TREES

With Jerry Pournelle:
FOOTFALL
LUCIFER'S HAMMER

Books published by The Random House Publishing Group
are available at quantity discounts on bulk purchases for
premium, educational, fund-raising, and special sales use.
For details, please call 1-800-733-3000.

FLATLANDER

Larry Niven

A Del Rey® Book

BALLANTINE BOOKS • NEW YORK

Sale of this book without a front cover may be unauthorized. If this book is coverless, it may have been reported to the publisher as "unsold or destroyed" and neither the author nor the publisher may have received payment for it.

A Del Rey® Book
Published by The Random House Publishing Group

Copyright © 1995 by Larry Niven

All rights reserved.

Published in the United States by Del Rey Books, an imprint of The Random House Publishing Group, a division of Random House, Inc., New York, and simultaneously in Canada by Random House of Canada Limited, Toronto.

DEL REY is a registered trademark and the Del Rey colophon is a trademark of Random House, Inc.

ISBN 978-0-345-39480-4

Printed in the United States of America

www.delreybooks.com

First Edition: June 1995

OPM   18   17   16   15   14   13

For Frederik Pohl
and the memory of John W. Campbell.

*

DEATH BY ECSTASY

First came the routine request for a breach of privacy permit. A police officer took down the details and forwarded the request to a clerk, who saw that the tape reached the appropriate civic judge. The judge was reluctant, for privacy is a precious thing in a world of eighteen billion, but in the end he could find no reason to refuse. On November 2, 2123, he granted the permit.

The tenant's rent was two weeks in arrears. If the manager of Monica Apartments had asked for eviction, he would have been refused. But Owen Jennison did not answer his doorbell or his room phone. Nobody could recall seeing him in many weeks. Apparently the manager only wanted to know that he was all right.

And so he was allowed to use his passkey, with an officer standing by.

And so they found the tenant of 1809.

And when they had looked in his wallet, they called me.

I was at my desk at ARM Headquarters, making useless notes and wishing it were lunchtime.

At this stage the Loren case was all correlate and wait. It involved an organlegging gang apparently run by a single man yet big enough to cover half the North American west coast. We had considerable data on the gang—methods of operation, centers of activity, a few former customers, even a tentative handful of names—but nothing that would give

1

us an excuse to act. So it was a matter of shoving what we had into the computer, watching the few suspected associates of the gang lord Loren, and waiting for a break.

The months of waiting were ruining my sense of involvement.

My phone buzzed.

I put the pen down and said, "Gil Hamilton."

A small dark face regarded me with soft black eyes. "I am Detective-Inspector Julio Ordaz of the Los Angeles Police Department. Are you related to an Owen Jennison?"

"Owen? No, we're not related. Is he in trouble?"

"You do know him, then."

"Sure I know him. Is he here, on Earth?"

"It would seem so." Ordaz had no accent, but the lack of colloquialisms in his speech made him sound vaguely foreign. "We will need positive identification, Mr. Hamilton. Mr. Jennison's ident lists you as next of kin."

"That's funny. I—back up a minute. Is Owen dead?"

"Somebody is dead, Mr. Hamilton. He carried Mr. Jennison's ident in his wallet."

"Okay. Now, Owen Jennison was a citizen of the Belt. This may have interworld complications. That makes it ARM's business. Where's the body?"

"We found him in an apartment rented under his own name. Monica Apartments, Lower Los Angeles, room 1809."

"Good. Don't move anything you haven't moved already. I'll be right over."

Monica Apartments was a nearly featureless concrete block, eighty stories tall, a thousand feet across the edges of its square base. Lines of small balconies gave the sides a sculptured look above a forty-foot inset ledge that would keep tenants from dropping objects on pedestrians. A hundred buildings just like it made Lower Los Angeles look lumpy from the air.

Inside, a lobby done in anonymous modern. Lots of metal and plastic showing, lightweight comfortable chairs without arms, big ashtrays, plenty of indirect lighting, a low ceiling, no wasted space. The whole room might have been stamped out with a die. It wasn't supposed to look small, but it did, and that warned you what the rooms would be like. You'd pay your rent by the cubic centimeter.

I found the manager's office and the manager, a soft-looking man with watery blue eyes. His conservative paper suit, dark red, seemed chosen to render him invisible, as did the style of his brown hair, worn long and combed straight back without a part. "Nothing like this has ever happened here," he confided as he led me to the elevator banks. "Nothing. It would have been bad enough without his being a Belter, but *now*—" He cringed at the thought. "Newsmen. They'll *smother* us."

The elevator was coffin-sized, but with the handrails on the inside. It went up fast and smooth. I stepped out into a long, narrow hallway.

What would Owen have been doing in a place like this? Machinery lived here, not people.

Maybe it wasn't Owen. Ordaz had been reluctant to commit himself. Besides, there's no law against picking pockets. You couldn't enforce such a law on this crowded planet. Everyone on Earth was a pickpocket.

Sure. Someone had died carrying Owen's wallet.

I walked down the hallway to 1809.

It was Owen who sat grinning in the armchair. I took one good look at him, enough to be sure, and then I looked away and didn't look back. But the rest of it was even more unbelievable.

No Belter could have taken that apartment. I was born in Kansas, but even I felt the awful anonymous chill. It would have driven Owen bats.

"I don't believe it," I said.

"Did you know him well, Mr. Hamilton?"

"About as well as two men can know each other. He and I spent three years mining rocks in the main asteroid belt. You don't keep secrets under those conditions."

"Yet you didn't know he was on Earth."

"That's what I can't understand. Why the blazes didn't he phone me if he was in trouble?"

"You're an ARM," said Ordaz. "An operative in the United Nations Police."

He had a point. Owen was as honorable as any man I knew, but honor isn't the same in the Belt. Belters think flatlanders are all crooks. They don't understand that to a flatlander, picking pockets is a game of skill. Yet a Belter sees smuggling as the same kind of game, with no dishonesty involved. He balances the thirty percent tariff against possible confiscation of his cargo, and if the odds are right, he gambles.

Owen could have been doing something that would look honest to him but not to me.

"He could have been in something sticky," I admitted. "But I can't see him killing himself over it. And ... not here. He wouldn't have come here."

Room 1809 was a living room and a bathroom and a closet. I'd glanced into the bathroom, knowing what I would find. It was the size of a comfortable shower stall. An adjustment panel outside the door would cause it to extrude various appurtenances in memory plastic, to become a washroom, a shower stall, a toilet, a dressing room, a steam cabinet. Luxurious in everything but size as long as you pushed the right buttons.

The living room was more of the same. A king bed was invisible behind a wall. The kitchen alcove, with basin and oven and grill and toaster, would fold into another wall; the sofa, chairs, and tables would vanish into the floor. One tenant and three guests would make a crowded cocktail party, a cozy dinner gathering, a closed poker game. Card table, dinner table, coffee table were all there, surrounded by the appropriate chairs, but only one set at a time would emerge from the floor. There was no refrigerator, no freezer, no bar. If a tenant needed food or drink, he phoned down and the supermarket on the third floor would send it up.

The tenant of such an apartment had his comfort. But he owned nothing. There was room for him; there was none for his possessions. This was one of the inner apartments. An age ago there would have been an air shaft, but air shafts took up expensive room. The tenant didn't even have a window. He lived in a comfortable box.

Just now the items extruded were the overstuffed reading armchair, two small side tables, a footstool, and the kitchen alcove. Owen Jennison sat grinning in the armchair. Naturally he grinned. Little more than dried skin covered the natural grin of his skull.

"It's a small room," Ordaz said, "but not too small. Millions of people live this way. In any case, a Belter would hardly be a claustrophobe."

"No. Owen flew a singleship before he joined us. Three months at a stretch in a cabin so small, you couldn't stand up with the air lock closed. Not claustrophobia, but—" I swept my arm about the room. "What do you see that's his?"

Small as it was, the closet was nearly empty. A set of street clothes, a paper shirt, a pair of shoes, a small brown overnight case. All new. The few items in the bathroom medicine chest had been equally new and equally anonymous.

Ordaz said, "Well?"

"Belters are transients. They don't own much, but what they do own, they guard. Small possessions, relics, souvenirs. I can't believe he wouldn't have had *something*."

"His space suit?"

"You think that's unlikely? It's not. The inside of his pressure suit is a Belter's home. Sometimes it's the only home he's got. He spends a fortune decorating it. If he loses his suit, he's not a Belter anymore.

"No, I don't insist he'd have brought his suit. But he'd have had *something*. His phial of Marsdust. The bit of nickel-iron they took out of his chest. Or, if he left all his souvenirs home, he'd have picked up things on Earth. But in this room—there's *nothing*."

"Perhaps," Ordaz suggested delicately, "he didn't notice his surroundings."

And somehow that brought it all home.

Owen Jennison sat grinning in a water-stained silk dressing gown. His space-darkened face lightened abruptly beneath his chin, giving way to normal suntan. His blond hair, too long, had been cut Earth style; no trace remained of the Belter strip cut he'd worn all his life. A month's growth of untended beard covered half his face. A small black cylinder protruded from the top of his head. An electric cord trailed from the top of the cylinder and ran to a wall socket.

The cylinder was a droud, a current addict's transformer.

I stepped closer to the corpse and bent to look. The droud was a standard make, but it had been altered. Your standard current addict's droud will pass only a trickle of current into the brain. Owen must have been getting ten times the usual charge, easily enough to damage his brain in a month's time.

I reached out and touched the droud with my imaginary hand.

Ordaz was standing quietly beside me, letting me make my examination without interruption. Naturally he had no way of knowing about my restricted psi powers.

With my imaginary fingertips I touched the droud in Owen's head, then ran them down to a tiny hole in his scalp and farther.

It was a standard surgical job. Owen could have had it done anywhere. A hole in his scalp, invisible under the hair, nearly impossible to find even if you knew what you were looking for. Even your best friends wouldn't know unless they caught you with the droud plugged in. But the tiny hole marked a bigger plug set in the bone of the skull. I touched the ecstasy plug with my imaginary fingertips, then ran them down the hair-fine wire going deep into Owen's brain, down into the pleasure center.

No, the extra current hadn't killed him. What had killed Owen was his lack of willpower. He had been unwilling to get up.

He had starved to death sitting in that chair. There were plastic squeezebottles all around his feet and a couple still on the end tables. All empty. They must have been full a month ago. Owen hadn't died of thirst. He had died of starvation, and his death had been planned.

Owen my crewmate. Why hadn't he come to me? I'm half a Belter myself. Whatever his trouble, I'd have gotten him out somehow. A little smuggling—what of it? Why had he arranged to tell me only after it was over?

The apartment was so clean, so clean. You had to bend close to smell the death; the air-conditioning whisked it all away.

He'd been very methodical. The kitchen was open so that a catheter could lead from Owen to the sink. He'd given himself enough water to last out the month; he'd paid his rent a month in advance. He'd cut the droud cord by hand, and he'd cut it short, deliberately tethering himself to a wall socket beyond reach of the kitchen.

A complex way to die, but rewarding in its way. A month of ecstasy, a month of the highest physical pleasure man can attain. I could imagine him giggling every time he remembered he was starving to death. With food only a few footsteps away . . . but he'd have to pull out the droud to reach it. Perhaps he had postponed the decision and postponed it again . . .

Owen and I and Homer Chandrasekhar, we had lived for three years in a cramped shell surrounded by vacuum. What was there to know about Owen Jennison that I hadn't known? Where was the weakness we didn't share? If Owen had done this, so could I. And I was afraid.

"Very neat," I whispered. "Belter neat."

"Typically Belter, would you say?"

"I would not. Belters don't commit suicide. Certainly not this way. If a Belter had to go, he'd blow his ship's drive and die like a star."

"Well," Ordaz said. "Well." He was uncomfortable. The facts spoke for themselves, yet he was reluctant to call me a liar. He fell back on formality.

"Mr. Hamilton, do you identify this man as Owen Jennison?"

"It's him." He'd always been a touch overweight, yet I'd recognized him the moment I saw him. "But let's be sure." I pulled the dirty dressing gown back from Owen's shoulder. A nearly-perfect circle of scar tissue, eight inches across, spread over the left side of his chest. "See that?"

"We noticed it, yes. An old burn?"

"Owen's the only man I know who could show you a meteor scar on his skin. It blasted him in the shoulder one day while he was outside the ship. Sprayed vaporized pressure-suit steel all over his skin. The doc pulled a tiny grain of nickel-iron from the center of the scar, just below the skin. Owen always carried that grain of nickel-iron. Always," I said, looking at Ordaz.

"We didn't find it."

"Okay."

"I'm sorry to put you through this, Mr. Hamilton. It was you who insisted we leave the body in situ."

"Yes. Thank you."

Owen grinned at me from the reading chair. I felt the pain in my throat and in the pit of my stomach. Once I had lost my right arm. Losing Owen felt the same way.

"I'd like to know more about this," I said. "Will you let me know the details as soon as you get them?"

"Of course. Through the ARM office?"

"Yes." This wasn't ARM business, despite what I'd told Ordaz, but ARM prestige would help. "I want to know why Owen died. Maybe he just cracked up . . . culture shock or something. But if someone hounded him to death, I'll have his blood."

"Surely the administration of justice is better left to—" Ordaz stopped, confused. Did I speak as an ARM or as a citizen?

I left him wondering.

The lobby held a scattering of tenants entering and leaving elevators or just sitting around. I stood outside the elevator for a moment, searching passing faces for the erosion of personality that must be there.

Mass-produced comfort. Room to sleep and eat and watch tridee but no room to *be* anyone. Living here, one would own nothing. What kind of people would live like that? They should have looked all alike, moved in unison, like the string of images in a barber's mirrors.

Then I spotted wavy brown hair and a dark red paper suit. The manager? I had to get close before I was sure. His face was the face of a permanent stranger.

He saw me coming and smiled without enthusiasm. "Oh, hello, Mr. . . . uh . . . Did you find . . ." He couldn't think of the right question.

"Yes," I said, answering it anyway. "But I'd like to know some things. Owen Jennison lived here for six weeks, right?"

"Six weeks and two days, before we opened his room."

"Did he ever have visitors?"

The man's eyebrows went up. We'd drifted in the direction of his office, and I was close enough to read the name on the door: JASPER MILLER, MANAGER. "Of course not," he said. "Anyone would have noticed that something was wrong."

"You mean he took the room for the express purpose of dying? You saw him once and never again?"

"I suppose he might . . . no, wait." The manager thought deeply. "No. He registered on a Thursday. I noticed the Belter tan, of course. Then on Friday he went out. I happened to see him pass."

"Was that the day he got the droud? No, skip it; you wouldn't know that. Was it the last time you saw him go out?"

"Yes, it was."

"Then he could have had visitors late Thursday or early Friday."

The manager shook his head very positively.

"Why not?"

"You see, Mr., uh . . ."

"Hamilton."

"We have a holo camera on every floor, Mr. Hamilton. It takes a picture of each tenant the first time he goes to his room and then never again. Privacy is one of the services a tenant buys with his room." The manager drew himself up a little as he said this. "For the same reason, the holo camera takes a picture of anyone who is *not* a tenant. The tenants are thus protected from unwarranted intrusions."

"And there were no visitors to any of the rooms on Owen's floor?"

"No, sir, there were not."

"Your tenants are a solitary bunch."

"Perhaps they are."

"I suppose a computer in the basement decides who is and is not a tenant."

"Of course."

"So for six weeks Owen Jennison sat alone in his room. In all that time he was totally ignored."

Miller tried to turn his voice cold, but he was too nervous. "We try to give our guests privacy. If Mr. Jennison had wanted help of any kind, he had only to pick up the house phone. He could have called me, or the pharmacy, or the supermarket downstairs."

"Well, thank you, Mr. Miller. That's all I wanted to know. I wanted to know how Owen Jennison could wait six weeks to die while nobody noticed."

Miller swallowed. "He was dying all that time?"

"Yah."

"We had no way of knowing. How could we? I don't see how you can blame us."

"I don't, either," I said, and brushed by. Miller had been close enough, so I had lashed out at him. Now I was ashamed. The man was perfectly right. Owen could have had help if he'd wanted it.

I stood outside, looking up at the jagged blue line of sky that showed between the tops of the buildings. A taxi floated into view, and I beeped my clicker at it, and it dropped.

* * *

I went back to ARM Headquarters. Not to work—I couldn't have done any work, not under the circumstances—but to talk to Julie.

Julie. A tall girl, pushing thirty, with green eyes and long hair streaked red and gold. And two wide brown forceps marks above her right knee, but they weren't showing now. I looked into her office through the one-way glass and watched her at work.

She sat in a contour couch, smoking. Her eyes were closed. Sometimes her brow would furrow as she concentrated. Sometimes she would snatch a glance at the clock, then close her eyes again.

I didn't interrupt her. I knew the importance of what she was doing.

Julie. She wasn't beautiful. Her eyes were a little too far apart, her chin too square, her mouth too wide. It didn't matter. Because Julie could read minds.

She was the ideal date. She was everything a man needed. A year ago, the day after the night I killed my first man, I had been in a terribly destructive mood. Somehow Julie had turned it into a mood of manic exhilaration. We'd run wild through a supervised anarchy park, running up an enormous bill. We'd hiked five miles without going anywhere, facing backward on a downtown slidewalk. At the end we'd been utterly fatigued, too tired to think . . . But two weeks ago it had been a warm, cuddly, comfortable night. Two people happy with each other, no more than that. Julie was what you needed, anytime, anywhere.

Her male harem must have been the largest in history. To pick up on the thoughts of a male ARM, Julie had to be in love with him. Luckily there was room in her for a lot of love. She didn't demand that we be faithful. A good half of us were married. But there had to be love for each of Julie's men, or Julie couldn't protect him.

She was protecting us now. Each fifteen minutes Julie was making contact with a specific ARM agent. Psi powers are notoriously undependable, but Julie was an exception. If we got in a hole, Julie was always there to get us out . . . provided that some idiot didn't interrupt her at work.

So I stood outside, waiting, with a cigarette in my imaginary hand.

The cigarette was for practice, to stretch the mental muscles. In its way my "hand" was as dependable as Julie's mind-touch, possibly because of its very limitations. Doubt your psi powers and they're gone. A rigidly defined third arm was more reasonable than some warlock ability to make objects move by wishing at them. I knew how an arm felt and what it would do.

Why do I spend so much time lifting cigarettes? Well, it's the biggest weight I can lift without strain. And there's another reason . . . something taught me by Owen.

At ten minutes to fifteen Julie opened her eyes, rolled out of the contour couch, and came to the door. "Hi, Gil," she said sleepily. "Trouble?"

"Yah. A friend of mine just died. I thought you'd better know." I handed her a cup of coffee.

She nodded. We had a date tonight, and this would change its character. Knowing that, she probed lightly.

"Jesus!" she said, recoiling. "How . . . how horrible. I'm terribly sorry, Gil. Date's off, right?"

"Unless you want to join the ceremonial drunk."

She shook her head vigorously. "I didn't know him. It wouldn't be proper. Besides, you'll be wallowing in your own memories, Gil. A lot of them will be private. I'd cramp your style if you knew I was there to probe. Now, if Homer Chandrasekhar were here, it'd be different."

"I wish he were. He'll have to throw his own drunk. Maybe with some of Owen's girls, if they're around."

"You know what I feel," she said.

"Just what I do."

"I wish I could help."

"You always help." I glanced at the clock. "Your coffee break's about over."

"Slave driver." Julie took my earlobe between thumb and

forefinger. "Do him proud," she said, and went back to her soundproof room.

She always helps. She doesn't even have to speak. Just knowing that Julie has read my thoughts, that someone understands . . . that's enough.

All alone at three in the afternoon, I started my ceremonial drunk.

The ceremonial drunk is a young custom, not yet tied down by formality. There is no set duration. No specific toasts must be given. Those who participate must be close friends of the deceased, but there is no set number of participants.

I started at the Luau, a place of cool blue light and running water. Outside it was fifteen-thirty in the afternoon, but inside it was evening in the Hawaiian Islands of centuries ago. Already the place was half-full. I picked a corner table with considerable elbow room and dialed for Luau grog. It came, cold, brown, and alcoholic, its straw tucked into a cone of ice.

There had been three of us at Cubes Forsythe's ceremonial drunk one black Ceres night four years ago. A jolly group we were, too, Owen and me and the widow of our third crewman. Gwen Forsythe blamed us for her husband's death. I was just out of the hospital with a right arm that ended at the shoulder, and I blamed Cubes and Owen and myself all at once. Even Owen had turned dour and introspective. We couldn't have picked a worse trio or a worse night for it.

But custom called, and we were there. Then as now, I found myself probing my own personality for the wound that was a missing crewman, a missing friend. Introspecting.

Gilbert Hamilton. Born of flatlander parents in April 2093 in Topeka, Kansas. Born with two arms and no sign of wild talents.

Flatlander: a Belter term referring to Earthmen, particularly to Earthmen who had never seen space. I'm not sure my parents ever looked at the stars. They managed the third largest farm in Kansas, ten square miles of arable land between two wide strips of city paralleling two strips of turnpike. We were city people, like all flatlanders, but when the crowds got to be too much for my brothers and me, we had vast stretches of land to be alone in. Ten square miles of playground, with nothing to hamper us but the crops and automachinery.

We looked at the stars, my brothers and I. You can't see stars from the city; the lights hide them. Even in the fields you couldn't see them around the lighted horizon. But straight overhead, they were there: black sky scattered with bright dots and sometimes a flat white moon.

At twenty I gave up my UN citizenship to become a Belter. I wanted stars, and the Belt government holds title to most of the solar system. There are fabulous riches in the rocks, riches belonging to a scattered civilization of a few hundred thousand Belters, and I wanted my share of that, too.

It wasn't easy. I wouldn't be eligible for a singleship license for ten years. Meanwhile I would be working for others and learning to avoid mistakes before they killed me. Half the flatlanders who join the Belt die in space before they can earn their licenses.

I mined tin on Mercury and exotic chemicals from Jupiter's atmosphere. I hauled ice from Saturn's rings and quicksilver from Europa. One year our pilot made a mistake pulling up to a new rock, and we damn near had to walk home. Cubes Forsythe was with us then. He managed to fix the com laser and aim it at Icarus to bring us help. Another time the mechanic who did the maintenance job on our ship forgot to replace an absorber, and we all got roaring drunk on the alcohol that built up in our breathing air. The three of us caught the mechanic six months later. I hear he lived.

Most of the time I was part of a three-man crew. The members changed constantly. When Owen Jennison joined us, he replaced a man who had finally earned his singleship license and couldn't wait to start hunting rocks on his own.

He was too eager. I learned later that he'd made one round trip and half of another.

Owen was my age but more experienced, a Belter born and bred. His blue eyes and blond cockatoo's crest were startling against the dark of his Belter tan, the tan that ended so abruptly where his neck ring cut off the space-intense sunlight his helmet let through. He was permanently chubby, but in free fall it was as if he'd been born with wings. I took to copying his way of moving, much to Cubes's amusement.

I didn't make my own mistake until I was twenty-six.

We were using bombs to put a rock in a new orbit. A contract job. The technique is older than fusion drives, as old as early Belt colonization, and it's still cheaper and faster than using a ship's drive to tow the rock. You use industrial fusion bombs, small and clean, and you set them so that each explosion deepens the crater to channel the force of later blasts.

We'd set four blasts already, four white fireballs that swelled and faded as they rose. When the fifth blast went off, we were hovering nearby on the other side of the rock.

The fifth blast shattered the rock.

Cubes had set the bomb. My own mistake was a shared one, because any of the three of us should have had the sense to take off right then. Instead, we watched, cursing, as valuable oxygen-bearing rock became nearly valueless shards. We watched the shards spread slowly into a cloud . . . and while we watched, one fast-moving shard reached us. Moving too slowly to vaporize when it hit, it nonetheless sheared through a triple crystal-iron hull, slashed through my upper arm, and pinned Cubes Forsythe to a wall by his heart.

A couple of nudists came in. They stood blinking among the booths while their eyes adjusted to the blue twilight, then converged with glad cries on the group two tables over. I watched and listened with an eye and an ear, thinking how different flatlander nudists were from Belter nudists. These all looked alike. They all had muscles, they had no interesting scars, they carried their credit cards in identical shoulder pouches, and they all shaved the same areas.

. . . We always went nudist in the big bases. Most people did. It was a natural reaction to the pressure suits we wore day and night while out in the rocks. Get him into a shirtsleeve environment, and your normal Belter sneers at a shirt. But it's only for comfort. Give him a good reason and your Belter will don shirt and pants as quickly as the next guy.

But not Owen. After he got that meteor scar, I never saw him wear a shirt. Not just in the Ceres domes but anywhere there was air to breathe. He just had to show that scar.

A cool blue mood settled on me, and I remembered . . .

. . . Owen Jennison lounging on a corner of my hospital bed, telling me of the trip back. I couldn't remember anything after that rock had sheared through my arm.

I should have bled to death in seconds. Owen hadn't given me the chance. The wound was ragged; Owen had sliced it clean to the shoulder with one swipe of a com laser. Then he'd tied a length of fiberglass curtain over the flat surface and knotted it tight under my remaining armpit. He told me about putting me under two atmospheres of pure oxygen as a substitute for replacing the blood I'd lost. He told me how he'd reset the fusion drive for four gees to get me back in time. By rights we should have gone up in a cloud of starfire and glory.

"So there goes my reputation. The whole Belt knows how I rewired our drive. A lot of 'em figure if I'm stupid enough to risk my own life like that, I'd risk theirs, too."

"So you're not safe to travel with."

"Just so. They're starting to call me Four Gee Jennison."

"You think you've got problems? I can just see how it'll be when I get out of this bed. 'You do something stupid, Gil?' The hell of it is, it *was* stupid."

"So lie a little."

"Uh huh. Can we sell the ship?"

"Nope. Gwen inherited a third interest in it from Cubes. She won't sell."

"Then we're effectively broke."

"Except for the ship. We need another crewman."

"Correction. *You* need *two* crewmen. Unless you want to fly with a one-armed man. I can't afford a transplant."

Owen hadn't tried to offer me a loan. That would have been insulting even if he'd had the money. "What's wrong with a prosthetic?"

"An iron arm? Sorry, no. I'm squeamish."

Owen had looked at me strangely, but all he'd said was, "Well, we'll wait a bit. Maybe you'll change your mind."

He hadn't pressured me. Not then and not later, after I'd left the hospital and taken an apartment while I waited to get used to a missing arm. If he thought I would eventually settle for a prosthetic, he was mistaken.

Why? It's not a question I can answer. Others obviously feel differently; there are millions of people walking around with metal and plastic and silicone parts. Part man, part machine, and how do they themselves know which is the real person?

I'd rather be dead than part metal. Call it a quirk. Call it, even, the same quirk that makes my skin crawl when I find a place like Monica Apartments. A human being should be all human. He should have habits and possessions peculiarly his own, he should not try to look like or behave like anyone but himself, and he should not be half robot.

So there I was, Gil the Arm, learning to eat with my left hand.

An amputee never entirely loses what he's lost. My missing fingers itched. I moved to keep from barking my missing elbow on sharp corners. I reached for things, then swore when they didn't come.

Owen had hung around, though his own emergency funds must have been running low. I hadn't offered to sell my third of the ship, and he hadn't asked.

There had been a girl. Now I'd forgotten her name. One night I had been at her place waiting for her to get dressed—a dinner date—and I'd happened to see a nail file she'd left on a table. I'd picked it up. I'd almost tried to file my nails but remembered in time. Irritated, I had tossed the file back on the table—and missed.

Like an idiot I'd tried to catch it with my right hand.

And I'd caught it.

I'd never suspected myself of having psychic powers. You have to be in the right frame of mind to use a psi power. But who had ever had a better opportunity than I did that night, with a whole section of brain tuned to the nerves and muscles of my right arm, and no right arm?

I'd held the nail file in my imaginary hand. I'd felt it, just as I'd felt my missing fingernails getting too long. I had run my thumb along the rough steel surface; I had turned the file in my fingers. Telekinesis for lift, esper for touch.

"That's it," Owen had said the next day. "That's all we need. One crewman, and you with your eldritch powers. You practice, see how strong you can get that lift. I'll go find a sucker."

"He'll have to settle for a sixth of net. Cubes's widow will want her share."

"Don't worry. I'll swing it."

"Don't worry!" I'd waved a pencil stub at him. Even in Ceres's gentle gravity it was as much as I could lift—then. "You don't think TK and esper can make do for a real arm, do you?"

"It's better than a real arm. You'll see. You'll be able to reach through your suit with it without losing pressure. What Belter can do that?"

"Sure."

"What the hell do you want, Gil? Someone should give you your arm back? You can't have that. You lost it fair and square, through stupidity. Now it's your choice. Do you fly with an imaginary arm, or do you go back to Earth?"

"I can't go back. I don't have the fare."

"Well?"

"Okay, okay. Go find us a crewman. Someone I can impress with my imaginary arm."

I sucked meditatively on a second Luau grog. By now all the booths were full, and a second layer was forming around the bar. The voices made a continuous hypnotic roar. Cocktail hour had arrived.

... He'd swung it, all right. On the strength of my imaginary arm, Owen had talked a kid named Homer Chandrasekhar into joining our crew.

He'd been right about my arm, too.

Others with similar senses can reach farther, up to halfway around the world. My unfortunately literal imagination had restricted me to a psychic hand. But my esper fingertips were more sensitive, more dependable. I could lift more weight. Today, in Earth's gravity, I can lift a full shot glass.

I found I could reach through a cabin wall to feel for breaks in the circuits behind it. In vacuum I could brush dust from the outside of my faceplate. In port I did magic tricks.

I'd almost ceased to feel like a cripple. It was all due to Owen. In six months of mining I had paid off my hospital bills and earned my fare back to Earth, with a comfortable stake left over.

"Finagle's black humor!" Owen had exploded when I had told him. "Of all places, why Earth?"

"Because if I can get my UN citizenship back, Earth will replace my arm. Free."

"Oh. That's true," he'd said dubiously.

The Belt had organ banks, too, but they were always undersupplied. Belters didn't give things away. Neither did the Belt government. They kept the prices on transplants as high as they would go. Thus they dropped the demand to meet the supply and kept taxes down to boot.

In the Belt I'd have to buy my own arm. And I didn't have the money. On Earth there was social security and a vast supply of transplant material.

What Owen had said couldn't be done, I'd done. I'd found someone to hand me my arm back.

Sometimes I'd wondered if Owen held the choice against me. He'd never said anything, but Homer Chandrasekhar had spoken at length. A Belter would have earned his arm or done without. Never would he have accepted charity.

Was that why Owen hadn't tried to call me?

I shook my head. I didn't believe it.

The room continued to lurch after my head stopped shaking. I'd had enough for the moment. I finished my third grog and ordered dinner.

Dinner sobered me for the next lap. It was something of a shock to realize that I'd run through the entire life span of my friendship with Owen Jennison. I'd known him for three years, though it had seemed like half a lifetime. And it was. Half my six-year life span as a Belter.

I ordered coffee grog and watched the man pour it: hot, milky coffee laced with cinnamon and other spices and high-proof rum poured in a stream of blue fire. This was one of the special drinks served by a human headwaiter, and it was the reason they kept him around. Phase two of the ceremonial drunk: blow half your fortune in the grand manner.

But I called Ordaz before I touched the drink.

"Yes, Mr. Hamilton? I was just going home for dinner."

"I won't keep you long. Have you found out anything new?"

Ordaz took a closer look at my phone image. His disapproval was plain. "I see that you have been drinking. Perhaps you should go home now and call me tomorrow."

I was shocked. "Don't you know *anything* about Belt customs?"

"I do not understand."

I explained the ceremonial drunk. "Look, Ordaz, if you know that little about the way a Belter thinks, then we'd better have a talk. Soon. Otherwise you're likely to miss something."

"You may be right. I can see you at noon, over lunch."

"Good. What have you got?"

"Considerable, but none of it is very helpful. Your friend landed on Earth two months ago, arriving on the *Pillar of Fire*, operating out of Outback Field, Australia. He was wearing a haircut in the style of Earth. From there—"

"That's funny. He'd have had to wait two months for his hair to grow out."

"That occurred even to me. I understand that a Belter commonly shaves his entire scalp except for a strip two inches wide running from the nape of his neck forward."

"The strip cut, yah. It probably started when someone decided he'd live longer if his hair couldn't fall in his eyes during a tricky landing. But Owen could have let his hair grow out during a singleship mining trip. There'd be nobody to see."

"Still, it seems odd. Did you know that Mr. Jennison has a cousin on Earth? One Harvey Peele, who manages a chain of supermarkets."

"So I wasn't his next of kin, even on Earth."

"Mr. Jennison made no attempt to contact him."

"Anything else?"

"I've spoken to the man who sold Mr. Jennison his droud and plug. Kenneth Graham owns an office and operating room on Gayley in Near West Los Angeles. Graham claims that the droud was a standard type, that your friend must have altered it himself."

"Do you believe him?"

"For the present. His permits and his records are all in order. The droud was altered with a soldering iron, an amateur's tool."

"Uh huh."

"As far as the police are concerned, the case will probably be closed when we locate the tools Mr. Jennison used."

"Tell you what. I'll wire Homer Chandrasekhar tomorrow. Maybe he can find out things—why Owen landed without a strip haircut, why he came to Earth at all."

Ordaz shrugged with his eyebrows. He thanked me for my trouble and hung up.

The coffee grog was still hot. I gulped at it, savoring the sugary, bitter sting of it, trying to forget Owen dead and remember him in life. He was always slightly chubby, I remembered, but he never gained a pound and never lost a pound. He could move like a whippet when he had to.

And now he was terribly thin, and his death grin was ripe with obscene joy.

I ordered another coffee grog. The waiter, a showman, made sure he had my attention before he lit the heated rum, then poured it from a foot above the glass. You can't drink that drink slowly. It slides down too easily, and there's the added spur that if you wait too long, it might get cold. Rum and strong coffee. Two of these and I'd be drunkenly alert for hours.

Midnight found me in the Mars Bar, running on scotch and soda. In between I'd been barhopping. Irish coffee at Bergin's, cold and smoking concoctions at the Moon Pool, scotch and wild music at Beyond. I couldn't get drunk, and I couldn't find the right mood. There was a barrier to the picture I was trying to rebuild.

It was the memory of the last Owen, grinning in an armchair with a wire leading down into his brain.

I didn't know that Owen. I had never met the man and never would have wanted to. From bar to nightclub to restaurant I had run from the image, waiting for the alcohol to break the barrier between present and past.

So I sat at a corner table, surrounded by 3D panoramic views of an impossible Mars. Crystal towers and long, straight blue canali, six-legged beasts and beautiful, impossibly slender men and women looked out at me across never-never land. Would Owen have found it sad or funny? He'd seen the real Mars and had not been impressed.

I had reached that stage where time becomes discontinuous, where gaps of seconds or minutes appear between the events you can remember. Somewhere in that period I found myself staring at a cigarette. I must have just lighted it, because it was near its original two-hundred-millimeter length. Maybe a waiter had snuck up behind me. There it was, at any rate, burning between my middle and index fingers.

I stared at the coal as the mood settled on me. I was calm, I was drifting, I was lost in time . . .

. . . We'd been two months in the rocks, our first trip out since the accident. Back we came to Ceres with a holdful of gold, fifty percent pure, guaranteed suitable for rustproof wiring and conductor plates. At nightfall we were ready to celebrate.

We walked along the city limits, with neon blinking and beckoning on the right, a melted rock cliff to the left, and stars blazing through the dome overhead. Homer Chandrasekhar was practically snorting. On this night his first trip out culminated in his first homecoming, and homecoming is the best part.

"We'll want to split up about midnight," he said. He didn't need to enlarge on that. Three men in company might conceivably be three singleship pilots, but chances are they're a ship's crew. They don't have their singleship licenses yet; they're too stupid or too inexperienced. If we wanted companions for the night—

"You haven't thought this through," Owen answered. I saw Homer's double take, then his quick look at where my shoulder ended, and I was ashamed. I didn't need my crewmates to hold my hand, and in this state I'd only slow them down.

Before I could open my mouth to protest, Owen went on. "We've got a draw here that we'd be idiots to throw away. Gil, pick up a cigarette. No, not with your left hand—"

I was drunk, gloriously drunk and feeling immortal. The attenuated Martians seemed to move in the walls, the walls that seemed to be picture windows on a Mars that never was. For the first time that night I raised my glass in a toast.

"To Owen, from Gil the Arm. Thanks."

I transferred the cigarette to my imaginary hand.

By now you've got the idea I was holding it in my imaginary fingers. Most people have the same impression, but it isn't so. I held it clutched ignominiously in my fist. The coal couldn't burn me, of course, but it still felt like a lead ingot.

I rested my imaginary elbow on the table, and that seemed to make it easier—which is ridiculous, but it works. Truly, I'd expected my imaginary arm to disappear after I got the transplant. But I'd found I could dissociate from the new arm to hold small objects in my invisible hand, to feel tactile sensations in my invisible fingertips.

I'd earned the title Gil the Arm that night in Ceres. It had started with a floating cigarette. Owen had been right. Everyone in the place eventually wound up staring at the floating cigarette smoked by the one-armed man. All I had to do was find the prettiest girl in the room with my peripheral vision, then catch her eye.

That night we had been the center of the biggest impromptu party ever thrown in Ceres Base. It wasn't planned that way at all. I'd used the cigarette trick three times so that each of us would have a date. But the third girl already had an escort, and he was celebrating something; he'd sold some kind of patent to an Earth-based industrial firm. He was throwing money around like confetti. So we let him stay. I did tricks, reaching esper fingers into a closed box to tell what was inside, and by the time I finished, all the tables had been pushed together and I was in the center, with Homer and Owen and three girls. Then we got to singing old songs, and the bartenders joined us, and suddenly everything was on the house.

Eventually about twenty of us wound up in the orbiting mansion of the First Speaker for the Belt Government. The goldskin cops had tried to bust us up earlier, and the First

Speaker had behaved very rudely indeed, then compensated
by inviting them to join us . . .

And that was why I used TK on so many cigarettes.

Across the width of the Mars Bar a girl in a peach-
colored dress sat studying me with her chin on her fist. I
got up and went over.

My head felt fine. It was the first thing I checked when
I woke up. Apparently I'd remembered to take a hangover
pill.

A leg was hooked over my knee. It felt good, though the
pressure had put my foot to sleep. Fragrant dark hair spilled
beneath my nose. I didn't move. I didn't want her to know
I was awake.

It's damned embarrassing when you wake up with a girl
and can't remember her name.

Well, let's see. A peach dress neatly hung from a door-
knob . . . I remembered a whole lot of traveling last night.
The girl at the Mars Bar. A puppet show. Music of all
kinds. I'd talked about Owen, and she'd steered me away
from that because it depressed her. Then—

Hah! Taffy. Last name forgotten.

"Morning," I said.

"Morning," she said. "Don't try to move; we're hooked
together . . ." In the sober morning light she was lovely.
Long black hair, brown eyes, creamy untanned skin. To be
lovely this early was a neat trick, and I told her so, and she
smiled.

My lower leg was dead meat until it started to buzz with
renewed circulation, and then I made faces until it calmed
down. Taffy kept up a running chatter as we dressed. "That
third hand is strange. I remember you holding me with two
strong arms and stroking the back of my neck with the
third. *Very* nice. It reminded me of a Fritz Leiber story."

" 'The Wanderer.' The panther girl."

"Mm hmm. How many girls have you caught with that
cigarette trick?"

"None as pretty as you."

"And how many girls have you told that to?"

"Can't remember. It always worked before. Maybe this time it's for real."

We exchanged grins.

A minute later I caught her frowning thoughtfully at the back of my neck. "Something wrong?"

"I was just thinking. You really crashed and burned last night. I hope you don't drink that much all the time."

"Why? You worried about me?"

She blushed, then nodded.

"I should have told you. In fact, I think I did, last night. When a good friend dies, it's obligatory to get smashed."

Taffy looked relieved. "I didn't mean to get—"

"Personal? Why not. You've the right. Anyway, I like—" *maternal types*, but I couldn't say that. "—people who worry about me."

Taffy touched her hair with some kind of complex comb. A few strokes snapped her hair instantly into place. Static electricity?

"It was a good drunk," I said. "Owen would have been proud. And that's all the mourning I'll do. One drunk and—" I spread my hands. "Out."

"It's not a bad way to go," Taffy mused reflectively. "Current stimulus, I mean. I mean, if you've got to bow out—"

"Now, drop that!" I don't know how I got so angry so fast. Ghoul-thin and grinning in a reading chair, Owen's corpse was suddenly vivid before me. I'd fought that image for too many hours. "Walking off a bridge is enough of a cop-out," I snarled. "Dying for a month while current burns out your brain is nothing less than sickening."

Taffy was hurt and bewildered. "But your friend did it, didn't he? You didn't make him sound like a weakling."

"Nuts," I heard myself say. "He didn't do it. He was—"

Just like that, I was sure. I must have realized it while I was drunk or sleeping. Of *course* he hadn't killed himself. *That* wasn't Owen. And current addiction wasn't Owen, either.

"He was murdered," I said. "Sure he was. Why didn't I see it?" And I made a dive for the phone.

"Good morning, Mr. Hamilton." Detective-Inspector Ordaz looked very fresh and neat this morning. I was suddenly aware that I hadn't shaved. "I see you remembered to take your hangover pills."

"Right. Ordaz, has it occurred to you that Owen might have been murdered?"

"Naturally. But it isn't possible."

"I think it might be. Suppose he—"

"Mr. Hamilton."

"Yah?"

"We have an appointment for lunch. Shall we discuss it then? Meet me at headquarters at twelve hundred."

"Okay. One thing you might take care of this morning. See if Owen registered for a nudist's license."

"Do you think he might have?"

"Yah. I'll tell you why at lunch."

"Very well."

"Don't hang up. You said you'd found the man who sold Owen his droud and plug. What was his name again?"

"Kenneth Graham."

"That's what I thought." I hung up.

Taffy touched my shoulder. "Do—do you really think he might have been—killed?"

"Yah. The whole setup depended on him not being able to—"

"No. Wait. I don't want to know about it."

I turned to look at her. She really didn't. The very subject of a stranger's death was making her sick to her stomach.

"Okay. Look, I'm a jerk not to at least offer you breakfast, but I've got to get on this right away. Can I call you a cab?"

When the cab came, I dropped a ten-mark coin in the slot and helped her in. I got her address before it took off.

ARM Headquarters hummed with early morning activity. Hellos came my way, and I answered them without stopping to talk. Anything important would filter down to me eventually.

As I passed Julie's cubicle, I glanced in. She was hard at work, limply settled in her contour couch, jotting notes with her eyes closed.

Kenneth Graham.

A hookup to the basement computer formed the greater part of my desk. Learning how to use it had taken me several months. I typed an order for coffee and doughnuts, then: INFORMATION RETRIEVAL. KENNETH GRAHAM. LIMITED LICENSE: SURGERY. GENERAL LICENSE: DIRECT CURRENT STIMULUS EQUIPMENT SALES. ADDRESS: NEAR WEST LOS ANGELES.

Tape chattered out of the slot, an instant response, loop after loop of it curling on my desk. I didn't need to read it to know I was right.

New technologies create new customs, new laws, new ethics, new crimes. About half the activity of the United Nations Police, the ARMs, dealt with control of a crime that hadn't existed a century ago. The crime of organlegging was the result of thousands of years of medical progress, of millions of lives selflessly dedicated to the ideal of healing the sick. Progress had brought these ideals to reality and, as usual, had created new problems.

1900 A.D. was the year Karl Landsteiner classified human blood into four types, giving patients their first real chance to survive a transfusion. The technology of transplants had grown with the growing of the twentieth century. Whole blood, dry bone, skin, live kidneys, live hearts could all be transferred from one body to another. Donors had saved tens of thousands of lives in that hundred years by willing their bodies to medicine.

But the number of donors was limited, and not many died in such a way that anything of value could be saved.

The deluge had come something less than a hundred years ago. One healthy donor (but of course there was no such animal) could save a dozen lives. Why, then, should a condemned murderer die for no purpose? First a few states, then most of the nations of the world had passed new laws. Criminals condemned to death must be executed in a hospital, with surgeons to save as much as could be saved for the organ banks.

The world's billions wanted to live, and the organ banks were life itself. A man could live forever as long as the doctors could shove spare parts into him faster than his own parts wore out. But they could do that only as long as the world's organ banks were stocked.

A hundred scattered movements to abolish the death penalty died silent, unpublicized deaths. Everybody gets sick sometime.

And still there were shortages in the organ banks. Still patients died for the lack of parts to save them. The world's legislators had responded to steady pressure from the world's people. Death penalties were established for first-, second-, and third-degree murder. For assault with a deadly weapon. Then for a multitude of crimes: rape, fraud, embezzlement, having children without a license, four or more counts of false advertising. For nearly a century the trend had been growing as the world's voting citizens acted to protect their right to live forever.

Even now there weren't enough transplants. A woman with kidney trouble might wait a year for a transplant: one healthy kidney to last the rest of her life. A thirty-five-year-old heart patient must live with a sound but forty-year-old heart. One lung, part of a liver, prosthetics that wore out too fast or weighed too much or did too little . . . there weren't enough criminals. Not surprisingly, the death penalty *was* a deterrent. People stopped committing crimes rather than face the donor room of a hospital.

For instant replacement of your ruined digestive system, for a *young* healthy heart, for a whole liver when you'd ruined yours with alcohol . . . you had to go to an organlegger.

There are three aspects to the business of organlegging. One is the business of kidnap-murder. It's risky. You can't fill an organ bank by waiting for volunteers. Executing condemned criminals is a government monopoly. So you go out and *get* your donors: on a crowded city slidewalk, in an air terminal, stranded on a freeway by a car with a busted capacitor . . . anywhere.

The selling end of the business is just as dangerous, because even a desperately sick man sometimes has a conscience. He'll buy his transplant, then go straight to the ARMs, curing his sickness and his conscience by turning in the whole gang. Thus the sales end is somewhat anonymous, but as there are few repeat sales, that hardly matters.

Third is the technical, medical aspect. Probably this is the safest part of the business. Your hospital is big, but you can put it anywhere. You wait for the donors, who arrive still alive; you ship out livers and glands and square feet of live skin, correctly labeled for rejection reactions.

It's not as easy as it sounds. You need doctors. Good ones.

That was where Loren came in. He had a monopoly.

Where did he get them? We were still trying to find out. Somehow, one man had discovered a foolproof way to recruit talented but dishonest doctors practically en masse. Was it really one man? All our sources said it was. And he had half the North American west coast in the palm of his hand.

Loren. No holographs, no fingerprints or retina prints, not even a description. All we had was that one name and a few possible contacts.

One of those was Kenneth Graham.

The hologram was a good one. Probably it had been posed in a portrait shop. Kenneth Graham had a long Scottish face with a lantern jaw and a small, dour mouth. In the holo he was trying to smile and look dignified simultaneously. He only looked uncomfortable. His hair was sandy and close cut. Above his light gray eyes his eyebrows were so light as to be nearly invisible.

My breakfast arrived. I dunked a doughnut and bit it and found out I was hungrier than I'd thought.

A string of holos had been reproduced on the computer tape. I ran through the others fairly quickly, eating with one hand and flipping the key with the other. Some were fuzzy; they had been taken by spy beams through the windows of Graham's shop. None of the prints were in any way incriminating. Not one showed Graham smiling.

He had been selling electrical joy for twelve years now.

A current addict has an advantage over his supplier. Electricity is cheap. With a drug, your supplier can always raise the price on you, but not with electricity. You see the ecstasy merchant once, when he sells you your operation and your droud, and never again. Nobody gets hooked by accident. There's an honesty to current addiction. The customer always knows just what he's getting into and what it will do for him—and to him.

Still, you'd need a certain lack of empathy to make a living the way Kenneth Graham did. Else he'd have had to turn away his customers. Nobody becomes a current addict gradually. He decides all at once, and he buys the operation before he has ever tasted its joy. Each of Kenneth Graham's customers had reached his shop after deciding to drop out of the human race.

What a stream of the hopeless and the desperate must have passed through Graham's shop! How could they help but haunt his dreams? And if Kenneth Graham slept well at night, then—

Then small wonder if he had turned organlegger.

He was in a good position for it. Despair is characteristic of the would-be current addict. The unknown, the unloved, the people nobody knew and nobody needed and nobody missed, these passed in a steady stream through Kenneth Graham's shop.

So a few didn't come out. Who'd notice?

I flipped quickly through the tape to find out who was in charge of watching Graham. Jackson Bera. I called down through the desk phone.

"Sure," Bera said, "we've had a spy beam on him about three weeks now. It's a waste of good salaried ARM agents. Maybe he's clean. Maybe he's been tipped somehow."

"Then why not stop watching him?"

Bera looked disgusted. "Because we've only been watching for three weeks. How many donors do you think he needs a year? Read the reports. Gross profit on a single donor is over a million UN marks. Graham can afford to be careful who he picks."

"Yah."

"At that, he wasn't careful enough. At least two of his customers disappeared last year. Customers with families. That's what put us on to him."

"So you could watch him for the next six months without a guarantee. He could be just waiting for the right guy to walk in."

"Sure. He has to write up a report on every customer. That gives him the right to ask personal questions. If the guy has relatives, Graham lets him walk out. Most people do have relatives, you know. Then again," Bera said disconsolately, "he could be clean. Sometimes a current addict disappears without help."

"How come I didn't see any holos of Graham at home? You can't be watching just his shop."

Jackson Bera scratched at his hair. Hair like black steel wool, worn long like a bushman's mop. "Sure we're watching his place, but we can't get a spy beam in there. It's an inside apartment. No windows. You know anything about spy beams?"

"Not much. I know they've been around awhile."

"They're as old as lasers. Oldest trick in the book is to put a mirror in the room you want to bug. Then you run a laser beam through a window, or even through heavy drapes, and bounce it off the mirror. When you pick it up, it's been distorted by the vibrations in the glass. That gives you a perfect recording of anything that's been said in that room. But for pictures you need something a little more sophisticated."

"How sophisticated can we get?"

"We can put a spy beam in any room with a window. We can send one through some kinds of wall. Give us an optically flat surface, and we can send one around corners."

"But you need an outside wall."

"Yup."

"What's Graham doing now?"

"Just a sec." Bera disappeared from view. "Someone just came in. Graham's talking to him. Want the picture?"

"Sure. Leave it on. I'll turn it off from here when I'm through with it."

The picture of Bera went dark. A moment later I was looking into a doctor's office. If I'd seen it cold, I'd have thought it was run by a podiatrist. There was the comfortable tilt-back chair with the headrest and the footrest; the cabinet next to it with instruments lying on top, on a clean white cloth; the desk over in one corner. Kenneth Graham was talking to a homely, washed-out-looking girl.

I listened to Graham's would-be-fatherly reassurances and his glowing description of the magic of current addiction. When I couldn't take it any longer, I turned the sound down. The girl took her place in the chair, and Graham placed something over her head.

The girl's homely face turned suddenly beautiful.

Happiness is beautiful all by itself. A happy person is beautiful per se. Suddenly and totally, the girl was full of joy, and I realized that I hadn't known everything about droud sales. Apparently Graham had an inductor to put the current where he wanted it, without wires. He *could* show a customer what current addiction felt like without first implanting the wires.

What a powerful argument that was!

Graham turned off the machine. It was as if he'd turned off the girl. She sat stunned for a moment, then reached frantically for her purse and started scrabbling inside.

I couldn't take any more. I turned it off.

Small wonder if Graham had turned organlegger. He had to be totally without empathy just to sell his merchandise.

Even there, I thought, he'd had a head start.

So he was a little more callous than the rest of the world's billions. But not much. Every voter had a bit of the organlegger in him. In voting the death penalty for so many crimes, the lawmakers had only bent to pressure from the voters. There was a spreading lack of respect for life, the evil side of transplant technology. The good side was a longer life for everyone. One condemned criminal could save a dozen deserving lives. Who could complain about that?

We hadn't thought that way in the Belt. In the Belt survival was a virtue in itself, and life was a precious thing, spread so thin among the sterile rocks, hurtling in single units through all that killing emptiness between the worlds.

So I'd had to come to Earth for my transplant.

My request had been accepted two months after I had landed. So quickly? Later I'd learned that the banks always have a surplus of certain items. Few people lose their arms these days. I had also learned, a year after the transplant had taken, that I was using an arm taken from a captured organlegger's storage bank.

That had been a shock. I'd hoped my arm had come from a depraved murderer, someone who'd shot fourteen nurses from a rooftop. Not at all. Some faceless, nameless victim had had the bad luck to encounter a ghoul, and I had benefited thereby.

Did I turn in my new arm in a fit of revulsion? No, surprising to say, I did not. But I had joined the ARMs, once the Amalgamation of Regional Militia, now the United Nations Police. Though I had stolen a dead man's arm, I would hunt the kin of those who had killed him.

The noble urgency of that resolve had been drowned in paperwork these last few years. Perhaps I was becoming callous, like the flatlanders—the *other* flatlanders around me, voting new death penalties year after year. *Income-tax evasion. Operating a flying vehicle on manual controls over a city.*

Was Kenneth Graham so much worse than they?

Sure he was. The bastard had put a wire in Owen Jennison's head.

I waited twenty minutes for Julie to come out. I could have sent her a memorandum, but there was plenty of time before noon and too little time to get anything accomplished, and . . . I wanted to talk to her.

"Hi," she said. "Thanks," taking the coffee. "How went the ceremonial drunk? Oh, I *see*. Mmmmm. Very good. Almost poetic." Conversation with Julie has a way of taking shortcuts.

Poetic, right. I remembered how inspiration had struck like lightning through a mild high glow. Owen's floating cigarette lure. What better way to honor his memory than to use it to pick up a girl?

"Right," Julie agreed. "But there's something you may have missed. What's Taffy's last name?"

"I can't remember. She wrote it down on—"

"What does she do for a living?"

"How should I know?"

"What religion is she? Is she a pro or an anti? Where did she grow up?"

"Dammit—"

"Half an hour ago you were very complacently musing on how depersonalized all us flatlanders are except you. What's Taffy, a person or a foldout?" Julie stood with her hands on her hips, looking up at me like a schoolteacher.

How many people is Julie? Some of us have never seen this guardian aspect. She's frightening, the guardian. If it ever appeared on a date, the man she was with would be struck impotent forever.

It never does. When a reprimand is deserved, Julie delivers it in broad daylight. This serves to separate her functions, but it doesn't make it easier to take.

No use pretending it wasn't her business, either.

I'd come here to ask for Julie's protection. Let me turn unlovable to Julie, even a little bit unlovable, and as far as Julie was concerned, I would have an unreadable mind.

How, then, would she know when I was in trouble? How could she send help to rescue me from whatever? My private life *was* her business, her single, vastly important job.

"I *like* Taffy," I protested. "I didn't care who she was when we met. Now I like her, and I think she likes me. What do you want from a first date?"

"You know better. You can remember other dates when two of you talked all night on a couch just from the joy of learning about each other." She mentioned three names, and I flushed. Julie knows the words that will turn you inside out in an instant. "Taffy is a person, not an episode, not a symbol of anything, not just a pleasant night. What's your judgment of her?"

I thought about it, standing there in the corridor. Funny: I've faced the guardian Julie on other occasions, and it has never occurred to me to just walk out of the unpleasant situation. Later I think of that. At the time I just stand there, facing the guardian/judge/teacher. I thought about Taffy . . .

"She's nice," I said. "*Not* depersonalized. Squeamish, even. She wouldn't make a good nurse. She'd want to help too much, and it would tear her apart when she couldn't. I'd say she was one of the vulnerable ones."

"Go on."

"I want to see her again, but I won't dare talk shop with her. In fact . . . I'd better not see her till this business of Owen is over. Loren might take an interest in her. Or . . . she might take an interest in me, and I might get hurt . . . have I missed anything?"

"I think so. You owe her a phone call. If you won't be dating her for a few days, call her and tell her so."

"Check." I spun on my heel, spun back. "Finagle's jest! I almost forgot. The reason I came here—"

"I know; you want a time slot. Suppose I check on you at oh nine forty-five every morning?"

"That's a little early. When I get in deadly danger, it's usually at night."

"I'm off at night. Oh nine forty-five is all I've got. I'm sorry, Gil, but it is. Shall I monitor you or not?"

"Sold. Nine forty-five."

"Good. Let me know if you get real proof Owen was murdered. I'll give you two slots. You'll be in a little more concrete danger then."

"Good."

Taffy wasn't home, of course, and I didn't know where she worked or even what she did. Her phone offered to take a message. I gave my name and said I'd call back.

And then I sat there sweating for five minutes.

It was half an hour to noon. Here I was at my desk phone. I couldn't decently see any way to argue myself out of sending a message to Homer Chandrasekhar.

I didn't want to talk to him, then or ever. He'd chewed me out but good last time I'd seen him. My free arm had cost me my Belter life, and it had cost me Homer's respect. I didn't want to talk to him even on a one-way message, and I most particularly didn't want to have to tell him Owen was dead.

But someone had to tell him.

And maybe he could find out something.

And I'd put it off nearly a full day.

For five minutes I sweated, and then I called long distance and recorded a message and sent it off to Ceres. More accurately, I recorded six messages before I was satisfied. I don't want to talk about it.

I tried Taffy again; she might come home for lunch. Wrong.

I hung up wondering if Julie had been fair. What had we bargained for, Taffy and I, beyond a pleasant night? And we'd had that and would have others, with luck.

But Julie would find it hard not to be fair. If she thought Taffy was the vulnerable type, she'd taken her information from my own mind.

Mixed feelings. You're a kid, and your mother has just laid down the law. But it *is* a law, something you can count on ... and she *is* paying attention to you ... and she *does*

care . . . when, for so many of those outside, nobody cares
at all.

"Naturally I thought of murder," Ordaz said. "I always
consider murder. When my sainted mother passed away after three years of the most tender care by my sister Maria
Angela, I actually considered searching for evidence of needle holes about the head."

"Find any?"

Ordaz's face froze. He put down his beer and started to
get up.

"Cool it," I said hurriedly. "No offense intended." He
glared a moment, then sat down half-mollified.

We'd picked an outdoor restaurant on the pedestrian
level. On the other side of a hedge (a real live hedge, green
and growing and everything) the shoppers were carried past
in a steady one-way stream. Beyond them a slidewalk carried a similar stream in the opposite direction. I had the
dizzy feeling that it was we who were moving.

A waiter like a bell-bottomed chess pawn produced
steaming dishes of chili from its torso, put them precisely
in front of us, and slid away on a cushion of air.

"Naturally I considered murder. Believe me, Mr. Hamilton, it does not hold up."

"I think I could make a pretty good case."

"You may try, of course. Better, I will start you on your
way. First, we must assume that Kenneth Graham the happiness peddler did not sell a droud and plug to Owen
Jennison. Rather, Owen Jennison was forced to undergo the
operation. Graham's records, including the written permission to operate, were forged. All this we must assume; is it
not so?"

"Right. And before you tell me Graham's escutcheon is
unblemished, let me tell you that it isn't."

"Oh?"

"He's connected with an organlegging gang. That's classified information. We're watching him, and we don't want
him tipped."

"That is news." Ordaz rubbed his jaw. "Organlegging. Well. What would Owen Jennison have to do with organlegging?"

"Owen's a Belter. The Belt's always drastically short of transplant materials."

"Yes, they import quantities of medical supplies from Earth. Not only organs in storage but also drugs and prosthetics. So?"

"Owen ran a good many cargoes past the goldskins in his day. He got caught a few times, but he's still way ahead of the government. He's on the records as a successful smuggler. If a big organlegger wanted to expand his market, he might very well send a feeler out to a Belter with a successful smuggling record."

"You never mentioned that Mr. Jennison was a smuggler."

"What for? All Belters are smugglers if they think they can get away with it. To a Belter, smuggling isn't immoral. But an organlegger wouldn't know that. He'd think Owen was already a criminal."

"Do you think your friend—" Ordaz hesitated delicately.

"No, Owen wouldn't turn organlegger. But he might, he just *might* try to turn one in. The rewards for information leading to the capture and conviction of, et cetera, are substantial. If someone contacted Owen, Owen might very well have tried to trace the contact by himself.

"Now, the gang we're after covers half the west coast of this continent. That's big. It's the Loren gang, the one Graham may be working for. Suppose Owen had a chance to meet Loren himself?"

"You think he might take it, do you?"

"I think he did. I think he let his hair grow out so he'd look like an Earthman to convince Loren he wanted to look inconspicuous. I think he collected as much information as he could, then tried to get out with a whole skin. But he didn't make it.

"Did you find his application for a nudist license?"

"No. I saw your point there," said Ordaz. He leaned

back, ignoring the food in front of him. "Mr. Jennison's tan was uniform except for the characteristic darkening of the face. I presume he was a practicing nudist in the Belt."

"Yah. We don't need licenses there. He'd have been one here, too, unless he was hiding something. Remember that scar. He never missed a chance to show it off."

"Could he really have thought to pass for a—" Ordaz hesitated. "—flatlander?"

"With that Belter tan? No! He was overdoing it a little with the haircut. Maybe he thought Loren would underestimate him. But he wasn't advertising his presence, or he wouldn't have left his most personal possessions home."

"So he was dealing with organleggers, and they found him out before he could reach you. Yes, Mr. Hamilton, this is well thought out. But it won't work."

"Why not? I'm not trying to prove it's murder. Not yet. I'm just trying to show you that murder is at least as likely as suicide."

"But it's not, Mr. Hamilton."

I looked the question.

"Consider the details of the hypothetical murder. Owen Jennison is drugged, no doubt, and taken to the office of Kenneth Graham. There, an ecstasy plug is attached. A standard droud is fitted and is then amateurishly altered with soldering tools. Already we see, on the part of the killer, a minute attention to details. We see it again in Kenneth Graham's forged papers of permission to operate. They were impeccable.

"Owen Jennison is then taken back to his apartment. It would be his own, would it not? There would be little point in moving him to another. The cord from his droud is shortened, again in amateurish fashion. Mr. Jennison is tied up—"

"I wondered if you'd see that."

"But why should he not be tied up? He is tied up and allowed to waken. Perhaps the arrangement is explained to him, perhaps not. That would be up to the killer. The killer then plugs Mr. Jennison into a wall. A current trickles through his brain, and Owen Jennison knows pure pleasure for the first time in his life.

"He is left tied up for, let us say, three hours. In the first few minutes he would be a hopeless addict, I think—"

"You must have known more current addicts than I have."

"Even I would not want to be pinned down. Your normal current addict is an addict after a few minutes. But then, your normal current addict asked to be made an addict, knowing what it would do to his life. Current addiction is symptomatic of despair. Your friend might have been able to fight free of a few minutes' exposure."

"So they kept him tied up for three hours. Then they cut the ropes." I felt sickened. Ordaz's ugly, ugly pictures matched mine in every detail.

"No more than three hours, by our hypothesis. They would not dare stay longer than a few hours. They would cut the ropes and leave Owen Jennison to starve to death. In the space of a month the evidence of his drugging would vanish, as would any abrasions left by ropes, lumps on his head, mercy needle punctures, and the like. A carefully detailed, well-thought-out plan, don't you agree?"

I told myself that Ordaz was not being ghoulish. He was just doing his job. Still, it was difficult to answer objectively.

"It fits our picture of Loren. He's been very careful with us. He'd love carefully detailed, well-thought-out plans."

Ordaz leaned forward. "But don't you see? A carefully detailed plan is all wrong. There is a crucial flaw in it. Suppose Mr. Jennison pulls out the droud?"

"Could he do that? Would he?"

"Could he? Certainly. A simple tug of the fingers. The current wouldn't interfere with motor coordination. Would he?" Ordaz pulled meditatively at his beer. "I know a good deal about current addiction, but I don't know what it *feels* like, Mr. Hamilton. Your normal addict pulls his droud out as often as he inserts it, but your friend was getting ten times normal current. He might have pulled the droud out a dozen times, and instantly plugged it back each time. Yet Belters are supposed to be strong-willed men, very individualistic. Who knows whether, even after a week of addiction, your friend might not have pulled the droud loose, coiled the cord, slipped it in his pocket, and walked away scot-free?

"There is the additional risk that someone might walk in on him—an automachinery serviceman, for instance. Or someone might notice that he had not bought any food in a month. A suicide would take that risk. Suicides routinely leave themselves a chance to change their minds. But a murderer?

"No. Even if the chance were one in a thousand, the man who created such a detailed plan would never have taken such a chance."

The sun burned hotly down on our shoulders. Ordaz suddenly remembered his lunch and began to eat.

I watched the world ride by beyond the hedge. Pedestrians stood in little conversational bunches; others peered into shop windows on the pedestrian strip or glanced over the hedge to watch us eat. There were the few who pushed through the crowd with set expressions, impatient with the ten-mile-per-hour speed of the slidewalk.

"Maybe they *were* watching him. Maybe the room was bugged."

"We searched the room thoroughly," Ordaz said. "If there had been observational equipment, we would have found it."

"It could have been removed."

Ordaz shrugged.

I remembered the spy-eyes in Monica Apartments. Someone would have had to physically enter the room to carry a bug out. He could ruin it with the right signal, maybe, but it would surely leave traces.

And Owen had had an inside room. No spy-eyes.

"There's one thing you've left out," I said presently.

"And what would that be?"

"My name in Owen's wallet, listed as next of kin. He

was directing my attention to the thing I was working on. The Loren gang."

"That is possible."

"You can't have it both ways."

Ordaz lowered his fork. "I *can* have it both ways, Mr. Hamilton. But you won't like it."

"I'm sure I won't."

"Let us incorporate your assumption. Mr. Jennison was contacted by an agent of Loren, the organlegger, who intended to sell transplant material to Belters. He accepted. The promise of riches was too much for him.

"A month later something made him realize what a terrible thing he had done. He decided to die. He went to an ecstasy peddler and had a wire put in his head. Later, before he plugged in the droud, he made one attempt to atone for his crime. He listed you as his next of kin so that you might guess why he had died and perhaps so that you could use that knowledge against Loren."

Ordaz looked at me across the table. "I see that you will never agree. I cannot help that. I can only read the evidence."

"Me, too. But I knew Owen. He'd never have worked for an organlegger, he'd never have killed himself, and if he had, he'd never have done it that way."

Ordaz didn't answer.

"What about fingerprints?"

"In the apartment? None."

"None but Owen's?"

"Even his were found only on the chairs and end tables. I curse the man who invented the cleaning robot. Every smooth surface in that apartment was cleaned exactly forty-four times during Mr. Jennison's tenancy." Ordaz went back to his chili.

"Then try this. Assume for the moment that I'm right. Assume Owen was after Loren, and Loren got him. Owen knew he was doing something dangerous. He wouldn't have wanted me to get onto Loren before he was ready. He wanted the reward for himself. But he might have left me something, just in case.

"Something in a locker somewhere, an airport or space-port locker. Evidence. Not under his own name, or mine, either, because I'm a known ARM. But—"

"Some name you both know."

"Right. Like Homer Chandrasekhar. Or—got it. Cubes Forsythe. Owen would have thought that was apt. Cubes is dead."

"We will look. You must understand that it will not prove your case."

"Sure. Anything you find, Owen could have arranged in a fit of conscience. Screw that. Let me know what you get," I said, and stood up and left.

I rode the slidewalk, not caring where it was taking me. It would give me a chance to cool off.

Could Ordaz be right? Could he?

But the more I dug into Owen's death, the worse it made Owen look.

Therefore, Ordaz was wrong.

Owen work for an organlegger? He'd rather have been a donor.

Owen getting his kicks from a wall socket? He never even watched tridee!

Owen kill himself? No. If so, not that way.

But even if I could have swallowed all that . . .

Owen Jennison letting me know he's worked with organleggers? Me, Gil the Arm Hamilton? Let *me* know *that*?

The slidewalk rolled along, past restaurants and shopping centers and churches and banks. Ten stories below, the hum of cars and scooters drifted faintly up from the vehicular level. The sky was a narrow, vivid slash of blue between black shadows of skyscraper.

Let *me* know *that*? Never.

But Ordaz's strangely inconsistent murderer was no better.

I thought of something even Ordaz had missed. Why would Loren dispose of Owen so elaborately? Owen need only disappear into the organ banks, never to bother Loren again.

The shops were thinning out now, and so were the crowds. The slidewalk narrowed, entered a residential area, and not a very good one. I'd let it carry me a long way. I looked around, trying to decide where I was.

And I was four blocks from Graham's place.

My subconscious had done me a dirty. I wanted to look at Kenneth Graham face to face. The temptation to go on was nearly irresistible, but I fought it off and changed direction at the next disk.

A slidewalk intersection is a rotating disk, its rim tangent to four slidewalks and moving with the same speed. From the center you ride up an escalator and over the slidewalks to reach stationary walks along the buildings. I could have caught a cab at the center of the disk, but I still wanted to think, so I just rode halfway around the rim.

I could have walked into Graham's shop and gotten away with it. Maybe. I'd have looked hopeless and bored and hesitant, told Graham I wanted an ecstasy plug, worried loudly about what my wife and friends would say, then changed my mind at the last moment. He'd have let me walk out, knowing I'd be missed. Maybe.

But Loren had to know more about the ARMs than we knew about him. Some time or other, had Graham been shown a holo of yours truly? Let a known ARM walk into his shop, and Graham would panic. It wasn't worth the risk.

Then, dammit, what *could* I do?

Ordaz's inconsistent killer. If we assumed Owen was murdered, we couldn't get away from the other assumptions. The care, the nitpicking detail—and then Owen left alone to pull out the plug and walk away, or to be discovered by a persistent salesman or a burglar, or—

No. Ordaz's hypothetical killer, and mine, would have watched Owen like a hawk. For a month.

That did it. I stepped off at the next disk and got a taxi.

The taxi dropped me on the roof of Monica Apartments. I took an elevator to the lobby.

If the manager was surprised to see me, he didn't show it as he gestured me into his office. The office seemed much roomier than the lobby had, possibly because there were things to break the anonymous modern decor: paintings on the wall, a small black worm track in the rug that must have been caused by a visitor's cigarette, a holo of Miller and his wife on the wide, nearly empty desk. He waited until I was settled, then leaned forward expectantly.

"I'm here on ARM business," I said, and passed him my ident.

He passed it back without checking it. "I presume it's the same business," he said without cordiality.

"Yah. I'm convinced Owen Jennison must have had visitors while he was here."

The manager smiled. "That's ridic—impossible."

"Nope, it's not. Your holo cameras take pictures of visitors, but they don't snap the tenants, do they?"

"Of course not."

"Then Owen could have been visited by any tenant in the building."

The manager looked shocked. "No, certainly not. Really, I don't see why you pursue this, Mr. Hamilton. If Mr. Jennison had been found in such a condition, it would have been reported!"

"I don't think so. Could he have been visited by any tenant in the building?"

"No. No. The cameras would have taken a picture of anyone from another floor."

"How about someone from the same floor?"

Reluctantly the manager bobbed his head. "Ye-es. As far as the holo cameras are concerned, that's possible. But—"

"Then I'd like to ask for pictures of any tenant who lived on the eighteenth floor during the last six weeks. Send them to the ARM Building, Central LA. Can do?"

"Of course. You'll have them within an hour."

"Good. Now, something else occurred to me. Suppose a

man got out on the nineteenth floor and walked down to the eighteenth. He'd be holoed on the nineteenth but not on the eighteenth, right?"

The manager smiled indulgently. "Mr. Hamilton, there are no stairs in this building."

"Just the elevators? Isn't that dangerous?"

"Not at all. There is a separate self-contained emergency power source for each of the elevators. It's common practice. After all, who would want to walk up eighty stories if the elevator failed?"

"Okay, fine. One last point. Could someone tamper with the computer? Could someone make it decide not to take a certain picture, for instance?"

"I . . . am not an expert on how to tamper with computers, Mr. Hamilton. Why don't you go straight to the company? Caulfield Brains, Inc."

"Okay. What's your model?"

"Just a moment." He got up and leafed through a drawer in a filing cabinet. "EQ 144."

"Okay."

That was all I could do here, and I knew it . . . and still I didn't have the will to get up. There ought to be *something* . . .

Finally Miller cleared his throat. "Will that be all, sir?"

"Yes," I said. "No. Can I get into 1809?"

"I'll see if we've rented it yet."

"The police are through with it?"

"Certainly." He went back to the filing cabinet. "No, it's still available. I'll take you up. How long will you be?"

"I don't know. No more than half an hour. No need to come up."

"Very well." He handed me the key and waited for me to leave. I did.

The merest flicker of blue light caught my eye as I left the elevator. I would have thought it was my optic nerve, not in the real world, if I hadn't known about the holo cam-

eras. Maybe it was. You don't need laser light to make a
holograph, but it does get you clearer pictures.

Owen's room was a box. Everything was retracted. There
was nothing but the bare walls. I had never seen anything
so desolate, unless it was some asteroidal rock too poor to
mine, too badly placed to be worth a base.

The control panel was just beside the door. I turned on
the lights, then touched the master button. Lines appeared,
outlined in red and green and blue. A great square on one
wall for the bed, most of another wall for the kitchen, various outlines across the floor. Very handy. You wouldn't
want a guest to be standing on the table when you expanded it.

I'd come here to get the feel of the place, to encourage
a hunch, to see if I'd missed anything. Translation: I was
playing. Playing, I reached through the control panel to find
the circuits. The printed circuitry was too small and too detailed to tell me anything, but I ran imaginary fingertips
along a few wires and found that they looped straight to
their action points, no detours. No sensors to the outside.
You'd have to be in the room to know what was expanded,
what retracted.

So a supposedly occupied room had had its bed retracted for six weeks. But you'd have to be in the room to
know it.

I pushed buttons to expand the kitchen nook and the
reading chair. The wall slid out eight feet; the floor humped
itself and took form. I sat down in the chair, and the kitchen
nook blocked my view of the door.

Nobody could have seen Owen from the hall.

If only someone had noticed that Owen wasn't ordering
food. That might have saved him.

I thought of something else, and it made me look around
for the air conditioner. There was a grill at floor level. I felt
behind it with my imaginary hand. Some of these apartment
air-conditioning units go on when the CO_2 level hits half a
percent. This one was geared to temperature and manual
control.

With the other kind, our careful killer could have tapped the air-conditioner current to find out if Owen was still alive and present. As it was, 1809 had behaved like an empty room for six weeks.

I flopped back in the reading chair.

If my hypothetical killer had watched Owen, he'd done it with a bug. Unless he'd actually lived on this floor for the four or five weeks it took Owen to die, there was no other way.

Okay, think about a bug. Make it small enough and nobody could find it except the cleaning robot, which would send it straight to the incinerator. You'd have to make it big so the robot wouldn't get it. No worry about Owen finding it! And then, when you knew Owen was dead, you'd use the self-destruct.

But if you burned it to slag, you'd leave a burn hole somewhere. Ordaz would have found it. So. An asbestos pad? You'd want the self-destruct to leave something that the cleaning robot would sweep up.

And if you'll believe that, you'll believe anything. It was too chancy. *Nobody* knows what a cleaning robot will decide is garbage. They're made stupid because it's cheaper. So they're programmed to leave large objects alone.

There had to be someone on this floor either to watch Owen himself or to pick up the bug that did the watching. I was betting everything I had on a human watcher.

I'd come here mainly to give my intuition a chance. It wasn't working. Owen had spent six weeks in this chair, and for at least the last week he'd been dead. Yet I couldn't feel it with him. It was just a chair with two end tables. He had left nothing in the room, not even a restless ghost.

The call caught me halfway back to headquarters.

"You were right," Ordaz told me over the wristphone. "We have found a locker at Death Valley Port registered to Cubes Forsythe. I am on my way there now. Will you join me?"

"I'll meet you there."

"Good. I am as eager as you to see what Owen Jennison left us."

I doubted that.

The port was something more than 230 miles away, an hour at taxi speeds. It would be a big fare. I typed out a new address on the destination board, then called in at headquarters. An ARM agent is fairly free; he doesn't have to justify every little move. There was no question of getting permission to go. At worst they might disallow the fare on my expense account.

"Oh, and there'll be a set of holos coming in from Monica Apartments," I told the man. "Have the computer check them against known organleggers and associates of Loren."

The taxi rose smoothly into the sky and headed east. I watched tridee and drank coffee until I ran out of coins for the dispenser.

If you go between November and May, when the climate is ideal, Death Valley can be a tourist's paradise. There is the Devil's Golf Course, with its fantastic ridges and pinnacles of salt; Zabriskie Point and its weird badlands topography; the old borax mining sites; and all kinds of strange, rare plants adapted to the heat and the death-dry climate. Yes, Death Valley has many points of interest, and someday I'm going to see them. So far all I'd seen was the spaceport. But the port was impressive in its own way.

The landing field used to be part of a sizable inland sea. It is now a sea of salt. Alternating red and blue concentric circles mark the field for ships dropping from space, and a century's developments in chemical, fission, and fusion reaction motors have left blast pits striped like rainbows by esoteric, often radioactive salts. But mostly the field retains its ancient glare-white.

And out across the salt are ships of many sizes and many shapes. Vehicles and machinery dance attendance, and if you're willing to wait, you may see a ship land. It's worth the wait.

The port building, at the edge of the major salt flat, is a

pastel green tower set in a wide patch of fluorescent orange concrete. No ship has ever landed on it—yet. The taxi dropped me at the entrance and moved away to join others of its kind. And I stood inhaling the dry, balmy air.

Four months of the year Death Valley's climate is ideal. One August the Furnace Creek Ranch recorded 134° Fahrenheit shade temperature.

A man behind a desk told me that Ordaz had arrived before me. I found him and another officer in a labyrinth of pay lockers, each big enough to hold two or three suitcases. The locker Ordaz had opened held only a lightweight plastic briefcase.

"He may have taken other lockers," he said.

"Probably not. Belters travel light. Have you tried to open it?"

"Not yet. It is a combination lock. I thought perhaps . . ."

"Maybe." I squatted to look at it.

Funny: I felt no surprise at all. It was as if I'd known all along that Owen's suitcase would be there. And why not? He was bound to try to protect himself somehow. Through me, because I was already involved in the UN side of organlegging. By leaving something in a spaceport locker, because Loren couldn't find the right locker or get into it if he did, and because I would naturally connect Owen with spaceports. Under Cubes's name, because I'd be looking for that and Loren wouldn't.

Hindsight is wonderful.

The lock had five digits. "He must have meant me to open it. Let's see . . ." I moved the tumblers to 42217. April 22, 2117, the day Cubes died, stapled suddenly to a plastic partition.

The lock clicked open.

Ordaz went instantly for the manila folder. More slowly, I picked up two glass phials. One was tightly sealed against Earth's air and half-full of an incredibly fine dust. So fine was it that it slid about like oil inside the glass. The other phial held a blackened grain of nickel-iron, barely big enough to see.

* * *

Other things were in that case, but the prize was that folder. The story was in there ... at least up to a point. Owen must have planned to add to it.

A message had been waiting for him in the Ceres mail dump when he returned from his last trip out. Owen must have laughed over parts of that message. Loren had taken the trouble to assemble a complete dossier of Owen's smuggling activities over the past eight years. Did he think he could ensure Owen's silence by threatening to turn the dossier over to the goldskins?

Maybe the dossier had given Owen the wrong idea. In any case, he'd decided to contact Loren and see what developed. Ordinarily he'd have sent me the entire message and let me try to track it down. I was the expert, after all. But Owen's last trip out had been a disaster.

His fusion drive had blown somewhere beyond Jupiter's orbit. No explanation. The safeties had blown his lifesystem capsule free of the explosion, barely. A rescue ship had returned him to Ceres. The fee had nearly broken him. He needed money. Loren might have known that and counted on it.

The reward for information leading to Loren's capture would have bought him a new ship.

He'd landed at Outback Field, following Loren's instructions. From there, Loren's men had moved him about a good deal: to London, to Bombay, to Amberg, Germany. Owen's personal, written story ended in Amberg. How had he reached California? He had not had a chance to say.

But in between he had learned a good deal. There were snatches of detail on Loren's organization. There was Loren's full plan for shipping illicit transplant materials to the Belt and for finding and contacting customers. Owen had made suggestions there. Most of them sounded reasonable and would be unworkable in practice. Typically Owen. I could find no sign that he'd overplayed his hand.

But of course he hadn't known it when he had.

And there were holos, twenty-three of them, each a

member of Loren's gang. Some of the pictures had markings on the back; others were blank. Owen had been unable to find out where each of them stood in the organization.

I leafed through them twice, wondering if one of them could be Loren himself. Owen had never known.

"It would seem you were right," Ordaz said. "He could not have collected such detail by accident. He must have planned from the beginning to betray the Loren gang."

"Just as I told you. And he was murdered for it."

"It seems he must have been. What motive could he have had for suicide?" Ordaz's round, calm face was doing its best to show anger. "I find I cannot believe in our inconsistent murderer, either. You have ruined my digestion, Mr. Hamilton."

I told him my idea about other tenants on Owen's floor. He nodded. "Possibly, possibly. This is your department now. Organlegging is the business of the ARMs."

"Right." I closed the briefcase and hefted it. "Let's see what the computer can do with these. I'll send you photocopies of everything in here."

"You'll let me know about the other tenants?"

"Of course."

I walked into ARM Headquarters swinging that precious briefcase, feeling on top of the world. Owen had been murdered. He had died with honor, if not—oh, definitely not—with dignity. Even Ordaz knew it now.

Then Jackson Bera, snarling and panting, went by at a dead run.

"What's up?" I called after him. Maybe I wanted a chance to brag. I had twenty-three faces, twenty-three organleggers, in my briefcase.

Bera slid to a stop beside me. "Where have *you* been?"

"Working. Honest. What's the hurry?"

"Remember that pleasure peddler we were watching?"

"Graham? Kenneth Graham?"

"That's the one. He's dead. We blew it." And Bera took off.

He'd reached the lab by the time I caught up with him.

Kenneth Graham's corpse was faceup on the operating table. His long, lantern-jawed face was pale and slack, without expression, empty. Machinery was in place above and below his head.

"How you doing?" Bera demanded.

"Not good," the doctor answered. "Not your fault. You got him into the deep freeze fast enough. It's just that the current—" He shrugged.

I shook Bera's shoulder. "What happened?"

Bera was panting a little from his run. "Something must have leaked. Graham tried to make a run for it. We got him at the airport."

"You could have waited. Put someone on the plane with him. Flooded the plane with TY-4."

"Remember the stink the last time we used TY-4 on civilians? Damn newscasters." Bera was shivering. I didn't blame him.

ARMs and organleggers play a funny kind of game. The organleggers have to turn their donors in alive, so they're always armed with hypo guns, firing slivers of crystalline anesthetic that melt instantly in the blood. We use the same weapon for somewhat the same reason: a criminal has to be saved for trial and then for the government hospitals. So no ARM ever expects to kill a man.

There was a day I learned the truth. A small-time organlegger named Raphael Haine was trying to reach a call button in his own home. If he'd reached it, all kinds of hell would have broken loose, Haine's men would have hypoed me, and I would have regained consciousness a piece at a time in Haine's organ-storage tanks. So I strangled him.

The report was in the computer, but only three human beings knew about it. One was my immediate superior, Lucas Garner. The other was Julie. So far he was the only man I'd ever killed.

And Graham was Bera's first killing.

"We got him at the airport," Bera said. "He was wearing a hat. I wish I'd noticed that; we might have moved faster. We started to close in on him with hypo guns. He turned and saw us. He reached under his hat, and then he fell."

"Killed himself?"

"Uh huh."

"How?"

"Look at his head."

I edged closer to the table, trying to stay out of the doctor's way. The doctor was going through the routine of trying to pull information from a dead brain by induction. It wasn't going well.

There was a flat oblong box on top of Graham's head. Black plastic, about half the size of a pack of cards. I touched it and knew at once that it was attached to Graham's skull.

"A droud. Not a standard type. Too big."

"Uh huh."

Liquid helium ran up my nerves. "There's a battery in it."

"Right."

"I often wonder what the vintners buy, et cetera. A cordless droud. Man, that's what *I* want for Christmas."

Bera twitched all over. "Don't *say* that."

"Did you know he was a current addict?"

"No. We were afraid to bug his home. He might have found it and been tipped. Take another look at that thing."

The shape was wrong, I thought. The black plastic case had been half melted.

"Heat," I mused. "Oh!"

"Uh huh. He blew the whole battery at once. Sent the whole killing charge right through his brain, right through the pleasure center of his brain. And Jesus, Gil, the thing I keep wondering is, What did it feel like? Gil, what could it possibly have *felt* like?"

I thumped him across the shoulders in lieu of giving him an intelligent answer. He'd be a long time wondering.

Here was the man who had put the wire in Owen's head. Had his death been momentary hell or all the delights of paradise in one singing jolt? Hell, I hoped, but I didn't believe it.

At least Kenneth Graham wasn't somewhere else in the world, getting a new face and new retinas and new fingertips from Loren's illicit organ banks.

"Nothing," the doctor said. "His brain's too badly burned. There's just nothing there that isn't too scrambled to make sense."

"Keep trying," Bera said.

I left quietly. Maybe later I'd buy Bera a drink. He seemed to need it. Bera was one of those with empathy. I knew that he could almost feel that awful surge of ecstasy and defeat as Kenneth Graham left the world behind.

The holos from Monica Apartments had arrived hours ago. Miller had picked not only the tenants who had occupied the eighteenth floor during the past six weeks but tenants from the nineteenth and seventeenth floors, too. It seemed an embarrassment of riches. I toyed with the idea of someone from the nineteenth floor dropping over his balcony to the eighteenth every day for five weeks. But 1809 hadn't had an outside wall, let alone a window, not to mention a balcony.

Had Miller played with the same idea? Nonsense. He didn't even know the problem. He'd just overkilled with the holos to show how cooperative he was.

None of the tenants during the period in question matched known or suspected Loren men.

I said a few appropriate words and went for coffee. Then I remembered the twenty-three possible Loren men in Owen's briefcase. I'd left them with a programmer, since I wasn't quite sure how to get them into the computer myself. He ought to be finished by now.

I called down. He was.

I persuaded the computer to compare them with the holos from Monica Apartments.

Nothing. Nobody matched anybody.

I spent the next two hours writing up the Owen Jennison case. A programmer would have to translate it for the machine. I wasn't that good yet.

We were back with Ordaz's inconsistent killer.

That and a tangle of dead ends. Owen's death had bought us a handful of new pictures, pictures which might even be obsolete by now. Organleggers changed their faces at the drop of a hat. I finished the case outline, sent it down to a programmer, and called Julie. I wouldn't need her protection now.

Julie had left for home.

I started to call Taffy, stopped with her number half-dialed. There are times not to make a phone call. I needed to sulk; I needed a cave to be alone in. My expression would probably have broken a phone screen. Why inflict it on an innocent girl?

I left for home.

It was dark when I reached the street. I rode the pedestrian bridge across the slidewalks, waited for a taxi at the intersection disk. Presently one dropped, the white FREE sign blinking on its belly. I stepped in and deposited my credit card.

Owen had collected his holos from all over the Eurasian continent. Most of them, if not all, had been Loren's foreign agents. Why had I expected to find them in Los Angeles?

The taxi rose into the white night sky. City lights turned the cloud cover into a flat white dome. We penetrated the clouds and stayed there. The taxi autopilot didn't care if I had a view or not.

. . . So what did I have now? Someone among dozens of tenants was a Loren man. That, or Ordaz's inconsistent killer, the careful one, had left Owen to die for five weeks, alone and unsupervised.

. . . Was the inconsistent killer so unbelievable?

He was, after all, my own hypothetical Loren. And Loren had committed murder, the ultimate crime. He'd murdered routinely, over and over, with fabulous profits. The ARMs hadn't been able to touch him. Wasn't it about time he started getting careless?

Like Graham. How long had Graham been selecting donors among his customers, choosing a few nonentities a year? And then, twice within a few months, he took clients who were missed. Careless.

Most criminals are not too bright. Loren had brains enough, but the men on his payroll would be about average. Loren would deal with the stupid ones, the ones who turned to crime because they didn't have enough sense to make it in real life.

If a man like Loren got careless, this was how it would happen. Unconsciously he would judge ARM intelligence by his own men. Seduced by an ingenious plan for murder, he might ignore the single loophole and go through with it. With Graham to advise him, he knew more about current addiction than we did, perhaps enough to trust the effects of current addiction on Owen.

Then Owen's killers had delivered him to his apartment and never seen him again. It was a small gamble Loren had taken, and it had paid off this time.

Next time he'd grow more careless. One day we'd get him.

The taxi settled out of the traffic pattern, touched down on the roof of my apartment building in the Hollywood Hills. I got out and moved toward the elevators.

An elevator opened. Someone stepped out.

Something warned me, something about the way he moved. I turned, quick drawing from the shoulder. The taxi might have made good cover—if it hadn't been already rising. Other figures had stepped from the shadows.

I think I got a couple before something stung my cheek.

Mercy bullets, slivers of crystalline anesthetics melting in my bloodstream. My head spun, and the roof spun, and the centrifugal force dropped me limply to the roof. Shadows loomed above me, then receded to infinity.

Fingers on my scalp shocked me awake.

I woke standing upright, bound like a mummy in soft, swaddling bandages. I couldn't so much as twitch a muscle below my neck. By the time I knew that much, it was too late. The man behind me had finished removing electrodes from my head and stepped into view, out of reach of my imaginary arm.

There was something of the bird about him. He was tall and slender, small-boned, and his triangular face reached a point at the chin. His wild, silken blond hair had withdrawn from his temples, leaving a sharp widow's peak. He wore impeccably tailored wool street shorts in orange and brown stripes. Smiling brightly, with his arms folded and his head cocked to one side, he stood waiting for me to speak.

And I recognized him. Owen had taken a holo of him somewhere.

"Where am I?" I groaned, trying to sound groggy. "What time is it?"

"Time? It's already morning," my captor said. "As for where you are, I'll let you wonder."

Something about his manner . . . I took a guess and said, "Loren?"

Loren bowed, not overdoing it. "And you are Gilbert Hamilton of the United Nations Police. Gil the Arm."

Had he said Arm or ARM? I let it pass. "I seem to have slipped."

"You underestimated the reach of my own arm. You also underestimated my interest."

I had. It isn't much harder to capture an ARM than any other citizen if you catch him off guard and if you're willing to risk the men. In this case his risk had cost him nothing. Cops use hypo guns for the same reason organleggers do. The men I'd shot, if I'd hit anyone in those few seconds of battle, would have come around long ago. Loren must have set me up in these bandages, then left me under "Russian sleep" until he was ready to talk to me.

The electrodes were the "Russian sleep." One goes on each eyelid, one on the nape of the neck. A small current goes through the brain, putting you right to sleep. You get a full night's sleep in an hour. If it's not turned off, you can sleep forever.

So this was Loren.

He stood watching me with his head cocked to one side, birdlike, with his arms folded. One hand held a hypo gun, rather negligently, I thought.

What time was it? I didn't dare ask again, because Loren might guess something. But if I could stall him until 0945, Julie could send help . . .

She could send help where?

Finagle in hysterics! Where was I? If I didn't know that, Julie wouldn't know, either!

And Loren intended me for the organ banks. One crystalline sliver would knock me out without harming any of the delicate, infinitely various parts that made me Gil Hamilton. Then Loren's doctors would take me apart.

In government operating rooms they flash-burn the criminal's brain for later urn burial. God knows what Loren would do with my brain. But the rest of me was young and healthy. Even considering Loren's overhead, I was worth more than a million UN marks on the hoof.

"Why me?" I asked. "It was me you wanted, not just any ARM. Why the interest in me?"

"It was you who were investigating the case of Owen Jennison. *Much* too thoroughly."

"Not thoroughly enough, dammit!"

Loren looked puzzled. "You really don't understand?"

"I really don't."

"I find that highly interesting," Loren mused. "Highly."

"All right, why am I still alive?"

"I was curious, Mr. Hamilton. I hoped you'd tell me about your imaginary arm."

So he'd said Arm, not ARM. I bluffed anyway. "My *what*?"

"No need for games, Mr. Hamilton. If I think I'm losing, I'll use this." He wiggled the hypo gun. "You'll never wake up."

Damn! He knew. The only things I could move were my ears and my imaginary arm, and Loren knew all about it! I'd never be able to lure him into reach.

Provided that he knew *all* about it.

I had to draw him out.

"Okay," I said, "but I'd like to know how you found out about it. A plant in the ARMs?"

Loren chuckled. "I wish it were so. No. We captured one of your men some months ago, quite by accident. When I realized what he was, I induced him to talk shop with me. He was able to tell me something about your remarkable arm. I hope you'll tell me more."

"Who was it?"

"Really, Mr. Hamil—"

"Who was it?"

"Do you really expect me to remember the name of every donor?"

Who had gone into Loren's organ banks? Stranger, acquaintance, friend? Does the manager of a slaughterhouse remember every slaughtered steer?

"So-called psychic powers interest me," Loren said. "I remembered you. And then, when I was on the verge of concluding an agreement with your Belter friend Jennison, I remembered something unusual about a crewman he had shipped with. They called you Gil the Arm, didn't they? Prophetic. In port your drinks came free if you could use your imaginary arm to drink them."

"Then damn you. You thought Owen was a plant, did you? Because of me! Me!"

"Breast-beating will earn you nothing, Mr. Hamilton." Loren put steel in his voice. "Entertain me, Mr. Hamilton."

I'd been feeling around for anything that might release

me from my upright prison. No such luck. I was wrapped like a mummy in bandages too strong to break. All I could feel with my imaginary hand were cloth bandages up to my neck and a bracing rod along my back to hold me upright. Beneath the swathing I was naked.

"I'll show you my eldritch powers," I told Loren, "if you'll loan me a cigarette." Maybe that would draw him close enough ...

He knew something about my arm. He knew its reach. He put one single cigarette on the edge of a small table on wheels and slid it up to me. I picked it up and stuck it in my mouth and waited hopefully for him to come light it. "My mistake," he murmured, and he pulled the table back and repeated the whole thing with a lighted cigarette.

No luck. At least I'd gotten my smoke. I pitched the dead one as far as it would go: about two feet. I have to move slowly with my imaginary hand. Otherwise what I'm holding simply slips through my fingers.

Loren watched in fascination. A floating, disembodied cigarette, obeying my will! His eyes held traces of awe and horror. That was bad. Maybe the cigarette had been a mistake.

Some people see psi powers as akin to witchcraft and psychic people as servants of Satan. If Loren feared me, then I was dead.

"Interesting," Loren said. "How far will it reach?"

He knew that. "As far as my real arm, of course."

"But why? Others can reach much farther. Why not you?"

He was clear across the room, a good ten yards away, sprawled in an armchair. One hand held a drink; the other held the hypo gun. He was superbly relaxed. I wondered if I'd ever see him move from that comfortable chair, much less come within reach.

The room was small and bare, with the look of a basement. Loren's chair and a small portable bar were the only furnishings unless there were others behind me.

A basement could be anywhere. Anywhere in Los Angeles or out of it. If it was really morning, I could be anywhere on Earth by now.

"Sure," I said, "others can reach farther than me. But they don't have my strength. It's an imaginary arm, sure enough, and my imagination won't make it ten feet long. Maybe someone could convince me it was if he tried hard enough. But maybe he'd ruin what belief I have. Then I'd have two arms, just like everyone else. I'm better off . . ." I let it trail away because Loren was going to take all my damn arms anyway.

My cigarette was finished. I pitched it away.

"Want a drink?"

"Sure, if you've got a jigger glass. Otherwise I can't lift it."

He found me a shot glass and sent it to me on the edge of the rolling table. I was barely strong enough to pick it up. Loren's eyes never left me as I sipped and put it down.

The old cigarette lure. Last night I'd used it to pick up a girl. Now it was keeping me alive.

Did I really want to leave the world with something gripped tightly in my imaginary fist? Entertaining Loren. Holding his interest until—

Where was I? Where?

And suddenly I knew. "We're at Monica Apartments," I said. "Nowhere else."

"I knew you'd guess that eventually." Loren smiled. "But it's too late. I got to you in time."

"Don't be so damn complacent. It was my stupidity, not your luck. I should have *smelled* it. Owen would never have come here of his own choice. You ordered him here."

"And so I did. By then I already knew he was a traitor."

"So you sent him here to die. Who was it that checked on him every day to see he'd stayed put? Was it Miller, the manager? He has to be working for you. He's the one who took your holograms out of the computer."

"He was the one," Loren said. "But it wasn't every day. I had a man watching Jennison every second, through a portable camera. We took it out after he was dead."

"And then waited a week. Nice touch." The wonder was that it had taken me so long. The atmosphere of the place . . . what kind of people would live in Monica Apartments? The faceless ones, the ones with no identity, the ones who would surely be missed by nobody. They would stay put in their apartments while Loren checked on them to see that they really did have nobody to miss them. Those who qualified would disappear, and their papers and possessions with them, and their holos would vanish from the computer.

Loren said, "I tried to sell organs to the Belters through your friend Jennison. I know he betrayed me, Hamilton. I want to know how badly."

"Badly enough." He'd guess that. "We've got detailed plans for setting up an organ-bank dispensary in the Belt. It wouldn't have worked anyway, Loren. Belters don't think that way."

"No pictures."

"No." I didn't want him changing his face.

"I was sure he'd left something," Loren said. "Otherwise we'd have made him a donor. Much simpler. More profitable, too. I needed the money, Hamilton. Do you know what it costs the organization to let a donor go?"

"A million or so. Why'd you do it?"

"He'd left something. There was no way to get at it. All we could do was try to keep the ARMs from looking for it."

"Ah." I had it then. "When anyone disappears without a trace, the first thing any idiot thinks of is organleggers."

"Naturally. So he couldn't just disappear, could he? The police would go to the ARMs, the file would go to you, and you'd start looking."

"For a spaceport locker."

"Oh?"

"Under the name of Cubes Forsythe."

"I knew that name," Loren said between his teeth. "I should have tried that. You know, after we had him hooked on current, we tried pulling the plug on him to get him to talk. It didn't work. He couldn't concentrate on anything but getting the droud back in his head. We looked high and low—"

"I'm going to kill you," I said, and meant every word.

Loren cocked his head, frowning. "On the contrary, Mr. Hamilton. Another cigarette?"

"Yah."

He sent it to me, lighted, on the rolling table. I picked it up, holding it a trifle ostentatiously. Maybe I could focus his attention on it—on his only way to find my imaginary hand.

Because if he kept his eyes on the cigarette and I put it in my mouth at a crucial moment, I'd leave my hand free without his noticing.

What crucial moment? He was still in the armchair. I had to fight the urge to coax him closer. Any move in that direction would make him suspicious.

What time was it? And what was Julie doing? I thought of a night two weeks past. Remembered dinner on the balcony of the highest restaurant in Los Angeles, just a fraction less than a mile up. A carpet of neon that spread below us to touch the horizon in all directions. Maybe she'd pick it up . . .

She'd be checking on me at 0945.

"You must have made a remarkable spaceman," Loren said. "Think of being the only man in the solar system who can adjust a hull antenna without leaving the cabin."

"Antennas take a little more muscle than I've got." So he knew I could reach through things. If he'd seen that far—"I should have stayed," I told Loren. "I wish I were on a mining ship right this minute. All I wanted at the time was two good arms."

"Pity. Now you have three. Did it occur to you that using psi powers against men was a form of cheating?"

"What?"

"Remember Raphael Haine?" Loren's voice had become uneven. He was angry and was holding it down with difficulty.

"Sure. Small-time organlegger in Australia."

"Raphael Haine was a friend of mine. I know he had you tied up at one point. Tell me, Mr. Hamilton: if your imaginary hand is as weak as you say, how did you untie the ropes?"

"I didn't. I couldn't have. Haine used handcuffs. I picked his pocket for the key ... with my imaginary hand, of course."

"You used psi powers against him. You had no right!"

Magic. Anyone who's not psychic himself feels the same way, just a little. A touch of dread, a touch of envy. Loren thought he could handle ARMs; he'd killed at least one of us. But to send warlocks against him was grossly unfair.

That was why he'd let me wake up. Loren wanted to gloat. How many men have captured a warlock?

"Don't be an idiot," I said. "I didn't volunteer to play your silly game or Haine's, either. *My* rules make you a wholesale murderer."

Loren got to his feet (what time was it?), and I suddenly realized my time was up. He was in a white rage. His silky blond hair seemed to stand on end.

I looked into the tiny needle hole in the hypo gun. There was nothing I could do. The reach of my TK was the reach of my fingers. I felt all the things I would never feel: the quart of Trastine in my blood to keep the water from freezing in my cells, the cold bath of half-frozen alcohol, the scalpels and the tiny, accurate surgical lasers. Most of all, the scalpels.

And my knowledge would die when they threw away my brain. I knew what Loren looked like. I knew about Monica Apartments and who knew how many others of the same kind? I knew where to go to find all the loveliness in Death Valley, and someday I was going to go. What time was it? What time?

Loren had raised the hypo gun and was sighting down the stiff length of his arm. Obviously he thought he was at target practice. "It really is a pity," he said, and there was only the slightest tremor in his voice. "You should have stayed a spaceman."

What was he waiting for? "I can't cringe unless you loosen these bandages," I snapped, and I jabbed what was left of my cigarette at him for emphasis. It jerked out of my grip, and I reached and caught it and—

And stuck it in my left eye.

At another time I'd have examined the idea a little more closely. But I'd still have done it. Loren already thought of me as his property. As live skin and healthy kidneys and lengths of artery, as parts in Loren's organ banks, I was property worth a million UN marks. And I was destroying my eye! Organleggers are always hurting for eyes; anyone who wears glasses could use a new pair, and the organleggers themselves are constantly wanting to change retina prints.

What I hadn't anticipated was the pain. I'd read somewhere that there are no sensory nerves in the eyeball. Then it was my lids that hurt. Terribly!

But I had to hold on only for a moment.

Loren swore and came for me at a dead run. He knew how terribly weak my imaginary arm was. What could I do with it? He didn't know; he'd never known, though it stared him in the face. He ran at me and slapped at the cigarette, a full swing that half knocked my head off my neck and sent the now-dead butt ricocheting off a wall. Panting, snarling, speechless with rage, he stood—within reach.

My eye closed like a small tormented fist.

I reached past Loren's gun, through his chest wall, and found his heart. And squeezed.

His eyes became very round, his mouth gaped wide, his larynx bobbed convulsively. There was time to fire the gun. Instead he clawed at his chest with a half-paralyzed arm. Twice he raked his fingernails across his chest, gaping upward for air that wouldn't come. He thought he was having a heart attack. Then his rolling eyes found my face.

My face. I was a one-eyed carnivore, snarling with the will to murder. I would have his life if I had to tear the heart out of his chest! How could he help but know?

He knew!

He fired at the floor and fell.

I was sweating and shaking with reaction and disgust. The scars! He was all scars; I'd felt them going in. His heart was a transplant. And the rest of him—he'd looked about thirty from a distance, but this close it was impossible to tell. Parts were younger, parts older. How much of Loren was Loren? What parts had he taken from others? And none of the parts quite matched.

He must have been chronically ill, I thought. And the Board wouldn't give him the transplants he needed. And one day he'd seen the answer to all his problems . . .

Loren wasn't moving. He wasn't breathing. I remembered the way his heart had jumped and wriggled in my imaginary hand and then suddenly given up.

He was lying on his left arm, hiding his watch. I was all alone in an empty room, and I still didn't know what time it was.

I never found out. It was hours before Miller finally dared to interrupt his boss. He stuck his round, blank face around the doorjamb, saw Loren sprawled at my feet, and darted back with a squeak. A minute later a hypo gun came around the jamb, followed by a watery blue eye. I felt the sting in my cheek.

"I checked you early," Julie said. She settled herself uncomfortably at the foot of the hospital bed. "Rather, you called me. When I came to work, you weren't there, and I wondered why, and *wham*. It was bad, wasn't it?"

"Pretty bad," I said.

"I've never sensed anyone so scared."

"Well, don't tell anyone about it." I hit the switch to raise the bed to the sitting position. "I've got an image to maintain."

My eye and the socket around it were bandaged and numb. There was no pain, but the numbness was obtrusive, a reminder of two dead men who had become part of me. One arm, one eye.

If Julie was feeling that with me, then small wonder if

she was nervous. She was. She kept shifting and twisting on the bed.

"I kept wondering what time it was. What time was it?"

"About nine-ten." Julie shivered. "I thought I'd faint when that—that vague little man pointed his hypo gun around the corner. Oh, don't! Don't, Gil. It's *over*."

That close? Was it *that* close? "Look," I said, "you go back to work. I appreciate the sick call, but this isn't doing either of us any good. If we keep it up, we'll both wind up in a state of permanent terror."

She nodded jerkily and got up.

"Thanks for coming. Thanks for saving my life, too."

Julie smiled from the doorway. "Thanks for the orchids."

I hadn't ordered them yet. I flagged down a nurse and got her to tell me that I could leave tonight, after dinner, provided that I went straight home to bed. She brought me a phone, and I used it to order the orchids.

Afterward I dropped the bed back and lay there awhile. It was nice being alive. I began to remember promises I had made, promises I might never have kept. Perhaps it was time to keep a few.

I called down to surveillance and got Jackson Bera. After letting him drag from me the story of my heroism, I invited him up to the infirmary for a drink. His bottle, but I'd pay. He didn't like that part, but I bullied him into it.

I had dialed half of Taffy's number before, as I had last night, I changed my mind. My wristphone was on the bedside table. No pictures.

" 'Lo."

"Taffy? This is Gil. Can you get a weekend free?"

"Sure. Starting Friday?"

"Good."

"Come for me at ten. Did you ever find out about your friend?"

"Yah. I was right. Organleggers killed him. It's over now; we got the guy in charge." I didn't mention the eye. By Friday the bandages would be off. "About that weekend. How would you like to see Death Valley?"

"You're kidding, right?"

"I'm kidding, wrong. Listen—"

"But it's hot! It's dry! It's as dead as the moon! You did say Death Valley, didn't you?"

"It's not hot this month. Listen . . ." And she did listen. She listened long enough to be convinced.

"I've been thinking," she said then. "If we're going to see a lot of each other, we'd better make a—a bargain. No shop talk. All right?"

"A good idea."

"The point is, I work in a hospital," Taffy said. "Surgery. To me, organic transplant material is just the tools of my trade, tools to use in healing. It took me a long time to get that way. I don't want to know where the stuff comes from, and I don't want to know anything about organleggers."

"Okay, we've got a covenant. See you at ten hundred Friday."

A doctor, I thought afterward. Well. The weekend was going to be a good one. Surprising people are always the ones most worth knowing.

Bera came in with a pint of J&B. "My treat," he said. "No use arguing, 'cause you can't reach your wallet, anyway." And the fight was on.

THE DEFENSELESS DEAD

The dead lay side by side beneath the glass. Long ago, in a roomier world, these older ones had been entombed each in his own double-walled casket. Now they lay shoulder to shoulder, more or less in chronological order, looking up, their features clear through thirty centimeters of liquid nitrogen sandwiched between two thick sheets of glass.

Elsewhere in the building some sleepers wore clothing, the formal costumery of a dozen periods. In two long tanks on another floor the sleepers had been prettied up with low-temperature cosmetics and sometimes with a kind of flesh-colored putty to fill and cover major wounds. A weird practice. It hadn't lasted beyond the middle of the last century. After all, these sleepers planned to return to life someday. The damage should show at a glance.

With these, it did.

They were all from the tail end of the twentieth century. They looked like hell. Some were clearly beyond saving, accident cases whose wills had consigned them to the freezer banks regardless. Each sleeper was marked by a plaque describing everything that was wrong with his mind and body, in script so fine and so archaic as to be almost unreadable.

Battered or torn or wasted by disease, they all wore the same look of patient resignation. Their hair was disintegrat-

71

ing very slowly. It had fallen in a thick gray crescent about each head.

"People used to call them *corpsicles*, frozen dead. Or *Homo snapiens*. You can imagine what would happen if you dropped one." Mr. Restarick did not smile. These people were in his charge, and he took his task seriously. His eyes seemed to look through rather than at me, and his clothes were ten to fifty years out of style. He seemed to be gradually losing himself here in the past. He said, "We've over six thousand of them here. Do you think we'll ever bring them back to life?" I was an ARM; I might know.

"Do you?"

"Sometimes I wonder." He dropped his gaze. "Not Harrison Cohn. Look at him, torn open like that. And *her*, with half her face shot off; she'd be a vegetable if you brought her back. The later ones don't look this bad. Up until 1989 the doctors couldn't freeze anyone who wasn't clinically dead."

"That doesn't make *sense*. Why not?"

"They'd have been up for murder. When what they were doing was *saving* lives." He shrugged angrily. "Sometimes they'd stop a patient's heart and then restart it to satisfy the legalities."

Sure, that made a lot of sense. I didn't dare laugh out loud. I pointed. "How about him?"

He was a rangy man of about forty-five, healthy-looking, with no visible marks of death, violent or otherwise. The long lean face still wore a look of command, though the deep-set eyes were almost closed. His lips were slightly parted, showing teeth straightened by braces in the ancient fashion.

Mr. Restarick glanced at the plaque. "Leviticus Hale, 1991. Oh, yes. Hale was a paranoid. He must have been the first they ever froze for *that*. They guessed right, too. If we brought him back now, we could cure him."

"If."

"It's been done."

"Sure. We only lose one out of three. He'd probably take

the chance himself. But then, he's crazy." I looked around at rows of long double-walled liquid nitrogen tanks. The place was huge and full of echoes, and this was only the top floor. The Vault of Eternity was ten stories deep in earthquake-free bedrock. "Six thousand, you said. But the vault was built for ten thousand, wasn't it?"

He nodded. "We're a third empty."

"Get many customers these days?"

He laughed at me. "You're joking. Nobody has himself frozen these days. He might wake up a piece at a time!"

"That's what I wondered."

"Ten years ago we were thinking of digging new vaults. All those crazy kids, perfectly healthy, getting themselves frozen so they could wake up in a brave new world. I had to watch while the ambulances came and carted them away for spare parts! We're a good third empty now since the Freezer Law passed!"

That business with the kids had been odd, all right. A fad or a religion or a madness, except that it had gone on for much too long.

The Freezeout Kids. Most of them were textbook cases of anomie, kids in their late teens who felt trapped in an imperfect world. History taught them (those who listened) that earlier times had been much worse. Perhaps they thought that the world was moving toward perfection.

Some had gambled. Not many in any given year, but it had been going on ever since the first experimental freezer vault revivals, a generation before I was born. It was better than suicide. They were young, they were healthy, they stood a better chance of revival than any of the frozen, damaged dead. They were poorly adapted to their society. Why not risk it?

Two years ago they had been answered. The General Assembly and the world vote had passed the Freezer Bill into law.

There were those in frozen sleep who had not had the foresight to set up a trust fund or who had selected the wrong trustee or invested in the wrong stocks. If medicine or a miracle had revived them now, they would have been on the dole, with no money and no trace of useful education and, in about half the cases, no evident ability to survive in *any* society.

Were they in frozen sleep or frozen death? In law there had always been that point of indecision. The Freezer Law cleared it up to some extent. It declared any person in frozen sleep who could not support himself should society choose to reawaken him to be dead in law.

And a third of the world's frozen dead, twelve hundred thousand of them, had gone into the organ banks.

"You were in charge then?"

The old man nodded. "I've been on the day shift at the vault for almost forty years. I watched the ambulances fly away with three thousand of my people. I think of them as my people," he said a bit defensively.

"The law can't seem to decide if they're alive or dead. Think of them any way you like."

"People who trusted me. What did those Freezeout Kids do that was worth killing them for?"

I thought: they wanted to sleep it out while others broke their backs turning the world into paradise. But it's no capital crime.

"They had nobody to defend them. Nobody but me." He trailed off. After a bit, and with visible effort, he pulled himself back to the present. "Well, never mind. What can I do for the United Nations Police, Mr. Hamilton?"

"Oh, I'm not here as an ARM agent. I'm just here to, to—" Hell, I didn't know myself. It was a news broadcast that had jarred me into coming here. I said, "They're planning to introduce another Freezer Bill."

"What?"

"A second Freezer Bill. Naming a different group. The communal organ banks must be empty again," I said bitterly.

Mr. Restarick started to shake. "Oh, no. No. They can't do that again. They, they can't."

I gripped his arm to reassure him or to hold him up. He

looked about to faint. "Maybe they can't. The first Freezer Law was supposed to stop organlegging, but it didn't. Maybe the citizens will vote this one down."

I left as soon as I could.

The second Freezer Bill made slow, steady progress without much opposition. I caught some of it in the boob cube. A perturbingly large number of citizens were petitioning the Security Council for confiscation of what they described as "The frozen corpses of a large number of people who were insane when they died. Parts of those corpses could possibly be recovered for badly needed organ replacements . . ."

They never mentioned that said corpses might someday be recovered whole and living. They often mentioned that said corpses could not be safely recovered *now*, and they could prove it with experts, and they had a thousand experts waiting their turns to testify.

They never mentioned biochemical cures for insanity. They spoke of the lack of a worldwide need for mental patients and insanity-carrying genes.

They hammered constantly on the need for organ transplant material.

I just about gave up watching news broadcasts. I was an ARM, a member of the United Nations police force, and I wasn't supposed to get involved in politics. It was none of my business.

It didn't become my business until I ran across a familiar name eleven months later.

Taffy was people watching. That demure look didn't fool me. A secretive glee looked out of her soft brown eyes, and they shifted left every time she raised her dessert spoon.

I didn't try to follow her eyes for fear of blowing her cover. Come, I will conceal nothing from you: I don't *care* who's eating at the next table in a public restaurant. Instead I lit a cigarette, shifted it to my imaginary hand (the weight tugging gently at my mind), and settled back to enjoy my surroundings.

High Cliffs is an enormous pyramidal city in a building in northern California. Midgard is on the first shopping level, way back near the service core. There's no view, but the restaurant makes up for it with a spectacular set of environment walls.

From inside, Midgard seems to be halfway up the trunk of an enormous tree, big enough to stretch from hell to heaven. Perpetual war is waged in the vasty distances, on various limbs of the tree, between warriors of oddly distorted size and shape. World-sized beasts show occasionally: a wolf attacks the moon, a sleeping serpent coils round the restaurant itself, the eye of a curious brown squirrel suddenly blocks one row of windows . . .

"Isn't that Holden Chambers?"

"Who?" The name sounded vaguely familiar.

"Four tables over, sitting alone."

I looked. He was tall and skinny and much younger than most of Midgard's clientele. Long blond hair, weak chin—he was really the type who ought to grow a beard. I was sure I'd never seen him before.

Taffy frowned. "I wonder why he's eating alone. Do you suppose someone broke a date?"

The name clicked. "Holden Chambers. Kidnapping case. Someone kidnapped him and his sister years ago. One of Bera's cases."

Taffy put down her dessert spoon and looked at me curiously. "I didn't know the ARM took kidnapping cases."

"We don't. Kidnapping would be a regional problem. Bera thought—" I stopped because Chambers looked around suddenly, right at me. He seemed surprised and annoyed.

I hadn't realized how rudely I was staring. I looked away, embarrassed. "Bera thought an organlegging gang might be involved. Some of the gangs turned to kidnapping about that time, after the Freezer Law slid their markets out from under them. Is Chambers still looking at me?" I felt his eyes on the back of my neck.

"Yah."

"I wonder why."

"*Do* you indeed?" Taffy knew, the way she was grinning. She gave me another two seconds of suspense, then said, "You're doing the cigarette trick."

"Oh. Right." I transferred the cigarette to a hand of flesh and blood. It's silly to forget how startling that can be: a cigarette or a pencil or a jigger of bourbon floating in mid-air. I've used it myself for shock effect.

Taffy said, "He's been in the boob cube a lot lately. He's the number eight corpsicle heir worldwide. Didn't you know?"

"Corpsicle heir?"

"You know what *corpsicle* means? When the freezer vaults first opened—"

"I know. I didn't know they'd started using the word again."

"Well, never mind *that*. The *point* is that if the second Freezer Bill passes, about three hundred thousand corpsicles will be declared formally dead. Some of those frozen dead men have money. The money will go to their next of kin."

"*Oh.* And Chambers has an ancestor in a vault some-where, does he?"

"Somewhere in Michigan. He's got an odd biblical name."

"Not Leviticus Hale?"

She stared. "Now, just how the bleep did you know that?"

"Just a stab in the dark." I didn't know what had made me say it. Leviticus Hale, dead, had a memorable face and a memorable name.

Strange, though, that I'd never thought of money as a motive for the second Freezer Bill. The first Freezer Law had applied only to the destitute, the Freezeout Kids.

Here are people who could not possibly adjust to any time in which they might be revived. They couldn't even ad-

just to their own times. Most of them weren't even sick; they didn't have that much excuse for foisting themselves on a nebulous future. Often they paid each other's way into the freezer vaults. If revived, they would be paupers, unemployable, uneducated by any possible present or future standards, permanent malcontents.

Young, healthy, useless to themselves and society. And the organ banks are always empty . . .

The arguments for the second Freezer Bill were not much different. The corpsicles named in group two had money, but they were insane. Today there were chemical cures for most forms of insanity. But the memory of having been insane, the habitual thought patterns formed by paranoia or schizophrenia, these would remain, these would require psychotherapy. And how to cure them in men and women whose patterns of experience were up to 140 years out of date to start with?

And the organ banks are always empty . . . Sure, I could see it. The citizens wanted to live forever. One day they'd work their way down to me, Gil Hamilton.

"You can't win," I said.

Taffy said, "How so?"

"If you're destitute, they won't revive you because you can't support yourself. If you're rich, your heirs want the money. It's hard to defend yourself when you're dead."

"Everyone who loved them is dead, too." She looked too seriously into her coffee cup. "I didn't really pay much attention when they passed the Freezer Law. At the hospital we don't even know where the spare parts come from: criminals, corpsicles, captured organleggers' stocks, it all looks the same. Lately I find myself wondering."

Taffy had once finished a lung transplant with hands and sterile steel after the hospital machines had quit at an embarrassing moment. A squeamish woman couldn't have done that. But the transplants themselves had started to bother her lately. Since she met me. A surgeon and an organlegger-hunting ARM, we made a strange pairing.

When I looked again, Holden Chambers was gone. We split the tab, paid, and left.

The first shopping level had an odd outdoor-indoor feel to it. We came out into a broad walk lined with shops and trees and theaters and sidewalk cafés, under a flat concrete sky forty feet up and glowing with light. Far away, an undulating black horizon showed in a narrow band between concrete sky and firmament.

The crowds had gone, but in some of the sidewalk cafés a few citizens still watched the world go by. We walked toward the black band of horizon, holding hands, taking our time. There was no way to hurry Taffy when she was passing shop windows. All I could do was stop when she did, wearing or not wearing an indulgent smile. Jewelry, clothing, all glowing behind plate glass—

She tugged my arm, turning sharply to look into a furniture store. I don't know what it was she saw. *I* saw a dazzling pulse of green light on the glass and a puff of green flame spurting from a coffee table.

Very strange. Surrealistic, I thought. Then the impressions sorted out, and I pushed Taffy hard in the small of the back and flung myself rolling in the opposite direction. Green light flashed briefly, very near. I stopped rolling. There was a weapon in my sporran the size of a double-barreled Derringer, two compressed-air cartridges firing clusters of anesthetic crystal slivers.

A few puzzled citizens had stopped to watch what I was doing.

I ripped my sporran apart with both hands. Everything spilled out, rolling coins and credit cards and ARM ident and cigarettes and—I snatched up the ARM weapon. The window reflection had been a break. Usually you can't tell *where* the pulse from a hunting laser might have come from.

Green light flashed near my elbow. The pavement cracked loudly and peppered me with particles. I fought an urge to fling myself backward. The afterimage was on my retina, a green line as thin as a razor's edge, pointing right at him.

He was in a cross street, poised kneeling, waiting for his gun to pulse again. I sent a cloud of mercy needles toward him. He slapped at his face, turned to run, and fell skidding.

I stayed where I was.

Taffy was curled on the pavement with her head buried in her arms. There was no blood around her. When I saw her legs shift, I knew she wasn't dead. I still didn't know if she'd been hit.

Nobody else tried to shoot at us.

The man with the gun lay where he was for almost a minute. Then he started twitching.

He was in convulsions when I got to him. Mercy needles aren't supposed to do that. I got his tongue out of his throat so he wouldn't choke, but I wasn't carrying medicines that could help. When the High Cliffs police arrived, he was dead.

Inspector Swan was a picture-poster cop, tri-racial and handsome as hell in an orange uniform that seemed tailored to him, so well did he fit it. He had the gun open in front of him and was probing at the electronic guts of it with a pair of tweezers. He said, "You don't have any idea why he was shooting at you?"

"That's right."

"You're an ARM. What do you work on these days?"

"Organlegging, mostly. Tracking down gangs that have gone into hiding." I was massaging Taffy's neck and shoulders, trying to calm her down. She was still shivering. The muscles under my hands were very tight.

Swan frowned. "Such an easy answer. But he couldn't be part of an organlegging gang, could he? Not with that gun."

"True." I ran my thumbs around the curve of Taffy's shoulder blades. She reached around and squeezed my hand.

The gun. I hadn't really expected Swan to see the implications. It was an unmodified hunting laser, right off the rack.

Officially, nobody in the world makes guns to kill people. Under the Conventions, not even armies use them, and the United Nations Police use mercy weapons with the intent that the criminals concerned should be unharmed for trial and, later, for the organ banks. The only killing weapons made are for killing animals. They are supposed to be, well, sportsmanlike.

A continuous-firing X-ray laser would be easy enough to make. It would chop down anything living, no matter how fast it fled, no matter what it hid behind. The beast wouldn't even know it was being shot at until you waved the beam through its body: an invisible sword blade a mile long.

But that's butchery. The prey should have a chance; it should at least know it's being shot at. A standard hunting laser fires a pulse of visible light and won't fire again for about a second. It's no better than a rifle, except in that you don't have to allow for windage, the range is close enough to infinite, you can't run out of bullets, it doesn't mess up the meat, and there's no recoil. That's what makes it sportsmanlike.

Against me it had been just sportsmanlike enough. He was dead. I wasn't.

"Not that it's so censored easy to modify a hunting laser," Swan said. "It takes some basic electronics. I could do it myself—"

"So could I. Why not? We've both had police training."

"The point is, I don't *know* anyone who couldn't *find* someone to modify a hunting laser, give it a faster pulse or even a continuous beam. Your friend must have been afraid to bring anyone else into it. He must have had a very personal grudge against you. You're sure you don't recognize him?"

"I never saw him before. Not with *that* face."

"And he's dead," Swan said.

"That doesn't really prove anything. Some people have allergic reactions to police anesthetics."

"You used a standard ARM weapon?"

"Yah. I didn't even fire both barrels. I *couldn't* have put a *lot* of needles in him. But there are allergic reactions."

"Especially if you take something to bring them on." Swan put the gun down and stood up. "Now, I'm just a city cop, and I don't know that much about ARM business. But I've heard that organleggers sometimes take something so they won't just go to sleep when an ARM anesthetic hits them."

"Yah. Organleggers don't like becoming spare parts themselves. I do have a theory, Inspector."

"Try me."

"He's a retired organlegger. A lot of them retired when the Freezer Bill passed. Their markets were gone, and they'd made their pile, some of them. They split up and became honest citizens. A respected citizen may keep a hunting laser on his wall, but it isn't modified. He could modify it if he had to with a day's notice."

"Then said respected citizen spotted an old enemy."

"Going into a restaurant, maybe. And he just had time to go home for his gun while we ate dinner."

"Sounds reasonable. How do we check it?"

"If you'll do a rejection spectrum on his brain tissue and send everything you've got to ARM Headquarters, we'll do the rest. An organlegger can change his face and fingerprints as he censored pleases, but he can't change his tolerance to transplants. Chances are he's on record."

"And you'll let me know."

"Right."

Swan was checking it with the radio on his scooter while I beeped my clicker for a taxi. The taxi settled at the edge of the walkway. I helped Taffy into it. Her movements were slow and jerky. She wasn't in shock, just depression.

Swan called from his scooter. "Hamilton!"

I stopped halfway into the taxi. "Yah?"

"He's a local," Swan boomed. His voice carried like an

orator's. "Mortimer Lincoln, ninety-fourth floor. Been living here since—" He checked again with his radio. "April 2123. I'd guess that's about six months after they passed the Freezer Law."

"Thanks." I typed an address on the cab's destination board. The cab hummed and rose.

I watched High Cliffs recede, a pyramid as big as a mountain, glowing with light. The city guarded by Inspector Swan was all in one building. It would make his job easier, I thought. Society would be a bit more organized.

Taffy spoke for the first time in a good while. "Nobody's ever shot at me before."

"It's all over now. I think he was shooting at me, anyway."

"I suppose." Suddenly she was shaking. I took her in my arms and held her. She talked into my shirt collar. "I didn't know what was happening. That green light; I thought it was *pretty*. I didn't know what happened until you knocked me down, and then that green line flashed at you and I heard the sidewalk go *ping*, and I didn't know what to *do*! I—"

"You did fine."

"I wanted to *help*! I didn't know; maybe you were dead, and there wasn't anything I could do. If you hadn't had a gun— Do you always carry a gun?"

"Always."

"I never knew." Without moving, she seemed to pull away from me a little.

At one time the Amalgamation of Regional Militia had been a federation of civil defense bodies in a number of nations. Later it had become the police force of the United Nations itself. They had kept the name. Probably they liked the acronym.

When I got to the office the next morning, Jackson Bera had already run the dead man to Earth. "No question about it," he told me. "His rejection spectrum checks perfectly. Anthony Tiller, known organlegger, suspected member of the Anubis gang. First came on the scene around 2120; he probably had another name and face before that. Disappeared April or May 2123."

"That fits. No, dammit, it doesn't. He must have been out of his mind. There he was, home free, rich and safe. Why would he blow it all to kill a man who never harmed a hair of his head?"

"You don't *really* expect an organlegger to behave like a well-adjusted member of society."

I answered Bera's grin. "I guess not ... Hey. You said *Anubis*, didn't you? The Anubis gang, not the Loren gang."

"That's what it says on the hard copy. Shall I query for probability?"

"Please." Bera programs a computer better than I do. I talked while he tapped at the keyboard in my desk. "Whoever the bleep he was, Anubis controlled the illicit medical facilities over a big section of the Midwest. Loren had a part of Eurasia, bigger area, bigger population. The difference is that I killed Loren myself by squeezing the life out of his heart with my imaginary hand, which is a very personal thing, as you will realize, Jackson. Whereas I never touched Anubis or any of his gang, or even interfered with his profits, to the best of my knowledge."

"I did," Bera said. "Maybe he thought I was you." Which is hilarious, because Bera is dark brown and a foot taller than me if you include the hair that puffs out around his head like a black powder explosion. "You missed something. Anubis was an intriguing character. He changed faces and ears and fingerprints whenever he got the urge. We're pretty sure he was male, but even that isn't worth a big bet. He's changed his height at least once. Full leg transplant."

"Loren couldn't do that. Loren was a pretty sick boy. He probably went into organlegging because he needed the transplant supply."

"Not Anubis. Anubis must have a sky-high rejection threshold."

"Jackson, *you're proud of Anubis*."

Bera was shocked to his core. "The hell! He's a dirty

murdering organlegger! If I'd *caught* him I'd be proud of Anubis—" He stopped because my desk screen was getting information.

The computer in the basement of the ARM Building gave Anthony Tiller no chance at all of being part of the Loren gang and a probability in the nineties that he had run with the Jackal God. One point was that Anubis and the rest had all dropped out of sight around the end of April 2123, when Anthony Tiller/Mortimer Lincoln changed his face and moved into High Cliffs.

"It could still have been revenge," Bera suggested. "Loren and Anubis knew each other. We know that much. They set up the boundary between their territories at least twelve years ago, by negotiation. Loren took over Anubis's territory when Anubis retired. And you killed Loren."

I scoffed. "And Tiller the Killer gave up his cover to get me two years after the gang broke up?"

"Maybe it wasn't revenge. Maybe Anubis wants to make a comeback."

"Or maybe this Tiller just flipped. Withdrawal symptoms. He hadn't killed anyone for almost two years, poor baby. I wish he'd picked a better time."

"Why?"

"Taffy was with me. She's still twitching."

"You didn't tell me that! She wasn't hit, was she?"

"No, just scared."

Bera relaxed. His hand caressed the interface where his hair faded into air, feather-lightly, in the nervous way another man might scratch his head. "I'd hate to see you two split up."

"Oh, it's not . . . ." Anything like that serious, I'd have told him, but he knew better. "Yah. We didn't get much sleep last night. It isn't just being shot at, you know."

"I know."

"Taffy's a surgeon. She thinks of transplant stocks as raw material. Tools. She'd be crippled without an organ bank. She doesn't think of the stuff as human . . . or she never used to, till she met me."

"I've never heard either of you talk about it."

"We don't, even to each other, but it's there. Most transplants are condemned criminals, captured by heroes such as you and me. Some of the stuff is respectable citizens captured by organleggers, broken up into illicit organ banks, and eventually recaptured by said heroes. They don't tell Taffy which is which. She works with pieces of people. I don't think she can live with me and not live with that."

"Getting shot at by an ex-organlegger couldn't have helped much. We'd better see to it that it doesn't happen again."

"Jackson, he was just a nut."

"He used to be with Anubis."

"I never had anything to do with Anubis." Which reminded me. "You did, though, didn't you? Do you remember anything about the Holden Chambers kidnapping?"

Bera looked at me peculiarly. "Holden and Charlotte Chambers, yah. You've got a good memory. There's a fair chance Anubis was involved."

"Tell me about it."

"There was a rash of kidnappings about that time all over the world. You know how organlegging works. The legitimate hospitals are always short of transplants. Some sick citizens are too much in a hurry to wait their turns. The gangs kidnap a healthy citizen, break him up into spare parts, throw away the brain, use the rest for illegal operations. That's the way it was until the Freezer Law cut the market out from under them."

"I remember."

"Some gangs turned to kidnapping for ransom. Why not? It's just what they were set up for. If the family couldn't pay off, the victim could always become a donor. It made people much more likely to pay off.

"The only strange thing about the Chambers kidnap was that Holden and Charlotte Chambers both disappeared about the same time, around six at night." Bera had been tapping at the computer controls. He looked at the screen and said, "Make that seven. March 21, 2123. But they were miles apart, Charlotte at a restaurant with a date, Holden at Washburn University attending a night class. Now, why would a kidnap gang think they needed them both?"

"Any ideas?"

"They might have thought that the Chambers trustees were more likely to pay off on both of them. We'll never know now. We never got any of the kidnappers. We were lucky to get the kids back."

"What made you think it was Anubis?"

"It was Anubis territory. The Chambers kidnap was only the last of half a dozen in that area. Smooth operations, no excitement, no hitches, victims returned intact after the ransom was paid." He glared. "No, I'm *not* proud of Anubis. It's just that he tended not to make mistakes, and he was used to making people disappear."

"Uh huh."

"They made themselves disappear, the whole gang, around the time of that last kidnap. We assume they were building up a stake."

"How much did they get?"

"On the Chambers kids? A hundred thousand."

"They'd have made ten times that selling them as transplants. They must have been hard up."

"You know it. Nobody was buying. What does all this have to do with your being shot at?"

"A wild idea. Could Anubis be interested in the Chambers kids *again*?"

Bera gave me a funny look. "No way. What for? They bled them white the first time. A hundred thousand UN marks isn't play money."

After Bera left, I sat there not believing it.

Anubis had vanished. Loren had acted immediately to take over Anubis's territory. Where had they gone, Anubis and the others? Into Loren's organ banks?

But there was Tiller/Lincoln.

I didn't *like* the idea that any random ex-organlegger might decide to kill me the instant he saw me. Finally I did something about it. I asked the computer for data on the Chambers kidnapping.

There wasn't much Bera hadn't told me. I wondered, though, why he hadn't mentioned Charlotte's condition.

When ARM police had found the Chambers kids drugged on a hotel parking roof, they had both been in good physical condition. Holden had been a little scared, a little relieved, just beginning to get angry. But Charlotte had been in catatonic withdrawal. At last notice she was still in catatonic withdrawal. She had never spoken with coherence about the kidnapping or about anything else.

Something had been done to her. Something terrible. Maybe Bera had taught himself not to think about it.

Otherwise the kidnappers had behaved almost with rectitude. The ransom had been paid; the victims had been returned. They had been on that roof, drugged, for less than twenty minutes. They showed no bruises, no signs of maltreatment . . . another sign that their kidnappers were organleggers. Organleggers aren't sadists. They don't have that much respect for the stuff.

I noted that the ransom had been paid by an attorney. The Chambers kids were orphans. If they'd both been killed, the executor of their estate would have been out of a job. From that viewpoint it made sense to capture them both . . . but not all *that* much sense.

And there couldn't be a motive for kidnapping them again. They didn't have the money. Except—

It hit me joltingly. *The second Freezer Bill.*

Holden Chambers's number was in the basement computer. I was dialing it when second thoughts interrupted. Instead I called downstairs and set a team to locating possible bugs in Chambers's home or phone. They weren't to interfere with the bugs or alert possible listeners. Routine stuff.

Once before the Chambers kids had disappeared. If we weren't lucky, they might disappear again. Sometimes the

ARM business was like digging a pit in quicksand. If you
dug hard enough, you could maintain a noticeable depression, but as soon as you stopped . . .

The Freezer Law of 2122 had given the ARM a field
day. Some of the gangs had simply retired. Some had tried
to keep going and wound up selling an operation to an
ARM plant. Some had tried to reach other markets, but
there weren't any, not even for Loren, who had tried to expand into the asteroid belt and found that they wouldn't
have him, either.

And some had tried kidnapping, but inexperience kept
tripping them up. The name of a victim points straight at a
kidnapper's only possible market. Too often the ARMs had
been waiting.

We'd cleaned them out. Organlegging should have been
an extinct profession this past year. The vanished jackals I
spent my days hunting should have posed no present threat
to society.

Except that the legitimate transplants released by the
Freezer Law were running out. And a peculiar thing was
happening. People had started to disappear from stalled vehicles, singles apartment houses, crowded city slidewalks.

Earth wanted the organleggers back.

No, that wasn't fair. Put it this way: Enough citizens
wanted to extend their own lives at any cost . . .

If Anubis was alive, he might well be thinking of going
back into business.

The point was that he would need backing. Loren had
taken over his medical facilities when Anubis had retired.
Eventually we'd located those and destroyed them. Anubis
would have to start over.

Let the second Freezer Bill pass, and Leviticus Hale
would be spare parts. Charlotte and Holden Chambers
would inherit . . . how much?

I got that via a call to the local NBA news department.
In 134 years Leviticus Hale's original 320,000 dollars had
become seventy-five million UN marks.

* * *

I spent the rest of the morning on routine. They call it legwork, though it's mostly done by phone and computer keyboard. The word covers some unbelievable long shots.

We were investigating every member of every Citizen's Committee to Oppose the second Freezer Bill in the world. The suggestion had come down from old man Garner. He thought we might find that a coalition of organleggers had pooled advertising money to keep the corpsicles off the market. The results that morning didn't look promising.

I half hoped it wouldn't work out. Suppose those committees *did* turn out to be backed by organleggers? It would make prime time news anywhere in the world. The second Freezer Bill would pass like *that*. But it had to be checked. There had been opposition to the first Freezer Bill, too, when the gangs had more money.

Money. We spent a good deal of computer time looking for unexplained money. The average criminal tends to think that once he's got the money, the game is over.

We hadn't caught a sniff of Loren or Anubis that way.

Where had Anubis spent his money? Maybe he'd just hidden it away somewhere, or maybe Loren had killed him for it. And Tiller had shot at me because he didn't like my face. Legwork is gambling, time against results.

It developed that Holden Chambers's environs were free of eavesdropping devices. I called him about noon.

There appeared within my phone screen a red-faced, white-haired man of great dignity. He asked to whom I wished to speak. I told him and displayed my ARM ident. He nodded and put me on hold.

Moments later I faced a weak-chinned young man who smiled distractedly at me and said, "Sorry about that. I've been getting considerable static from the news lately. Zero acts as a kind of, ah, buffer."

Past his shoulder I could see a table with things on it: a tape viewer, a double handful of tape spools, a tape recorder the size of a man's palm, two pens, and a stack of paper, all neatly arranged. I said, "Sorry to interrupt your studying."

"That's all right. It's tough getting back to it after Year's End. Maybe you remember. Haven't I seen you—? *Oh.* The floating cigarette."

"That's right."

"How did you do that?"

"I've got an imaginary arm." And it's a great conversational device, an icebreaker of wondrous potency. I was a marvel, a talking sea serpent, the way the kid was looking at me. "I lost an arm once, mining rocks in the Belt. A sliver of asteroidal rock sheared it off clean to the shoulder."

He looked awed.

"I got it replaced, of course. But for a year I was a one-armed man. Well, here was a whole section of my brain developed to control a right arm, and no right arm. Psychokinesis is easy enough to develop when you live in a low-gravity environment." I paused just less than long enough for him to form a question. "Somebody tried to kill me outside Midgard last night. That's why I called."

I hadn't expected him to burst into a fit of the giggles. "Sorry," he got out. "It sounds like you lead an active life!"

"Yah. It didn't seem that funny at the time. I don't suppose you noticed anything unusual last night?"

"Just the usual shootings and muggings, and there was one guy with a cigarette floating in front of his face." He sobered before my clearly deficient sense of humor. "Look, I *am* sorry, but one minute you're talking about a meteor shearing your arm off, and the next it's bullets whizzing past your ear."

"Sure, I see your point."

"I left before you did. I know censored well I did. What happened?"

"Somebody shot at us with a hunting laser. He was probably just a nut. He was also part of the gang that kidnapped—" He looked stricken. "Yah, them. There's probably no connection, but we wondered if you might have noticed anything. Like a familiar face."

He shook his head. "They change faces, don't they?"

"Usually. How did you leave?"

"Taxi. I live in Bakersfield, about twenty minutes from High Cliffs. Where did all this happen? I caught my taxi on the third shopping level."

"That kills it. We were on the first."

"I'm not really sorry. He might have shot at me, too."

I'd been trying to decide whether to tell him that the kidnap gang might be interested in him again. Whether to scare the lights out of him on another long shot or leave him off guard for a possible kidnap attempt. He seemed stable enough, but you never knew.

I temporized. "Mister Chambers, we'd like you to try to identify the man who tried to kill me last night. He probably did change his face—"

"Yah." He was uneasy. Many citizens would be if asked to look a dead man in the face. "But I suppose you've got to try it. I'll stop in tomorrow afternoon, after class."

So. Tomorrow we'd see what he was made of.

He asked, "Imaginary arm? I've never heard of a psi talking that way about his talent."

"I wasn't being cute," I told him. "My limited imagination. I can feel things out with my fingertips, but not if they're farther away than an arm can reach."

"But most psis can reach farther. Why not try a hypnotist?"

"And lose the whole arm? I don't want to risk that."

He looked disappointed in me. "What can you do with an imaginary arm that you can't do with a real one?"

"I can pick up hot things without burning myself."

"Yah!" He hadn't thought of that.

"And I can reach through walls. I can reach two ways through a phone screen. Fiddle with the works or—here, I'll show you."

It doesn't always work. But I was getting a good picture. Chambers showed life-sized, in color and stereo, through four square feet of screen. It looked like I could reach right into it. So I did. I reached into the screen with my imaginary hand, picked a pencil off the table in front of him, and twirled it like a baton.

He threw himself backward out of his chair. He landed rolling. I saw his face, pale gray with terror, before he rolled away and out of view. A few seconds later the screen went blank. He must have turned the knob from offscreen.

If I'd touched his face, I could have understood it. But all I'd done was lift a pencil. What the hell?

My fault, I guessed. Some people see psi powers as supernatural, eerie, threatening. I shouldn't have been showing off like that. But Holden hadn't looked the type. Brash, a bit nervous, but fascinated rather than repulsed by the possibilities of an invisible, immaterial hand.

Then, terror.

I didn't try to call him back. I dithered about putting a guard on him, decided not to. A guard might be noticed. But I ordered a tracer implanted in him.

Anubis might pick Chambers up at any time. He needn't wait for the General Assembly to declare Leviticus Hale dead.

A tracer needle was a useful thing. It would be fired at Chambers from ambush. He'd probably never notice the sting, the hole would be only a pinprick, and it would tell us just where he was from then on.

I thought Charlotte Chambers could use a tracer, too, so I picked up a palm-size pressure implanter downstairs. I also traded the discharged barrel on my sidearm for a fresh one. The feel of the gun in my hand sent vivid green lines sizzling past my mind's eye.

Last, I ordered a standard information package, C priority, on what Chambers had been doing for the last two years. It would probably arrive in a day or so.

The winter face of Kansas had great dark gaps in it, a town nestled in each gap. The weather domes of various townships had shifted kilotons of snow outward, to deepen the drifts across the flat countryside. In the light of early sunset the snowbound landscape was orange-white, striped with the broad black shadows of a few cities within buildings. It all seemed eerie and abstract, sliding west beneath the folded wings of our plane.

We slowed hard in midair. The wings unfolded, and we settled over downtown Topeka.

This was going to look odd on my expense account. All this way to see a girl who hadn't spoken sense in three years. Probably it would be disallowed . . . yet she was as much a part of the case as her brother. Anyone planning to recapture Holden Chambers for reransom would want Charlotte, too.

Menninger Institute was a pretty place. Besides the twelve stories of glass and mock brick which formed the main building, there were at least a dozen outbuildings of varied ages and designs that ran from boxlike rectangles to free-form organics poured in foam plastic. They were all wide apart, separated by green lawns and trees and flower beds. A place of peace, a place with elbow room. Pairs and larger groups passed me on the curving walks: an aide and a patient or an aide and several less disturbed patients. The aides were obvious at a glance.

"When a patient is well enough to go outside for a walk, then he needs the greenery and the room," Doctor Hartman told me. "It's part of his therapy. Going outside is a giant step."

"Do you get many agoraphobes?"

"No, that's not what I was talking about. It's the *lock* that counts. To anyone else that lock is a prison, but to many patients it comes to represent security. Someone else to make the decisions, to keep the world outside."

Doctor Hartman was short and round and blond. A comfortable person, easygoing, patient, sure of himself. Just the man to trust with your destiny, assuming you were tired of running it yourself.

I asked, "Do you get many cures?"

"Certainly. As a matter of fact, we generally won't take patients unless we feel we can cure them."

"That must do wonders for the record."

He was not offended. "It does even more for the patients.

Knowing that we know they can be cured makes them feel the same way. And the incurably insane . . . can be damned depressing." Momentarily he seemed to sag under an enormous weight. Then he was himself again. "They can affect the other patients. Fortunately, there aren't many incurables these days."

"Was Charlotte Chambers one of the curables?"

"We thought so. After all, it was only shock. There was no previous history of personality disturbances. Her blood psychochemicals were near enough normal. We tried everything in the records. Stroking. Fiddling with her chemistry. Psychotherapy didn't get very far. Either she's deaf or she doesn't listen, and she won't talk. Sometimes I think she hears everything we say . . . but she doesn't respond."

We had reached a powerful-looking locked door. Doctor Hartman searched through a key ring, touched a key to the lock. "We call it the violent ward, but it's more properly the severely disturbed ward. I wish to hell we *could* get some violence out of some of them. Like Charlotte. They won't even *look* at reality, much less try to fight it . . . here we are."

Her door opened outward into the corridor. My nasty professional mind tagged the fact: if you tried to hang yourself from the door, anyone could see you from either end of the corridor. It would be very public.

In these upper rooms the windows were frosted. I suppose there's good reason why some patients shouldn't be reminded that they are twelve stories up. The room was small but well lighted and brightly painted, with a bed and a padded chair and a tridee screen set flush with the wall. There wasn't a sharp corner anywhere in the room.

Charlotte was in the chair, looking straight ahead of her, her hands folded in her lap. Her hair was short and not particularly neat. Her yellow dress was of some wrinkleproof fabric. She looked resigned, I thought, resigned to some ultimately awful thing. She did not notice us as we came in.

I whispered, "Why is she still here if you can't cure her?"

Doctor Hartman spoke in a normal tone. "At first we

thought it was catatonic withdrawal. That we could have cured. This isn't the first time someone has suggested moving her. She's still here because I want to know what's *wrong* with her. She's been like this ever since they brought her in."

She still hadn't noticed us. The doctor talked as if she couldn't hear us. "Do the ARMs have any idea what was done to her? If we knew that, we might be better able to treat her."

I shook my head. "I was going to ask you. What *could* they have done to her?"

He shook his head.

"Try another angle, then. What couldn't they have done to her? There were no bruises, broken bones, anything like that."

"No internal injuries, either. No surgery was performed on her. There was the evidence of drugging. I understand they were organleggers."

"It looks likely." She could have been pretty, I thought. It wasn't the lack of cosmetics or even the gaunt look. It was the empty eyes, isolated above high cheekbones, looking at nothing. "Could she be blind?"

"No. The optic nerves function perfectly."

She reminded me of a wirehead. You can't get a wirehead's attention, either, when house current is trickling down a fine wire from the top of his skull into the pleasure center of his brain. But no, the pure egocentric joy of a wirehead hardly matched Charlotte's egocentric misery.

"Tell me," Doctor Hartman said. "How badly could an organlegger frighten a young girl?"

"We don't get many citizens back from organleggers. I . . . honestly can't think of any upper limit. They could have taken her on a tour of the medical facilities. They could have made her watch while they broke up a prospect for stuff." I didn't like what my imagination was doing. There are things you don't think about, because the point is to protect the prospects, keep the Lorens and the Anubises from reaching them at all. But you can't help thinking about them anyway, so you push them back, push them back. These things must have been in my head for a long time. "They had the facilities to partly break her up and put her back together again and leave her conscious the whole time. You wouldn't have found scars. The only scars they can't cure with modern medicine are in the bone itself. They could have done any kind of temporary transplant—and they must have been bored, Doctor. Business was slow. But—"

"Stop." He was gray around the edges. His voice was weak and hoarse.

"But organleggers aren't sadists generally. They don't have that much respect for the stuff. They wouldn't play that kind of game unless they had something special against her."

"My God, you play rough games. How can you sleep nights, knowing what you know?"

"None of your business, Doctor. In your opinion, is it likely that she was frightened into this state?"

"Not all at once. We could have brought her out of it if it had happened all at once. I suppose she may have been frightened repeatedly. How long did they have her?"

"Nine days."

Hartman looked worse yet. Definitely he was not ARM material.

I dug in my sporran for the pressure implanter. "I'd like your permission to put a tracer needle in her. I won't hurt her."

"There's no need to whisper, Mr. Hamilton—"

"Was I?" Yes, dammit, I'd been holding my voice low, as if I were afraid to disturb her. In a normal voice I said, "The tracer could help us locate her in case she disappears."

"Disappears? Why should she do that? You can see for yourself—"

"That's the worst of it. The same gang of organleggers that got her the first time may be trying to kidnap her again. Just how good is your ... security ..." I trailed off.

Charlotte Chambers had turned around and was looking at me.

Hartman's hand closed hard on my upper arm. He was warning me. Calmly, reassuringly, he said, "Don't worry, Charlotte. I'm Doctor Hartman. You're in good hands. We'll take care of you."

Charlotte was half out of her chair, twisted around to search my face. I tried to look harmless. Naturally I knew better than to try to guess what she was thinking. Why should her eyes be big with hope? Frantic, desperate hope. When I'd just uttered a terrible threat.

Whatever she was looking for, she didn't find it in my face. What looked like hope gradually died out of her eyes, and she sank back in her chair, looking straight ahead of her without interest. Doctor Hartman gestured, and I took the hint and left.

Twenty minutes later he joined me in the visitors' waiting room. "Hamilton, that's the first time she's ever shown that much awareness. What could possibly have sparked it?"

I shook my head. "I wanted to ask, Just how good is your security?"

"I'll warn the aides. We can refuse to permit her visitors unless accompanied by an ARM agent. Is that good enough?"

"It may be, but I want to plant a tracer in her. Just in case."

"All right."

"Doctor, what was that in her expression?"

"I thought it was hope. Hamilton, I will just bet it was your voice that did it. You may sound like someone she knows. Let me take a recording of your voice, and we'll see if we can find a psychiatrist who sounds like you."

When I put the tracer in her, she never so much as twitched.

All the way home her face haunted me. As if she'd waited two years in that chair, not bothering to move or think, until I came. Until finally I came.

* * *

My right side seems weightless. It throws me off stride as I back away, back away. My right arm ends at the shoulder. Where my left eye was is an empty socket. Something vague shuffles out of the dark, looks at me with its one left eye, reaches for me with its one right arm. I back away, back away, fending it off with my imaginary arm. It comes closer, I touch it, I reach into it. Horrible! The scars! Loren's pleural cavity is a patchwork of transplants. I want to snatch my hand away. Instead I reach deeper and find his borrowed heart and squeeze. And squeeze.

How can I sleep nights, knowing what I know? Well, Doctor, some nights I dream.

Taffy opened her eyes to find me sitting up in bed, staring at a dark wall. She said, "What?"

"Bad dream."

"Oh." She scratched me under the ear for reassurance. "How awake are you?"

She sighed. "Wide awake."

"Corpsicle. Where did you hear the word *corpsicle*? In the boob cube? From a friend?"

"I don't remember. Why?"

"Just a thought. Never mind. I'll ask Luke Garner."

I got up and made us some hot chocolate with bourbon flavoring. It knocked us out like a cluster of mercy needles.

Lucas Garner was a man who had won a gamble with fate. Medical technology had progressed as he grew older, so that his expected life span kept moving ahead of him. He was not yet the oldest living member of the Struldbrugs' Club, but he was getting on, getting on.

His spinal nerves had worn out long since, marooning him in a ground-effect travel chair. His face hung loose from his skull, in folds. But his arms were apishly strong, and his brain still worked. He was my boss.

"Corpsicle," he said. "Corpsicle. Right. They've been saying it on tridee. I didn't notice, but you're right. It's funny they should start using that word again."

"How did it get started?"

"Popsicle. A Popsicle was frozen sherbet on a stick. You licked it off."

I winced at the mental picture that evoked. Leviticus Hale, covered with frost, a stake up his anus, a gigantic tongue—

"A *wooden* stick." Garner had a grin to scare babies. Grinning, he was almost a work of art: an antique, a hundred eighty-odd years old, like a Hannes Bok illustration of Lovecraft. "That's how long ago it was. They didn't start freezing people until the nineteen sixties or seventies, but we were still putting wooden sticks in Popsicles. Why would anyone use it now?"

"Who uses it? Newscasters? I don't watch the boob cube much."

"Newscasters, yah, and lawyers . . . How are you making out on the Committees to Oppose the Second Freezer Bill?"

It took me a moment to make the switch. "No positive results. The program's still running, and results are slow in some parts of the world, Africa, the Middle East . . . They all seem to be solid citizens."

"Well, it's worth a try. We've been looking into the other side of it, too. If organleggers are trying to block the second Freezer Bill, they might well try to intimidate or kill off anyone who *backs* the second Freezer Bill. Follow me?"

"I suppose."

"So we have to know who to protect. It's strictly business, of course. The ARM isn't supposed to get involved in politics."

Garner reached sideways to tap one-handed at the computer keyboard in his desk. His bulky floating chair wouldn't fit under the keyboard. Tape slid from the slot, two feet of it. He handed it to me.

"Mostly lawyers," he said. "A number of sociologists and humanities professors. Religious leaders pushing their own brand of immortality; we've got religious factions on both sides of the question. These are the people who publicly back the second Freezer Bill. I'd guess they're the ones who started using the word *corpsicle*."

"Thanks."

"Cute word, isn't it? A joke. If you said *frozen sleep*, someone might take you seriously. Someone might even wonder if they were really dead. Which is the key question, isn't it? The corpsicles they want are the ones who were healthiest, the ones who have the best chance of being brought back to life some day. These are the people they want revived a piece at a time. By me that's lousy."

"Me, too." I glanced down at the list. "I presume you haven't actually warned any of these people."

"No, you idiot. They'd go straight to a newscaster and tell him that all their opponents are organleggers."

I nodded. "Thanks for the help. If anything comes of this—"

"Sit down. Run your eyes down those names. See if you spot anything."

I didn't know most of them, of course, not even in the Americas. There were a few prominent defense lawyers, and at least one federal judge, and Raymond Sinclair the physicist, and a string of newscast stations, and— "Clark and Nash? The advertising firm?"

"A number of advertising firms in a number of countries. Most of these people are probably sincere enough, and they'll talk to *anyone*, but the coverage has to come from somewhere. It's coming from these firms. That word *corpsicle has* to be an advertising stunt. The publicity on the corpsicle heirs: they may have had a hand in that, too. You know about the corpsicle heirs?"

"Not a lot."

"NBA Broadcasting has been running down the heirs to the richest members of Group II, the ones who were committed to the freezer vaults for reasons that don't harm their value as—stuff." Garner spat the word. It was organlegger slang. "The paupers all went into the organ banks on the first Freezer Law, of course, so Group II boasts some considerable wealth. NBA found a few heirs who would never have turned up otherwise. I imagine a lot of them will be voting for the second Freezer Bill—"

"Yah."

"Only the top dozen have been getting the publicity. But it's still a powerful argument, isn't it? If the corpsicles are in frozen sleep, that's one thing. If they're *dead*, then people are being denied their rightful inheritance."

I asked the obvious question. "Who's paying for the advertising?"

"Now, we wondered about that. The firms wouldn't say. We dug a little farther."

"And?"

"They don't know, either." Garner grinned like Satan. "They were hired by firms that aren't listed anywhere. A number of firms, whose representatives only appeared once. They paid their fees in lump sums."

"It sounds like—no. They're on the wrong side."

"Right. Why would an organlegger be *pushing* the second Freezer Bill?"

I thought it over. "How about this? A number of old, sickly, wealthy men and women set up a fund to see to it that the public supply of spare parts isn't threatened. It's legal, at least, which dealing with an organlegger isn't. With enough of them it might even be cheaper."

"We thought of that. We're running a program on it. I've been asking some subtle questions around the Struldbrugs' Club, just because I'm a member. It had to be subtle. Legal it may be, but they wouldn't want publicity."

"No."

"And then I got your report this morning. Anubis and the Chambers kid, huh? Wouldn't it be nice if it went a bit farther than that?"

"I don't follow you."

At this moment Garner looked like something that was ready to pounce. "Wouldn't it be wonderful if a federation of organleggers was backing the second Freezer Bill? The idea would be to kidnap *all* of the top corpsicle heirs *just before the Bill passes.* Most people worth kidnapping can afford to protect themselves. Guards, house alarms, wrist alarms. A corpsicle heir can't do that yet."

Garner leaned forward in his chair, doing the work with his arms. "If we could prove this and give it some publicity, wouldn't it shoot hell out of the second Freezer Law?"

There was a memo on my desk when I got back. The data package on Holden Chambers was in the computer memory, waiting for me. I remembered that Holden himself would be here this afternoon unless the arm trick had scared him off.

I punched for the package and read it through, trying to decide just how sane the kid was. Most of the information had come from the college medical center. They'd been worried about him, too.

The kidnapping had interrupted his freshman year at Washburn. His grades had dropped sharply afterward, then sloped back to marginally passing. In September he'd changed his major from architecture to biochemistry. He'd made the switch easily. His grades had been average or better during these last two years.

He lived alone in one of those tiny apartments whose furnishings are all memory plastic, extruded as needed. Technology was cheaper than elbow room. The apartment house did have some communal facilities—sauna, pool, cleaning robots, party room, room-service kitchen, clothing dispensary . . . I wondered why he didn't get a roommate. It would have saved him money, for one thing. But his sex life had always been somewhat passive, and he'd never been gregarious, according to the file. He'd just about pulled the hole in after him for some months after the kidnapping. As if he'd lost all faith in humanity.

If he'd been off the beam then, he seemed to have recovered. Even his sex life had improved. That information had not come from the college medical center but from records from the communal kitchen (breakfast for two, late-night room service) and some recent recorded phone messages. All quite public; there was no reason for me to be feeling like a peeping Tom. The publicity on the corpsicle heirs may have done him some good, started girls chasing him for a change. A few had spent the night, but he didn't seem to be seeing anyone steadily.

I had wondered how he could afford a servant. The answer made me feel stupid. The secretary named Zero turned out to be a computer construct, an answering service.

Chambers was not penniless. After the ransom had been paid, the trust fund had contained about twenty thousand marks. Charlotte's care had eaten into that. The trustees were giving Holden enough to pay his tuition and still live comfortably. There would be some left when he graduated, but it would be earmarked for Charlotte.

I turned off the screen and thought about it. He'd had a jolt. He'd recovered. Some do, some don't. He'd been in perfect health, which has a lot to do with surviving emotional shock. If he was your friend today, you would avoid certain subjects in his presence.

And he'd thrown himself backward in blind terror when a pencil rose from his desk and started to pinwheel. How normal was that? I just didn't know. I was too used to my imaginary arm.

Holden himself appeared at about fourteen hundred.

Anthony Tiller was in a cold box. His face had been hideously contorted during his last minutes, but it showed none of that now. He was as expressionless as any dead man. The frozen sleepers at the Vault of Eternity had looked like that. Superficially, most of them had been in worse shape than he was.

Holden Chambers studied him with interest. "So that's what an organlegger looks like."

"An organlegger looks like anything he wants to."

He grimaced at that. He bent close to study the dead man's face. He circled the cold box with his hands clasped behind his back. He wanted to look nonchalant, but he was still walking wide of me. I didn't think the dead man bothered him.

He said the same thing I'd said two nights ago. "Nope. Not with that face."

"Well, it was worth a try. Let's go to my office. It's more comfortable."

He smiled. "Good."

He dawdled in the corridors. He looked into open offices, smiled at anyone who looked up, asked me mostly intelligent questions in a low voice. He was enjoying himself: a tourist in ARM Headquarters. But he trailed back when I tried to take the middle of the corridor, so that we wound up walking on opposite sides. Finally I asked him about it.

I thought he wasn't going to answer. Then, "It was that pencil trick."

"What about it?"

He sighed, as one who despairs of ever finding the right words does. "I don't like to be touched. I mean, I get along with girls all right, but generally I don't like to be touched."

"I didn't—"

"But you *could* have. And without my *knowing*. I couldn't see it, I might not even feel it. It just bothered the censored hell out of me, you reaching out of a phone screen like that! A phone call isn't supposed to be that, that *personal*." He stopped suddenly, looking down the corridor. "Isn't that Lucas Garner?"

"Yah."

"Lucas Garner!" He was awed and delighted. "He runs it all, doesn't he? How old is he now?"

"In his hundred and eighties." I thought of introducing him, but Luke's chair slid off in a different direction.

My office is just big enough for me, my desk, two chairs, and an array of spigots in the wall. I poured him tea and me coffee. I said, "I went to visit your sister."

"Charlotte? How is she?"

"I doubt she's changed since the last time you saw her. She doesn't notice anything around her . . . except for one incident, when she turned around and stared at me."

"Why? What did you do? What did you say?" he demanded.

Well, here it came. "I was telling her doctor that the same gang that kidnapped her once might want her again."

Strange things happened around his mouth. Bewilderment, fear, disbelief. "What the bleep made you say that?"

"It's a possibility. You're both corpsicle heirs. Tiller the Killer could have been watching you when he spotted *me* watching you. He couldn't have that."

"No, I suppose not . . ." He was trying to take it lightly, and he failed. "Do you seriously think they might want me—us—again?"

"It's a possibility," I repeated. "If Tiller was inside the restaurant, he could have spotted me by my floating cigarette. It's more distinctive than my face. Don't look so worried. We've got a tracer on you; we could track him anywhere he took you."

"In me?" He didn't like that much better—too personal?—but he didn't make an issue of it.

"Holden, I keep wondering what they could have done to your sister—"

He interrupted coldly. "I stopped wondering that long ago."

"—that they didn't do to you. It's more than curiosity. If the doctors knew what was done to her, if they knew what it is in her memory—"

"Dammit! Don't you think I want to help her? She's my sister!"

"All right." What was I playing psychiatrist for, anyway? Or was it detective I was playing? He didn't know anything. He was at the eye of several storms at once, and he must be getting sick and tired of it. I ought to send him home.

He spoke first. I could barely hear him. "You know what they did to me? A nerve block at the neck. A little widget taped to the back of my neck with surgical skin. I couldn't feel anything below the neck, and I couldn't move. They put that on me, dumped me on a bed, and left me. For nine days. Every so often they'd turn me on again and let me drink and eat something and go to the bathroom."

"Did anyone tell you they'd break you up for stuff if they didn't get the ransom?"

He thought about it. "N-no. I could pretty well guess it. They never said anything to me at all. They treated me like I was dead. They examined me for, oh, it felt like hours, poking and prodding me with their hands and their instruments, rolling me around like dead meat. I couldn't feel any of it, but I could see it all. If they did that to Charlotte . . . maybe she thinks she's dead." His voice rose. "I've been through this again and again, with the ARMs, with Doctor Hartman, with the Washburn medical staff. Let's drop it, shall we?"

"Sure. I'm sorry. We don't learn tact in this business. We learn to ask questions. Any questions."

And yet, and yet, the look on her face.

I asked him one more question as I was escorting him out. Almost offhandedly. "What do you think of the second Freezer Bill?"

"I don't have a UN vote yet."

"That's not what I asked."

He faced me belligerently. "Look, there's a lot of money involved. A *lot* of money. It would pay for Charlotte the rest of her life. It would fix my face. But Hale, Leviticus Hale—" He pronounced the name accurately, and with no flicker of a smile. "He's a relative, isn't he? My great-to-the-third-grandfather. They could bring him back someday; it's possible. So what do I do? If I had a vote, I'd have to decide. But I'm not twenty-five yet, so I don't have to worry about it."

"Interviews."

"I don't give interviews. You just got the same answer everyone else gets. It's on tape, on file with Zero. Goodbye, Mr. Hamilton."

Other ARM departments had thinned our ranks during the lull following the first Freezer Law. Over the next couple of weeks they began to trickle back. We needed operatives to implant tracers in unsuspecting victims and afterward to monitor their welfare. We needed an augmented staff to follow their tracer blips on the screens downstairs.

We were sorely tempted to tell all the corpsicle heirs what was happening and have them check in with us at regular intervals, say, every fifteen minutes. It would have made things much easier. It might also have influenced their votes, altered the quality of the interviews they gave out.

But we didn't want to alert our quarry, the still hypothetical coalition of organleggers now monitoring the same corpsicle heirs we were interested in. And the backlash vote would be ferocious if we were wrong. And we weren't supposed to be interested in politics.

We operated without the knowledge of the corpsicle heirs. There were two thousand of them in all parts of the world, almost three hundred in the western United States, with an expected legacy of fifty thousand UN marks or more—a limit we set for our own convenience, because it was about all we could handle.

One thing helped the manpower situation. We had reached another lull. Missing persons complaints had dropped to near zero all over the world.

"We should have been expecting that," Bera commented. "For the last year or so most of their customers must have stopped going to organleggers. They're waiting to see if the second Freezer Bill will go through. Now all the gangs are stuck with full organ banks and no customers. If they learned anything from last time, they'll pull in their horns and wait it out. Of course I'm only guessing." But it looked likely enough. At any rate, we had the men we needed.

We monitored the top dozen corpsicle heirs twenty-four hours a day. The rest we checked at random intervals. The tracers could only tell us where they were, not who they were with or whether they wanted to be there. We had to keep checking to see if anyone had disappeared.

We sat back to await results.

* * *

The Security Council passed the second Freezer Bill on February 3, 2125. Now it would go to the world vote in late March. The voting public numbered ten billion, of whom perhaps sixty percent would bother to phone in their votes.

I took to watching the boob cube again.

NBA Broadcasting continued its coverage of the corpsicle heirs and its editorials in favor of the bill. Proponents took every opportunity to point out that many corpsicle heirs still remained to be discovered. (And YOU might be one.) Taffy and I watched a parade in New York in favor of the bill: banners and placards (SAVE THE LIVING, NOT THE DEAD . . . IT'S *YOUR* LIFE AT STAKE . . . CORPSICLES KEEP BEER COLD) and one censored big mob of chanting people. The transportation costs must have been formidable.

The various committees to oppose the bill were also active. In the Americas they pointed out that although about forty percent of people in frozen sleep were in the Americas, the spare parts derived would go to the world at large. In Africa and Asia it was discovered that the Americas had most of the corpsicle heirs. In Egypt an analogy was made between the pyramids and the freezer vaults: both bids for immortality. It didn't go over well.

Polls indicated that the Chinese sectors would vote against the bill. NBA newscasters spoke of ancestor worship and reminded the public that six ex-chairmen resided in Chinese freezer vaults, alongside myriad lesser ex-officials. Immortality was a respected tradition in China.

The committees to oppose reminded the world's voting public that some of the wealthiest of the frozen dead had heirs in the Belt. Were Earth's resources to be spread indiscriminately among the asteroidal rocks? I started to hate both sides. Fortunately, the UN cut that line off fast by threatening an injunction. Earth needed Belt resources too heavily.

Our own results began to come in.

Mortimer Lincoln, alias Anthony Tiller, had not been at Midgard the night he had tried to kill me. He'd eaten alone in his apartment, a meal sent from the communal kitchen. Which meant that he himself could not have been watching Chambers.

We found no sign of anyone lurking behind Holden Chambers or behind any of the other corpsicle heirs, publicized or not, with one general exception. Newsmen. The media were unabashedly and constantly interested in the corpsicle heirs, priority based on the money they stood to inherit. We faced a depressing hypothesis: the potential kidnappers were spending all their time watching the boob cube, letting the media do their tracking for them. But perhaps the connection was closer.

We started investigating newscast stations.

In mid-February I pulled Holden Chambers in and had him examined for an outlaw tracer. It was a move of desperation. Organleggers don't use such tools. They specialize in medicine. Our own tracer was still working, and it was the only tracer in him. Chambers was icily angry. We had interrupted his studying for a midterm exam.

We managed to search three of the top dozen when they had medical checkups. Nothing.

Our investigations of the newscast stations turned up very little. Clark and Nash was running a good many one-time spots through NBA. Other advertising firms had similar lines of possible influence over other stations, broadcasting companies, and cassette newszines. But we were looking for newsmen who had popped up from nowhere, with backgrounds forged or nonexistent. Ex-organleggers in new jobs. We didn't find any.

I called Menninger's one empty afternoon. Charlotte Chambers was still catatonic. "I've got Lowndes of New York working with me," Hartman told me. "He has precisely your voice and good qualifications, too. Charlotte hasn't responded yet. We've been wondering: could it have been the *way* you were talking?"

"You mean the accent? It's Kansas with an overlay of west coast and Belter."

"No, Lowndes has that, too. I mean organlegger slang."

"I use it. Bad habit."

"That could be it." He made a face. "But we can't act on it. It might just scare her completely into herself."

"That's where she is now. I'd risk it."

"You're not a psychiatrist," he said.

I hung up and brooded. Negatives, all negatives.

I didn't hear the hissing sound until it was almost on me. I looked up then, and it was Luke Garner's ground-effect travel chair sliding accurately through the door. He watched me a moment, then said, "What are you looking so grim about?"

"Nothing. All the nothing we've been getting instead of results."

"Uh huh." He let the chair settle. "It's beginning to look like Tiller the Killer wasn't on assignment."

"That would blow the whole thing, wouldn't it? I did a lot of extrapolating from two beams of green light. One ex-organlegger tries to make holes in one ARM agent, and now we've committed tens of thousands of man-hours and seventy or eighty computer-hours on the strength of it. If they'd been planning to tie us up, they couldn't have done it better."

"You know, I think you'd take it as a personal insult if Tiller shot at you just because he didn't like you."

I had to laugh. "How personal can you get?"

"That's better. Now, will you stop sweating this? It's just another long shot. You know what legwork is like. We bet a lot of man-effort on this one because the odds looked good. Look how many organleggers would have to be in on it if it were true! We'd have a chance to snaffle them all. But if it doesn't work out, why sweat it?"

"The second Freezer Bill," I said, as if he didn't know.

"The will of the people be done."

"Censor the people! They're murdering those dead men!"

Garner's face twitched oddly. I said, "What's funny?"

He let the laugh out. It sounded like a chicken screaming for help. "*Censor. Bleep.* They didn't used to be swear words. They were euphemisms. You'd put them in a book or on TV when you wanted a word they wouldn't let you use."

I shrugged. "Words are funny. *Damn* used to be a technical term in theology, if you want to look at it that way."

"I know, but they *sound* funny. When you start saying *bleep* and *censored*, it ruins your masculine image."

"Censor my masculine image. What do we do about the corpsicle heirs? Call off the surveillance?"

"No. There's too much in the pot already." Garner looked broodingly into one bare wall of my office. "Wouldn't it be nice if we could persuade ten billion people to use prosthetics instead of transplants?"

Guilt glowed in my right arm, my left eye. I said, "Prosthetics don't feel. I might have settled for a prosthetic arm—" Dammit, I'd had the choice! "—but an eye? Luke, suppose it was possible to graft new legs on you. Would you take them?"

"Oh, dear, I do wish you hadn't asked me that," he said venomously.

"Sorry. I withdraw the question."

He brooded. It was a lousy thing to ask a man. He was still stuck with it; he couldn't spit it out.

I asked, "Did you have any special reason for dropping in?"

Luke shook himself. "Yah. I got the impression you were taking all this as a personal defeat. I stopped down to cheer you up."

We laughed at each other. "Listen," he said, "there are worse things than the organ bank problem. When I was young—your age, my child—it was almost impossible to get anyone convicted of a capital crime. Life sentences weren't for life. Psychology and psychiatry, such as they were, were concerned with curing criminals, returning them to society. The United States Supreme Court almost voted the death penalty unconstitutional."

"Sounds wonderful. How did it work out?"

"We had an impressive reign of terror. A lot of people

got killed. Meanwhile, transplant techniques were getting better and better. Eventually Vermont made the organ banks the official means of execution. That idea spread very damn fast."

"Yah." I remembered history courses.

"Now we don't even *have* prisons. The organ banks are always short. As soon as the UN votes the death penalty for a crime, most people stop committing it. Naturally."

"So we get the death penalty for having children without a license, or cheating on income tax, or running too many red traffic lights. Luke, I've seen what it *does* to people to keep voting more and more death penalties. They lose their respect for life."

"But the other situation was just as bad, Gil. Don't forget it."

"So now we've got the death penalty for being poor."

"The Freezer Law? I won't defend it. Except that that's the penalty for being poor and *dead*."

"Should it be a capital crime?"

"No, but it's not too bright, either. If a man expects to be brought back to life, he should be prepared to pay the medical fees. Now, hold it. I know a lot of the pauper group had trust funds set up. They were wiped out by depressions, bad investments. Why the hell do you think banks take interest for a loan? They're being paid for the *risk*. The risk that the loan won't be paid back."

"Did you vote for the Freezer Law?"

"No, of course not."

"I must be spoiling for a fight. I'm glad you dropped by, Luke."

"Don't mention it."

"I keep thinking the ten billion voters will eventually work their way down to me. Go ahead, grin. Who'd want *your* liver?"

Garner cackled. "Somebody could murder me for my skeleton. Not to put inside him. For a museum."

We left it at that.

* * *

The news broke a couple of days later. Several North American hospitals had been reviving corpsicles.

How they kept the secret was a mystery. Those corpsicles who survived the treatment—twenty-two of them out of thirty-five attempts—had been clinically alive for some ten months, conscious for shorter periods.

For the next week it was all the news there was. Taffy and I watched interviews with the dead men, with the doctors, with members of the Security Council. The move was not illegal. As publicity against the second Freezer Bill, it may have been a mistake.

All the revived corpsicles had been insane. Else why risk it?

Some of the casualties had died because their insanity was caused by brain damage. The rest were cured, but only in a biochemical sense. All had been insane long enough for their doctors to decide that there was no hope. Now they were stranded in a foreign land, their homes forever lost in the mists of time. Revivification had saved them from an ugly, humiliating death at the hands of most of the human race, a fate that smacked of cannibalism and ghouls. The paranoids were hardly surprised. The rest reacted like paranoids.

In the boob cube they came across as a bunch of frightened mental patients.

One night we watched a string of interviews on the big screen in Taffy's bedroom wall. They weren't well handled. Too much "How do you feel about the wonders of the present?" when the poor boobs hadn't come out of their shells long enough to know or care. Many wouldn't believe anything they were told or shown. Others didn't care about anything but space exploration—a largely Belter activity which Earth's voting public tended to ignore. Too much of it was at the level of this last one: an interviewer explaining to a woman that a boob cube was not a *cube*, that the word referred only to the three-dimensional effect. The poor woman was badly rattled and not too bright in the first place.

Taffy was sitting cross-legged on the bed, combing out her long, dark hair so that it flowed over her shoulders in shining curves. "She's an early one," she said critically. "There may have been oxygen starvation of the brain during freezing."

"That's what *you* see. All the average citizen sees is the way she acts. She's obviously not ready to join society."

"Dammit, Gil, she's *alive*. Shouldn't that be miracle enough for anyone?"

"Maybe. Maybe the average voter liked her better the other way."

Taffy brushed at her hair with angry vigor. "They're *alive*."

"I wonder if they revived Leviticus Hale."

"Leviti—? Oh. Not at Saint John's." Taffy worked there. She'd know.

"I haven't seen him in the cube. They should have revived him," I said. "With that patriarchal visage he'd make a *great* impression. He might even try the Messiah bit. 'Yea, brethren, I have returned from the dead to lead you—' None of the others have tried that yet."

"Good thing, too." Her strokes slowed. "A lot of them died in the thawing process and afterward. From cell wall ruptures."

Ten minutes later I got up and used the phone. Taffy showed her amusement. "Is it that important?"

"Maybe not." I dialed the Vault of Eternity in New Jersey. I knew I'd be wondering until I did.

Mr. Restarick was on night watch. He seemed glad to see me. He'd have been glad to see anyone who would talk back. His clothes were the same mismatch of ancient styles, but they didn't look as anachronistic now. The boob cube had been infested with corpsicles wearing approximations of their own styles.

Yes, he remembered me. Yes, Leviticus Hale was still in place. The hospitals had taken two of his wards, and both had survived, he told me proudly. The administrators had wanted Hale, too; they'd liked his looks and his publicity value, dating as he did from the last century but one. But they hadn't been able to get permission from the next of kin.

Taffy watched me watching a blank phone screen. "What's wrong?"

"The Chambers kid. Remember Holden Chambers, the corpsicle heir? He lied to me. He refused permission for the hospitals to revive Leviticus Hale. A *year* ago."

"Oh." She thought it over, then reacted with a charity typical of her. "It's a lot of money just for not signing a paper."

The cube was showing an old flick, a remake of a Shakespeare play. We turned it to landscape and went to sleep.

I back away, back away. The composite ghost comes near, using somebody's arm and somebody's eye and Loren's pleural cavity containing somebody's heart and somebody's lung and somebody's other lung, and I can feel it all inside him. Horrible. I reach deeper. Somebody's heart leaps like a fish in my hand.

Taffy found me in the kitchen making hot chocolate. For two. I know damn well she can't sleep when I'm restless. She said, "Why don't you tell me about it?"

"Because it's ugly."

"I think you'd better tell me." She came into my arms, rubbed her cheek against mine.

I said to her ear, "Get the poison out of my system. Sure, and into yours."

"All right." I could take it either way.

The chocolate was ready. I disengaged myself and poured it, added meager splashes of bourbon. She sipped reflectively. She said, "Is it always Loren?"

"Yah. Damn him."

"Never this one you're after now?"

"Anubis? I never dealt with him. He was Bera's assignment. Anyway, he retired before I was properly trained. Gave his territory to Loren. The market in stiffs was so bad that Loren had to double his territory just to keep going."

I was talking too much. I was desperate to talk to someone, to get back my grip on reality.

"What did they do, flip a coin?"

"For what? Oh. No, there was never a question about who was going to retire. Loren was a sick man. It must have been why he went into the business. He needed the supply of transplants. And he couldn't get out because he needed constant shots. His rejection spectrum must have been a bad joke. Anubis was different."

She sipped at her chocolate. She shouldn't have to know this, but I couldn't stop talking. "Anubis changed body parts at whim. We'll never get him. He probably made himself over completely when he . . . retired."

Taffy touched my shoulder. "Let's go back to bed."

"All right." But my own voice ran on in my head. *His only problem was the money. How could he hide a fortune that size? And the new identity. A new personality with lots of conspicuous money . . . and, if he tried to live somewhere else, a foreign accent, too. But there's less privacy here, and he's known . . .* I sipped the chocolate, watching the landscape in the boob cube. *What could he do to make a new identity convincing?* The landscape scene was night on some mountaintop, bare tumbled rock backed by churning clouds. Restful.

I thought of something he could do.

I got out of bed and called Bera.

Taffy watched me in amazement. "It's three in the morning," she pointed out.

"I know."

Lila Bera was sleepy and naked and ready to kill someone. Me. She said, "Gil, it better be good."

"It's good. Tell Jackson I can locate Anubis."

Bera popped up beside her, demanded, "Where?" His hair was miraculously intact, a puffy black dandelion ready to blow. He was squint-eyed and grimacing with sleep and as naked as . . . as I was, come to that. This thing superseded good manners.

I told him where Anubis was.

I had his attention then. I talked fast, sketching in the intermediate steps. "Does it sound reasonable? I can't tell. It's three in the morning. I may not be thinking straight."

Bera ran both hands through his hair, a swift, violent gesture that left his natural in shreds. "Why didn't I think of that? Why didn't *anyone* think of that?"

"The waste. When the stuff from one condemned ax murderer can save a dozen lives, it just doesn't occur to you—"

"Right right right. Skip that. What do we do?"

"Alert headquarters. Then call Holden Chambers. I may be able to tell just by talking to him. Otherwise we'll have to go over."

"Yah." Bera grinned through the pain of interrupted sleep. "He's not going to like being called at three in the morning."

The white-haired man informed me that Holden Chambers was not to be disturbed. He was reaching for a (mythical) cutoff switch when I said, "ARM business, life and death," and displayed my ARM ident. He nodded and put me on hold.

Very convincing. But he'd gone through some of the same motions every time I'd called.

Chambers appeared, wearing a badly wrinkled cloth sleeping jacket. He backed up a few feet (wary of ghostly intrusions?) and sat down on the uneasy edge of a water bed. He rubbed his eyes and said, "Censor it, I was up past midnight studying. What now?"

"You're in danger. Immediate danger. Don't panic, but don't go back to bed, either. We're coming over."

"You're kidding." He studied my face in the phone screen. "You're not, are you? A-a-all right, I'll put some clothes on. What kind of danger?"

"I can't tell you that. Don't go anywhere."

I called Bera back.

He met me in the lobby. We used his taxi. An ARM ident in the credit slot turns any cab into a police car. Bera said, "Couldn't you tell?"

"No, he was too far back. I had to say *something*, so I warned him not to go anywhere."

"I wonder if that was a good idea."

"It doesn't matter. Anubis only has about fifteen minutes to act, and even then we could follow him."

There was no immediate answer to our ring. Maybe he was surprised to see us outside his door. Ordinarily you can't get into the parking roof elevator unless a tenant lets you in, but an ARM ident unlocks most locks.

Bera's patience snapped. "I think he's gone. We'd better call—"

Chambers opened the door. "All right, what's it all about? Come—" He saw our guns.

Bera hit the door hard and branched right; I branched left. Those tiny apartments don't have many places to hide. The water bed was gone, replaced by an L-shaped couch and coffee table. There was nothing behind the couch. I covered the bathroom while Bera kicked the door open.

Nobody here but us. Chambers lost his astonished look, smiled, and clapped for us. I bowed.

"You *must* have been serious," he said. "What kind of danger? Couldn't it have waited for morning?"

"Yah, but I couldn't have slept," I said, coming toward him. "I'm going to owe you a big fat apology if this doesn't work out."

He backed away.

"Hold still. This will only take a second." I advanced on him. Bera was behind him now. He hadn't hurried. His long legs give him deceptive speed.

Chambers backed away, backed away, backed into Bera, and squeaked in surprise. He dithered, then made a break for the bathroom.

Bera reached out, wrapped one arm around Chambers's waist, and pinned his arms with the other. Chambers struggled like a madman. I stepped wide around them, moved in sideways to avoid Chambers's thrashing legs, reached out to touch his face with my imaginary hand.

He froze. Then he screamed.

"That's what you were afraid of," I told him. "You never dreamed I could reach through a phone screen to do *this*." I reached into his head, felt smooth muscle and grainy bone and sinus cavities like bubbles. He tossed his head, but my hand went with it. I ran imaginary fingertips along the smooth inner surface of his skull. It was there. A ridge of scar, barely raised above the rest of the bone, too fine for X rays. It ran in a closed curve from the base of his skull up through the temples to intersect his eye sockets.

"It's him," I said.

Bera screamed in his ear. "You *pig*!"

Anubis went limp.

"I can't find a joining at the brain stem. They must have transplanted the spinal cord, too: the whole central nervous system." I found scars along the vertebrae. "That's what they did, all right."

Anubis spoke almost casually, as if he'd lost a chess game. "All right, that's a gotcha. I concede. Let's sit down."

"Sure." Bera threw him at the couch. He hit it, more or less. He adjusted himself, looking astonished at Bera's bad behavior. What was the man so excited about?

Bera told him. "You pig. Coring him like that, making a vehicle out of the poor bastard. We never thought of a brain transplant."

"It's a wonder I thought of it myself. The stuff from one donor is worth over a million marks in surgery charges. Why should anyone use a whole donor for one transplant? But once I thought of it, it made all kinds of sense. The stuff wasn't selling, anyway."

Funny: they both talked as if they'd known each other a long time. There aren't many people an organlegger will regard as *people*, but an ARM is one of them. We're organleggers, too, in a sense.

Bera was holding a sonic on him. Anubis ignored it. He said, "The only problem was the money."

"Then you thought of the corpsicle heirs," I said.

"Yah. I went looking for a rich corpsicle with a young, healthy direct-line heir. Leviticus Hale seemed made for the part. He was the first one I noticed."

"He's pretty noticeable, isn't he? A healthy middle-aged man sleeping there among all those battered accident cases. Only two heirs, both orphans, one kind of introverted, the other . . . What did you do to Charlotte?"

"Charlotte Chambers? We drove her mad. We had to. She was the only one who'd notice if Holden Chambers suddenly got too different."

"What did you *do* to her?"

"We made a wirehead out of her."

"The hell. Someone would have noticed the contact in her scalp."

"No, no, no. We used one of those induction helmets you find in the ecstasy shops. We kept her in the helmet for nine days, on full. When we stopped the current, she just wasn't interested in anything anymore."

"How did you know it would work?"

"Oh, we tried it out on a few prospects. It worked fine. It didn't hurt them after they were broken up."

"Okay." I went to the phone and dialed ARM Headquarters.

"It solved the money problem beautifully," he ran on. "I plowed most of it into advertising charges. And there's nothing suspicious about Leviticus Hale's money. When the second Freezer Bill goes through—well, I guess not. Not now. Unless—"

"No," Bera said for both of us.

I told the man on duty where we were, and to stop monitoring the tracers, and to call in the operatives watching corpsicle heirs. Then I hung up.

"I spent six months studying Chambers's college courses. I didn't want to blow his career. Six months! Answer me one," Anubis said, curiously anxious. "Where did I go wrong? What gave me away?"

"You were beautiful," I told him wearily. "You never went out of character. You should have been an actor.

Would have been safer, too. We didn't suspect anything until—" I looked at my watch. "Forty-five minutes ago."

"Censored dammit! You would say that. When I saw you looking at me in Midgard, I thought that was it. That floating cigarette. You'd got Loren, now you were after me."

I couldn't help it. I roared. Anubis sat there, taking it. He was beginning to blush.

They were shouting something, something I couldn't make out. Something with a beat. *DAdadadaDAdadada* . . .

There was just room for me and Jackson Bera and Luke Garner's travel chair on the tiny balcony outside Garner's office. Far below, the marchers flowed past the ARM building in half-orderly procession. Teams of them carried huge banners. LET THEM STAY DEAD, one suggested, and another in small print: *Why not revive them a bit at a time?* FOR YOUR FATHER'S SAKE, a third said with deadly logic.

They were roped off from the spectators, roped off into a column down the middle of Wilshire. The spectators were even thicker. It looked like all of Los Angeles had turned out to watch. Some of them carried placards, too. THEY WANT TO LIVE TOO, and ARE YOU A FREEZER VAULT HEIR?

"What is it they're shouting?" Bera wondered. "It's not the marchers; it's the spectators. They're drowning out the marchers."

DAdadadaDAdadadaDAdadada. It rippled up to us on stray wind currents.

"We could see it better inside, in the boob cube," Garner said without moving. What held us was a metaphysical force, the knowledge that one is *there*, a witness.

Abruptly, Garner asked, "How's Charlotte Chambers?"

"I don't know." I didn't want to talk about it.

"Didn't you call Menninger Institute this morning?"

"I mean I don't know how to take it. They've done a wirehead operation on her. They're giving her just enough current to keep her interested. It's working, I mean she's talking to people, but . . ."

"It's got to be better than being catatonic," Bera said.

"Does it? There's no way to turn off a wirehead. She'll have to go through life with a battery under her hat. When she comes back far enough into the real world, she'll find a way to boost the current and bug right out again."

"Think of her as walking wounded." Bera shrugged, shifting an invisible weight on his shoulders. "There *isn't* any good answer. She's been *hurt*, man!"

"There's more to it than that," Luke Garner said. "We need to know if she can be cured. There are more wireheads every day. It's a new vice. We need to learn how to control it. What the bleep is happening down there?"

The bystanders were surging against the ropes. Suddenly they were through in a dozen places, converging on the marchers. It was a swirling mob scene. They were still chanting, and suddenly I caught it.

ORganleggersORganleggersORganleggers . . .

"That's it!" Bera shouted in pleased surprise. "Anubis is getting too much publicity. It's good versus evil!"

The rioters started to collapse in curved ribbon patterns. Copters overhead were spraying them with sonic stun cannon.

Bera said, "They'll never pass the second Freezer Bill now."

Never is a long time to Luke Garner. He said, "Not this time, anyway. We ought to start thinking about that. A lot of people have been applying for operations. There's quite a waiting list. When the second Freezer Bill fails—"

I saw it. "They'll start going to organleggers. We can keep track of them. Tracers."

"That's what I had in mind."

✳
ARM

The ARM Building had been abnormally quiet for some months now.

We'd needed the rest—at first. But these last few mornings the silence had had an edgy quality. We waved at each other on our paths to our respective desks, but our heads were elsewhere. Some of us had a restless look. Others were visibly, determinedly busy.

Nobody wanted to join a mother hunt.

This past year we'd managed to cut deep into the organlegging activities in the West Coast area. Pats on the back all around, but the results were predictable: other activities were going to increase. Sooner or later the newspapers would start screaming about stricter enforcement of the Fertility Laws, and then we'd all be out hunting down illegitimate parents ... all of us who were not involved in something else.

It was high time I got involved in something else.

This morning I walked to my office through the usual edgy silence. I ran coffee, carried it to my desk, punched for messages at the computer terminal. A slender file slid from the slot. A hopeful sign. I picked it up one-handed so that I could sip coffee as I went through it and let it fall open in the middle.

Color holographs jumped out at me. I was looking down through a pair of windows over two morgue tables.

124

Stomach to brain: LURCH! What a hell of an hour to be looking at people with their faces burned off! Get eyes to look somewhere else and don't try to swallow that coffee. Why don't you change jobs?

They were hideous. Two of them, a man and a woman. Something had burned their faces away down to the skulls and beyond: bones and teeth charred, brain tissue cooked.

I swallowed and kept looking. I'd seen the dead before. These had just hit me at the wrong time.

Not a laser weapon, I thought . . . though that was chancy. There are thousands of jobs for lasers and thousands of varieties to do the jobs. Not a hand laser, anyway. The pencil-thin beam of a hand laser would have chewed channels in the flesh. This had been a wide, steady beam of some kind.

I flipped back to the beginning and skimmed.

Details: They'd been found on the Wilshire slidewalk in West Los Angeles around 4:30 A.M. People don't use the slidewalks that late. They're afraid of organleggers. The bodies could have traveled up to a couple of miles before anyone saw them.

Preliminary autopsy: They'd been dead three or four days. No signs of drugs or poisons or puncture marks. Apparently the burns had been the only cause of death.

It must have been quick, then: a single flash of energy. Otherwise they'd have tried to dodge, and there'd be burns elsewhere. There were none. Just the faces and char marks around the collars.

There was a memo from Bates, the coroner. From the look of them, they might have been killed by some new weapon. So he'd sent the file over to us. Could we find anything in the ARM files that would fire a blast of heat or light a foot across?

I sat back and stared into the holos and thought about it.

A light weapon with a beam a foot across? They make lasers in that size, but as war weapons, used from orbit. One of those would have vaporized the heads, not charred them.

There were other possibilities. Death by torture, with the heads held in clamps in the blast from a commercial attitude jet. Or some kind of weird industrial accident: a flash explosion that had caught them both looking over a desk or something. Or even a laser beam reflected from a convex mirror.

Forget about its being an accident. The way the bodies were abandoned reeked of guilt, of something to be covered up. Maybe Bates was right. A new illegal weapon.

And I could be deeply involved in searching for it when the mother hunt started.

The ARM has three basic functions. We hunt organleggers. We monitor world technology: new developments that might create new weapons or that might affect the world economy or the balance of power among nations. And we enforce the Fertility Laws.

Come, let us be honest with ourselves. Of the three, protecting the Fertility Laws is probably the most important.

Organleggers don't aggravate the population problem.

Monitoring of technology is necessary enough, but it may have happened too late. There are enough fusion power plants and fusion rocket motors and fusion crematoriums and fusion seawater distilleries around to let any madman or group thereof blow up the Earth or any selected part of it.

But if a lot of people in one region started having illegal babies, the rest of the world would scream. Some nations might even get mad enough to abandon population control. Then what? We've got eighteen billion on Earth now. We couldn't handle more.

So the mother hunts are necessary. But I hate them. It's no fun hunting down some poor sick woman so desperate to have children that she'll go through hell to avoid her six-month contraceptive shots. I'll get out of it if I can.

I did some obvious things. I sent a note to Bates at the coroner's office. *Send all further details on the autopsies and let me know if the corpses are identified.* Retinal prints and brain-wave patterns were obviously out, but they might get something on gene patterns and fingerprints.

I spent some time wondering where two bodies had been kept for three to four days, and why, before being abandoned in a way that could have been used three days earlier. But that was a problem for the LAPD detectives. Our concern was with the weapon.

So I started writing a search pattern for the computer: find me a widget that will fire a beam of a given description. From the pattern of penetration into skin and bone and brain tissue, there was probably a way to express the frequency of the light as a function of the duration of the blast, but I didn't fool with that. I'd pay for my laziness later, when the computer handed me a foot-thick list of light-emitting machinery and I had to wade through it.

I had punched in the instructions and was relaxing with more coffee and a cigarette when Ordaz called.

Detective-Inspector Julio Ordaz was a slender, dark-skinned man with straight black hair and soft black eyes. The first time I saw him in a phone screen, he had been telling me of a good friend's murder. Two years later I still flinched when I saw him.

"Hello, Julio. Business or pleasure?"

"Business, Gil. It is to be regretted."

"Yours or mine?"

"Both. There is murder involved, but there is also a machine . . . Look, can you see it behind me?" Ordaz stepped out of the field of view, then reached invisibly to turn the phone camera.

I looked into somebody's living room. There was a wide circle of discoloration in the green indoor grass rug. In the center of the circle, a machine and a man's body.

Was Julio putting me on? The body was old, half-mummified. The machine was big and cryptic in shape, and it glowed with a subdued, eerie blue light.

Ordaz sounded serious enough. "Have you ever seen anything like this?"

"No. That's some machine." Unmistakably an experimental device: no neat plastic case, no compactness, no assembly-line welding. Too complex to examine through a phone camera, I decided. "Yah, that looks like something for us. Can you send it over?"

Ordaz came back on. He was smiling, barely. "I'm afraid we cannot do that. Perhaps you should send someone here to look at it."

"Where are you now?"

"In Raymond Sinclair's apartment on the top floor of the Rodewald Building in Santa Monica."

"I'll come myself," I said. My tongue suddenly felt thick.

"Please land on the roof. We are holding the elevator for examination."

"Sure." I hung up.

Raymond Sinclair!

I'd never met Raymond Sinclair. He was something of a recluse. But the ARM had dealt with him once in connection with one of his inventions, the FyreStop device. And everyone knew that he had lately been working on an interstellar drive. It was only a rumor, of course . . . but if someone had killed the brain that held that secret . . .

I went.

The Rodewald Building was forty stories of triangular prism with a row of triangular balconies going up each side. The balconies stopped at the thirty-eighth floor.

The roof was a garden. There were rosebushes in bloom along one edge, full-grown elms nestled in ivy along another, and a miniature forest of bonsai trees along the third. The landing pad and carport were in the center. A squad car floated down ahead of my taxi, then slid under the carport to give me room to land.

A cop in a vivid orange uniform came out to watch me come down. He was carrying a deep-sea fishing pole, still in its kit.

He said, "May I see some ID, please?"

I had my ARM ident in my hand. He checked it in the

console in the squad car, then handed it back. "The inspector's waiting downstairs," he said.

"What's the pole for?"

He smiled suddenly, almost secretively. "You'll see."

We left the garden smells via a flight of concrete stairs. They led down into a small room half-full of gardening tools and a heavy door with a spy-eye in it. Ordaz opened the door for us. He shook my hand briskly, glanced at the cop. "You found something? Good."

The cop said, "There's a sporting goods store six blocks from here. The manager let me borrow it. He made sure I knew the name of the store."

"Yes, there will certainly be publicity on this matter. Come, Gil." Ordaz took my arm. "You should examine this before we turn it off."

No garden smells here, but there was something—a whiff of something long dead—that the air-conditioning hadn't quite cleared away. Ordaz walked me into the living room.

It looked like somebody's idea of a practical joke.

The indoor grass covered Sinclair's living room floor, wall to wall. In a perfect fourteen-foot circle between the sofa and the fireplace, the rug was brown and dead. Elsewhere it was green and thriving.

A man's mummy, dressed in stained slacks and turtleneck, lay on its back in the center of the circle. At a guess it had been about six months dead. It wore a big wristwatch with extra dials on the face and a fine-mesh platinum band, loose now around a wrist of bones and brown skin. The back of the skull had been smashed open, possibly by the classic blunt instrument lying next to it.

If the fireplace was false—it almost had to be; nobody burns wood—the fireplace instruments were genuine nineteenth- or twentieth-century antiques. The rack was missing a poker. A poker lay inside the circle, in the dead grass next to the disintegrating mummy.

The glowing device sat just in the center of the magic circle.

I stepped forward, and a man's voice spoke sharply. "Don't go inside that circle of rug. It's more dangerous than it looks."

It was a man I knew: Officer-One Valpredo, a tall man with a small, straight mouth and a long, narrow Italian face.

"Looks dangerous enough to me," I said.

"It is. I reached in there myself," Valpredo told me, "right after we got here. I thought I could flip the switch off. My whole arm went numb. Instantly. No feeling at all. I yanked it away fast, but for a minute or so after that my whole arm was dead meat. I thought I'd lost it. Then it was all pins and needles, like I'd slept on it."

The cop who had brought me in had almost finished assembling the deep-sea fishing pole.

Ordaz waved into the circle. "Well? Have you ever seen anything like this?"

I shook my head, studying the violet-glowing machinery. "Whatever it is, it's brand-new. Sinclair's really done it this time."

An uneven line of solenoids was attached to a plastic frame with homemade joins. Blistered spots on the plastic showed where other objects had been attached and later removed. A breadboard bore masses of heavy wiring. There were six big batteries hooked in parallel and a strange, heavy piece of sculpture in what we later discovered was pure silver, with wiring attached at three curving points. The silver was tarnished almost black, and there were old file marks at the edges.

Near the center of the arrangement, just in front of the silver sculpture, were two concentric solenoids embedded in a block of clear plastic. They glowed blue shading to violet. So did the batteries. A less perceptible violet glow radiated from everywhere on the machine, more intensely in the interior parts.

That glow bothered me more than anything else. It was too theatrical. It was like something a special effects man might add to a cheap late-night thriller to suggest a mad scientist's laboratory.

I moved around to get a closer look at the dead man's watch.

"Keep your head out of the field!" Valpredo said sharply.

I nodded. I squatted on my heels outside the borderline of dead grass.

The dead man's watch was going like crazy. The minute hand was circling the dial every seven seconds or so. I couldn't find the second hand at all.

I backed away from the arc of dead grass and stood up. Interstellar drive, hell. This blue-glowing monstrosity looked more like a time machine gone wrong.

I studied the single-throw switch welded to the plastic frame next to the batteries. A length of nylon line dangled from the horizontal handle. It looked like someone had tugged the switch on from outside the field by using the line, but he'd have had to hang from the ceiling to tug it off that way.

"I see why you couldn't send it over to ARM Headquarters. You can't even touch it. You stick your arm or your head in there for a second, and that's ten minutes without a blood supply."

Ordaz said, "Exactly."

"It looks like you could reach in there with a stick and flip that switch off."

"Perhaps. We are about to try that." He waved at the man with the fishing pole. "There was nothing in this room long enough to reach the switch. We had to send—"

"Wait a minute. There's a problem."

He looked at me. So did the cop with the fishing pole.

"That switch could be a self-destruct. Sinclair was supposed to be a secretive bastard. Or the field might hold considerable potential energy. Something might go blooey."

Ordaz sighed. "We must risk it. Gil, we have measured the rotation of the dead man's wristwatch. One hour per seven seconds. Fingerprints, footprints, laundry marks, residual body odor, stray eyelashes, all disappearing at an hour per seven seconds." He gestured, and the cop moved in and began trying to hook the switch.

"Already we may never know just when he was killed," Ordaz said.

The tip of the pole wobbled in large circles, steadied beneath the switch, made contact. I held my breath. The pole bowed. The switch snapped up, and suddenly the violet glow was gone. Valpredo reached into the field, warily, as if the air might be red hot. Nothing happened, and he relaxed.

Then Ordaz began giving orders, and quite a lot happened. Two men in lab coats drew a chalk outline around the mummy and the poker. They moved the mummy onto a stretcher, put the poker in a plastic bag, and put it next to the mummy.

I said, "Have you identified that?"

"I'm afraid so," Ordaz said. "Raymond Sinclair had his own autodoc—"

"*Did* he? Those things are expensive."

"Yes. Raymond Sinclair was a wealthy man. He owned the top two floors of this building and the roof. According to records in his 'doc, he had a new set of bud teeth implanted two months ago." Ordaz pointed to the mummy, to the skinned-back dry lips and the buds of new teeth that were just coming in.

Right. That was Sinclair.

That brain had made miracles, and someone had smashed it with a wrought-iron rod. The interstellar drive . . . that glowing Goldberg device? Or had it been still inside his head?

I said, "We'll have to get whoever did it. We'll *have* to. Even so . . ." Even so. No more miracles.

"We may have her already," Julio said.

I looked at him.

"There is a girl in the autodoc. We think she is Dr. Sinclair's great-niece, Janice Sinclair."

It was a standard drugstore autodoc, a thing like a giant coffin with walls a foot thick and a headboard covered with dials and red and green lights. The girl's face was calm, her breathing shallow. Sleeping Beauty. Her arms were in the guts of the 'doc, hidden by bulky rubbery sleeves.

She was lovely enough to stop my breath. Soft brown hair showing around the electrode cap; small, perfect nose and mouth; smooth pale blue skin shot with silver threads . . .

That last was an evening dye job. Without it the impact of her would have been much lessened. The blue shade varied slightly to emphasize the shape of her body and the curve of her cheekbones. The silver lines varied, too, being denser in certain areas, guiding the eye in certain directions: to the tips of her breasts or across the slight swell of abdominal muscle to a lovely oval navel.

She'd paid high for that dye job. But she would be beautiful without it.

Some of the headboard lights were red. I punched for a readout and was jolted. The 'doc had been forced to amputate her right arm. Gangrene.

She was in for a hell of a shock when she woke up.

"All right," I said. "She's lost her arm. That doesn't make her a killer."

Ordaz asked, "If she were homely, would it help?"

I laughed. "You question my dispassionate judgment? Men have died for less!" Even so, I thought he could be right. There was good reason to think that the killer was now missing an arm.

"What do you think happened here, Gil?"

"Well . . . any way you look at it, the killer had to want to take Sinclair's, ah, time machine with him. It's priceless, for one thing. For another, it looks like he tried to set it up as an alibi. Which means that he knew about it before he came here." I'd been thinking this through. "Say he made sure some people knew where he was a few hours before he got here. He killed Sinclair within range of the . . . call it a generator. Turned it on. He figured Sinclair's own watch would tell him how much time he was gaining. Afterward he could set the watch back and leave with the generator. There'd be no way the police could tell he wasn't killed six hours earlier, or any number you like."

"Yes. But he did not do that."

"There was that line hanging from the switch. He must have turned it on from outside the field ... probably because he didn't want to sit with the body for six hours. If he tried to step outside the field after he'd turned it on, he'd bump his nose. It'd be like trying to walk through a wall, going from field time to normal time. So he turned it off, stepped out of range, and used that nylon line to turn it on again. He probably made the same mistake Valpredo did: he thought he could step back in and turn it off."

Ordaz nodded in satisfaction. "Exactly. It was very important for him—or her—to do that. Otherwise he would have no alibi and no profit. If he continued to try to reach into the field—"

"Yah, he could lose the arm to gangrene. That'd be convenient for us, wouldn't it? He'd be easy to find. But look, Julio: the girl could have done the same thing to herself trying to *help* Sinclair. He might not have been that obviously dead when she got home."

"He might even have been alive," Ordaz pointed out.

I shrugged.

"In point of fact, she came home at one-ten, in her own car, which is still in the carport. There are cameras mounted to cover the landing pad and carport. Doctor Sinclair's security was thorough. This girl was the only arrival last night. There were no departures."

"From the roof, you mean."

"Gil, there are only two ways to leave these apartments. One is from the roof, and the other is by elevator, from the lobby. The elevator is on this floor, and it was turned off. It was that way when we arrived. There is no way to override that control from elsewhere in this building."

"So someone could have taken it up here and turned it off afterward ... or Sinclair could have turned it off before he was killed ... I see what you mean. Either way, the killer has to be still here." I thought about that. I didn't like its taste. "No, it doesn't fit. How could she be bright enough to work out that alibi, then dumb enough to lock herself in with the body?"

Ordaz shrugged. "She locked the elevator before killing her uncle. She did not want to be interrupted. Surely that was sensible? After she hurt her arm, she must have been in a great hurry to reach the 'doc."

One of the red lights turned green. I was glad for that. She didn't look like a killer. I said half to myself, "Nobody looks like a killer when he's asleep."

"No. But she is where a killer ought to be. *Qué lástima.*"

We went back to the living room. I called ARM Headquarters and had them send a truck.

The machine hadn't been touched. While we waited, I borrowed a camera from Valpredo and took pictures of the setup in situ. The relative positions of the components might be important.

The lab men were in the brown grass, using aerosol sprays to turn fingerprints white and give a vivid yellow glow to faint traces of blood. They got plenty of fingerprints on the machine, none at all on the poker. There was a puddle of yellow in the grass where the mummy's head had been and a long yellow snail track ending at the business end of the poker. It looked like someone had tried to drag the poker out of the field after it had fallen.

Sinclair's apartments were roomy and comfortable and occupied the entire top floor. The lower floor was the laboratory where Sinclair had produced his miracles. I went through it with Valpredo. It wasn't that impressive. It looked like an expensive hobby setup. These tools would assemble components already fabricated, but they would not build anything complex.

Except for the computer terminal. That was like a little womb, with a recline chair inside a 360-degree wraparound holovision screen and enough banked controls to fly the damn thing to Alpha Centauri.

The secrets there must be in that computer! But I didn't try to use it. We'd have to send an ARM programmer to break whatever fail-safe codes Sinclair had put in the memory banks.

The truck arrived. We dragged Sinclair's legacy up the stairs to the roof in one piece. The parts were sturdily mounted on their frame, and the stairs were wide and not too steep.

I rode home in the back of the truck. Studying the generator. That massive piece of silver had something of the look of *Bird in Flight*: a triangle operated on by a topology student with wires at what were still the corners. I wondered if it was the heart of the machine or just a piece of misdirection. Was I really riding with an interstellar drive? Sinclair could have started that rumor himself to cover whatever this was. Or . . . there was no law against his working two projects simultaneously.

I was looking forward to Bera's reaction.

Jackson Bera came upon us moving it through the halls of ARM Headquarters. He trailed along behind us. Nonchalant. We pulled the machine into the main laboratory and started checking it against the holos I'd taken in case something had been jarred loose. Bera leaned against the doorjamb, watching us, his eyes gradually losing interest until he seemed about to go to sleep.

I'd met him three years ago, when I had returned from the asteroids and joined the ARM. He was twenty then, and two years an ARM, but his father and grandfather had both been ARMs. Much of my training had come from Bera. And as I learned to hunt men who hunt other men, I had watched what it was doing to him.

An ARM needs empathy. He needs the ability to piece together a picture of the mind of his prey. But Bera had too much empathy. I remember his reaction when Kenneth Graham killed himself: a single surge of current through the plug in his skull and down the wire to the pleasure center of his brain. Bera had been twitchy for weeks. And the Anubis case early last year. When we realized what the man had done, Bera had been close to killing him on the spot. I wouldn't have blamed him.

Last year Bera had had enough. He'd gone into the technical end of the business. His days of hunting organleggers were finished. He was now running the ARM laboratory.

He *had* to want to know what this oddball contraption was. I kept waiting for him to ask . . . and he watched, faintly smiling. Finally it dawned on me. He thought it was a pratical joke, something I'd cobbled together for his own discomfiture.

I said, "Bera."

And he looked at me brightly and said, "Hey, man, what is it?"

"You ask the most embarrassing questions."

"Right, I can understand your feeling that way, but what *is* it? I love it, it's neat, but what is this· that you have brought me?"

I told him all I knew, such as it was. When I finished, he said, "It doesn't sound much like a new space drive."

"Oho, you heard that, too, did you? No, it doesn't. Unless—" I'd been wondering since I first saw it. "Maybe it's supposed to accelerate a fusion explosion. You'd get greater efficiency in a fusion drive."

"They get better than ninety percent now, and that widget looks *heavy*." He reached to touch the bent silver triangle gently with long, tapering fingers. "Huh. Well, we'll dig out the answers."

"Good luck. I'm going back to Sinclair's place."

"Why? The action is here." Often enough he'd heard me talking wistfully of joining an interstellar colony. He must know how I'd feel about a better drive for the interstellar slowboats.

"It's like this," I said. "We've got the generator, but we don't know anything about it. We might wreck it. I'm going to have a whack at finding someone who knows something about Sinclair's generator."

"Meaning?"

"Whoever tried to steal it. Sinclair's killer."

"If you say so." But he looked dubious. He knew me too

well. He said, "I understand there's a mother hunt in the offing."

"Oh?"

He smiled. "Just a rumor. You guys are lucky. When my dad first joined, the business of the ARM was *mostly* mother hunts. The organleggers hadn't really got organized yet, and the Fertility Laws were new. If we hadn't enforced them, nobody would have obeyed them at all."

"Sure, and people threw rocks at your father. Bera, those days are *gone*."

"They could come back. Having children is basic."

"Bera, I did not join the ARM to hunt unlicensed parents." I waved and left before he could answer. I could do without the call to duty from Bera, who had done with hunting men and mothers.

I'd had a good view of the Rodewald Building while dropping toward the roof this morning. I had a good view now from my commandeered taxi. This time I was looking for escape paths.

There were no balconies on Sinclair's floors, and the windows were flush to the side of the building. A cat burglar would have trouble with them. They didn't look like they'd open.

I tried to spot the cameras Ordaz had mentioned as the taxi dropped toward the roof. I couldn't find them. Maybe they were mounted in the elms.

Why was I bothering? I hadn't joined the ARM to chase mothers or machinery or common murderers.

I'd joined the ARM to hunt organleggers.

The ARM doesn't deal in murder per se. The machine was out of my hands now. A murder investigation wouldn't keep me out of a mother hunt. And I'd never met the girl. I knew nothing of her beyond the fact that she was where a killer ought to be.

Was it just that she was pretty?

Poor Janice. When she woke up . . . For a solid month

I'd wakened to that same stunning shock, the knowledge that my right arm was gone.

The taxi settled. Valpredo was waiting below.

I speculated . . . Cars weren't the only things that flew. But anyone flying one of those tricky ducted-fan flycycles over a city, where he could fall on a pedestrian, wouldn't have to worry about a murder charge. They'd feed him to the organ banks regardless. And anything that flew would leave traces anywhere but on the landing pad itself. It would crush a rosebush or a bonsai tree or be flipped over by an elm.

The taxi took off in a whisper of air.

Valpredo was grinning at me. "The thinker. What's on your mind?"

"I was wondering if the killer could have come down on the carport roof."

He turned to study the situation. "There are two cameras mounted on the edge of the roof. If his vehicle was light enough, sure, he could land there, and the cameras wouldn't spot him. Roof wouldn't hold a car, though. Anyway, nobody did it."

"How do you know?"

"I'll show you. By the way, we inspected the camera system. We're pretty sure the cameras weren't tampered with. Nobody even landed here until seven this morning. Look here." We had reached the concrete stairs that led down into Sinclair's apartments. Valpredo pointed at a glint of light in the sloping ceiling, at heart level. "This is the only way down. The camera would get anyone coming in or out. It might not catch his face, but it'd show if someone passed. It takes sixty frames a minute."

I went on down. A cop let me in.

Ordaz was on the phone. The screen showed a young man with a deep tan and shock showing through the tan. Ordaz waved at me, a shushing motion, and went on talking. "Fifteen minutes? That will be a great help to us. Please land on the roof. We are still working on the elevator."

He hung up and turned to me. "Andrew Porter, Janice Sinclair's lover. He tells us that he and Janice spent the evening at a party. She dropped him off at his home around one o'clock."

"Then she came straight home, if that's her in the 'doc."

"I think it must be. Mr. Porter says she was wearing a blue skin-dye job." Ordaz was frowning. "He put on a most convincing act, if it was that. I think he really was not expecting any kind of trouble. He was surprised that a stranger answered, shocked when he learned of Doctor Sinclair's death, and horrified when he learned that Janice had been hurt."

With the mummy and the generator removed, the murder scene had become an empty circle of brown grass marked with random streaks of yellow chemical and outlines of white chalk.

"We had some luck," Ordaz said. "Today's date is June 4, 2124. Dr. Sinclair was wearing a calendar watch. It registered January 17, 2125. If we switched the machine off at ten minutes to ten—which we did—and if it was registering an hour for every seven seconds that passed outside the field, then the field must have gone on at around one o'clock last night, give or take a margin of error."

"Then if the girl didn't do it, she must have just missed the killer."

"Exactly."

"What about the elevator? Could it have been jiggered?"

"No. We took the workings apart. It was on this floor and locked by hand. Nobody could have left by elevator . . ."

"Why did you trail off like that?"

Ordaz shrugged, embarrassed. "This peculiar machine really does bother me, Gil. I found myself thinking, Suppose it can reverse time? Then the killer could have gone down in an elevator that was going up."

He laughed with me. I said, "In the first place, I don't

believe a word of it. In the second place, he didn't have the machine to do it with. Unless . . . he made his escape before the murder. Dammit, now you've got me doing it."

"I would like to know more about the machine."

"Bera's investigating it now. I'll let you know as soon as we learn anything. And *I'd* like to know more about how the killer couldn't possibly have left."

He looked at me. "Details?"

"Could someone have opened a window?"

"No. These apartments are forty years old. The smog was still bad when they were built. Dr. Sinclair apparently preferred to depend on his air-conditioning."

"How about the apartment below? I presume it has a different set of elevators."

"Yes, of course. It belongs to Howard Rodewald, the owner of this building—of this chain of buildings, in fact. At the moment he is in Europe. His apartment has been loaned to friends."

"There's no stairs down to there?"

"No. We searched these apartments thoroughly."

"All right. We know the killer had a nylon line, because he left a strand of it on the generator. Could he have climbed down to Rodewald's balcony from the roof?"

"Thirty feet? Yes, I suppose so." Ordaz's eyes sparked. "We must look into that. There is still the matter of how he got past the camera and whether he could have gotten inside once he was on the balcony."

"Yah."

"Try this, Gil. Another question. How did he *expect* to get away?" He watched for my reaction, which must have been satisfying, because it *was* a damn good question. "You see, if Janice Sinclair murdered her great-uncle, then neither question applies. If we are looking for someone else, we have to assume that his plans misfired. He had to improvise."

"Uh huh. He could still have been planning to use Rodewald's balcony. And that would mean he had a way past the camera . . ."

"Of course he did. The generator."

Right. If he came to steal the generator . . . and he'd have to steal it regardless, because if we found it here, it would shoot his alibi sky high. So he'd leave it on while he trundled it up the stairs. Say it took him a minute; that's only an eighth of a second of normal time. One chance in eight that the camera would fire, and it would catch nothing but a streak . . . "Uh oh."

"What is it?"

"He had to be planning to steal the machine. Is he really going to lower it to Rodewald's balcony by *rope*?"

"I think it unlikely," Ordaz said. "It weighed more than fifty pounds. He could have moved it upstairs. The frame would make it portable. But to lower it by rope . . ."

"We'd be looking for one hell of an athlete."

"At least you will not have to search far to find him. We assume that your hypothetical killer came by elevator, do we not?"

"Yah." Nobody but Janice Sinclair had arrived by the roof last night.

"The elevator was programmed to allow a number of people to enter it and to turn away all others. The list is short. Doctor Sinclair was not a gregarious man."

"You're checking them out? Whereabouts, alibis, and so forth?"

"Of course."

"There's something else you might check on," I said. But Andrew Porter came in, and I had to postpone it.

Porter came casual, in a well-worn translucent one-piece jumpsuit he must have pulled on while running for a taxi. The muscles rolled like boulders beneath the loose fabric, and his belly muscles showed like the plates on an armadillo. Surfing muscles. The sun had bleached his hair nearly white and burned him as brown as Jackson Bera. You'd think a tan that dark would cover for blood draining out of a face, but it doesn't.

"Where is she?" he demanded. He didn't wait for an answer. He knew where the 'doc was, and he went there. We trailed in his wake.

Ordaz didn't push. He waited while Porter looked down at Janice, then punched for a readout and went through it in detail. Porter seemed calmer then, and his color was back. He turned to Ordaz and said, "What happened?"

"Mr. Porter, did you know anything of Dr. Sinclair's latest project?"

"The time compressor thing? Yah. He had it set up in the living room when I got here yesterday evening—right in the middle of that circle of dead grass. Any connection?"

"When did you arrive?"

"Oh, about six. We had some drinks, and Uncle Ray showed off his machine. He didn't tell us much about it. Just showed what it could do." Porter showed us flashing white teeth. "It *worked*. That thing can compress time! You could live your whole life in there in two months! Watching him move around inside the field was like trying to keep track of a hummingbird. Worse. He struck a match—"

"When did you leave?"

"About eight. We had dinner at Cziller's House of Irish Coffee, and—Listen, what *happened* here?"

"There are some things we need to know first, Mr. Porter. Were you and Janice together for all of last evening? Were there others with you?"

"Sure. We had dinner alone, but afterward we went to a kind of party. On the beach at Santa Monica. Friend of mine has a house there. I'll give you the address. Some of us wound up back at Cziller's around midnight. Then Janice flew me home."

"You have said that you are Janice's lover. Doesn't she live with you?"

"No. I'm her steady lover, you might say, but I don't have any strings on her." He seemed embarrassed. "She lives here with Uncle Ray. Lived. Oh, *hell*." He glanced into the 'doc. "Look, the readout said she'll be waking up any minute. Can I get her a robe?"

"Of course."

We followed Porter to Janice's bedroom, where he picked out a peach-colored negligee for her. I was beginning to like the guy. He had good instincts. An evening dye job was not the thing to wear on the morning of a murder. And he'd picked one with long, loose sleeves. Her missing arm wouldn't show so much.

"You call him Uncle Ray," Ordaz said.

"Yah. Because Janice did."

"He did not object? Was he gregarious?"

"Gregarious? Well, no, but *we* liked each other. We both liked puzzles, you understand? We traded murder mysteries and jigsaw puzzles. Listen, this may sound silly, but are you sure he's dead?"

"Regrettably, yes. He is dead, and murdered. Was he expecting someone to arrive after you left?"

"Yes."

"He said so?"

"No. But he was wearing a shirt and pants. When it was just us, he usually went naked."

"Ah."

"Older people don't do that much," Porter said. "But Uncle Ray was in good shape. He took care of himself."

"Have you any idea whom he might have been expecting?"

"No. Not a woman; not a date, I mean. Maybe someone in the same business."

Behind him, Janice moaned.

Porter was hovering over her in a flash. He put a hand on her shoulder and urged her back. "Lie still, love. We'll have you out of there in a jiffy."

She waited while he disconnected the sleeves and other paraphernalia. She said, "What happened?"

"They haven't told me yet," Porter said with a flash of anger. "Be careful sitting up. You've had an accident."

"What kind of—? *Oh!*"

"It'll be all right."

"My *arm!*"

Porter helped her out of the 'doc. Her arm ended in pink

flesh two inches below the shoulder. She let Porter drape
the robe around her. She tried to fasten the sash, quit when
she realized she was trying to do it with one hand.

I said, "Listen, I lost my arm once."

She looked at me. So did Porter.

"I'm Gil Hamilton. With the UN Police. You really don't
have anything to worry about. See?" I raised my right arm,
opened and closed the fingers. "The organ banks don't get
much call for arms. You probably won't even have to wait.
I didn't. It feels just like the arm I was born with, and it
works just as well."

"How did you lose it?" she asked.

"Ripped away by a meteor," I said.

Ordaz said to her, "Do you remember how you lost your
own arm?"

"Yes." She shivered. "Could we go somewhere where I
could sit down? I feel a bit weak."

We moved to the living room. Janice dropped onto the
couch a bit too hard. It might have been shock, or the missing arm might be throwing her balance off. I remembered.
She said, "Uncle Ray's dead, isn't he?"

"Yes."

"I came home and found him that way. Lying next to
that time machine of his, and the back of his head all
bloody. I thought maybe he was still alive, but I could see
the machine was going; it had that violet glow. I tried to get
hold of the poker. I wanted to use it to switch the machine
off, but I couldn't get a grip. My arm wasn't just numb; it
wouldn't move. You know, you can try to wiggle your toes
when your foot's asleep, but . . . I could get my hands on
the handle of the damn poker, but when I tried to pull, it
just slid off."

"You kept trying?"

"For a while. Then . . . I backed away to think it over. I
wasn't about to waste any time with Uncle Ray maybe
dying in there. My arm felt stone dead . . . I guess it was,
wasn't it?" She shuddered. "Rotting meat. It smelled that

way. And all of a sudden I felt so weak and dizzy, like I was dying myself. I barely made it into the 'doc."

"Good thing you did," I said. The blood was leaving Porter's face again as he realized what a close thing it had been.

Ordaz said, "Was your great-uncle expecting visitors last night?"

"I think so."

"Why do you think so?"

"I don't know. He just—acted that way."

"We are told that you and some friends reached Cziller's House of Irish Coffee around midnight. Is that true?"

"I guess so. We had some drinks, then I took Drew home and came home myself."

"Straight home?"

"Yes." She shivered. "I put the car away and went downstairs. I knew something was wrong. The door was open. Then there was Uncle Ray lying next to that machine! I knew better than to just run up to him. He'd told us not to step into the field."

"Oh? Then you should have known better than to reach for the poker."

"Well, yes. I could have used the tongs," she said as if the idea had just occurred to her. "It's just as long. I didn't think of it. There wasn't *time*. Don't you understand? He was dying in there, or dead!"

"Yes, of course. Did you interfere with the murder scene in any way?"

She laughed bitterly. "I suppose I moved the poker about two inches. Then, when I felt what was happening to me, I just ran for the 'doc. It was awful. Like dying."

"Instant gangrene," Porter said.

Ordaz said, "You did not, for example, lock the elevator?"

Damn! I should have thought of that.

"No. We usually do when we lock up for the night, but I didn't have time."

Porter said, "Why?"

"The elevator was locked when we arrived," Ordaz told him.

Porter ruminated that. "Then the killer must have left by the roof. You'll have pictures of him."

Ordaz smiled apologetically. "That is our problem. No cars left the roof last night. Only one car arrived. That was yours, Miss Sinclair."

"But," Porter said, and he stopped.

"What happened was this," Ordaz said. "Around five-thirty this morning, the tenants in—" He stopped to remember. "—in 36A called the building maintenance man about a smell as of rotting meat coming through the air-conditioning system. He spent some time looking for the source, but once he reached the roof, it was obvious. He—"

Porter pounced. "He reached the roof in what kind of vehicle?"

"Mr. Steeves says that he took a taxi from the street. There is no other way to reach Dr. Sinclair's private landing pad, is there?"

"No. But why would he do that?"

"Perhaps there have been other times when strange smells came from Dr. Sinclair's laboratory. We will ask him."

"Do that."

"Mr. Steeves followed the smell through the doctor's open door. He called us. He waited for us on the roof."

"What about his taxi?" Porter was hot on the scent. "Maybe the killer just waited till that taxi got here, then took it somewhere else when Steeves finished with it."

"It left immediately after Steeves had stepped out. He had a taxi clicker if he wanted another. The cameras were on it the entire time it was on the roof." Ordaz paused. "You see the problem?"

Apparently Porter did. He ran both hands through his white-blond hair. "I think we ought to put off discussing it until we know more."

He meant Janice. Janice looked puzzled; she hadn't caught on. But Ordaz nodded at once and stood up. "Very well. There is no reason Miss Sinclair cannot go on living here. We may have to bother you again," he told her. "For now, our condolences."

He made his exit. I trailed along. So, unexpectedly, did Drew Porter. At the top of the stairs he stopped Ordaz with a big hand around the inspector's upper arm. "You're thinking Janice did it, aren't you?"

Ordaz sighed. "I must consider the possibility."

"She didn't have any reason. She loved Uncle Ray. She's lived with him on and off these past twelve years. She hasn't got the slightest reason to kill him."

"Is there no inheritance?"

His expression went sour. "All right, *yes*, she'll have some money coming. But Janice wouldn't care about anything like that!"

"Ye-es. Still, what choice have I? Everything we now know tells us that the killer could not have left the scene of the killing. We searched the premises immediately. There was only Janice Sinclair and her murdered uncle."

Porter bit back an answer, chewed it . . . He must have been tempted. Amateur detective, one step ahead of the police all the way. Yes, Watson, these gendarmes have a talent for missing the obvious . . . But he had too much to lose. Porter said, "And the maintenance man. Steeves."

Ordaz lifted one eyebrow. "Yes, of course. We shall have to investigate Mr. Steeves."

"How did he get that call from, uh, 36A? Bedside phone or pocket phone? Maybe he was already on the roof."

"I don't remember what he said. But we have pictures of his taxi landing."

"He had a taxi clicker. He could have just called it down."

"One more thing," I said, and Porter looked at me hopefully. "Porter, the elevator wouldn't take anyone up unless they were on its list."

"Or unless Uncle Ray buzzed down. There's an intercom in the lobby. But at that time of night he probably wouldn't let anyone up unless he was expecting him."

"So if Sinclair was expecting a business associate, he or she was probably in the tape. How about going down? Would the elevator take you down to the lobby if you weren't in the tape?"

"I'd . . . think so."

"It would," Ordaz said. "The elevator screens entrances, not departures."

"Then why didn't the killer use it? I don't mean Steeves necessarily. I mean *anyone*, whoever it might have been. Why didn't he just go down in the elevator? Whatever he did do, that had to be easier."

They looked at each other, but they didn't say anything.

"Okay." I turned to Ordaz. "When you check out the people in the tape, see if any of them shows a damaged arm. The killer might have pulled the same stunt Janice did: ruined her arm trying to turn off the generator. And I'd like a look at who's in that tape."

"Very well," Ordaz said, and we moved toward the squad car under the carport. We were out of earshot when he added, "How does the ARM come into this, Mr. Hamilton? Why your interest in the murder aspect of this case?"

I told him what I'd told Bera: that Sinclair's killer might be the only living expert on Sinclair's time machine. Ordaz nodded. What he'd really wanted to know was: Could I justify giving orders to the Los Angeles Police Department in a local matter? And I had answered yes.

The rather simple-minded security system in Sinclair's elevator had been built to remember the thumbprints and the facial bone structures (which it scanned by deep radar, thus avoiding the problems raised by changing beard styles and masquerade parties) of up to a hundred people. Most people know about a hundred people, plus or minus ten or so. But Sinclair had only listed a dozen, including himself.

RAYMOND SINCLAIR
ANDREW PORTER
JANICE SINCLAIR

EDWARD SINCLAIR, SR.
EDWARD SINCLAIR III
HANS DRUCKER
GEORGE STEEVES
PAULINE URTHIEL
BERNATH PETERFI
LAWRENCE MUHAMMAD ECKS
BERTHA HALL
MURIEL SANDUSKY

Valpredo had been busy. He'd been using the police car and its phone setup as an office while he guarded the roof. "We know who some of these are," he said. "Edward Sinclair Third, for instance, is Edward Senior's grandson, Janice's brother. He's in the Belt, in Ceres, making something of a name for himself as an industrial designer. Edward Senior is Raymond's brother. He lives in Kansas City. Hans Drucker and Bertha Hall and Muriel Sandusky all live in the Greater Los Angeles area; we don't know what their connection with Sinclair is. Pauline Urthiel and Bernath Peterfi are technicians of sorts. Ecks is Sinclair's patent attorney."

"I suppose we can interview Edward Third by phone." Ordaz made a face. A phone call to the Belt wasn't cheap. "These others—"

I said, "May I make a suggestion?"

"Of course."

"Send me along with whoever interviews Ecks and Peterfi and Urthiel. They probably knew Sinclair in a business sense, and having an ARM along will give you a little more clout to ask a little more detailed questions."

"I could take those assignments," Valpredo volunteered.

"Very well." Ordaz still looked unhappy. "If this list were exhaustive, I would be grateful. What if Doctor Sinclair's visitor simply used the intercom in the lobby and asked to be let in?"

* * *

Bernath Peterfi wasn't answering his phone.

We got Pauline Urthiel via her pocket phone. A brusque contralto voice, no picture. We'd like to talk to her in connection with a murder investigation; would she be at home this afternoon? No. She was lecturing that afternoon but would be home around six.

Ecks answered dripping wet and not smiling. So sorry to get you out of a shower, Mr. Ecks. We'd like to talk to you in connection with a murder investigation.

"Sure, come on over. Who's dead?"

Valpredo told him.

"Sinclair? *Ray* Sinclair? You're sure?"

We were.

"Oh, lord. Listen, he was working on something important. An interstellar drive, if it works out. If there's any possibility of salvaging the hardware—"

I reassured him and hung up. If Sinclair's patent attorney thought it was a star drive ... maybe it was.

"Doesn't sound like he's trying to steal it," Valpredo said.

"No. And even if he'd got the thing, he couldn't have claimed it was his. If he's the killer, that's not what he was after."

We were moving at high speed, police-car speed. The car was on automatic, of course, but it could need manual override at any instant. Valpredo concentrated on the passing scenery and spoke without looking at me.

"You know, you and the detective-inspector aren't looking for the same thing."

"I know. I'm looking for a hypothetical killer. Julio's looking for a hypothetical visitor. It could be tough to prove there wasn't one, but if Porter and the girl were telling the truth, maybe Julio can prove the visitor didn't do it."

"Which would leave the girl," he said.

"Whose side are you on?"

"Nobody's. All I've got is interesting questions." He looked at me sideways. "But you're pretty sure the girl didn't do it."

"Yah."

"Why?"

"I don't know. Maybe because I don't think she's got the brains. It wasn't a simple killing."

"She's Sinclair's niece. She can't be a complete idiot."

"Heredity doesn't work that way. Maybe I'm kidding myself. Maybe it's her arm. She's lost an arm; she's got enough to worry about." And I borrowed the car phone to dig into records in the ARM computer.

PAULINE URTHIEL. Born Paul Urthiel. Ph.D. in plasma physics, University of California at Irvine. Sex change and legal name change, 2111. Six years ago she'd been in competition for a Nobel prize for research into the charge suppression effect in the Slaver disintegrator. Height: 5′ 9″. Weight: 135. Married Lawrence Muhammad Ecks, 2117. Had kept her (loosely speaking) maiden name. Separate residences.

BERNATH PETERFI. Ph.D. in subatomics and related fields, MIT. Diabetic. Height: 5′ 8″. Weight: 145. Application for exemption to the Fertility Laws denied, 2119. Married 2118, divorced 2122. Lived alone.

LAWRENCE MUHAMMAD ECKS. Master's degree in physics. Member of the bar. Height: 6′ 1″. Weight: 190. Artificial left arm. Vice president, CET (Committee to End Transplants).

Valpredo said: "Funny how the human arm keeps cropping up in this case."

"Yah." Including one human ARM who didn't really belong there. "Ecks has a master's. Maybe he could have talked people into thinking the generator was his. Or maybe he thought he could."

"He didn't try to snow *us*."

"Suppose he blew it last night? He wouldn't necessarily want the generator lost to humanity, now, would he?"

"How did he get out?"

I didn't answer.

* * *

Ecks lived in a tapering tower almost a mile high. At one time Lindstetter's Needle must have been the biggest thing ever built, before they started with the arcologies. We landed on a pad a third of the way up, then took a drop shaft ten floors down.

He was dressed when he answered the door in blazing yellow pants and a net shirt. His skin was very dark, and his hair was a puffy black dandelion with threads of gray in it. On the phone screen I hadn't been able to tell which arm was which, and I couldn't now. He invited us in, sat down, and waited for the questions.

Where was he last night? Could he produce an alibi? It would help us considerably.

"Sorry, nope. I spent the night going through a rather tricky case. You wouldn't appreciate the details."

I told him I would. He said, "Actually, it involves Edward Sinclair—Ray's great-nephew. He's a Belt immigrant, and he's done an industrial design that could be adapted to Earth. Swivel for a chemical rocket motor. The trouble is, it's not *that* different from existing designs, it's just *better*. His Belt patent is good, but the UN laws are different. You wouldn't believe the legal tangles."

"Is he likely to lose out?"

"No, it just might get sticky if a firm called FireStorm decides to fight the case. I want to be ready for that. In a pinch I might even have to call the kid back to Earth. I'd hate to do that, though. He's got a heart condition."

Had he made any phone calls, say, to a computer, during his night of research?

Ecks brightened instantly. "Oh, sure. Constantly, all night. Okay, I've got an alibi."

No point in telling him that such calls could have been made from anywhere. Valpredo asked, "Do you have any idea where your wife was last night?"

"No, we don't live together. She lives three hundred stories over my head. We've got an open marriage . . . maybe too open," he added wistfully.

There seemed a good chance that Raymond Sinclair was expecting a visitor last night. Did Ecks have any idea—?

"He knew a couple of women," Ecks said. "You might ask them. Bertha Hall is about eighty, about Ray's age. She's not too bright, not by Ray's standards, but she's as much of a physical fitness nut as he is. They go backpacking, play tennis, maybe sleep together, maybe not. I can give you her address. Then there's Muriel something. He had a crush on her a few years ago. She'd be thirty now. I don't know if they still see each other or not."

Did Sinclair know other women?

Ecks shrugged.

Who did he know professionally?

"Oh, lord, that's an endless list. Do you know anything about the way Ray worked?" He didn't wait for an answer. "He used computer setups mostly. Any experiment in his field was likely to cost millions or more. What he was good at was setting up a computer analogue of an experiment that would tell him what he wanted to know. Take, oh . . . I'm sure you've heard of the Sinclair molecule chain."

Hell, yes. We used it for towing in the Belt; nothing else was light enough and strong enough. A loop of it was nearly invisibly fine, but it would cut steel.

"He didn't start working with chemicals until he was practically finished. He told me he spent four years doing molecular designs by computer analogue. The tough part was the ends of the molecule chain. Until he got that, the chain would start disintegrating from the end points the minute you finished making it. When he finally had what he wanted, he hired an industrial chemical lab to make it for him.

"That's what I'm getting at," Ecks continued. "He hired other people to do the concrete stuff once he knew what he had. And the people he hired had to know what they were doing. He knew the top physicists and chemists and field theorists everywhere on Earth and in the Belt."

Like Pauline? Like Bernath Peterfi?

"Yah, Pauline did some work for him once. I don't think

she'd do it again. She didn't like having to give him all the credit. She'd rather work for herself. I don't blame her."

Could he think of anyone who might want to murder Raymond Sinclair?

Ecks shrugged. "I'd say that was your job. Ray never liked splitting the credit with anyone. Maybe someone he worked with nursed a grudge. Or maybe someone was trying to steal this latest project of his. Mind you, I don't know much about what he was trying to do, but if it worked, it would have been fantastically valuable, and not just in money."

Valpredo was making noises like he was about finished. I said, "Do you mind if I ask a personal question?"

"Go ahead."

"Your arm. How'd you lose it?"

"Born without it. Nothing in my genes, just a bad prenatal situation. I came out with an arm and a turkey wishbone. By the time I was old enough for a transplant, I knew I didn't want one. You want the standard speech?"

"No, thanks, but I'm wondering how good your artificial arm is. I'm carrying a transplant myself."

Ecks looked me over carefully for signs of moral degeneration. "I suppose you're also one of those people who keep voting the death penalty for more and more trivial offenses?"

"No, I—"

"After all, if the organ banks ran out of criminals, you'd be in trouble. You might have to live with your mistakes."

"No, I'm one of those people who blocked the second corpsicle law, kept that group from going into the organ banks. And I hunt organleggers for a living. But I don't have an artificial arm, and I suppose the reason is that I'm squeamish."

"Squeamish about being part mechanical? I've heard of that," Ecks said. "But you can be squeamish the other way, too. What there is of me is all me, not part of a dead man. I'll admit the sense of touch isn't quite the same, but it's just as good. And—look."

He put a hand on my upper forearm and squeezed.

It felt like the bones were about to give. I didn't scream, but it took an effort. "That isn't all my strength," he said. "And I could keep it up all day. This arm doesn't get tired."

He let go.

I asked if he would mind my examining his arms. He didn't. But then, Ecks didn't know about my imaginary hand.

I probed the advanced plastics of Ecks's false arm, the bone and muscle structure of the other. It was the real arm I was interested in.

When we were back in the car, Valpredo said, "Well?"

"Nothing wrong with his real arm," I said. "No scars."

Valpredo nodded.

But the bubble of accelerated time wouldn't hurt plastic and batteries, I thought. And if he'd been planning to lower fifty pounds of generator two stories down on a nylon line, his artificial arm had the strength for it.

We called Peterfi from the car. He was in. He was a small man, dark-complected, mild of face, his hair straight and shiny black around a receding hairline. His eyes blinked and squinted as if the light were too bright, and he had the scruffy look of a man who has slept in his clothes. I wondered if we had interrupted an afternoon nap.

Yes, he would be glad to help the police in a murder investigation.

Peterfi's condominium was a slab of glass and concrete set on a Santa Monica cliff face. His apartment faced the sea. "Expensive, but worth it for the view," he said, showing us to chairs in the living room. The drapes were closed against the afternoon sun. Peterfi had changed clothes. I noticed the bulge in his upper left sleeve where an insulin capsule and automatic feeder had been anchored to the bone of the arm.

"Well, what can I do for you? I don't believe you mentioned who had been murdered."

Valpredo told him.

He was shocked. "Oh, my. Ray Sinclair. But there's no telling how this will affect—" and he stopped suddenly.

"Please go on," said Valpredo.

"We were working on something together. Something revolutionary."

An interstellar drive?

He was startled. He debated with himself, then said, "Yes. It was supposed to be secret."

We admitted to having seen the machine in action. How did a time compression field serve as an interstellar drive?

"That's not exactly what it is," Peterfi said. Again he debated with himself. Then, "There have always been a few optimists around who thought that just because mass and inertia have always been associated in human experience, it need not be a universal law. What Ray and I have done is to create a condition of low inertia. You see—"

"An inertialess drive!"

Peterfi nodded vigorously at me. "Essentially yes. Is the machine intact? If not—"

I reassured him on that point.

"That's good. I was about to say that if it had been destroyed, I could recreate it. I did most of the work of building it. Ray preferred to work with his mind, not with his hands."

Had Peterfi visited Sinclair last night?

"No. I had dinner at a restaurant down the coast, then came home and watched the holo wall. What times do I need alibis for?" he asked jokingly.

Valpredo told him. The joking look turned into a nervous grimace. No, he'd left the Mail Shirt just after nine; he couldn't prove his whereabouts after that time.

Had he any idea who might have wanted to murder Raymond Sinclair?

Peterfi was reluctant to make outright accusations. Surely we understood. It might be someone he had worked with in the past or someone he'd insulted. Ray thought most of humanity were fools. Or we might look into the matter of Ray's brother's exemption.

Valpredo said, "Edward Sinclair's exemption? What about it?"

"I'd really prefer that you get the story from someone else. You may know that Edward Sinclair was refused the right to have children because of an inherited heart condition. His grandson has it, too. There is some question as to whether he really did the work that earned him the exemption."

"But that must have been forty to fifty years ago. How could it figure in a murder now?"

Peterfi explained patiently. "Edward had a child by virtue of an exemption to the Fertility Laws. Now there are two grandchildren. Suppose the matter came up for review? His grandchildren would lose the right to have children. They'd be illegitimate. They might even lose the right to inherit."

Valpredo was nodding. "Yah. We'll look into that, all right."

I said, "You applied for an exemption yourself not long ago. I suppose your, uh—"

"Yes, my diabetes. It doesn't interfere with my life at all. Do you know how long we've been using insulin to handle diabetes? Almost two hundred years! What does it matter if I'm a diabetic? If my children are?"

He glared at us, demanding an answer. He got none.

"But the Fertility Laws refuse me children. Do you know that I lost my wife because the board refused me an exemption? I deserved it. My work on plasma flow in the solar photosphere— Well, I'd hardly lecture you on the subject, would I? But my work can be used to predict the patterns of proton storms near any G-type star. Every colony world owes something to my work!"

That was an exaggeration, I thought. Proton storms affected mainly asteroidal mining operations. "Why don't you move to the Belt?" I asked. "They'd honor you for your work, and they don't have Fertility Laws."

"I get sick off Earth. It's biorhythms; it has nothing to do with diabetes. Half of humanity suffers from biorhythm upset."

I felt sorry for the guy. "You could still get the exemption. For your work on the inertialess drive. Wouldn't that get you your wife back?"

"I . . . don't know. I doubt it. It's been two years. In any case, there's no telling which way the board will jump. I thought I'd have the exemption last time."

"Do you mind if I examine your arms?"

He looked at me. "What?"

"I'd like to examine your arms."

"That seems a most curious request. Why?"

"There seems a good chance that Sinclair's killer damaged his arm last night. Now, I'll remind you that I'm acting in the name of the UN Police. If you've been hurt by the side effects of a possible space drive, one that might be used by human colonists, then you're concealing evidence in a—" I stopped, because Peterfi had stood up and was taking off his tunic.

He wasn't happy, but he stood still for it. His arms looked all right. I ran my hands along each arm, bent the joints, massaged the knuckles. Inside the flesh I ran my imaginary fingertips along the bones.

Three inches below the shoulder joint the bone was knotted. I probed the muscles and tendons . . .

"Your right arm is a transplant," I said. "It must have happened about six months ago."

He bridled. "You may not be aware of it, but surgery to reattach my own arm would show the same scars."

"Is that what happened?"

Anger made his speech more precise. "Yes. I was performing an experiment, and there was an explosion. The arm was nearly severed. I tied a tourniquet and got to a 'doc before I collapsed."

"Any proof of this?"

"I doubt it. I never told anyone of this accident, and the 'doc wouldn't keep records. In any case, I think the burden of proof would be on you."

"Uh huh."

Peterfi was putting his tunic back on. "Are you quite finished here? I'm deeply sorry for Ray Sinclair's death, but I don't see what it could possibly have to do with my stupidity of six months ago."

I didn't, either. We left.

Back in the car. It was seventeen-twenty; we could pick up a snack on the way to Pauline Urthiel's place. I told Valpredo, "I think it was a transplant. And he didn't want to admit it. He must have gone to an organlegger."

"Why would he do that? It's not that tough to get an arm from the public organ banks."

I chewed that. "You're right. But if it was a normal transplant, there'll be a record. Well, it could have happened the way he said it did."

"Uh huh."

"How about this? He was doing an experiment, and it was illegal. Something that might cause pollution in a city or even something to do with radiation. He picked up radiation burns in his arm. If he'd gone to the public organ banks, he'd have been arrested."

"That would fit, too. Can we prove it on him?"

"I don't know. I'd like to. He might tell us how to find whoever he dealt with. Let's do some digging: maybe we can find out what he was working on six months ago."

Pauline Urthiel opened the door the instant we rang. "Hi! I just got in myself. Can I make you drinks?"

We refused. She ushered us into a smallish apartment with a lot of fold-into-the-ceiling furniture. A sofa and coffee table were showing now; the rest existed as outlines on the ceiling. The view through the picture window was breathtaking. She lived near the top of Lindstetter's Needle, some three hundred stories up from her husband.

She was tall and slender, with a facial structure that would have been effeminate on a man. On a woman it was a touch masculine. The well-formed breasts might be flesh or plastic but were surgically implanted in either case.

She finished making a large drink and joined us on the couch. And the questions started.

Had she any idea who might have wanted Raymond Sinclair dead?

"Not really. How did he die?"

"Someone smashed in his skull with a poker," Valpredo said. If he wasn't going to mention the generator, neither was I.

"How quaint." Her contralto turned acid. "His own poker, too, I presume. Out of his own fireplace rack. What you're looking for is a traditionalist." She peered at us over the rim of her glass. Her eyes were large, the lids decorated in semipermanent tattoos as a pair of flapping UN flags. "That doesn't help much, does it? You might try whoever was working with him on whatever his latest project was."

That sounded like Peterfi, I thought. But Valpredo said, "Would he necessarily have a collaborator?"

"He generally works alone at the beginning. But somewhere along the line he brings in people to make the hardware. He never made anything real by himself. It was all just something in a computer bank. It took someone else to make it real. And he never gave credit to anyone."

Then his hypothetical collaborator might have found out how little credit he was getting for his work, and— But Urthiel was shaking her head. "I'm talking about a psychotic, not someone who's really been cheated. Sinclair never *offered* anyone a share in anything he did. He always made it damn plain what was happening. I knew what I was doing when I set up the FyreStop prototype for him, and I knew what I was doing when I quit. It was all him. He was using my training, not my brain. I wanted to do something original, something *me*."

Did she have any idea what Sinclair's present project was?

"My husband would know. Larry Ecks, lives in this same building. He's been dropping cryptic hints, and when I want more details, he has this grin—" She grinned herself suddenly. "You'll gather I'm interested. But he won't say."

Time for me to take over or we'd never get certain questions asked. "I'm an ARM. What I'm about to tell you is secret," I said. And I told her what we knew of Sinclair's generator. Maybe Valpredo was looking at me disapprovingly, maybe not.

"We know that the field can damage a human arm in a few seconds. What we want to know," I said, "is whether the killer is now wandering around with a half-decayed hand or arm—or foot, for that—"

She stood and pulled the upper half of her body stocking down around her waist.

She looked very much a real woman. If I hadn't known—and why would it matter? These days the sex change operation is elaborate and perfect. Hell with it; I was on duty. Valpredo was looking nonchalant, waiting for me.

I examined both of her arms with my eyes and my three hands. There was nothing. Not even a bruise.

"My legs, too?"

I said, "Not if you can stand on them."

Next question. Could an artificial arm operate within the field?

"Larry? You mean *Larry*? You're out of your teeny mind."

"Take it as a hypothetical question."

She shrugged. "Your guess is as good as mine. There aren't any experts on inertialess fields."

"There was one. He's dead," I reminded her.

"All I know is what I learned watching the Gray Lensman show in the holo wall when I was a kid." She smiled suddenly. "That old space opera."

Valpredo laughed. "You, too? I used to watch that show in study hall on a little pocket phone. One day the principal caught me at it."

"Sure. And then we outgrew it. Too bad. Those inertialess ships ... I'm sure an inertialess ship wouldn't behave like those did. You couldn't possibly get rid of the time compression effect." She took a long pull on her drink, set it down, and said, "Yes and no. He could reach in, but—you see the problem? The nerve impulses that move the motors in Larry's arm, they're coming into the field too slowly."

"Sure."

"But if Larry closed his fist on something, say, and reached into the field with it, it would probably stay closed. He could have brained Ray with—no, he couldn't. The poker wouldn't be moving any faster than a glacier. Ray would just dodge."

And he couldn't pull a poker out of the field, either. His fist wouldn't close on it after it was inside. But he could have tried and still left with his arm intact, I thought.

Did Urthiel know anything of the circumstances surrounding Edward Sinclair's exemption?

"Oh, that's an old story," she said. "Sure, I heard about it. How could it possibly have anything to do with, with Ray's murder?"

"I don't know," I confessed. "I'm just thrashing around."

"Well, you'll probably get it more accurately from the UN files. Edward Sinclair did some mathematics on the fields that scoop up interstellar hydrogen for the cargo ramrobots. He was a shoo-in for the exemption. That's the surest way of getting it: make a breakthrough in anything that has anything to do with the interstellar colonies. Every time you move one man away from Earth, the population drops by one."

"What was wrong with it?"

"Nothing anyone could prove. Remember, the Fertility Restriction Laws were new then. They couldn't stand a real test. But Edward Sinclair's a pure math man. He works with number theory, not practical applications. I've seen Edward's equations, and they're closer to something Ray would come up with. And Ray didn't need the exemption. He never wanted children."

"So you think—"

"I don't *care* which of them redesigned the ramscoops. Diddling the Fertility Board like that, that takes *brains*." She swallowed the rest of her drink, set the glass down. "Breeding for brains is never a mistake. It's no challenge to the Fertility Board, either. The people who do the damage are the ones who go into hiding when their shots come due, have their babies, then scream to high heaven when the board has to sterilize them. Too many of those and we won't have Fertility Laws anymore. And *that*—" She didn't have to finish.

Had Sinclair known that Pauline Urthiel was once Paul?

She stared. "Now just what the bleep has that got to do with anything?"

I'd been toying with the idea that Sinclair might have been blackmailing Urthiel with that information. Not for money but for credit in some discovery they'd made together. "Just thrashing around," I said.

"Well . . . all right. I don't know if Ray knew or not. He never raised the subject, but he never made a pass, either, and he must have researched me before he hired me. And, say, listen: Larry doesn't know. I'd appreciate it if you wouldn't blurt it out."

"Okay."

"See, he had his children by his first wife. I'm not denying him children . . . Maybe he married me because I had a touch of, um, masculine insight. Maybe. But he doesn't know it, and he doesn't want to. I don't know whether he'd laugh it off or kill me."

I had Valpredo drop me off at ARM Headquarters.

This peculiar machine really does bother me, Gil . . . Well it should, Julio. The Los Angeles Police were not trained to deal with a mad scientist's nightmare running quietly in the middle of a murder scene.

Granted that Janice wasn't the type. Not for this murder. But Drew Porter was precisely the type to evolve a perfect murder around Sinclair's generator, purely as an intellectual exercise. He might have guided her through it; he might even have been there and used the elevator before she shut it off. It was the one thing he forgot to tell her: not to shut off the elevator.

Or: he outlined a perfect murder to her, purely as a puzzle, never dreaming she'd go through with it—badly.

Or: one of them killed Janice's uncle on impulse. No telling what he'd said that one of them couldn't tolerate. But the machine had been right there in the living room, and Drew had wrapped his big arm around Janice and said, *Wait, don't do anything yet; let's think this out* . . .

Take any of these as the true state of affairs, and a prosecutor could have a hell of a time proving it. He could show that no killer could possibly have left the scene of the crime without Janice Sinclair's help, and therefore . . . But what about that glowing thing, that time machine built by the dead man? *Could* it have freed a killer from an effectively locked room? How could a judge know its power?

Well, could it?

Bera might know.

The machine was running. I caught the faint violet glow as I stepped into the laboratory and a flickering next to it . . . and then it was off, and Jackson Bera stood suddenly beside it, grinning, silent, waiting.

I wasn't about to spoil his fun. I said, "Well? Is it an interstellar drive?"

"Yes!"

A warm glow spread through me. I said, "Okay."

"It's a low-inertia field," said Bera. "Things inside lose most of their inertia . . . not their mass, just the resistance to movement. Ratio of about five hundred to one. The interface is sharp as a razor. We think there are quantum levels involved."

"Uh huh. The field doesn't affect time directly?"

"No, it . . . I shouldn't say that. Who the hell knows what time really is? It affects chemical and nuclear reactions, energy release of all kinds . . . but it doesn't affect the speed of light. You know, it's kind of kicky to be measuring the speed of light at 370 miles per second with honest instruments."

Dammit. I'd been half hoping it was an FTL drive. I

said, "Did you ever find out what was causing that blue glow?"

Bera laughed at me. "Watch." He'd rigged a remote switch to turn the machine on. He used it, then struck a match and flipped it toward the blue glow. As it crossed an invisible barrier, the match flared violet-white for something less than an eye blink. I blinked. It had been like a flashbulb going off.

I said, "Oh, *sure*. The machinery's warm."

"Right. The blue glow is just infrared radiation being boosted to violet when it enters normal time."

Bera shouldn't have had to tell me that. Embarrassed, I changed the subject. "But you said it was an interstellar drive."

"Yah. It's got drawbacks," Bera said. "We can't just put a field around a whole starship. The crew would think they'd lowered the speed of light, but so what? A slowboat doesn't get that close to lightspeed anyway. They'd save a little trip time, but they'd have to live through it five hundred times as fast."

"How about if you just put the field around your fuel tanks?"

Bera nodded. "That's what they'll probably do. Leave the motor and the life support system outside. You could carry a god-awful amount of fuel that way . . . Well, it's not our department. Someone else'll be designing the starships," he said a bit wistfully.

"Have you thought of this thing in relation to robbing banks? Or espionage?"

"If a gang could afford to build one of these jobs, they wouldn't need to rob banks." He ruminated. "I hate making anything this big a UN secret. But I guess you're right. The average government could afford a whole stable of the things."

"Thus combining James Bond and the Flash."

He rapped on the plastic frame. "Want to try it?"

"Sure," I said.

Heart to brain: THUD! What're you doing? You'll get us

*all killed! I knew we should never have put you in charge
of things* . . . I stepped up to the generator, waited for Bera
to scamper beyond range, then pulled the switch.

Everything turned deep red. Bera became a statue.

Well, here I was. The second hand on the wall clock had
stopped moving. I took two steps forward and rapped with
my knuckles. Rapped, hell: it was like rapping on contact
cement. The invisible wall was tacky.

I tried leaning on it for a minute or so. That worked fine
until I tried to pull away, and then I knew I'd done something stupid. I was embedded in the interface. It took me
another minute to pull loose, and then I went sprawling
backward; I'd picked up too much inward velocity, and it
all came into the field with me.

At that, I'd been lucky. If I'd leaned there a little longer,
I'd have lost my leverage. I'd have been sinking deeper and
deeper into the interface, unable to yell to Bera, building up
more and more velocity outside the field.

I picked myself up and tried something safer. I took out
my pen and dropped it. It fell normally: thirty-two feet per
second per second, field time. Which scratched one theory
as to how the killer had thought he would be leaving.

I switched the machine off. "Something I'd like to try,"
I told Bera. "Can you hang the machine in the air, say by
a cable around the frame?"

"What have you got in mind?"

"I want to try standing on the bottom of the field."

Bera looked dubious.

It took us twenty minutes to set it up. Bera took no
chances. He lifted the generator about five feet. Since the
field seemed to center on that oddly shaped piece of silver,
that put the bottom of the field just a foot in the air. We
moved a stepladder into range, and I stood on the stepl-
der and turned on the generator.

I stepped off.

Walking down the side of the field was like walking in
progressively stickier taffy. When I stood on the bottom, I
could just reach the switch.

My shoes were stuck solid. I could pull my feet out of them, but there was no place to stand except in my own shoes. A minute later my feet were stuck, too: I could pull one loose, but only by fixing the other ever more deeply in the interface. I sank deeper, and all sensation left the soles of my feet. It was scary, though I knew nothing terrible could happen to me. My feet wouldn't die out there; they wouldn't have time.

But the interface was up to my ankles now, and I started to wonder what kind of velocity they were building up out there. I pushed the switch up. The lights flashed bright, and my feet slapped the floor hard.

Bera said, "Well? Learn anything?"

"Yah. I don't want to try a real test: I might wreck the machine."

"What kind of real test—?"

"Dropping it forty stories with the field on. Quit worrying; I'm not going to do it."

"Right. You aren't."

"You know, this time compression effect would work for more than just spacecraft. After you're on the colony world, you could raise full-grown cattle from frozen fertilized eggs in just a few minutes."

"Mmm ... Yah." The happy smile flashing white against darkness, the infinity look in Bera's eyes ... Bera liked playing with ideas. "Think of one of these mounted on a truck, say on Jinx. You could explore the shoreline regions without ever worrying about the Bandersnatchi attacking. They'd never move fast enough. You could drive across any alien world and catch the whole ecology laid out around you, none of it running from the truck. Predators in midleap, birds in midflight, couples in courtship."

"Or larger groups."

"I ... think that habit is unique to humans." He looked at me sideways. "You wouldn't spy on *people*, would you? Or shouldn't I ask?"

"That five-hundred-to-one ratio. Is that constant?"

He came back to here and now. "We don't know. Our

theory hasn't caught up to the hardware it's supposed to fit. I wish to hell we had Sinclair's notes."

"You were supposed to send a programmer out there."

"He came back," Bera said viciously. "Clayton Wolfe. Clay says the tapes in Sinclair's computer were all wiped before he got there. I don't know whether to believe him or not. Sinclair was a secretive bastard, wasn't he?"

"Yah. One false move on Clay's part and the computer might have wiped everything. But he says different?"

"He says the computer was blank, a newborn mind all ready to be taught. Gil, is that possible? Could whoever have killed Sinclair have wiped the tapes?"

"Sure, why not? What he couldn't have done is left afterward." I told him a little about the problem. "It's even worse than that, because as Ordaz keeps pointing out, he thought he'd be leaving with the machine. I thought he might have been planning to roll the generator off the roof, step off with it, and float down. But that wouldn't work. Not if it falls five hundred times as fast. He'd have been killed."

"Losing the machine maybe saved his life."

"But *how did he get out*?"

Bera laughed at my frustration. "Couldn't his niece be the one?"

"Sure, she could have killed her uncle for the money. But I can't see how she'd have a motive to wipe the computer. Unless—"

"Something?"

"Maybe. Never mind." Did Bera ever miss this kind of manhunting? But I wasn't ready to discuss this yet; I didn't know enough. "Tell me more about the machine. Can you vary that five-hundred-to-one ratio?"

He shrugged. "We tried adding more batteries. We thought it might boost the field strength. We were wrong; it just expanded the boundary a little. And using one less battery turns it off completely. So the ratio seems to be constant, and there do seem to be quantum levels involved. We'll know better when we build another machine."

"How so?"

"Well, there are all kinds of good questions," Bera said. "What happens when the fields of two generators intersect? They might just add, but maybe not. That quantum effect . . . And what happens if the generators are right next to each other, operating in each other's accelerated time? The speed of light could drop to a few feet per second. Throw a punch and your hand gets shorter!"

"That'd be kicky, all right."

"Dangerous, too. Man, we'd better try that one on the moon!"

"I don't see that."

"Look, with one machine going, infrared light comes out violet. If two machines were boosting each other's performance, what kind of radiation would they put out? Anything from X rays to antimatter particles."

"An expensive way to build a bomb."

"Well, but it's a bomb you can use over and over again."

I laughed. "We did find you an expert," I said. "You may not need Sinclair's tapes. Bernath Peterfi says he was working with Sinclair. He could be lying—more likely he was working *for* him, under contract—but at least he knows what the machine does."

Bera seemed relieved at that. He took down Peterfi's address. I left him there in the laboratory, playing with his new toy.

The file from the city morgue was sitting on my desk, open, waiting for me since this morning. Two dead ones looked up at me through sockets of blackened bone, but not accusingly. They had patience. They could wait.

The computer had processed my search pattern. I braced myself with a cup of coffee, then started leafing through the thick stack of printout. When I knew what had burned away two human faces, I'd be close to knowing who. Find the tool, find the killer. And the tool must be unique or close to it.

Lasers, lasers—more than half the machine's suggestions

seemed to be lasers. Incredible the way lasers seemed to breed and mutate throughout human industry. Laser radar. The laser guidance system on a tunneling machine. Some suggestions were obviously unworkable, and one was a lot too workable.

A standard hunting laser fires in pulses. But it can be jiggered for a much longer pulse or even a continuous burst.

Set a hunting laser for a long pulse and put a grid over the lens. The mesh has to be optically fine, on the order of angstroms. Now the beam will spread as it leaves the grid. A second of pulse will vaporize the grid, leaving no evidence. The grid would be no bigger than a contact lens; if you didn't trust your aim, you could carry a pocketful of them.

The grid-equipped laser would be less efficient, as a rifle with a silencer is less efficient. But the grid would make the murder weapon impossible to identify.

I thought about it and got cold chills. Assassination is already a recognized branch of politics. If this got out— But that was the trouble; someone seemed to have thought of it already. If not, someone would. Someone always did.

I wrote up a memo for Lucas Garner. I couldn't think of anyone better qualified to deal with this kind of sociological problem.

Nothing else in the stack of printout caught my eye. Later I'd have to go through it in detail. For now I pushed it aside and punched for messages.

Bates, the coroner, had finished the autopsies on the two charred corpses. Nothing new. But records had identified the fingerprints. Two missing persons, disappeared six and eight months ago. Ah ha!

I knew that pattern. I didn't even look at the names; I just skipped on to the gene coding.

Right. The fingerprints did not match the genes. All twenty fingertips must be transplants. And the man's scalp was a transplant; his own hair had been blond.

I leaned back in my chair, gazing fondly down at holograms of charred skulls.

You evil sons of bitches. Organleggers, both of you. With all that raw material available, most organleggers change their fingerprints constantly—and their retina prints—but we'd never get prints from those charred eyeballs. So, weird weapon or no, they were ARM business. My business.

And we still didn't know what had killed them, or who.

It could hardly have been a rival gang. For one thing, there was no competition. There must be plenty of business for every organlegger left alive after the ARM swept through them last year. For another, why had they been dumped on a city slidewalk? Rival organleggers would have taken them apart for their own organ banks. Waste not, want not.

On that same philosophy, I had something to be deeply involved in when the mother hunt broke. Sinclair's death wasn't ARM business, and his time compression field wasn't in my field. This was both.

I wondered what end of the business the dead ones had been in. The file gave their estimated ages: forty for the man, forty-three for the woman, give or take three years each. Too old to be raiding the city street for donors. That takes youth and muscle. I billed them as doctors, culturing the transplants and doing the operations, or salespersons, charged with quietly letting prospective clients know where they could get an operation without waiting two years for the public organ banks to come up with material.

So they'd tried to sell someone a new kidney and had been killed for their impudence. That would make the killer a hero.

So why hide them for three days, then drag them out onto a city slidewalk in the dead of night?

Because they'd been killed with a fearsome new weapon?

I looked at the burned faces and thought: fearsome, right. Whatever did that *had* to be strictly a murder weapon. As the optical grid over a laser lens would be strictly a murder technique.

So a secretive scientist and his deformed assistant, fearful of rousing the wrath of the villagers, had dithered over the bodies for three days, then disposed of them in that clumsy fashion because they panicked when the bodies started to smell. Maybe.

But a prospective client needn't have used his shiny new terror weapon. He had only to call the cops after they were gone. It read better if the killer was a prospective *donor*; he'd fight with anything he could get his hands on.

I flipped back to full shots of the bodies. They looked to be in good condition. Not much flab. You don't collect a donor by putting an armlock on him; you use a needle gun. But you still need muscle to pick up the body and move it to your car, and you have to do that damn quick. Hmmm ...

Someone knocked at my door.

I shouted, "Come on in!"

Drew Porter came in. He was big enough to fill the office, and he moved with a grace he must have learned on a board. "Mr. Hamilton? I'd like to talk to you."

"Sure. What about?"

He didn't seem to know what to do with his hands. He looked grimly determined. "You're an ARM," he said. "You're not actually investigating Uncle Ray's murder. That's right, isn't it?"

"That's right. Our concern is with the generator. Coffee?"

"Yes, thanks. But you know all about the killing. I thought I'd like to talk to you, straighten out some of my own ideas."

"Go ahead." I punched for two coffees.

"Ordaz thinks Janice did it, doesn't he?"

"Probably. I'm not good at reading Ordaz's mind. But it seems to narrow down to two distinct groups of possible killers: Janice and everyone else. Here's your coffee."

"Janice didn't do it." He took the cup from me, gulped at it, set it down on my desk, and forgot about it.

"Janice and X," I said. "But X couldn't have left. In fact,

X couldn't have left even if he'd had the machine he came for. And we still don't know why he didn't just take the elevator."

He scowled as he thought that through. "Say he had a way to leave," he said. "He wanted to take the machine—he *had* to want that, because he tried to use the machine to set up an alibi. But even if he couldn't take the machine he'd still use his alternative way out."

"Why?"

"It'd leave Janice holding the bag if he knew Janice was coming home. If he didn't know that, he'd be leaving the police with a locked room."

"Locked room mysteries are good clean fun, but I never heard of one happening in real life. In fiction they usually happen by accident." I waved aside his protest. "Never mind. How did he get out?"

Porter didn't answer.

"Would you care to look at the case against Janice Sinclair?"

"She's the only one who could have done it," he said bitterly. "But she didn't. She couldn't kill anyone, not in that cold-blooded, prepackaged way, with an alibi all set up and a weird machine at the heart of it. Look, that machine is too *complicated* for Janice."

"No, she isn't the type. But—no offense intended—you are."

He grinned at that. "Me? Well, maybe I am. But why would I want to?"

"You're in love with her. I think you'd do anything for her. Aside from that, you might enjoy setting up a perfect murder. And there's the money."

"You've got a funny idea of a perfect murder."

"Say I was being tactful."

He laughed at that. "All right. Say I set up a murder for the love of Janice. Damn it, if she had that much hate in her, I wouldn't love her! Why would she want to kill Uncle Ray?"

I dithered about whether to drop that on him. Decided

ARM   175

yes. "Do you know anything about Edward Sinclair's exemption?"

"Yah, Janice told me something about . . ." He trailed
off.

"Just what did she tell you?"

"I don't have to say."

That was probably intelligent. "All right," I said. "For
the sake of argument, let's assume it was Raymond Sinclair
who worked out the math for the new ramrobot scoops, and
Edward took the credit, with Raymond's connivance. It was
probably Raymond's idea. How would that sit with
Edward?"

"I'd think he'd be grateful forever," Porter said. "Janice
says he is."

"Maybe. But people are funny, aren't they? Being grateful for fifty years could get on a man's nerves. It's not a
natural emotion."

"You're so young to be so cynical," Porter said pityingly.

"I'm trying to think this out like a prosecution lawyer. If
these brothers saw each other too often, Edward might get
to feeling embarrassed around Raymond. He'd have a hard
time relaxing with him. The rumors wouldn't help . . . Oh,
yes, there are rumors. I've been told that Edward couldn't
have worked out those equations because he doesn't have
the ability. If that kind of thing got back to Edward, how
would he like it? He might even start avoiding his brother.
Then Ray might remind brother Edward of just how much
he owed him . . . and that's the kiss of death."

"Janice says no."

"Janice could have picked up the hate from her father.
Or she might have started worrying about what would happen if Uncle Ray changed his mind one day. It could happen any time if things were getting strained between the
elder Sinclairs. So one day she shut his mouth—"

Porter growled in his throat.

"I'm just trying to show you what you're up against.
One more thing: the killer may have wiped the tapes in
Sinclair's computer."

"Oh?" Porter thought that over. "Yah. Janice could have done that just in case there were some notes in there, notes on Ed Sinclair's ramscoop field equations. But look: X could have wiped those tapes, too. Stealing the generator doesn't do him any good unless he wipes it out of Uncle Ray's computer."

"Shall we get back to the case against X?"

"With pleasure." He dropped into a chair. Watching his face smooth out, I added, *and with great relief.*

I said, "Let's not call him X. Call him K for killer." We already had an Ecks involved . . . and his family name probably *had* been X once upon a time. "We've been assuming K set up Sinclair's time compression effect as an alibi."

Porter smiled. "It's a lovely idea. *Elegant*, as a mathematician would say. Remember, I never saw the actual murder scene. Just chalk marks."

"It was—macabre. Like a piece of surrealism. A very bloody practical joke. K could have deliberately set it up that way if his mind is twisted enough."

"If he's that twisted, he probably escaped by running himself down the garbage disposal."

"Pauline Urthiel thought he might be a psychotic. Someone who worked with Sinclair who thought he wasn't getting enough credit." Like Peterfi, I thought, or Pauline herself.

"I like the alibi theory."

"It bothers me. Too many people knew about the machine. How did he expect to get away with it? Lawrence Ecks knew about it. Peterfi knew about it. Peterfi knew enough about the machine to rebuild it from scratch. Or so he says. You and Janice saw it in action."

"Say he's crazy, then. Say he hated Uncle Ray enough to kill him and then set him up in a makeshift Dali painting. He'd still have to get *out.*" Porter was working his hands together. The muscles bulged and rippled in his arms. "If the elevator hadn't been locked and on Uncle Ray's floor, there wouldn't be a problem."

"So?"

"So. Janice came home, called the elevator up, and locked it. She does that without thinking. She had a bad shock last night. This morning she didn't remember."

"And this evening it could come back to her."

Porter looked up sharply. "I wouldn't—"

"You'd better think long and hard before you do. If Ordaz is sixty percent sure of her now, he'll be a hundred percent sure when she lays that on him."

Porter was working his muscles again. In a low voice he said, "It's possible, isn't it?"

"Sure. It makes things a lot simpler, too. But if Janice said it now, she'd sound like a liar."

"But it's *possible*."

"I give up. Sure, it's possible."

"Then who's our killer?"

There wasn't any reason I shouldn't consider the question. It wasn't my case at all. I did, and presently I laughed. "Did I say it'd make things simpler? Man, it throws the case *wide open*! *Anyone* could have done it. Uh, anyone but Steeves. Steeves wouldn't have had any reason to come back this morning."

Porter looked glum. "Steeves wouldn't have done it anyway."

"He was your suggestion."

"Oh, in pure mechanical terms, he's the only one who didn't need a way out. But you don't know Steeves. He's a big, brawny guy with a beer belly and no brains. A nice guy, you understand, I *like* him, but if he ever killed anyone, it'd be with a beer bottle. And he was proud of Uncle Ray. He liked having Raymond Sinclair in his building."

"Okay, forget Steeves. Is there anyone you'd particularly like to pin it on? Bearing in mind that now *anyone* could get in to do it."

"Not anyone. Anyone in the elevator computer, plus anyone Uncle Ray might have let up."

"Well?"

He shook his head.

"You make a hell of an amateur detective. You're afraid to accuse anyone."

He shrugged, smiling, embarrassed.

"What about Peterfi? Now that Sinclair's dead, he can claim they were equal partners in the, uh, time machine. And he tumbled to it awfully fast. The moment Valpredo told him Sinclair was dead, Peterfi was his partner."

"Sounds typical."

"Could he be telling the truth?"

"I'd say he's lying. Doesn't make him a killer, though."

"No. What about Ecks? If he didn't know Peterfi was involved, he might have tried the same thing. Does he need money?"

"Not hardly. And he's been with Uncle Ray for longer than I've been alive."

"Maybe he was after the exemption. He's had kids, but not by his present wife. He may not know she can't have children."

"Pauline *likes* children. I've seen her with them." Porter looked at me curiously. "I don't see having children as that big a motive."

"You're young. Then there's Pauline herself. Sinclair knew something about her. Or Sinclair might have told Ecks, and Ecks blew up and killed him for it."

Porter shook his head. "In red rage? I can't think of anything that'd make Larry do that. Pauline, maybe. Larry, no."

But, I thought, there are men who would kill if they learned that their wives had gone through a sex change. I said, "Whoever killed Sinclair, if he wasn't crazy, he had to want to take the machine. One way might have been to lower it by rope . . ." I trailed off. Fifty pounds or so, lowered two stories by nylon line. Ecks's steel and plastic arm . . . or the muscles now rolling like boulders in Porter's arms. I thought Porter could have managed it.

Or maybe he'd thought he could. He hadn't actually had to go through with it.

My phone rang.

It was Ordaz. "Have you made any progress on the time machine? I'm told that Dr. Sinclair's computer—"

"Was wiped, yah. But that's all right. We're learning quite a lot about it. If we run into trouble, Bernath Peterfi can help us. He helped build it. Where are you now?"

"At Dr. Sinclair's apartment. We had some further questions for Janice Sinclair."

Porter twitched. I said, "All right, we'll be right over. Andrew Porter's with me." I hung up and turned to Porter. "Does Janice know she's a suspect?"

"No. Please don't tell her unless you have to. I'm not sure she could take it."

I had the taxi drop us at the lobby level of the Rodewald Building. When I told Porter I wanted a ride in the elevator, he just nodded.

The elevator to Raymond Sinclair's penthouse was a box with a seat in it. It would have been comfortable for one, cozy for two good friends. With me and Porter in it, it was crowded. Porter hunched his knees and tried to fold into himself. He seemed used to it.

He probably was. Most apartment elevators are like that. Why waste room on an elevator shaft when the same space can go into apartments?

It was a fast ride. The seat was necessary; it was two gees going up and a longer period at half a gee slowing down while lighted numbers flickered past. Numbers but no doors.

"Hey, Porter. If this elevator jammed, would there be a door to let us out?"

He gave me a funny look and said he didn't know. "Why worry about it? If it jammed at this speed, it'd come apart like a handful of shredded lettuce."

It was just claustrophobic enough to make me wonder. K hadn't left by elevator. Why not? Because the ride up had terrified him? *Brain to memory: dig into the medical records of that list of suspects. Claustrophobia.* Too bad the el-

evator brain didn't keep records. We could find out which
of them had used the boxlike elevator once or not at all.

In which case we'd be looking for K_2. By now I was
thinking in terms of three groups. K_1 killed Sinclair, then
tried to use the low-inertia field as both loot and alibi. K_2
was crazy; he hadn't wanted the generator at all, except as
a way to set up his macabre tableau. K_3 was Janice and
Drew Porter.

Janice was there when the doors slid open. She was wan,
and her shoulders slumped. But when she saw Porter, she
smiled like sunlight and ran to him. Her run was wobbly,
thrown off by the missing weight of her arm.

The wide brown circle was still there in the grass,
marked with white chalk and the yellow chemical that picks
up bloodstains. White outlines to mark the vanished body,
the generator, the poker.

Something knocked at the back door of my mind. I
looked from the chalk outlines, to the open elevator, to the
chalk . . . and a third of the puzzle fell into place.

So simple. We were looking for K_1 . . . and I had a pretty
good idea who he was.

Ordaz was asking me, "How did you happen to arrive
with Mr. Porter?"

"He came to my office. We were talking about a hypothetical killer—" I lowered my voice slightly. "—a killer
who isn't Janice."

"Very good. Did you reason out how he must have left?"

"Not yet. But play the game with me. Say there was a
way."

Porter and Janice joined us, their arms about each other's
waists. Ordaz said, "Very well. We assume there was a way
out. Did he improvise it? And why did he not use the elevator?"

"He must have had it in mind when he got here. He
didn't use the elevator because he was planning to take the
machine. It wouldn't have fit."

They all stared at the chalk outline of the generator. So

simple. Porter said, "Yah! Then he used it anyway and left you a locked room mystery!"

"That may have been his mistake," Ordaz said grimly. "When we know his escape route, we may find that only one man could have used it. But of course we do not even know that the route exists."

I changed the subject. "Have you got everyone on the elevator tape identified?"

Valpredo dug out his spiral notebook and flipped to the jotted names of the people permitted to use Sinclair's elevator. He showed it to Porter. "Have you seen this?"

Porter studied it. "No, but I can guess what it is. Let's see ... Hans Drucker was Janice's lover before I came along. We still see him. In fact, he was at that beach party last night at the Randalls'."

"He flopped on the Randalls' rug last night," Valpredo said. "Him and four others. One of the better alibis."

"Oh, *Hans* wouldn't have anything to do with this!" Janice exclaimed. The idea horrified her.

Porter was still looking at the list. "You know about most of these people already. Bertha Hall and Muriel Sandusky were lady friends of Uncle Ray's. Bertha goes backpacking with him."

"We interviewed them, too," Valpredo told me. "You can hear the tapes if you like."

"No, just give me the gist. I already know who the killer is."

Ordaz raised his eyebrows at that, and Janice said, "Oh, good! Who?" which question I answered with a secretive smile. Nobody actually called me a liar.

Valpredo said, "Muriel Sandusky's been living in England for almost a year. Married. Hasn't seen Sinclair in years. Big, beautiful redhead."

"She had a crush on Uncle Ray once," Janice said. "And vice versa. I think his lasted longer."

"Bertha Hall is something else again," Valpredo continued. "Sinclair's age and in good shape. Wiry. She says that when Sinclair was on the home stretch on a project, he gave up everything: friends, social life, exercise. Afterward he'd call Bertha and go backpacking with her to catch up with himself. He called her two nights ago and set a date for next Monday."

I said, "Alibi?"

"Nope."

"Really!" Janice said indignantly. "Why, we've known Bertha since I was that high! If you know who killed Uncle Ray, why don't you just say so?"

"Out of this list, I sure do, given certain assumptions. But I don't know how he got out, or how he expected to, or whether we can prove it on him. I can't accuse anyone *now*. It's a damn shame he didn't lose his arm reaching for that poker."

Porter looked frustrated. So did Janice.

"You would not want to face a lawsuit," Ordaz suggested delicately. "What of Sinclair's machine?"

"It's an inertialess drive, sort of. Lower the inertia, time speeds up. Bera's already learned a lot about it, but it'll be a while before he can really . . ."

"You were saying?" Ordaz asked when I trailed off.

"Sinclair was *finished* with the damn thing."

"Sure he was," Porter said. "He wouldn't have been showing it around otherwise."

"Or calling Bertha for a backpacking expedition. Or spreading rumors about what he had. Yeah. Sure, he knew everything he could learn about that machine. Julio, you were cheated. It all depends on the machine. And the bastard did wrack up his arm, and we can prove it on him."

We piled into Ordaz's commandeered taxi: me and Ordaz and Valpredo and Porter. Valpredo set the thing for conventional speeds so he wouldn't have to worry about driving. We'd turned the interior chairs to face each other.

"This is the part I won't guarantee," I said, sketching rapidly in Valpredo's borrowed notebook. "But remember, he had a length of line with him. He must have expected to use it. Here's how he planned to get out."

I sketched in a box to represent Sinclair's generator, a

stick figure clinging to the frame. A circle around them to represent the field. A bowknot tied to the machine, with one end trailing up through the field.

"See it? He goes up the stairs with the field on. The camera has about one chance in eight of catching him while he's moving at that speed. He wheels the machine to the edge of the roof, ties the line to it, throws the line a good distance away, pushes the generator off the roof, and steps off with it. The line falls at thirty-two feet per second squared, normal time, plus a little more because the machine and the killer are tugging down on it. Not hard, because they're in a low-inertia field. By the time the killer reaches ground, he's moving at something more than, uh, twelve hundred feet per second over five hundred . . . uh, say three feet per second internal time, and he's got to pull the machine out of the way fast, because the rope is going to hit like a bomb."

"It looks like it would work," Porter said.

"Yah. I thought for a while that he could just stand on the bottom of the field. A little fooling with the machine cured me of that. He'd smash both legs. But he could hang on to the frame; it's strong enough."

"But he didn't have the machine," Valpredo pointed out.

"That's where you got cheated. What happens when two fields intersect?"

They looked blank.

"It's not a trivial question. Nobody knows the answer yet. *But Sinclair did.* He had to; he was *finished.* He must have had two machines. The killer took the second machine."

Ordaz said, "Ahh."

Porter said, "Who's K?"

We were settling on the carport. Valpredo knew where we were, but he didn't say anything. We left the taxi and headed for the elevators.

"That's a lot easier," I said. "He expected to use the machine as an alibi. That's silly, considering how many people knew it existed. But if he didn't know that Sinclair was ready to start showing it to people—specifically to you and Janice—who's left? Ecks only knew it was some kind of interstellar drive."

The elevator was uncommonly large. We piled into it.

"And," Valpredo said, "there's the matter of the arm. I think I've got that figured, too."

"I gave you enough clues," I told him.

Peterfi was a long time answering our buzz. He may have studied us through the door camera, wondering why a parade was marching through his hallway. Then he spoke through the grid. "Yes? What is it?"

"Police. Open up," Valpredo said.

"Do you have a warrant?"

I stepped forward and showed my ident to the camera. "I'm an ARM. I don't need a warrant. Open up. We won't keep you long." *One way or another.*

He opened the door. He looked neater now than he had this afternoon despite informal brown indoor pajamas. "Just you," he said. He let me in, then started to close the door on the others.

Valpredo put his hand against the door. "Hey—"

"It's okay," I said. Peterfi was smaller than I was, and I had a needle gun. Valpredo shrugged and let him close the door.

My mistake. I had two-thirds of the puzzle, and I thought I had it all.

Peterfi folded his arms and said, "Well? What is it you want to search this time? Would you like to examine my legs?"

"No, let's start with the insulin feeder on your upper arm."

"Certainly," he said, and startled the hell out of me.

I waited while he took off his shirt—unnecessary, but he needn't know that—then ran my imaginary fingers through the insulin feed. The reserve was nearly full. "I should have known," I said. "Dammit. You got six months worth of insulin from the organlegger."

His eyebrows went up. "Organlegger?" He pulled loose. "Is this an accusation, Mr. Hamilton? I'm taping this for my attorney."

And I was setting myself up for a lawsuit. The hell with it. "Yah, it's an accusation. You killed Sinclair. Nobody else could have tried that alibi stunt."

He looked puzzled—honestly, I thought. "Why not?"

"If anyone else had tried to set up an alibi with Sinclair's generator, Peterfi, you, would have told the police all about what it was and how it worked. But you were the only one who knew that until last night, when he started showing it around."

There was only one thing he could say to that kind of logic, and he said it. "Still recording, Mr. Hamilton."

"Record and be damned. There are other things we can check. Your grocery delivery service. Your water bill."

He didn't flinch. He was smiling. Was it a bluff? I sniffed the air. Six months worth of body odor emitted in one night? By a man who hadn't taken more than four or five baths in six months? But his air-conditioning was too good.

The curtains were open now to the night and the ocean. They'd been closed this afternoon, and he'd been squinting. But it wasn't evidence. The lights: he only had one light burning now, and so what?

The big, powerful campout flashlight sitting on a small table against a wall. I hadn't even noticed it this afternoon. Now I was sure I knew what he'd used it for, but how to prove it?

Groceries . . . "If you didn't buy six months worth of groceries last night, you must have stolen them. Sinclair's generator is perfect for thefts. We'll check the local supermarkets."

"And link the thefts to me? How?"

He was too bright to have kept the generator. But come to think of it, where could he abandon it? He was *guilty*. He couldn't have covered *all* his tracks—

"Peterfi? I've got it."

He believed me. I saw it in the way he braced himself. Maybe he'd worked it out before I did. I said, "Your contraceptive shots must have worn off six months early. Your organlegger couldn't get you that; he's got no reason to keep contraceptives around. You're dead, Peterfi."

"I might as well be. Damn you, Hamilton! You've cost me the exemption!"

"They won't try you right away. We can't afford to lose what's in your head. You know too much about Sinclair's generator."

"Our generator! We built it together!"

"Yah."

"You won't try me at all," he said more calmly. "Are you going to tell a court how the killer left Ray's apartment?"

I dug out my sketch and handed it to him. While he was studying it, I said, "How did you like going off the roof? You couldn't have *known* it would work."

He looked up. His words came slowly, reluctantly. I guess he had to tell someone, and it didn't matter now. "By then I didn't care. My arm hung like a dead rabbit, and it stank. It took me three minutes to reach the ground. I thought I'd die on the way."

"Where'd you dig up an organlegger that fast?"

His eyes called me a fool. "Can't you guess? Three years ago. I was hoping diabetes could be cured by a transplant. When the government hospitals couldn't help me, I went to an organlegger. I was lucky he was still in business last night."

He drooped. It seemed that all the anger went out of him. "Then it was six months in the field, waiting for the scars to heal. In the dark. I tried taking that big campout flashlight in with me." He laughed bitterly. "I gave that up after I noticed the walls were smoldering."

The wall above that little table had a scorched look. I should have wondered about that earlier.

"No baths," he was saying. "I was afraid to use up that

much water. No exercise, practically. But I had to eat, didn't I? And all for nothing."

"Will you tell us how to find the organlegger you dealt with?"

"This is your big day, isn't it, Hamilton? All right, why not. It won't do you any good."

"Why not?"

He looked up at me very strangely.

Then he spun about and ran.

He caught me flat-footed. I jumped after him. I didn't know what he had in mind; there was only one exit to the apartment, excluding the balcony, and he wasn't headed there. He seemed to be trying to reach a blank wall with a small table set against it and a camp flashlight on it and a drawer in it. I saw the drawer and thought, *Gun!* And I surged after him and got him by the wrist just as he reached the wall switch above the table.

I threw my weight backward and yanked him away from there . . . and then the field came on.

I held a hand and arm up to the elbow. Beyond was a fluttering of violet light: Peterfi was thrashing frantically in a low-inertia field. I hung on while I tried to figure out what was happening.

The second generator was here somewhere. In the wall? The switch seemed to have been recently plastered in, now that I saw it close. Figure a closet on the other side and the generator in it. Peterfi must have drilled through the wall and fixed that switch. Sure, what else did he have to do with six months of spare time?

No point in yelling for help. Peterfi's soundproofing was too modern. And if I didn't let go, Peterfi would die of thirst in a few minutes.

Peterfi's feet came straight at my jaw. I threw myself down, and the edge of a boot sole nearly tore my ear off. I rolled forward in time to grab his ankle. There was more violet fluttering, and his other leg thrashed wildly outside the field. Too many conflicting nerve impulses were pouring into the muscles. The leg flopped about like something dying. If I didn't let go, he'd break it in a dozen places.

He'd knocked the table over. I didn't see it fall, but suddenly it was lying on its side. The top, drawer included, must have been well beyond the field. The flashlight lay just beyond the violet fluttering of his hand.

Okay. He couldn't reach the drawer; his hand wouldn't get coherent signals if it left the field. I could let go of his ankle. He'd turn off the field when he got thirsty enough.

And if I didn't let go, he'd die in there.

It was like wrestling a dolphin one-handed. I hung on anyway, looking for a flaw in my reasoning. Peterfi's free leg seemed broken in at least two places . . . I was about to let go when something must have jarred together in my head.

Faces of charred bone grinned derisively at me.

Brain to hand: HANG ON! Don't you understand? He's trying to reach the flashlight!

I hung on.

Presently Peterfi stopped thrashing. He lay on his side, his face and hands glowing blue. I was trying to decide whether he was playing possum when the blue light behind his face quietly went out.

I let them in. They looked it over. Valpredo went off to search for a pole to reach the light switch. Ordaz asked, "Was it necessary to kill him?"

I pointed to the flashlight. He didn't get it.

"I was overconfident," I said. "I shouldn't have come in alone. He's already killed two people with that flashlight. The organleggers who gave him his new arm. He didn't want them talking, so he burned their faces off and then dragged them out onto a slidewalk. He probably tied them to the generator and then used the line to pull it. With the field on, the whole setup wouldn't weigh more than a couple of pounds."

"With a flashlight?" Ordaz pondered. "Of course. It

would have been putting out five hundred times as much light. A good thing you thought of that in time."

"Well, I do spend more time dealing with these oddball science fiction devices than you do."

"And welcome to them," Ordaz said.

*

PATCHWORK GIRL

1. CITY OF MIRRORS

We fell east to west, dipping toward the moon in the
usual shallow, graceful arc. Our pilot had turned off the
cabin lights to give us a view. The sun set as we fell. I
peered past Tom Reinecke and let my eyes adjust.

It was black below. There wasn't even Earthlight; the
"new" Earth was a slender sliver in the eastern sky. The
black shadows of mountains emerged form the western horizon and came toward us.

Reinecke had fallen silent.

That was a new development. Tom Reinecke had been
trying to interview me even before we left Outback Field,
Australia. Thus:

What was it like out there among the flying mountains?
Had I really killed an organlegger by using psychic powers? As a man of many cultures—Kansas farm boy, seven
years mining the asteroids, five years in the United Nations
Police—didn't I consider myself the ideal delegate to a
Conference to Review Lunar Law? How did I feel about
what liberals called "the organ bank problem"? Would I
demonstrate my imaginary arm, please? Et cetera.

I'd admitted to being a liberal and denied being the solar
system's foremost expert on lunar law, inasmuch as I'd
never been on the moon. Beyond that, I'd managed to get
him talking about himself. He'd never stopped.

The flatlander reporter was a small, rounded man in his early twenties, brown-haired and smooth-shaven. Born in Australia, schooled in England, he'd never been in space. He'd gone from journalism school straight into a job with the BBC. He'd told me about himself at length. This young and he was on his way to the moon! To witness deliberations that could affect all of future history! He seemed eager and innocent. I wondered how many older, more experienced newstapers had turned down his assignment.

Now, suddenly, he was quiet. More: he was leaving fingerprints in the hard plastic chair arms.

The black shadows of the D'Alembert Mountains were coming right at us: broken teeth in a godling's jaw, ready to chew us up.

We passed low over the mountains, almost between the peaks, and continued to fall. Now the land was chewed by new and old meteorite craters. Light ahead of us became a long line of lighted windows, the west face of Hovestraydt City. Slowing, we passed north of the city and curved around. The city was a square border of light, and peculiar reflections flashed from within the border: mostly greens, some reds, yellows, browns.

The ship hovered and settled east of the city, at the edge of Grimalde's rim wall. No dust sprayed around us as we touched down. Too many ships had landed here over the last century. The dust was all gone.

Tom Reinecke let go of his chair arms and resumed breathing. He forced a smile. "Thrill a minute."

"Hey, you weren't *worried*, were you? You can't even *imagine* the *real* problems with making this kind of landing."

"What? What do you mean? I—"

I laughed. "Relax, I was kidding. People have been landing on the moon for a hundred and fifty years, and they've only had two accidents."

We fought politely for room to struggle into our pressure suits.

With a little more warning I would have had a skintight pressure suit made at the taxpayers' expense. But skintight suits have to be carefully fitted, and that takes time. Luke Garner had given me just ten days to get ready. I'd spent the time on research. I was half-certain that Garner had picked someone else for the job and that he or she had died or gotten sick or pregnant.

Be that as it may: I had bought an inflated suit on the expense account. The other passengers—reporters and conference delegates—were also getting into inflated suits.

Half a dozen lunies and Belters waited to greet us when we climbed down from the air lock. I could see fairly well into the bubble helmets. Taffy wasn't among them. I recognized people I'd seen only on phone screens. And a familiar voice: cheerful, cordial, mildly accented.

"Welcome to Hovestraydt City," said the voice of Mayor Hove Watson. "You've arrived near dinnertime by the city clocks. I hope to show you around a bit before you begin your work tomorrow." I had no trouble picking him out of the crowd: a lunie over eight feet tall with thinning blond hair and a cordial smile showing through his helmet and a flowering ash tree on his chest. "You've already been assigned rooms, and—before I forget—the city computer's command name is *Chiron*. It will be keyed to your voice. Shall we postpone introductions until we can get into shirtsleeves?" He turned to lead the way.

So Taffy hadn't made it. I wondered if she'd left a message and how long it would be before I reached a phone.

We trooped toward the lights a few hundred yards away. No moondust softened our footfalls. My first look at the moon, and I wasn't seeing much. Black night around us and a glare of light from the city. But the sky was the sky I remembered, the Belter's sky, stars by the hundred thousand, so hard and bright, you could reach up and feel their heat. I lagged behind to get the full effect. It was like homecoming.

We were Belters and flatlanders and lunies, and there was no problem telling us apart.

All the flatlanders were wearing inflated suits in bright primary colors. They hampered movement, made us clumsy. Even I was having trouble.

I'd talked to the other United Nations delegates just before the flight. Jabez Stone was a cross between tall black Watusi and long-jawed white New Englander. He'd been a prosecution lawyer before going into politics. He represented the General Assembly. Octavia Budrys of the Security Council had very white skin and very black hair. She was overweight but with the muscle tension to carry it well. You sensed their awareness of their own power. On Earth they had walked like rulers. Here—

Their dignity suffered. Budrys bounced like a big rubber ball. Stone fought the lower gravity with a kind of shuffle. They veered from side to side and into each other. I heard their panting in my earphones.

The Belters found their stride easily. Through the bubble helmets you saw Belter crests on both men and women: hair running in a strip from forehead to nape of neck, the scalp shaved on both sides. They wore silvered cloaks against the cold of lunar night. Under the cloaks were skintights: membranous elastic cloth that would pass sweat and fitted like a coat of paint.

Paintings glowed across their chests and bellies. A Belter's pressure suit is his real home, and he will spend a fortune on a good torso painting. The brawny redheaded woman wearing the gold of the Belt Police had to be Marion Shaeffer. Her torso showed an eagle-clawed dragon stooping on a tiger. A broad-shouldered black-haired man, Chris Penzler, wore a copy of a Bonnie Dalzell griffin, the one in the New York Metropolitan: mostly gold and bronze with a cloudy Earth clutched in one claw.

I had abandoned a Belter suit when I returned to Earth. The chest painting showed a great brass-bound door opening on a lush world with two suns. I missed it.

The lunies wore skintights, but they would never be taken for Belters. They stood seven and eight feet tall. Their suits were in bright monochrome colors to stand out against a bright and confusing lunar background. Their chest paintings were smaller and generally not as good and tended to feature one dominant color, as Mayor Watson's ash tree painting was mostly green. The lunies hardly walked; they flew in shallow arcs, effortlessly, and it was beautiful to watch.

One hundred fifty-seven years after the first landing on the Earth's moon, you could almost believe that mankind was dividing into different species. We were three branches of humanity, trooping toward the lights.

Most of Hovestraydt City was underground. That square of light was only the top of it. Three sides of the square were living quarters; I had seen light spilling through windows. But the whole east face of the city was given over to the mirror works.

We passed telescope mirrors in the polishing stage, with mobile screens to shield them. Silicate ore stood in impressively tall conical heaps. Spindly lunies in skintights and silver cloaks stopped work to watch us pass. They didn't smile.

Under a roof that had rock and moondust piled high atop it for meteor protection, a wide stretch of the east face was open to vacuum. Here were big, fragile paraboloids and lightweight telescope assemblies for Belter ships; widgetry for polishing and silvering mirrors and more widgetry for measuring their curvature; garage space for wide-wheeled motorcycles, bubble-topped buses, and special trucks to carry lenses and radar reflectors. There were more lunies at work. I'd expected to see amusement at the way we walked, but they weren't amused. Was that resentment I saw within the bubble helmets?

I could guess what was bothering them. The conference.

Tom Reinecke veered away to peer through a glass wall. I followed him. Lunie workmen were looking this way; I was afraid he'd get in trouble.

He was looking down through thick glass. Beyond and below, an assembly line was birthing acre-sized sheets of silvered fabric, rolling the fabric into tubes with the silvering on the inside, sealing the ends, and folding them into relatively tiny packets.

"City of mirrors," Tom said reflectively.

"You know it," said a woman's voice. Belt accent, specifically Confinement Asteroid. I found her at my shoulder. Within the bubble helmet she was young and pretty and very black: Watusi genes, skin blackened further by the unfiltered sunlight of space. She was almost as tall as a lunie, but the style of her suit made her a Belter. I liked her torso painting. Against the pastel glow of the Veil Nebula, a slender woman's silhouette showed in uttermost black, save for two glowing greenish-white eyes.

"City of mirrors. There are Hove City mirrors everywhere in space, everywhere you look," she told us. "Not just telescopes. You know what they're doing down there? Those are solar reflectors. They're shipped out flat. We inflate them. Then we spray foam plastic struts on them. They don't have to be strong. We cut them up and get cylindrical mirrors for solar power."

"I've been a Belt miner," I said.

She looked at me curiously. "I'm Desiree Porter, newstaper for the Vesta Beam."

"Tom Reinecke, BBC."

"Gil Hamilton, ARM delegate, and we're being abandoned."

Her teeth flashed like lightning in a black sky. "Gil the Arm! I know about you!" She looked where I was pointing and added, "Yah, we'll talk later. I want to interview you."

We jumped to join the last of the line as it cycled through the air lock.

We crowded into different elevators and rejoined on the sixth level, the dining facility. Mayor Watson again took the lead. You couldn't get lost following Mayor Watson. Eight feet two inches tall, topped with ash blond hair and a nose like the prow of a ship and a smile that showed a good many very white teeth.

By now we were talking away like old friends . . . some of us, anyway. Clay and Budrys and the other UN delegates still had to keep all their attention on their feet, and they still bounded too high. And I got my first look at the Garden, but I didn't get a chance to study it till we were seated.

We were three delegates from the United Nations, three from the Belt, and four representing the moon itself, plus Porter and Reinecke, and Mayor Watson as our host.

The dining hall was crowded, and the noise level was high. Mayor Watson was out of earshot at the other end of the table. He'd tried to mix us up a little. The reporters seemed to be interviewing each other and liking what they learned. I found myself between Chris Penzler, Fourth Speaker for the Belt, and a Tycho Dome official named Bertha Carmody. She was intimidating: seven feet three with a spreading crown of tightly curled white hair, a strong jaw, and a penetrating voice.

The Garden ran vertically through Hovestraydt City: a great pit lined with ledges. A bedspring-shaped ramp ran up the center, and narrower ramps fed into it at all levels, including this one. The plants that covered the ledges were crops, but that didn't keep them from being pretty. Melons hung along one ledge. A ledge of glossy green ground cover turned out to be raspberries and strawberries. There were ledges of ripe corn and unripe wheat and tomatoes. The orange and lemon trees lower down were blooming.

Chris Penzler caught me gaping. "Tomorrow," he said. "You're seeing it by sunlamps now. By daylight it's quite beautiful."

I was surprised. "Didn't you just get here? Like the rest of us?"

"No, I've been here a week. And I was here at the first conference twenty years ago. They've dug the city deeper since. The Garden, too." Penzler was a burly Belter nearing fifty. His immense, sloping shoulders made his otherwise acceptable legs look spindly. He must have spent much of his life in free fall. His Belter crest was still black, but it had thinned on top to leave an isolated tuft on his forehead. His brows formed a single furry black ridge across his eyes.

I said, "I'd think direct sunlight would kill plants."

When Penzler started to answer, Bertha Carmody rode him down. "Direct sunlight would. The convex mirrors on the roof thin the sunlight and spread it about. We set more mirrors at the bottom of the pit and the sides to direct the sunlight everywhere. Every city on the moon uses essentially the same system." She refrained from adding that I should have done my research before I came, but I could almost hear her thinking it.

Lunies were bringing us plates and food. Special service. The other diners were all getting their own from a ledge, buffet style. I plied my chopsticks. They had splayed ends, and they worked better than a spoon and fork in low gravity. Dinner was mostly vegetables, roughly Chinese in approach and quite good. When I found chicken meat, I turned again to the Garden. There were birds flying between the ledges, though most had settled for the night. Pigeons and chickens. Chickens fly very well in low gravity.

A dark-haired young man was talking to the mayor.

I admit to being abnormally curious, but how could I help but stare? The kid was the mayor's height, a couple of inches over eight feet, and even thinner. Age hard to estimate, say eighteen plus or minus three. They looked like Tolkien elves. Elfish king and elfish prince in well-mannered disagreement. They were not enjoying their inaudible conversation, and they cut it short as quickly as possible.

My eyes followed the kid back to his table. A table for two, across the width of the Garden. His companion was an extraordinarily beautiful woman . . . a flatlander. As he sat down, the woman darted a look of pure poison in our direction.

For an instant our eyes locked.

It was Naomi Horne!

She knew me. Our eyes held . . . and we broke the lock and went back to eating. It had been fourteen years since I last felt the urge to talk to Naomi Horne, and I didn't have it now.

We ended with melon and coffee. Most of us were heading for the elevator when Chris Penzler took my arm. "Look down into the Garden," he said.

I did. It was another nine stories to the bottom; I counted. A tree was growing down there. Its top was only two levels below us. The ramp spiraled down around the trunk.

"That redwood," Chris said, "was planted when Hovestraydt City was first occupied. It's much taller now than it was when I first came. They transplant it whenever they dig the Garden deeper."

We turned away. I asked, "What's it going to be like, this conference?"

"Less hectic than the last one, I hope. Twenty years ago we carved out the general body of law that now rules the moon." He frowned. "I have my doubts. Some of the lunar citizenry think we are meddling in their internal affairs."

"They've got a point."

"Of course they do. We face other opportunities for embarrassment, too. The holding tanks were expensive. Worse, the lunar delegates are in a position to claim that they serve no useful purpose."

"Chris, I'm a last-minute replacement. I only had ten days to bone up."

"Ah. Well, the first conference was twenty years ago. It wasn't easy finding compromises between three ways of life. You flatlanders saw no reason why lunar law shouldn't send all felons to the organ banks. Belt law is considerably more lenient. The death penalty is so damned *permanent.* Suppose it turns out that you broke up the wrong person?"

"I know about the holding tanks," I said.

"They were our most important point of compromise."

"Six months, isn't it? The convict stays in suspended animation for six months before they break him up. If the conviction is reversed, he's revived."

"That's right. What you may not know," Chris said, "is

that no convict has been revived in the past twenty years. The moon had to pay half the cost of the holding tanks . . . well, we could have made them pay the whole bill. And there were some bugs in the prototypes. We know four convicts died and had to be broken up at once, and half the organs were lost."

We crowded into the elevator with the rest. We lowered our voices. "And all for nothing?"

"By lunie standards, yes. But how diligently were the rights of the convicts guarded? Well. As I say, the conference may be more hectic than one would hope."

We all got off on zero level. I gathered that few lunies wanted to live on the surface. These rooms were mostly for transients. I left Penzler at his door and walked two down to my own.

2. VIEW THROUGH A WINDOW

Wherever you go in space, shirtsleeve environments tend to be cramped. My room was bigger than I expected. There was a bed, narrow but long, and a table with four collapsed chairs, and a tub. There was a phone screen, and I made for that.

Taffy wasn't in, but she'd left a message. She wore a paper surgical coverall and sounded a bit breathless. "Gil, I can't meet you. You'll get in about ten minutes after I go on duty. I get off at the usual ungodly hour, in this case 0600, city time. Can you meet me for breakfast? Ten past six, in oh-fifty-three, in the north face on zero level. There's room service. Isn't Garner lovely?"

The picture smiled enchantingly and froze. Chiron asked, "Will there be an answer, sir?" and beeped.

I was still feeling ruffled and mean. I had to force the eager smile. "Chiron, message. Ten past six, your room. I'll come to you by Earthlight, though hell should bar the way." Called off the phone and lost the smile.

For getting me this chance to see Taffy again after two

and a half months of separation . . . yeah, Garner was lovely.

Taffy and I had been roommates for three years when she got this chance to practice surgery on the moon. Exchange program. It wasn't something she could turn down: too useful to her career and too much fun. They'd been rotating her among the lunar cities. She'd been in Hovestraydt City almost two weeks now.

She'd taken to dating a lunie GP, McCavity by name. I refuse to admit that that irritated me, but the way her schedule had messed up our first meeting did. So did the thought of the conference meeting tomorrow at nine-thirty. I'd heard angry voices at dinner. Clay and Budrys hadn't mastered the art of walking yet, and it would affect their tempers.

And my own feet kept getting tangled.

What I needed was a soak in a hot bath.

The bathtub was strange. It was right out in the open, next to the bed, with a view of the phone screen and the picture window. It wasn't long, but it stood four feet high, with a rim that curved inward, and the back rose six feet before curving over. The overflow drain was only halfway up. I started water running, then watched, fascinated. The water looked like it was actively trying to escape.

I tried some commands. The door lock, the closet lock, the lights all responded to my voice and the Chiron command. The water closet lock was manual.

Presently the bath was full to the overflow line. I got in carefully and stretched out. The water dipped in a meniscus around me, reluctant to wet me, until I added soap.

I played with the water, jetting it up between my hands, watching it slowly rise and slowly fall back. I stopped when I'd gotten too much on the ceiling and it was dripping back in fat globules. I was feeling a lot better. I found tiny holes under me and tried calling, "Chiron, activate spa." Water and air bubbles churned around me, battering muscles strained by low-gravity walking.

The phone rang.

Taffy? I called, "Chiron, spa off. Answer phone." The screen rotated to face me. It was Naomi.

In low gravity her long, soft golden hair floated around her with every motion. Her cheekbones were high in an oval face. She was made up in recent flatlander style, so that her blue eyes were patterns on the wings of a great gaudy butterfly. Her mouth was small, her face just a touch fuller than I remembered.

Her body was still athletic, tall and slender by flatlander standards. Her dress was soft blue, and it clung to her as if by static electricity. She'd changed in fourteen years, but not much . . . not enough.

It was unrequited love, and it had lasted half of a spring and all of summer, until the day I invested my scanty fortune to loft myself from Earth and outfit myself as an asteroid miner. The scar on my heart had healed over. Of course it had. But I'd known her across a crowded restaurant. At that distance a stranger would barely have known her for a flatlander.

She smiled a bit nervously. "Gil. I saw you at dinner. Do you remember me?"

"Naomi Horne. Hi."

"Hi. Naomi Mitchison now. What are you doing on the moon, Gil?" She sounded a bit breathless. She'd always talked like that, eager to get the words out, as if someone might interrupt.

"Conference to Review Lunar Law. I represent the ARM. How about you?"

"I'm sightseeing. My life kind of came apart a while back . . . I remember now, you were on the news. You'd caught some kind of organlegging kingpin—"

"Anubis."

"Right." Pause. "Can we meet for a drink?"

I'd already made that decision. "Sure, we'll squeeze it in somewhere. I don't know just how busy I'll be. See, I actually came here following my ex-roommate. She's a surgeon on loan to the hospital here. Between Taffy's weird hours and the conference itself—"

"You're likely to meet yourself in the halls. Yes, I see."

"But I'll call you. Hey, who was your date?"

She laughed. "Alan Watson. He's Mayor Hove's son. I don't think the mayor approves of his dating a flatlander. Lunies are a bit prudish, don't you think?"

"I haven't had a chance to find out. I can't seem to guess a lunie's age."

"He's nineteen." She was teasing me a little. "They can't tell our ages, either. He's nice, Gil, but he's very serious. Like you were."

"Uh huh. Okay, I'll leave a message if I get loose. Would you object to a foursome? For dinner?"

"Sounds good. Chiron, phone off."

I scowled at the blank screen. I had an erection under the water. She still affected me that way. She couldn't have seen it; the camera angle was wrong. "Chiron, spa," I said, and the evidence disappeared in bubbles.

Strange. She thought it was *funny* that a man would want to take her to bed. I'd told myself that fourteen years ago, but I don't think I believed it. I'd thought it was me.

And strange: Naomi was clearly relieved when I told her about Taffy. So why had she called? Not because she wanted a date!

I stood up in the tub. A half-inch sheath of water came up with me. I scraped most of it back into the tub with the edges of my hands, then toweled myself off from the top down.

The picture window was jet black but for a small glowing triangle.

"Chiron, lights off," I said. Blind, I took a chair and waited for my eyes to adjust. Gradually the view took form. Starlight glazed the battered lands to the west. Dawn was creeping down the highest peak. A floating mountain seemed to flame among the stars. I watched until I saw a second peak come alight. Then I set the alarm and went to bed.

* * *

"Phone call, Mr. Hamilton," a neuter voice was saying. "Phone call, Mr. Hamilton. Phone c—"

"Chiron, answer phone!" I had trouble sitting up. There was a broad strap across my chest; I unfastened it. The phone screen showed Tom Reinecke and Desiree Porter bending low to put her face next to his. "It better be good," I said.

"It's not good, but it's not dull," Tom said. "Would an ARM be interested in the attempted murder of a conference delegate?"

I rubbed my eyes. "He would. Who?"

"Chris Penzler. Fourth Speaker for the Belt."

"Does nudity offend you?"

Desiree laughed. Tom said, "No. It bothers lunies."

"Okay. Tell me about it." I got up and started putting clothes on while they talked. The screen and camera rotated to follow me.

"We're next to Penzler's room," Desiree said. "At least Tom is. The walls are thin. We heard a kind of god-awful slosh-*thump* and sort of a feeble scream. We went and pounded on his door. No answer. I stayed while Tom phoned the lunie cops."

"I phoned them, then Marion Shaeffer," Tom said. "She's a Belter, too, the goldskin delegate. Okay, she showed up, then the cops, and they talked the door open. Penzler was faceup in his bathtub with a big hole in his chest. He was still alive when they kicked us out."

"My fault," Desiree said. "I took some pictures."

I had my clothes on and my hair brushed. "I'll be there. Chiron, phone off."

Penzler's door was closed. Desiree said, "They've got my camera. Can you get it back for me?"

"I'll try." I pushed the bell.

"And the pictures?"

"I'll try."

Marion Shaeffer was in uniform. She was my height, muscular, with broad shoulders and heavy breasts. Her ancestors would have been strong farm wives. Her deep tan ended sharply at the throat. "Come in, Hamilton, but stay out of the way. It's not really your territory."

"Nor yours."

"He's one of my people."

Chris Penzler's room was much like mine. It seemed crowded. Three of the six people present were lunies, and that made a difference. I got an impression of too many elbows flashing in my personal space. One was a redheaded, heavily freckled lunie policeman in orange marked with black. He was working the phone. The blond man in informal pajamas was just watching, and he was Mayor Watson himself. The third was a doctor, and he was working on Penzler.

They'd wheeled up a mobile autodoc, a heavy, dauntingly complex machine armed with scalpels, surgical lasers, clamps, hypos, suction tubes, sensor fingers ending in tiny bristles, all mounted on a huge adjustable stand. That took up room, too. The lunie was hard at work monitoring the keyboard and screen set into the 'doc, sometimes typing rapid-fire commands with his long, fragile-looking fingers.

Penzler was on his back on the bed. The bed was wet with water and blood. A pressure bottle was feeding blood into Penzler's arm; you can't use gravity feed on the moon. We watched as the autodoc finished spraying foam over Penzler until it covered him from his chin to his navel.

I swore under my breath, but I couldn't really claim they should have waited for me.

"Here." Marion Shaeffer elbowed me in the ribs and handed me three holograms. "The reporters took pictures. Good thing. Nobody else had a camera."

The first picture showed Penzler on the bed. His whole chest was an ugly deep red, beginning to blister around the edges but burned worse than that in the center. White and black showed where a charred hole had been burned deep into the bone of the sternum, an inch wide and an inch deep. The wound must have been sponged out before the picture was taken.

The second holo showed him faceup in bloody bathwater. The wounds were the same, and he looked dead.

The third was a shot through the picture window, taken over the rim of the tub.

"I don't get this," I said.

Penzler turned his head a bare minimum and looked at me with suffering eyes. "Laser. Shot me through the window."

"Most laser wounds don't spread like this. The wound would be narrower and deeper, wouldn't it, Doctor?"

The doctor jerked his chin down and up without looking around. But Penzler made a strong effort to face me. The doctor stopped him with a hand on his shoulder.

"Laser. I saw. Stood up in the tub. Saw someone out there on the moon." Penzler stopped to pant a bit, then, "Red light. Blast bounced me back in the water. Laser!"

"Chris, did you see only one person?"

"Yah," he grunted.

Mayor Watson spoke for the first time. "How? It's night out there. How could you see anything?"

"I saw him," Penzler said thickly. "Three hundred, four hundred meters. Past the big tilted rock."

I asked, "What was he? Lunie, Belter, flatlander? What was he wearing?"

"Couldn't see. It happened too fast. I stood up, I looked out, then *flash*. I thought . . . for a second . . . I couldn't tell."

"Let him rest now," the doctor said.

Nuts. Penzler should have seen that much. Not that it would prove anything. A Belter could wear a pressure suit. A flatlander could get a skintight made, though you'd expect to find records. A lunie . . . well, there exist short lunies, shorter than, for instance, Desiree Porter, who was a Belter.

I stepped past the tub to reach the window. The tub was still full of pink water. Penzler would have bled to death or drowned if Tom and Desiree hadn't acted so quickly.

I looked out on the moon.

Dawn had crawled down the peaks to touch their bases. Most of the lowlands were still puddles of black, and the shadow of Hovestraydt City seemed to stretch away forever. Out of the city's shadow, 190 yards away to left of center, was a massive monolith that could be Penzler's "big tilted rock." It was the shape of an elongated egg and smooth. Perhaps the surface had been polished by the blast that had made Grimalde Crater.

"It's a wonder he saw anything at all," I said. "Why didn't the killer just keep to the shadows? The sun wasn't up yet."

Nobody answered. Penzler was unconscious now. The doctor patted his shoulder and said, "Three or four days, the foam will start to peel off. He can come to me then and I'll remove it. It'll be longer than that before the bone heals, though."

He turned to us. "It was close. A few minutes later and he would have been dead. The beam charred part of the sternum and cooked tissue underneath. I had to replace parts of his esophagus, the superior vena cava, some mesentery . . . scrape out the charred bone and fill it full of pins . . . it was a mess. On Earth he wouldn't move for a week, and then he'd want a wheelchair."

I asked, "Suppose the beam had been three inches lower?"

"Heart cooked, pleural cavity ruptured. Are you Gil Hamilton?" He stuck out a hand. "I believe we have a friend in common. I'm Harry McCavity."

I smiled and shook his hand (carefully, fighting temptation; those long fingers did look fragile). My thoughts were only mildly malicious. Doctor McCavity wasn't with Taffy either tonight.

McCavity had fluffy brown hair and a nose like an eagle's beak. He was short for a lunie, but he still looked like he'd grown up on a stretch rack. Only lunies look like that. Belters raise their children in great bubble structures spun up to an Earth gravity, places like Confinement and Farmer's Asteroid. McCavity was handsome in an elvish, eerie fashion. In no way did he seem freakish.

"Weird," he said. "Do you know what saved his life?" He jerked a long thumb at the bathtub. "He stood up, and a lot of water came up with him. The laser beam plowed into the water. Live steam exploded all over his chest, but it saved his life, too. The water spread the beam. It didn't go deep enough to kill him right away. The steam explosion threw him back in the tub, so the killer didn't get a second chance."

I remembered how the water had sheathed me when I had stood up in the tub. But— "Would it spread that much? Mayor, could the glass in the window cut some of the light?"

The mayor shook his head. "He said red light. The window wouldn't stop red light. It filters raw sunlight, but mainly in the blue and ultraviolet and X-ray range."

"We ought to let him sleep," McCavity said. We followed him out.

The corridor was high because lunies are high, and wide for a touch of luxury. Windows looked down into the Garden.

The newstapers were waiting. Desiree Porter confronted Marion Shaeffer. "I'd like my camera back, please."

Shaeffer handed over the bulky two-handed instrument. "And my holos?"

She jerked a thumb at the freckled, seven-foot-high lunie cop. "Captain Jefferson's got 'em. They're evidence."

Tom Reinecke confronted Harry McCavity. "Doctor, what is Chris Penzler's condition? Is it murder or attempted murder?"

McCavity smiled. "Attempted. He'll be all right. He should rest tomorrow, but I think he'll be well enough to attend the conference afterward. Mayor, are you through with me? I'm tired."

Captain Jefferson said, "We'll need your evidence on the nature of the wound, but not just now."

McCavity waved and departed, leaping down the corridor like a frog, both feet pushing at the floor at the same time.

Mayor Hove Watson watched him go. His face was puzzled, thoughtful. He came to himself with a start. "What about it, Gil? What would the ARM be doing if this were Los Angeles?"

"Nothing. Murder isn't ARM business unless it involves organlegging or esoteric technology. I've investigated some murders, though. Mainly we'd try to track the weapon."

"We'll do that. Chris said red light. That probably means it was a message laser, and they're guarded. The police use them for weapons as well as senders."

"Guarded how?" I noticed that both newstapers were listening quietly.

"The locks are controlled by the same computer that operates your own apartment, including the door lock. It's a different program, of course."

"Okay. What about opportunity? There was a killer out on the moon. He can't stay out forever."

Mayor Hove turned to the lunie cop. "We have no secrets, Jefferson."

"Yessir. We were lucky," Jefferson told us. "First, it's city night *and* lunar night. Well, predawn. Most of the population is in their apartments, and we can account for some of the rest. One flatlander tourist is out on the moon, and nobody else as far as we can tell. We're checking the night shift at the mirror works. If it were daylight, we'd have hundreds of suspects. Second, the Watchbird Two satellite rose ten minutes ago. I've had the projection room made ready for us."

"Very good." Mayor Hove rubbed his eyes. "Proceed with your investigations, Captain. Detectives Hamilton and Shaeffer may accompany you if they wish. The reporters . . . well, use your own judgment." He dropped his voice to tell me, "I thought it politic to let Mr. Penzler see me concerned in his behalf, but I'd be of no more use here . . ." And he jumped off down the corridor.

The rest of us followed Jefferson to an elevator.

3. THE PROJECTION ROOM

The projection room was a big box set into Levels Six and Seven, underground, in the south side. The police had a projection going when we arrived. They were wading knee deep in miniature lunar landscape.

I think the newstapers were jolted. I know I was.

Jefferson beamed at us. "The Watchbird Two satellite is just over us now. It sends us a picture, and we project it in real time."

He waded out into the moon, and we followed, thigh deep and a hundred feet tall. I could see my feet through the flat stone surface of Grimalde Crater if I concentrated.

Dawn had fully arrived. The sun flared on the eastern horizon, not far below the crescent Earth. The crater-pocked landscape west of us was all glaring ridges and black shadows. Hovestraydt City was a dollhouse. Tiny figures in bright orange skintights with police insignia were leaving an air lock in the south face, on the road that led across the badlands to the Belt Trading Post.

Someone was walking toward them down the middle of the road. I bent close above the doll figure, looking for details. An inflated suit, sky blue, shorter than the approaching lunie cops. Blond hair in the bubble helmet.

I heard a satisfied "Ah." When I turned, Marion Shaeffer added, "I was pretty sure it would be a flatlander."

Penzler's room would be second from the end in the west face. I picked it out, then traced a line to a tilted rock like an elongated egg. Past that point it was mostly shadows. I saw nobody anywhere in that whole stretch of moonscape, save for a sky blue suit and four orange ones, converging.

"We seem to have only one suspect," Captain Jefferson said. "Even a puffer wouldn't take a killer out of range that fast."

Shaeffer asked, "Puffer?"

"Basically two wheels and a motor and a saddle. We use them a lot."

"Ah. What about a spacecraft?"

"We checked, of course. The only spacecraft in the vicinity came nowhere near here."

I was thinking along different lines. "What's a message laser look like? Our little blue suspect doesn't seem to be carrying anything."

"We'd see it. A message laser is about yay long—" Jefferson's hands were a yard, or meter, apart. "—and masses nine kilos."

"Well, those shadows could hide anything. Mind if I feel around in there? I might turn up the weapon."

Tom and Desiree grinned at each other. Shaeffer stared. Jefferson said. "What? What did you say?"

The newstapers laughed outright. Desiree said, "He's Gil the Arm. Haven't you ever heard of Gil the Arm?"

"He's got an imaginary arm," Tom added.

With impressive restraint Jefferson said, "Oh?"

"Combination of psychic powers," I told him. "But it's all limited by my imagination. As if I had a ghost arm and hand."

I didn't bother to add that psychic powers are notoriously undependable. What gave me confidence this time was that I was already trying it: running my imaginary hand lightly over the smooth surface of the Grimalde plain, feeling its texture—cooled magma, cracked everywhere, the cracks filled by moondust—then plunging my hand in and running the ghostly rock between my fingers like water. Hard rock here; pools of moondust in the rough land beyond Grimalde's rim wall; here beneath the dust, an oxygen tank split down the middle by internal pressure. "It'd help if I knew what a message laser looks like," I added.

Captain Jefferson used his belt phone to summon someone with a message laser. "While we're waiting," he said, "maybe you'd like to feel around in here?" He patted at the southeast corner of the hologram city.

I reached into the wall. I found a small room, cramped, lined with racks. The only door felt thick, massive. It opened into the mirror works, in vacuum. I found varied equipment on the racks: armored inflated suits, personal jet packs, a heavy two-handed cutting torch. I described what I was finding. My audience could be expected to include skeptics.

And I tried not to think about what was actually happening: my own disembodied sense of touch reaching through rock walls to roam through a locked room seven floors above me. If I stopped believing, it couldn't happen.

The racks held a score of things like bulky rifles.

I pinched one between my thumb and two fingers. Riflestock frame, compact excitation barrel, tingle of battery power, and a scope just big enough to feel as a bump. The message laser felt both light and heavy: no mass at all yet impossible to move.

A cop came in carrying the real thing. I held it in my hands and ran my imaginary hand over it, then through it. There was a dimmer switch and a cord that would plug into a pressure suit's microphone.

You could talk with it. I wouldn't have been surprised either way. Calling a deadly police weapon a message laser could have been no more than good public relations.

I waded west into the choppy cratered land our would-be killer must have fired from. The newstapers and lunie cops were watching me intently. God knows what they expected to see. I swept my imaginary hand back and forth through the landscape, like sifting intangible sand. The killer might well have dumped his weapon into a dust pool. He might equally well be hiding in one of those shadows, I thought, with a stock of air tanks and spare batteries. I sifted them.

Pools and lakes of shadow felt very cold and showed nothing, though I could feel the shapes of the rocks. Once I felt something like a twelve-foot artillery shell smashed against a crater rim. I asked Jefferson about it. He said it was probably from the rescue attempt after the Blowout eighteen years ago. It would have held water or air.

There was a high ridge, a crater wall. I felt around in the shadows behind it. The killer couldn't have been placed farther back than this. The ridge would have blocked him, and it was already farther than Chris Penzler's "three hundred, four hundred meters."

I turned and went back over the same territory again. By now I was feeling foolish. No laser, no hidden killer, and the beginning of a headache.

The neon orange dolls had collected the blue doll and were going through the air lock. I waded back to where the others waited. I said, "I quit."

The others didn't hide their disappointment. Then Desiree brightened and said, "You'll have to testify, won't you? No weapon and no other suspect."

"I guess I will. Let's go see who they've got."

The desk sergeant was a lunie woman with rounded oriental features and big boobs.

Forgive me! Later I got to know Laura Drury fairly well, but I was seeing her for the first time, and I admit I stared. On her spare, attenuated frame her attractive, ample breasts became her dominant feature. You don't picture a Tolkien elf that way.

We stopped in the doorway, not wanting to interfere. Sergeant Drury asked, "Is this your first visit to the moon, Ms. Mitchison?"

And I went numb.

Naomi's eyes flicked to us and away. It was the desk sergeant who concerned her. She knew she was in trouble, and it made her voice brittle. "No, I was at the museum in Mare Tranquilitatis four years ago."

"Did you see much of the moon then?"

The shock was getting through to me. One suspect had been in position to fire through Chris Penzler's window. I would have to testify that nobody was hiding out there in the shadows. I'd eliminated everyone but Naomi.

It was insane. What could Naomi have to do with Chris Penzler? But I remembered a vindictive glare directed toward our dinner table last night. For Penzler?

Her golden hair was still rumpled from the pressure suit helmet. The rest of the suit was still on her. The big gaudy blue butterfly still covered her eyelids. She sat on the forward edge of a web chair. "I only stayed a week that time," she said. "I . . . was in the mood for a dead world, but I was wrapped up in myself, too. My husband and my little girl had just died. I guess I spent most of my time staring out the window of my room."

"You left Hovestraydt City alone this evening," the desk sergeant said. "You've been out four and a half hours. For a tourist that is reckless. Did you keep to known paths?"

"No, I played tourist. I wandered. I spent some time on the big road, but I ducked into the shadows and the craters every so often. Why not? I couldn't get lost. I could see Earth."

"Did you take a signal laser?"

"No. Nobody told me to. Have I broken some fool regulation, Sergeant?"

The lunie woman's lips twitched. "In a manner of speaking. You are accused of having stationed yourself several hundred meters west of the city, of having located Fourth Speaker Chris Penzler's window and kept watch until he stood up in his bathtub, at which time you fired a signal laser into his chest. Did you do that?"

Naomi was amazed, then horrified . . . or she was a fine actress. "No. Why would I?" She turned. "Gil? Are you in on this?"

"Only as an observer," I half lied. Marion was looking at me with distrust. Clearly the suspect knew me.

The desk sergeant asked, "Ms. Mitchison? Do you *know* Chris Penzler?"

"I used to. He's a Belter. My husband and I met him on Earth almost five years ago. He was negotiating with the UN about some kind of jurisdictional problem. Is he dead?"

"No. He is badly injured."

"And you're really accusing me of attempted murder? With a message laser?"

"We are, yes."

"But . . . I don't have any reason. I don't have a message

laser, either. Why me?" Her eyes flicked about the room: a butterfly fluttering against a window. "Gil?"

I flinched. "I'm not in this. It's not my jurisdiction."

"Gil, is attempted murder an organ bank crime? On the moon?"

Sergeant Drury answered for me. "Why would we give a clumsy killer a second chance?"

"You can refuse to answer questions," I said.

Naomi shook her head. "That's all right. But . . . is that a news camera?"

Jefferson crooked his finger at Tom and Desiree. The newstapers looked at each other and somehow agreed that resistance would be futile. They followed Jefferson out.

The desk sergeant's eyes flicked to Marion. "Who might you be?"

"Marion Shaeffer, Captain, Belt Police. The man who was shot is a Belt citizen."

Drury's eyes questioned me, and I answered. "Gil Hamilton, operative, ARM, here for the conference. I know Ms. Mitchison. I'd like to stay."

"Have you any suggestions?"

"Yes. Naomi, one problem is that we can't find anyone else who could have been in the right place. You were. You've said you didn't shoot Chris—"

"With *what*?"

"Who cares? If you're not our clumsy killer, then you're our only witness. Did you see anything unusual out there?"

She thought about it. "I'm handicapped, Gil. I don't know the moon, and it was night. I didn't see anyone else."

"Did you drop anything, or brush against anything, or break anything? Is there some way we could tell just where you were?"

"You could examine my suit." Hostility was creeping into her voice.

"Oh, we'll do that. We'd also like to examine your route. You'd have to lead us. We can't make you do that."

"Gil, can I get some sleep first?"

I looked at Sergeant Drury, who said, "Of course. You

may find it easier when the sun's higher." She sent Naomi
off with another cop.

"We've got men out there," she said briskly. "There
won't be anyone tampering with evidence. What do you
know about her?"

"I haven't seen Naomi in ten years. I wouldn't have said
she was the killer type. When you take her outside, may I
go along?"

"We'll alert you. And you, Ms. Shaeffer."

"Thanks. Make that Marion."

"Okay. I'm Laura Drury. Make it Laura."

We waited for the elevators. Marion said, "Gil, what do
you consider the killer type?"

"Yeah, that's a hard one, isn't it? But Naomi strikes me
as more the murder *victim* type."

"What do you mean?"

She sounded like she was questioning a suspect. I put it
down to habit, I said, "Once upon a time I might have
killed her myself. Naomi has a way of . . . inviting a pass,
then slapping the passer down hard. I really think she gets
a charge out of leaving a man horny and frustrated. This
isn't just subjective, Marion. I've heard other guys talk
about it. Still . . . it was ten years ago, and she got married
and had a little girl. So your guess is as good as mine."

The elevator came. We got in. Marion said, "I don't have
to guess. She was the only one out there, and she's a flatlander."

"So?"

She smiled. "The wound was too high. Eight, nine centimeters above the heart. Why?"

"The rim of the tub was too high."

"Right. Now, there aren't any tubs in the Belt, except in
the bubble worlds. A flatlander wouldn't expect a lunie
bathtub to stand so tall. When it came time to make her
move, Naomi couldn't see Penzler's heart. She just took her
best shot."

I shook my head. "A lunie would know how tall the tub was, but he wouldn't expect Penzler to be so short."

"He must have *seen* Penzler."

"Sure, and Naomi's seen lunie bathtubs, too." While she was mulling that, I added, "Maybe it was a Belter. You said it yourself; the only tubs in the Belt are in the bubble worlds. You spin those for an Earth gravity. Belt bathtubs are just like Earth's."

Marion grinned. "Got me."

"And we're still missing the main point. Why didn't the killer just wait till Penzler got out of the tub? If it was Naomi, she'd already been waiting most of four hours."

"Now, that is a *damn* good question," Marion said. And we parted on that note, her to her room, me to mine. I could catch two or three hours on my back before 0610.

At exactly 0610 I rang Taffy's doorbell.

"Gil! Are you alone?"

The long stretch of hall was quite empty. "At this hour, what sane man would be up?"

"Chiron, open door."

I walked in. And she was already in flight! I leaned far forward to catch her weight and managed not to bounce back into the hall. We took a long time over our first kiss. Tasting each other. By and by I noticed that she was wearing a surgeon's paper coverall. Those things are intended to be used only once.

"Can I rip this off you?"

"Be my guest."

I tore it off in handfuls, with sound effects: the roar of an unendurably frustrated male. The paper was tough. A lunie couldn't have done it. I swept her in my arms and leapt for the bed and bounced off again. Pulled my own clothes off more sedately, moved back to the bed, and had some trouble.

She whispered in my ear. "Let me dominate, okay? I've had some practice. The missionary position doesn't work at all."

"What do I have to know?"

Partly she told me, partly she showed me. We had to use our muscles to keep us together; gravity wouldn't help. We bounced. We spent considerable time above the bed. Taffy told me not to worry about falling off, and I didn't. Old and accustomed partners danced a new dance, with Taffy leading.

We rested. Then I made love to her standing up, with Taffy's strong legs wrapped around my hips, one arm out to clutch the edge of the tub. In lunar gravity that position is almost restful. And I studied her face, joyful, glowing, familiar.

We rested again. Sweat stayed where it was; it wouldn't drip. Taffy stirred in my arms and asked, "Hungry?"

"Yes!"

There was a tray on the table. Scrambled eggs, chicken wings, toast, coffee. "It may have cooled off," she said. "It had to get here before you did. Otherwise we'd have to be dressed."

We ate. I asked, "What is it with lunies? I keep hearing remarks. It's the kind of thing you'd expect in the eighteenth century, with social diseases and no contraceptives."

She nodded and swallowed and said, "Harry tried to explain it to me. People have been living on the moon for a hundred twenty years or so, but even eighty years ago there were only a few hundred. Human beings haven't really adapted biologically to having children in low gravity. Maybe someday, but for now . . . they marry early and have two or three children and never use a contraceptive at all. Two or three children and a dozen or two dozen pregnancies that don't come to term. The children are precious. It's very important who the father is."

"Uh *huh*."

"That's the official position. But there are contraceptives, and *somebody's* buying them. And long engagements are normal, and children born seven or eight months after the ceremony are also normal. I'd guess they try each other out, just like we do, but one at a time, and what they're looking for is fertility, not compatibility. And they don't talk about even that."

"Except Harry."

She nodded. "Harry likes flatlander women. Society kind of frowns on that, but Harry's too good a doctor to be fired." She grinned at me. "That's his story. He's actually damned good. And he's sterile, guaranteed. There are a fair number of men like that, and women, too. They're in a special position. Not really considered a threat, if you follow."

I wanted to know more about that relationship. I tried an oblique approach. "Would you recommend that I take a lunie lover?"

She didn't smile. "Don't fail to seduce a lunie, Gil. What I mean is, *don't fail*. Don't ask unless the answer is yes. In fact—" Now she smiled. "Don't ask. You can let yourself be seduced. Everyone knows flatlanders are easy."

"Are we?"

"Sure. Now, would you like to meet Harry McCavity? Is that what you were getting at? You'd like him, and he doesn't consider you a threat. Quite the reverse."

"What?"

"You're a good cover. You and I are roommates of long standing. Hove City society would really prefer that Harry keep his relationships purely social."

"Oh. Okay, I'd like to meet him socially. I met him officially last night. He was repairing a hole in a Belt delegate." I told her about Penzler.

She didn't like it. "Gil, if someone's shooting at offworld conference delegates, shouldn't you start wearing a mirror vest? And me, too?"

"Not to worry. They've got a suspect."

"That's a relief. The right suspect?"

"She was the only one out there." I discovered that I didn't want to talk to Taffy about Naomi. "They'll be expecting to call me in my room. And I need some sleep. When shall we twain meet again?"

"It looks like Thursday, same time, unless someone changes my schedule again."

"Same time. Lord."

"I thought you were used to my funny hours. Look, I'll leave you a message if it looks like we can get together with Harry. Lunch or dinner, okay?"

"Okay."

It was nine when I reached my room. I called the mayor's office, got his secretary, and was told the conference had been postponed for that day but that the conference room would be open for informal discussions.

Interesting. Chris was that important? But two other delegates had been up late into the night, and others could be suffering from time lag. I was just as glad they'd called it off.

I slept till noon. Then Laura Drury called. She was just going off duty, and a team of lunie police were leaving with Naomi in ten minutes.

4. THE CRATERED LANDS

I got into my suit in a hell of a hurry, then stopped and made myself go through the checkout routine. I was long out of practice. I reached the south face air lock and found the rest of the party still in sight on the road. I bounced after them.

There were seven of us: Naomi, Marion Shaeffer, me, and four tall lunie cops. The freckled redhead was Jefferson. The face above the tallest of the orange suits was also familiar. I'd seen him talking to the mayor last night at dinner.

"Alan Watson?"

"Yes, that's right. You're one of the conference delegates."

"Gil Hamilton. ARM." We shook gloves. He was a thin young man with straight black hair, a narrow nose, thick shaggy eyebrows, blunt-fingered hands as strong as mine. He couldn't make himself smile. Frightened for Naomi? The smallish painting on his chest showed an esoteric spacecraft nearing the North America nebula, all in reds and blacks.

We set off, Naomi leading. The road west was a trade road; it sometimes carried heavy equipment, up to the size of a damaged spacecraft. It was broad and smooth but not straight. Follow it far enough and you would reach the Belt Trading Post.

We had come four or five hundred yards without much conversation when Naomi said, "I turned off here. I wanted to climb that rock."

She was pointing at a faceted lump a considerable distance away. It was the tallest point around. I had first seen it glowing in darkness, lit by imminent dawn, when I had looked out my window last night.

We followed Naomi toward it. Marion asked, "Did you climb it?"

"Yes."

The sun was only six degrees up in the sky. We walked in shadow most of the time. It would have been like wading through ink but for our headlamps. The footing was chancy. Naomi stumbled as often as I did, more often than the lunies. Marion had trouble, too.

She stopped Naomi at one point where our only route of approach would round a spur of black volcanic glass. "Okay, what's around this turn?"

"I don't know," Naomi said. "It was dark; it was all different. I'm not even sure this is the way I came."

The peak was a thousand feet high and not particularly steep. It would give a good view of Hove City, I thought, but we were north of where Chris Penzler had spotted his assassin. A cop directed Naomi to climb it.

She wasn't exactly agile in unfamiliar gravity, with the inflated suit restricting her movements. But she didn't have any trouble till she was three hundred feet up. Then she started yelping. She came down dangerously fast.

"It's hot!" she complained. "It burned me right through the suit!"

"Where?" Alan Watson demanded.

"My chest and arms. It's okay now, I think, but I can't climb it in daylight. Shall I try the other side?"

Marion said, "No, skip it. Where next?"

Naomi led us south. I wondered if we would learn anything this way. Whether or not she was lying, her answer would be the same: it was dark, I don't know the moon, this probably isn't the way I came. Tentatively, she had lied already. When I'd climbed out of my tub, the peak had been sunlit for the upper hundred feet. Why had she tried to climb the sunlit side today if she'd had the chance to learn better last night?"

Of course she could have started earlier yesterday ... and climbed in total darkness. I didn't like that, either.

And I hated where she was leading us.

This was familiar territory. I had sifted it in miniature, felt its contours with my imaginary hand. I half remembered landmarks large or strange, and so, it seemed, did Naomi.

Like a hill-sized boulder that had split nicely down the middle, leaving flat planes uppermost, Naomi described it before we reached it. She pointed out one half of the split monolith and said, "I climbed up on that one. I lay on my back and looked at the stars and sometimes at Hove City. More than half the windows were dark by then. There was nice backlighting from behind, from the spaceport and the mirror works."

She moved to climb up on it, but Marion yanked her back. The orange-clad cops searched with headlamps and powerful flashlights for boot scrapes, footprints, anything Naomi might have dropped. When they gave up on the sides, Watson and Jefferson reached the top in one leap and searched that. Slanted sunlight made the lamps unnecessary.

Marion jumped up and joined them. She balanced on boot toes and fingertips and searched with her face two inches from the rock.

"Nothing," she said. "Are you sure you were in this territory?"

"I was right up there on that rock!"

Marion looked satisfied; Jefferson looked grim; Alan Watson had a haunted look. I climbed up after them, knowing.

It was roomy and almost flat. It would be a good place to stretch out and watch stars. I looked toward the city, and Chris Penzler's "tilted rock" was almost in my line of sight, assuming I had the right rock. I could look right into Chris's window around four hundred yards away. The sun made me squint. But at night that window would make a fine shooting gallery.

I thought it over for a few seconds. Then I said, "Hamilton speaking. I'd like to try a couple of things if nobody has any objection. First, I'd like to test fire a message laser."

I used Jefferson's. He showed me how to hook the transceiver cable into my helmet mike and how to aim the thing, first making sure the dimmer switch was at full dim. If you turned it up, the safety gave you five minutes and then turned it down again. Otherwise you could accidentally vaporize whoever you were trying to call. You never used full power, Jefferson explained, for anything closer than an orbiting spacecraft.

He showed me how to find and call the Watchbird One satellite, using the scope. I got a computer. It gave me a news update. Spacecraft *Chili Bird* had safely departed the Belt Trading Post for Confinement Asteroid. Sunspot activity was on the increase, but no solar flares had yet formed.

I asked Jefferson, "These things do function as weapons, don't they?"

"In an emergency, yes."

"How?"

He showed me how to turn the dimmer switch to full bright. I fired at a darkish rock. I got a half-second burst of red flame and a hole three inches deep and a quarter of an inch wide.

"Half a second isn't much of a message," I said.

So he showed me how to override the safety. "It burns

out the sender, of course, and you get just enough time to yell 'Help! Blowout!' That can be enough."

I handed it back, "Second," I said, "I'd like to go straight back to Hove City from here, and I'd like to take an escort. Officer Watson, would you care for a stroll?"

He said, "All right. See you later, Naomi, and don't worry."

She nodded jerkily, wearing the same stony expression she'd worn all this time.

We hadn't gone far when Watson said, "Operative Hamilton, we can adjust our helmet mikes so we won't disturb the others."

"I know how. Call me Gil."

"I'm Alan."

We set our radios for privacy. I said, "It finally hit me that I was missing the point. You and I aren't looking for the same killer as the rest of them. We think Naomi's not guilty, right?"

"She'd never kill a man from ambush."

"So we're looking for someone else. Sticking to Naomi's route won't give him to us. She never saw him."

He bought it. He relaxed just a little. "She can't even tell us where he wasn't. That place where she watched the stars . . . he could have come after she left. Penzler saw his killer, didn't he? Jefferson says he did."

I'd known Naomi ten years ago, but Alan Watson knew her *now*. He believed her. Could I be wrong?

I filed the question. "Penzler says he saw something, but he can't even describe the suit. Something human, past the tilted rock. So let's walk toward the tilted rock, taking our time and looking around."

We walked through pools of glare and shadow, with almost no in-between. The colors were mostly browns and grays and whites. Alan said, "I wish I knew what to look for. It's a shame she didn't lose something."

I shrugged that off. "We aren't looking for anything Naomi dropped. This is where the killer had to be. We check the high points because he had to have a view of Chris's window. We look for tracks of a vehicle or burn marks from a rocket, anything that could get him out of here before the police started looking for him. He had ten minutes or more. And look for pieces of a laser. I would have found a laser, but it could have been broken up."

"Your imaginary arm?"

Skeptical. He'd have his chance to sneer at my imaginary arm when I testified for the prosecution against Naomi.

The thought of Naomi being broken up for spare parts gave me the creeps. I could never be neutral where Naomi was concerned. But say that love and hate could add to make indifference ... say I could feel nothing for Naomi. It would *still* be like taking scissors to a George Barr painting. Vandalism.

Alan said, "That flat-topped rock where she watched the stars would have been perfect, wouldn't it?"

"Yeah. A beautiful view of Chris's window. What I don't believe is that she'd lead us there. Alan, would a lunie go sightseeing on the moon at night?"

He laughed. "A lunie can always wait two weeks. A tourist has to go home." The grim look returned. "Most tourists pick daytime. It does look funny. Dammit."

Light and shadow. All moonscape and no clues. Every time we walked into full sunlight, I had to blink against the glare. My visor took a fraction of a second to darken, and it was too long. We took the easy paths, but we stopped to climb obvious vantage points.

The silence was getting to me. I asked, "Was your father named after the city itself?"

"Oh ... partly. *The* Jacob Hovestraydt, the man who founded the city, was my great-grandfather. And he had two daughters, and one didn't have children, and the other had Dad and my three aunts. So we're the direct genetic line. Dad was practically *born* mayor. We've talked about it, how he grew up ... Hey, stay away from there. You don't know how deep it is."

I'd been about to wade through a dust pool, scuffing my

feet, looking for pieces of a laser. But he was right, of course.

I said, "I'd like another crack at the projection room. Could you get me that?"

"I think so."

"Did you ever show Naomi the projection room?"

He stopped walking. "How'd you know?"

"I just wondered."

We marched our crooked path in silence for a time. Then Alan said, "Every time some offworlder bigwig showed up, he had to meet the kid. Me. Once upon a time I told Dad I didn't like it. He said he went through the same thing when his grandfather was mayor. And his mother picked his school courses for him. Political science, air cycle engineering, ecology, economics. His first job was in the Garden. Then he was in maintenance, tending the air system."

"And you? Are you being groomed for mayor?"

"Maybe. Dad was in the police, too, for a while. I'm not sure I'll ever want to run Hovestraydt City . . . and I'm sure Dad wouldn't force me, and I'm not sure I could. I don't want to now. I want to travel. Look, Gil, we've almost reached the tilted rock. That's too close."

"I wonder. In the first place, I don't trust a Belter's sense of distance on the moon."

"Mmm . . . yes. In fact . . . the closer the killer was, the better the chance Penzler would see him. And Naomi wouldn't have, because she was farther west. He could have been just behind the rock."

"Yeah, and we'll look."

"He'd have had to be in sunlight, wouldn't he, for Penzler to see him?" Alan squatted, then leapt. Soared. Graceful as all hell. His parabola peaked at the rock's rounded tip, and he clutched it with all four limbs, then began his own investigations.

To me it seemed a precarious perch for an aspiring marksman.

From Chris's window the tilted rock had looked like an elongated egg. But the side in darkness was almost flat. I played my headlamp over it. The surface was rough and white.

I scraped my gloved fingers over it. Crumbly white stuff adhered to my fingers. It disappeared as I watched. What the hell?

"No laser parts, no footprints, no puffer tracks, nothing," Alan said. "And there's too much dust around. If he has any brains, the killer wouldn't have been walking where there's dust. Gil, we'll have to backtrack."

"I don't think so. I don't think Chris saw his killer."

"What?"

"Why would the killer be in sunlight? He'd be half-blind in the glare. It was just dawn, with most of this region in shadow. He'd have had to go *looking* for sunlight to stand in so Chris could see him. It's plain silly."

"Then what *did* he see?"

"I don't know yet. I want another look at Chris's room."

"Gil, what's your stake in this?"

"Aesthetic. She's too beautiful to be broken up." Too flippant. I tried again. "I loved her once, and I hated her once. Now she's an old friend in trouble. You?"

"I love her."

We weren't looking for clues now. The tilted rock was behind us; Penzler couldn't have seen anything here. Like the keen-eyed Indian in his forest or the street-wise mugger on his home turf, Alan Watson knew this part of the moon. He'd see anything worth seeing. To me it was all moonscape.

I did get him talking about the conference.

"Six out of ten of you are offworlders," he said. "We don't even have a voting majority. I can see why some citizens don't like that. But they're wrong. The moon is a kind of halfway house between the mud and the sky . . . between Earth and the Belt. We gain some advantages from that, but we have to keep you both satisfied, too. The organ bank problem doesn't make that any easier."

His lecturer's manner made him seem older, somehow. If he went into politics, he'd succeed at it.

"Might I ask, are these your father's views, too?"

"We've talked about it, but I'm not just quoting him." He smiled. "The last conference established the holding tanks. Even if Naomi's convicted, she still goes into a holding tank for six months. Six months to prove she's innocent, and I'm very glad of that."

"Wups. Alan, does she know that? She may be more scared than she has to be."

"Oh, good lord!" He was horrified.

"So you never told her. So make an opportunity. Can she have visitors?"

"She's in her own room with the phone turned off and the door geared to reject her voice. I'm sure a policeman could visit her. I just didn't think. The trial's set for day after tomorrow, and she thinks that's it, the end. I'll tell her, Gil. Gil, what are you doing?"

We had reached Hovestraydt City, and I was hard up against Chris Penzler's window. I said, "Checking the scene of the crime from the other side, kid."

I noted with approval that I was in the fields of three cameras. Our clumsy killer might conceivably want to plant a small bomb on the window.

I peered in. Chris was on his back on the bed, covered with foam plastic from chin to navel and armpit to armpit. The mobile autodoc was standing above him like a polished steel nursemaid.

"Alan, come here a second. Do you see anything like a miniature hologram in there? On a wall or the table?"

"No."

"Neither do I. Dammit."

"Why?"

"Maybe it was moved. I still can't see our half-competent marksman sticking his face into sunlight, blinding himself, just before he fired. I thought maybe Chris had a holo of his mother or someone on the wall and saw it reflected in the window just before he got shot. But there's nothing."

"No."

The door opened and closed behind Harry McCavity. The doctor prodded his unconscious patient for a bit, then moved to the autodoc screen and typed, read the screen for a bit, typed again ... ran his hands through his fluffy brown hair in a swift gesture that changed nothing ... turned around, and jumped a yard in the air when he saw faces peering in the window.

I gestured in a curve to the left. *We'll come through the air lock.* He glared and gestured back. *Up Uranus!*

A few minutes later we knocked at the door, and he let us in. "We were looking around," Alan said lamely.

"For what?" McCavity demanded.

I said, "A hologram portrait. My idea. Have you seen anything that might fit?"

"No."

"It's important."

"No!"

"Can he answer questions?" I waved at Chris Penzler.

"No. Let him alone; he's doing fine. He'll be mobile tomorrow ... not comfortable but mobile. Ask him then. Gil, are you booked for dinner?"

"No. What time do you like?"

"Say half an hour. We can check with Ms. Grimes, see if she's off duty. Perhaps she can join us."

5. THE CONFERENCE TABLE

We'd chosen a table in a far corner of the dining level. Lunie diners tended to cluster around the Garden. We could barely see the Garden, and nobody was in eavesdropping distance.

"It isn't just that we aren't man and wife," McCavity said, stabbing the air with splay-ended chopsticks. "We can't even keep the same hours. We enjoy each other ... don't we?"

Taffy nodded happily.

"I need constant reassurance, my dear. Gil, we enjoy each other, but when we see each other, it's generally over an open patient. I'm glad for Taffy that you're here. Isn't this kind of thing supposed to be normal on Earth?"

"Well," I said, "it's normal where I've lived . . . California, Kansas, Australia . . . Over most of the Earth we tend to keep recreational sex separate from having children. There are the Fertility Laws, of course. The government doesn't tell people *how* to use their birthrights, but we do check the baby's tissue rejection spectrum to see *which* father has used up a birthright. Don't get the idea that Earth is all one culture. The Arabs are back to *harems*, for God's sake, and so were the Mormons, for a while."

"Harems? What about the birthrights?"

"The harems are recreation as far as the sheikh is concerned, and of course he uses up his own birthrights. When they're gone, the ladies take sperm from some healthy genius with an unlimited birthright and the right skin color, and the sheikh raises the children as the next generation of aristocrats."

Harry ate while he thought. Then, "It sounds wonderful, by Allah! But for us, having children is a big thing. We tend to stay faithful. I'm the freak. And I know of a lunie who fathered a child for two good friends . . . but I could maybe get killed for naming them."

I said, "Okay, we're a ménage à at least trois. But you would like it noised abroad that Taffy and I are steady roommates."

"It would be convenient."

"Would it be convenient for *me*? Harry, I gather lunies don't like that sort of thing. There are four lunie delegates in the conference. I can't alienate them."

Taffy was frowning. "Futz! I hadn't thought of that."

Harry said, "I did. Gil, it'll *help* you. What the lunie citizen *really* wants to know is that you aren't running around compromising the honor of lunie women."

I looked at Taffy. She said, "I think he's right. I can't swear to it."

"Okay."

We ate. It was mostly vegetables, fresh, with good variety. I had almost finished a side dish, beef with onions and green pepper over rice, before I wondered. Beef?

I looked up into Harry's grin. "Imported," he said, and laughed as my jaw dropped. "No, not from Earth! Can you imagine the delta-V? Imported from Tycho. They've got an underground bubble big enough to graze cattle. It costs like blazes, of course. We're fairly wealthy here."

Dessert was strawberry shortcake with whipped cream from Tycho. The coffee *was* imported from Earth, but freeze-dried. I wondered if they saved anything that way, given that the water in coffee beans had to be imported anyway ... then kicked myself. Lunies don't import water. They import hydrogen. They run the hydrogen past heated oxygen-bearing rock to get water vapor.

So I sipped my coffee and asked, "May we talk business?"

"None of us are squeamish," McCavity said.

"The wound, then. Would a layer of bathwater spread the beam that much?"

"I don't know. Nobody knows. It's never happened before."

"Your best guess, then."

"Gil, it had to be enough, unless you've got another explanation."

"Mmm ... there was a case in Warsaw where a killer put a dot of oil over the aperture of a laser. The beam was supposed to spread a little, just enough that the police couldn't identify the weapon. It would have worked fine if he hadn't got drunk and bragged about it."

McCavity shrugged. "Not here. Any damn fool would *guess* it was a message laser."

"We know the beam spread. We're speculating."

Harry's eyes went distant and dreamy. "Would the oil vaporize?"

"Sure. Instantly."

"The beam would constrict in midburn. That would fit. The hole in Penzler's chest looked like the beam changed width in the middle of the burn."

"It constricted?"

"It constricted, or expanded, or there's something we haven't thought of."

"Futz. Okay. Do you know Naomi Mitchison?"

"Vaguely." Harry seemed to withdraw a little.

"Not intimately?"

"No."

Taffy was looking at him. We waited.

"I grew up here," Harry said abruptly. "I *never* make proposals to a woman unless I have reason to think they'll be accepted. Okay, I must have read the signals wrong. She reacted like an insulted married lunie woman! So I apologized and went away, and we haven't spoken since. You're right; flatlanders aren't all the same. A week ago I would have said we were friends. Now . . . no, I don't know the lady."

"Do you hate her?"

"What? No."

Taffy said, "Maybe your killer doesn't care if Penzler lives or dies. Maybe it's Naomi he wants to hurt."

I mulled that. "I don't like it. First, how would he know he could make it stick? There *might* have been someone else out there. Second, it gives us a whole damn *city* full of suspects." I noticed, or imagined, Harry's uneasiness. "Not you, Harry. You sweated blood to save Chris. It would have been trivial to kill him while the 'doc was cutting him up."

Harry grinned. "So what? It was already an organ bank crime for Naomi."

"Yes, but he saw something. He might remember more."

Taffy asked, "Who else wouldn't want to frame Naomi?"

"I'm really not taking the idea too seriously," I said, "but I guess I'd want to know who she insulted. Who made passes and got slapped down and who took it badly."

Harry said, "You won't find many lunie suspects."

"The men are too careful?"

"That, and— No offense, my dear, but Naomi isn't beautiful by lunie standards. She's stocky."

"What," Taffy wondered, "does that make me?"

Harry grinned at her. "Stocky. I told you I was a freak."

She grinned back at that tall, narrow offshoot of human stock . . . and I found myself grinning, too. They did get along. It was a pleasure to watch them.

We broke it up soon afterward. Taffy was on duty, and I needed my sleep.

The city hall complex was four stories deep, with the mayor's office on the ground level. A room on the second level was reserved for the conference.

I got there at 0800. Eight-foot-tall Bertha Carmody was in animated discussion with a small, birdlike Belt woman in late middle age. They broke off long enough to introduce the stranger: Hildegarde Quifting, Fourth Speaker for the Belt Government.

Chris Penzler was in a bulky armchair equipped with safety straps and a ground-effect skirt. Soft foam covered his chest. He seemed to be brooding on his wrongs.

I said hello anyway. He looked up. "You'll find coffee and rolls on the side table," he said, and tried to wave in the right direction. "Ow!"

"Hurts?"

"Yah."

I got coffee in a small-mouthed bottle with a foam plastic sleeve. Other delegates trickled in until we were all present.

A lunie I hadn't met, Charles Ward of Copernicus, moved to elect a chairman, then nominated Bertha Carmody of Tycho Dome. With four lunies out of ten delegates, the chairman was bound to be a lunie, so I voted for Bertha. So did everybody else. The lunies seemed surprised at their easy victory. But Bertha was a good choice; she had the loudest voice among us.

We spent the morning covering old ground.

Belt and moon and United Nations each had its own ax to grind. Officially the moon was a satellite of Earth and was subject to United Nations law, in which even minor crimes carried the death penalty: laws designed not only to punish the guilty but also to supply transplant organs to the innocent voting public.

The ethical gap between Earth and Belt was as vast as the physical gap. On Earth the hospitals had been supplied by criminals for well over a hundred years. When Luke Garner was young the death penalty had been revived for murder, kidnapping, treason, and the like. As medical techniques had improved and spread to the have-not nations, demands on the public organ banks had grown. The death penalty was imposed for armed robbery, rape, burglary. A plea of insanity became worthless. Eventually felons died for income tax evasion or driving while high on funny chemicals.

Belt hospitals kept organ banks, but there were major differences. The Belt used fewer transplants. Belters tend to let evolution take care of the careless ones; they are not egalitarians. Space accidents don't tend to leave medical cases, anyway. The Belt didn't perform its own executions. Up to twenty years ago their practice had been to ship convicts to Earth and buy the organs back. In theory, their law would not be affected by the flatlanders' greed for life.

The moon's shallower gravity well made it a far better choice as the Belt's place of execution.

So the first conference was called, and strange were the results.

There had been major compromises at the conference of 2105. The biggest was the holding tanks. They were unique. The Belt had insisted that they be built, and the UN had capitulated. The holding tanks would hold a convict inactivated, but alive and healthy, for six months. If new evidence was found, the convict could be revived.

Twenty years later that solution was under fire.

Hildegarde Quifting wanted a rundown on the past

twenty years of lunar jurisprudence. In particular, had the holding tanks ever been forced to disgorge a living felon?

Charles Ward obliged. He was six-eleven or so, in his late thirties, a frail dark man with a receding hairline. In a colorless voice he told us that over the past twenty years some six thousand felons had passed through the lunar courts and hospitals. Just under a thousand were lunies. The Belt felons had been convicted by Belt courts; lunar hospitals served only as execution grounds. No conviction had yet been reversed.

Ward represented Copernicus Dome, actually a complex of domes plus a metals mine, the site of one of the moon's three major hospital complexes. Ward had come armed with graphs and maps and statistics. Average of 120 executions a year, mostly Belters shipped in via the Belt Trading Post and the mass driver in Grimalde Crater. The hospital took nearly four hundred patients a year, mostly lunies, the numbers rising over the years as the lunar population increased. I listened carefully. Copernicus was where Naomi would be sent if she was convicted.

Lunch was delivered around noon. We talked in low voices while we ate, until Carmody called us to order. At once Marion Shaeffer demanded to know whether the lunar hospitals shipped as much transplant material out as came to them through the Belt courts.

Ward answered, a bit superciliously, that Belt transplants tended to be not quite the right shape, that bones and muscles from Belter arms and legs, for instance, would be drastically too short for a lunie. This seemed obvious enough, but it wasn't what Marion meant. She wanted to know how much transplant material the moon shipped to Earth.

Quite a lot.

The conference was polarizing. Belters and flatlanders were opposite poles, with the lunies in the middle. To frail old Hildegarde Quifting, our approach to the organ bank problem was monstrous: death penalties imposed at every opportunity to keep the voting citizens alive and healthy. To Jabez Stone of the General Assembly, a criminal was lucky to redeem himself in *any* way, and Belters need not act so damn superior. When a man orders a steak, a steer must be mutilated, then murdered. How many transplants were keeping Quifting alive?

Carmody ruled that out of order. Quifting insisted on answering it anyway. She had *never* had a transplant, she said belligerently. I noticed uncomfortable expressions among the delegates. Maybe they noticed mine.

It was a long session. The break for dinner came none too soon.

I fell in beside Chris Penzler's softly whispering air-cushion chair. "You didn't say much. Are you up to this?"

"Oh, I'm up to it." He smiled a passable smile that faded. "I feel mortal," he said. "Having a hole shot through him can make a man think. I could *die*. I have one daughter. I never had time for more; I was too busy making money, making a career, and then ... there was a solar flare while I was en route to Mercury, and now I'm sterile. When I die, she'll be all that's left of me. Almost."

I said, "The quality of their lives is as important as their number."

Trite, but he nodded thoughtfully. Then, "Somebody hates me enough to kill me."

"Does Naomi Mitchison hate you that much?"

He scowled. "She has no reason. Oh, she's strange enough, and she doesn't like me, but ... I wish I knew. I hope to God it's her."

Of course. If it wasn't Naomi, then the clumsy killer was still loose.

I asked, "Do you keep holograms in your room? Or statues of any kind?"

He stared. "No."

"Futz. Is your phone working all right?"

"Yah, it's working well. Why?"

"Just a thought. Now, you said you were looking past a big tilted rock when you saw somebody. Which side of the rock?"

"I don't remember." He considered. "That's very strange. I *don't* remember. *Mayor Hove?*" he bellowed.

Hove was just coming up a spiral stairwell at the end of the hall. He turned, startled. "Hello, Chris, Gil. How's the conference going?"

I said, "There's a certain amount of friction—"

Chris interrupted. "Can you let us into your office?"

"Of course. Why?"

"I want to look out the window." He seemed feverishly excited.

The mayor shrugged. He led the way upstairs.

His office was big, roomy. The computer terminal built into the desk hooked into the hologram wall and into two more screens. There was a foot and a half of keyboard with a rolltop cover. A hologram wall looked out on Jovian storms, seen from closer than Amalthea, swirling like a million shades of paint poured into a whirlpool. Endless storms big enough to swallow the Earth. Hovestraydt Watson must have a big ego, I thought. How else could he live and work next to *that*?

The picture window looked south into a blazing moonscape. Chris edged as close as he could to the window. "I can't see it. We'll have to go to my room."

"What's it all about?" the mayor asked.

"I was looking past a large boulder just before the beam burned me. I must have seen the killer to one side or the other, but I can't—"

"Are you sure he wasn't closer than the rock?"

Penzler screwed his eyes shut. After a moment he said, "Almost. He'd have to be a midget to show that small, that close. I wish I could be sure."

I said, "Chris, I thought maybe you saw a reflection from a small hologram in your room or maybe from the phone screen. Is that possible?"

Chris shrugged. Mayor Hove said, "The phone would have to be on, wouldn't it? It would have been facing Chris if it was working right. Chris, did you call anyone while you were in the tub?"

"No. And my phone system is working."

So we went down the hall to Chris's room, all three of us. Chris pointed out the tilted rock Alan Watson and I had investigated. We studied it for a good minute before he said, "I simply cannot remember. But he was almost twice as far as the rock."

I called from my room. "I want to talk to Naomi Mitchison," I told the desk sergeant, "preferably in person."

He looked at me. "You're not her lawyer."

"I didn't claim to be."

He took his time thinking it over. "I'll put you through to her lawyer." He rang, waited, then said, "Mr. Boone isn't there. His answering bug says he's in conference with a client."

"So let me talk to them both."

He went into a brown study. I said, "Then put me through to Sergeant Drury, if *that's* possible."

His relief showed. He made the call. The phone screen went blank, and Laura Drury's voice said, "Just a minute. Gil Hamilton, isn't it?"

"Yes. I'm trying to get permission to talk to Ms. Mitchison. The desk sergeant is giving me static."

"Let's see, her lawyer is supposed to be with her. I'll call him on her phone. He's a public defender, Artemus Boone."

"Lunie?"

"Yes. Did you learn anything from going over her course?"

"Nothing conclusive."

The screen lighted. Laura Drury was just completing the act of zipping up a pale gold jumpsuit. I gathered the picture had caught her a split second too soon. The zipper had hesitated at her bosom, and well it might. She looked flustered; she tugged hard; the zipper went up. I repressed a smile.

"Jefferson thinks she was lying," she said, "but he can't tell what she was lying about."

I thought so, too. "I'd like to know more about that trek

myself," I said. "I have to go through this Boone, is that right? If you can't convince him, may I talk to him myself? I'd like to help her."

"I'll find out. Stand by." She put me on hold.

She called back a minute later. "They won't see you. They won't talk to you, either. I'm sorry."

"Futz! Is that just her lawyer's word?"

"I think he talked to her first, off camera."

"Thanks, Laura." I called the phone off. I debated schemes for getting through to her anyway and gave up on them. I didn't really have a lot to say to Naomi.

6. THE LUNAR LAW

The committee met again at 0800. I'd had breakfast with Taffy, but the rest of us were sipping and munching when Bertha Carmody called us to order.

Charles Ward asked for the floor. "It strikes me that our differences are all concerned with matters of the lunar law and the manner in which it is enforced. Is this the case?"

He got noises signifying agreement. "Then let me remind you all," said that frail dark beanpole, "that the trial of Naomi Mitchison for the attempted murder of Chris Penzler begins in one hour. Some of us are likely to be called as witnesses. Mr. Penzler, in particular, is still recovering from his wounds. His mind is likely to be on the trial."

Chris nodded and winced in pain. "You may be right. I wouldn't be concentrating."

Ward spread his hands wide. "Then in the interests of actually observing lunar justice in action, why don't we all adjourn to the courtroom?"

We voted eight to two in favor. We adjourned to the courtroom.

The courtroom was a place of beauty. Its design was standard: high podium for the judge, rails separating the spectators from the accused and the jury. It was the thousand-year-old English courtroom design, originally intended to protect the accused from the victim's family. But one whole wall was glass, and it overlooked the Garden.

Mirrors caught the raw lunar sunlight and diffused it down upon dozens of ledges of plants, down along the great redwood to its long, tangled roots. The air was full of wings. No plant grew that didn't have a use, but the prettiest plants, artichokes and apple trees and so forth, were the most accessible, and the dancing fountains weren't only for irrigation, and the winding paths weren't only for the farmers. The Garden was designed for pleasure.

I thought how terrible it must be to look out on the Garden and wait to be condemned to death.

Naomi was watching the Garden. Her golden hair was piled high in a coiled arrangement that must have represented hours of work. She had taken particular care with dress and cosmetics. The butterfly tattoo was gone. She seemed composed, with terror hiding underneath. When her lunie lawyer whispered to her, her answers were curt. She must know that if she started screaming, they would fill her full of tranquilizers.

Was she guilty? My judgment would never be impartial where Naomi was concerned.

Chris Penzler thought she was. He watched Naomi's eyes while he gave his testimony. "I was taking a bath. I stood up and reached for a towel. I thought I saw something outside the window, a man or a woman. Then there was a flare of red light. It struck me in the chest, threw me back in the water, and knocked me unconscious."

The prosecuting lawyer was a pale blond woman over seven feet tall, massing no more than I do. She had an elfish triangular face, quite lovely, quite perfect, and quite without human weakness. She asked, "What color was the suit? Did it have markings on it?"

Penzler shook his head. "I didn't have time to see."

"But you saw only one person."

"Yes," he said, and looked at Naomi.

She probed. "Was it a local? We tend to be taller and thinner."

Chris didn't laugh, though others did. "I don't know. It was less than a second, then ... it was like being run through with a red-hot jousting lance."

"How far away?"

"Three to four hundred meters. I can't judge distances here."

"Would Naomi Mitchison have any reason to hate you?"

"I've wondered about that." Chris hesitated, then said, "Four years ago Mrs. Mitchison applied for emigration to the Belt. Her application was turned down." Again he hesitated. "By me."

Naomi's surprise and anger were obvious.

Prosecution asked, "Why?"

"I knew her. She wasn't qualified. The Belt environment kills careless people. She would have been a danger to herself and everyone around her." Chris Penzler's ears and neck were quite pink.

Prosecution was through with him. Naomi's lawyer cross-examined him briefly. "You say you knew Mrs. Mitchison. How well?"

"I knew Naomi and Itch Mitchison briefly, five years ago, when I was on Earth. We attended a few parties together. Itch wanted to know about buying mining stocks, and I got him some details."

Naomi was moving her lips without sound. I read the words on her lips: *Liar, liar.*

"You believe you saw your assassin out on the moon. Could you be mistaken, or could you have missed others out there?"

Chris laughed. "I saw a human shape blazing against the dark. It was *night on the moon*! There could have been an army hidden in the shadows. For that matter, perhaps I only saw a pattern of reflections. I only saw it for a split second, then *bang*."

Prosecution dismissed Chris and called a lunie cop I didn't know. He testified that there was indeed a message laser missing from the weapons room. Defense tried to get him to say that the door would open only to the police.

What the cop said was that the lock responded to voice and retina prints and that it was governed by the Hovestraydt City computer, the same one that operated every door and safe lock in the city, not to mention the water and air.

Prosecution then asked that Naomi's records, beamed from Earth, be read into the record. I remembered: Naomi had been a computer programmer.

The elf woman turned with floating grace in lunar gravity. "Call Gilbert Hamilton."

I was aware that I moved to the witness chair with a flat-lander's clumsiness, treading air and half falling at every step.

"Your name and occupation?"

"Gilbert Gilgamesh Hamilton. I'm an ARM."

"Are you here on the moon in that capacity?"

"It's not my regular beat," I said, and got suppressed laughter. "I'm here for the Conference to Review Lunar Law."

She didn't need to go into that. The judge and three jurors were all lunies; they'd have been following the conference via the boob cube. She led me through the details of Tuesday night: the midnight call, the scene in Penzler's room, the trek to the projection room.

Then she asked, "Are you sometimes called Gil the Arm?"

"Yes."

"Why?"

"I've got an imaginary arm." I had to smile at the baffled looks. I explained, hoping I didn't sound too glib.

"Returning to the projection room," she said. "Did you search the landscape in an attempt to find any suspect who might have been overlooked?"

"For a suspect or for a discarded weapon, yes."

"In what fashion did you search?"

"I ran my imaginary fingers through the projected moon-scape." There was a whisper of giggling from the audience. I'd expected that. "I sifted shadows, dust pools, anything big enough to hide a message laser."

"Or a human being? Would you have found a human being, or were you, let us say, tuned only to the shape and feel of a message laser?"

"I'd have found a human being."

She turned me over to defense.

Artemus Boone stood seven feet plus, with craggy features, a full black beard, and thick black hair. To me he looked like a wandering ghoul, but I was biased. The lunie jurors might be seeing an elongated Abe Lincoln.

"You came for the Conference to Review Lunar Law. When did it begin?"

"Yesterday."

"Have you revised many of our laws yet?" He'd decided I was an adverse witness.

"We haven't had time to revise anything," I said.

"Not even regarding the holding tanks?"

Hey, weren't our doings supposed to be secret? But nobody objected. I said, "That one may never be settled."

"How were you chosen to represent the United Nations viewpoint, Mr. Hamilton?"

"I was a Belt miner for seven years. Now I'm an ARM. It gives me two of the three crucial viewpoints. I'm picking up the lunie viewpoint as best I can."

"As best you can," Boone said dubiously. "Well, then. The pleasantly convenient manner in which Naomi Mitchison has supplied us with exactly one suspect may have led us to overlook something. You were present when she was brought in. Was she carrying a weapon?"

"No."

"You say you searched for a message laser. Just how much imaginary moonscape did you run your imaginary fingers through?"

"I searched the badlands west of the city, the area Chris Penzler could have seen from his bathtub. I searched as far as the western peaks and some of the far slopes."

"You found no weapon?"

"None."

"Psychic powers have always been undependable,

haven't they? Science was reluctant even to recognize their existence, and the law was slow in allowing psychics to testify. Tell me, Mr. Hamilton: If your unusual talent missed finding a message laser, could you not have overlooked a man?"

"It's possible, certainly."

Defense was through with me. The cold-eyed elf woman asked me, "What if the gun had been broken up and the pieces discarded? Would you have found it?"

"I don't know."

They let me go, and I sat down.

Prosecution called an expert witness, an oriental-seeming man who turned out to be a lunie cop. He was actually shorter than I am. He testified that he had examined Naomi's pressure suit and found it to be working satisfactorily. In the course of tests he had worn the suit outside. "It was a tight fit," he said.

"Did you notice anything else?"

"I noticed the smell. The suit is some years old, and the molecular filter badly needs cleaning. After some hours of wear certain fatigue poisons build up in the recycled air, and it begins to smell."

They called Octavia Budrys, and I started to catch on.

"The police handed me a pressure suit," she said, "and told me to gear up. I did. I suppose they chose me because I'm not used to space. I barely know how to put on a pressure suit."

"Did you notice anything?"

"Yes, there was a faint chemical smell, not so much unpleasant as, well, ominous. I would have had it repaired before I tried to wear it outside."

The killer fired as soon as Chris Penzler stood up in his tub. He'd already waited a good long while. Why not wait a moment longer while Penzler got out?

Because the smell in Naomi Mitchison's suit made her think her air supply was going bad. She was afraid to wait.

I wasn't convinced. Any given killer might have lost patience, waiting in lunar discomfort while Chris wallowed in his tub. But it was a point against Naomi.

The court broke for lunch. After lunch the defense called Naomi Mitchison.

Boone kept it short. He asked Naomi if she had stolen a message laser and tried to kill Chris Penzler with it. She swore she hadn't. He asked her what she was doing during the period in question. She told the court more or less what she'd told us, adding details. She swore that she had never had any reason to dislike Chris Penzler until now.

Boone mentioned that he might have further questions and turned her over to the prosecution.

The elf woman did not waste our time.

"On September 6, 2121, did you apply for emigration to the asteroid belt society?"

"I did."

"Why?"

"Things had gone all wrong," Naomi said. "I wanted out."

"How did they go wrong?"

"My husband tried to kill me. I got to one of the bathrooms, locked the door, and went out the window. He killed our little girl and then himself. That was in June."

"Why did he do it?"

"I don't know. I've thought about it. I don't know."

"Let me see if I can help," the elf woman said. "The records show that Itch Mitchison was a professional comedian. The basis of his humor was an image that used to be called macho: a man who expects sexual exclusivity from his woman and who expects of himself unlimited potency and attractiveness to women. Was that the case?"

"More or less."

"What was he like in his private life?"

"Pretty much the same. Some of that was a put-on, but I think that's the way he was."

"You had a little girl?"

"Miranda. Born January 4, 2117. She was four and a half years old when Itch killed her." Her calm had cracked.

"Had you and your husband applied for a second child?"

"Yes. But by then Itch's grandmother was in the organ banks. She . . . is this necessary?"

"No. It will be read into the record."

"Just say she went crazy, then. The Fertility Board decided it was congenital. They had his record of asthma trouble, childhood diseases . . . The upshot was that I could have children but Itch couldn't, and he bloody well didn't want me to. We talked about my using artificial insemination. He got terribly angry. That old macho image wasn't just about seduction; did you know that?" Brittle laughter. "When you sire a *lot* of babies, then you're macho."

"Was your love life affected by these developments?"

"It was killed dead. And he did have that congenital tendency. Eventually he . . . he snapped."

"Three months later you applied to the Belt."

"Yes."

"And Chris Penzler blocked you."

"I didn't know that. I never had reason to hate Chris Penzler," she said. "I didn't know why my application was turned down. But that vindictive bastard had reason to hate me! He made a pass at me once, and I slapped him down good!"

"Physically? Did you actually strike him?"

"No, of course not. I told him to go to hell. I told him that if he ever came near me again I'd tell Itch. Itch would have knocked him silly. That's macho, too."

I guessed she'd made a point in her favor. Lunies wouldn't be familiar with open marriages.

The elf woman thought differently. "Very well, Mr. Penzler made indecent proposals to you, a married woman. Surely that might be reason for you to hate and despise him? Especially after what later happened to your marriage."

Naomi shook her head. "He didn't cause that."

The prosecution dismissed her and called Alan Watson.

* * *

Of the team that had tried to follow Naomi's ill-timed attempt to play tourist, four were called as witnesses. They did Naomi little good. Naomi had led them straight to the scene of the crime. Her knowledge of the terrain was spotty at best. The best reason for believing her was that she would have had to be crazy to lie.

I ate dinner alone and went back to my room. It was my mind that was exhausted; I'd had no exercise, yet I felt like sleeping for a week. But I checked my phone before I dropped off.

I had messages from Taffy and from Desiree Porter.

Taffy and Harry were both free Friday. They planned to explore the shops of the Belt Trading Post. Would I like to join them? Feel free to add a friend, female preferred. I phoned back, but Taffy wasn't in and neither was Harry. I left a message: Sorry, I was tied up in the conference and a murder trial.

I tried to call Naomi's room. Her phone refused my call. I wasn't up to fighting with Artemus Boone.

And I didn't want to talk to a newstaper. I called off the lights and flopped back. And the phone said, "Phone call, Mr. Hamilton. Pho—"

"Chiron, answer phone."

Tom Reinecke was standing behind the seated Desiree, their faces level. It was a nice effect, and they knew it. I said, "What do you two want?"

"News," Desiree said. "Are you getting anywhere with the conference?"

"Secret. Anyway, we postponed it."

"We heard that. Do you think Naomi Mitchison will be convicted?"

"Up to the jury."

"You're a big help."

Tom cut in smoothly. "It's the speed of the trial that impressed us. Why do you suppose it went so fast?"

"Oh, hell." I was fully awake. "They think they've got a locked room murder. One suspect, locked out on the moon.

If they could eliminate Naomi, they'd invent themselves a real problem. *No* suspects. So they aren't really trying."

"How would you go about it?" Tom asked, while Desiree was saying, "Would you change the law?"

They'd caught me half asleep and gotten me talking. It served me right. "Changing the law wouldn't make anything different. How would I get her off? I'd prove she wasn't there, or I'd prove someone else was, or maybe I'd prove the killer wasn't where we thought he was."

Tom asked, "How would you do that?"

"I'm tired. Go away and leave me alone."

Desiree asked, "Is she guilty?"

"Chiron, phone off. No calls for eight hours."

I didn't know.

Getting to sleep took a long time.

7. LAST NIGHT AND MORNING AFTER

We discussed the trial over our rolls and coffee next morning. Belters and flatlanders both expressed surprise at its speed and at the number of jurors.

The lunies were affronted. They asserted that the accused's agony of anticipation should be as brief as possible. As for the jury, the moon had never had a large population with vast leisure. Three were enough. A larger jury would only get tangled in a dozen different viewpoints, like any committee. Like our own.

It got rather heated.

Chris Penzler was out of his travel chair, but foam bandaging still bulked out his shirt, and he moved like an old man. He wasn't inclined to join the discussions. Neither was I. Once I tried to suggest that the length of a trial should depend on the complexity of the case. Nobody much liked that, and in fact Marion Shaeffer insisted that I was biased in the accused's favor. I dropped it.

Presently Bertha Carmody called us to order, said a few words intended to soothe ruffled feelings, and adjourned us to the courtroom.

* * *

I wasn't called again. Chris Penzler was. He testified at length as to his relationship to Itch and Naomi on Earth.

He said he had seen Naomi when she had arrived at Hovestraydt City. She had given him a cold glare, and he had returned it, and they had avoided each other since. He repeated that he couldn't describe what he saw before he was shot. Lunie, Belter, flatlander: he couldn't say.

He didn't seem to be trying to hurt Naomi. It was as if he were trying to work out a puzzle with the court's help.

Defense called Dr. Harry McCavity, who testified that from the nature of the wound, the beam must have spread abnormally. Asked to agree that something other than a message laser had been used—something cobbled together by an amateur, for instance, so that it didn't collimate very well—McCavity dithered. The hole in Penzler was not *that* much too big. And, damn him, he raised my suggestion of a drop of oil on the aperture.

They wrapped it up faster than I would have believed.

At eleven hundred the elf woman started her summing up. She pointed out that Naomi had motive, method, and opportunity.

Jurisprudence did not require that motive be proved (I had wondered if that was true in lunar law), but Naomi had motive enough. Circumstances had struck Naomi a terrible blow; she had made a half-mad attempt to escape an intolerable environment; Chris Penzler had blocked it for his own motives. Prosecution made no excuse for Penzler, but his vindictive act had been the straw that broke her mind.

Method? Naomi had been a top computer programmer. Breaking the code of the Hovestraydt City computer wouldn't be easy, but her needs were not great. She needed only to enter a computer-guarded gun room without leaving a record in the computer memory.

Opportunity? Someone had fired at Penzler from the badlands west of Hovestraydt City. Penzler had seen her; a known psychic had testified that nobody else was in the vicinity. Had Naomi Mitchison fired that beam? Who else?

During his own summing up Boone made a big thing of
the missing weapon. The jury must disregard Gil "the
Arm's" testimony as to the absence of other suspects or ac-
cept that there was no weapon, either, and thus no murder.
The nature of the wound indicated that the weapon was
homemade, using skills Naomi Mitchison didn't have. Gil
Hamilton's talent had missed it and the killer, too.

Prosecution's counterargument was concise. There had
been a laser. Ignore the nature of both weapon and
would-be killer; if Hamilton couldn't find it, the weapon
must have been broken up. There were dust pools to hide
the parts. Jury must disregard the absence of the laser and
consider the presence of a suspect caught out on the moon
with an air system going sour.

By shortly after noon the judge was instructing the jury.
By thirteen hundred the jury had retired.

We straggled off to lunch. I wasn't hungry, of course, but
I managed to get Bertha Carmody talking around her sandwich.

"I wonder if they've really got enough information to
make a decision," I ventured. "The summing up seemed so
quick."

"They've got everything they need," Bertha said.
"They've got a computer with access to all the records of
the trial, dossiers for everyone who was so much as mentioned, and anything in the city library. If a point of law
comes up, they can call the judge day or night until they
bring in a verdict. What more do they need?"

They needed to have been in love with Naomi
Mitchison.

I couldn't concentrate during the afternoon session. I was
trying to outguess a jury several floors away. Talk flowed
past me . . .

"I wonder if you're not a bit quick to convict," Octavia
Budrys said, "knowing that a conviction can be reversed."

"You've watched a trial," Bertha Carmody said. "Did
you have any quarrel with the proceedings?"

"Only that it was so quick. I'll admit that the case seems open and shut. What will happen to her now?"

The delegate from Clavius said, "We've been through that. She'll spend six months in the holding tank. It's the same technology used on the slowboats, the interstellar starships, and it's quite safe. Then, barring a reversal, she'll be broken up."

"She won't be touched until then?"

"Barring an emergency, no."

"What does the lunar law call an emergency?"

That was the question that snapped me wide awake.

Ward gave us details. There *had* been emergencies. Six years ago a quake had ripped one of the domes open at Copernicus. The doctors had used everything they could get their hands on, including holding tanks. They'd preserved the felons' central nervous systems until their grace time was up. They'd done the same after the Blowout of eighteen years ago. Two years ago there was a patient whose odd tissue rejection patterns matched a holding tank felon's . . .

Rare and unlikely events. Yeah. Maybe we didn't really have six months.

There were calls waiting on my phone from Sergeant Laura Drury and Artemus Boone. I took Drury's call first.

She was sitting cross-legged on a bed, quite naked. I hadn't thought lunies were that casual. Naked, she was a sheer delight: brown hair three feet long floating in the room's air currents; a long, slender, graceful body with lines of hard muscle; heavy breasts that floated, too; and legs that went on forever. But her words drove all prurient thoughts out of my mind.

"Gil, forgive the voice-only. I called to tell you the jury's come back," she said. "I thought you should hear it from someone you know. It's a conviction. She'll be flown to Copernicus tomorrow morning. I'm sorry."

There was no shock. I'd been expecting it.

The phone asked, "Will there be a reply?"

"Chiron, record reply. Thanks for calling, Laura. I appreciate it. Chiron, phone off."

I stared out the window for a minute before I remembered the other call.

The black-bearded lawyer was seated behind an ancient computer terminal in an equally ancient windowless office. His message was short. "My client has asked me to ask you to call her. Her number is two-seven-one-one. You may have to get it through the police. I apologize for refusing your calls earlier, but in my judgment it was best."

Her timing was silly. The trial was over. Oh, well. "Chiron, phone, call two-seven-one-one."

"Please identify yourself."

"Gilbert Hamilton."

I waited while the city computer compared voice prints, while it called Naomi's room, while Naomi—"Gil! Hello!"

She looked awful. She looked like a once-lovely woman coming out of a year on the wire. Her gaiety was a brittle mask. I said, "Hello. Isn't your timing a little off? I might have been able to do something."

She brushed it off. "Gil, will you spend my last night with me? We used to be good friends, and I don't want to be alone."

I would have preferred a night on the rack. "There's Alan Watson. There's your lawyer."

"I've seen enough of Artemus Boone to last—Gil, he's all tied up in my mind with the trial. Please?" She hadn't even mentioned Alan.

"I'll call you back," I said.

A last night with Naomi. The thought terrified me.

Taffy wasn't answering her phone. I tried Harry McCavity's room and got Harry.

"She's in a brush-up class on trace element dietary deficiencies," he said. "I took it last year. Flatlanders don't need it except in places like Brazil. What's up?"

"Naomi Mitchison's been convicted."

"Is she guilty?"

"For all I know. She's been lying about *something*. She wants me to spend her last night with her."

"Well? You're old friends, aren't you?"

"How would Taffy feel about that?"

He looked puzzled. "You know her. She doesn't think she owns either of us. Anyway, it's a mission of mercy. You're sitting up with a sick friend. There isn't anyone sicker than Naomi Mitchison right now." When he got no response, he asked, "What do you want to hear?"

"I want someone to talk me out of it."

He thought it over. Then, "Taffy wouldn't try. But she'll want to hold your hand when it's over, I think. I'll tell her. Maybe she can get some time early tomorrow. Shall I let you know?"

"Futz!"

"Witness is unresponsive. Does it help if I tell you I sympathize? I'll get drunk with you if she's not free."

"I may need that. Chiron, phone off. Chiron, phone, call two-seven-one-one." Futz. I was going to have to go through with it.

I found a cop outside her door. He took my retina prints and checked them with the city computer. He grinned down at me and started to say something, looked again, and changed his mind. He said instead, "You look like they're about to break *you* up."

"It feels like they already did."

He let me past.

It was party time. Naomi wore floating luminous transparencies, blue with flashes of scarlet. The butterfly fluttering on her eyelids had iridescent blue wings. She smiled and ushered me in, and for a moment I forgot why I was here. Then her eyes flicked to the clock, and mine followed. 1810, city time.

0628, city time. Early morning. Two orange hemispheres looked me in the eye as I emerged. I looked up. The cop guarding Naomi's door had been replaced by Laura Drury.

I asked, "How long has she got?"

"Half an hour."

Futz, I already knew that. The landscape within my skull was blanketed in fog. Later I remembered the chill in Drury's voice. I was in no shape to notice then.

I said, "I hate to let her sleep, and I hate to wake her up. What do I do?"

"I don't know her. If she went to sleep happy; let her sleep."

"Happy?" I shook my head. She hadn't been happy. Should I wake her? No. I said, "I want to thank you for calling. It was kind."

"That's all right."

I considered telling Laura that she'd better get her phone fixed or stop mumbling the commands. I was almost that woozy. Tell a lunie she'd exposed her nakedness to a flatlander? Not me. I waved and turned away and staggered to the elevators.

At the ground floor level I decided I wanted to be alone. I aimed myself toward my room. I changed my mind before I got there.

Taffy studied me for a moment. Then she pulled me in, worked my rumpled clothes off, got me facedown on the bed, poured oil on me, and started a massage. When she felt some of the tension leaving me, she spoke. "Do you want to talk about it?"

"Um. I don't think so."

"What do you want? Coffee? Sleep?"

"More massage," I said. "She was the perfect hostess."

"It was her last chance."

"It was reminiscence time. She wanted to cover a ten-year gap in one night. We did a lot of talking."

She said nothing.

"Taffy? Do you want to have children?"

Her hands stopped, then resumed kneading my calf muscle and Achilles tendon. "Some day."

"With me?"

"What brought this on?"

"Naomi. Chris Penzler. They both waited too long. I wouldn't want to wait too long."

She said, "Pregnant women don't make good surgeons. They turn clumsy. I'd have to drop my career for six or seven months. I'd want to think about that."

"Right."

"And I'd want to finish my tour here."

"Right."

"I'd want to get married. A fifteen-year contract. I wouldn't want to raise a child alone."

In my fatigue-doped state I hadn't thought that far. Fifteen years! Still— "Sounds reasonable. How many birthrights do you have?"

"Just the two."

"Good. Me, too. Why don't we use them both? More efficient."

She kissed the small of my back, then went back to working the bones and joints of my feet. She asked, "What did she say that got you so worked up about children?"

I tried to remember . . .

Naomi fluttered around the bar in a cloud of blue and scarlet transparencies. She made navy grogs in huge balloon glasses with constricted rims. I gathered we weren't expected to stay sober. She asked, "What have you been doing for ten years?"

I told her how I had fled Earth for the Belt, emphasizing her part in it. I thought she'd like that. I told her how we'd set a bomb to move a small asteroid, how the asteroid had shattered— "I usually just say a meteor got me. But it was our own meteor."

She wanted me to show her my imaginary arm. In lunar gravity it was possible to heft the weight of the glass now that it was nearly empty.

She told me about life with Itch. He was savagely jealous and an inconsiderate lover, and he slept with women who looked like genetic failures next to Naomi herself. He had the fragile ego of any half-successful comic.

"So why did you marry him?"

She shrugged.

I spoke before I thought. "Did you like him being jealous? Maybe it kept other men at just the right distance."

"I didn't like being slapped around for it!" I was looking for a change of subject when she added, "When I was climbing out of that bathroom window, I swore I'd never let a man father a child on me again. That was even before I knew Miranda was dead."

"It's a big thing to give up."

For an instant her look was wary, secretive. Then, "Maybe I'm a loser in the evolution game. You don't have children yourself, do you?"

"Not yet."

"Are you out of the evolution game?"

"Not yet." I hefted my empty glass in my imaginary hand. "Every so often someone almost kills me. Maybe . . . maybe it's time."

Naomi got up so energetically that for a moment she floated. "Futz this. Let's see what's for dinner."

"There were subjects she shied away from," I told Taffy.

She was working on my shoulders. "That's not surprising."

"Granted. The organ banks, Penzler getting shot at . . . and children. She chopped that off fast, and that's not surprising, either, I guess."

"Gil, you didn't *grill* her, did you?"

"No!" But I'd flinched. Guilt? "I only noticed things. I think she lied on the stand. I know she did. But why?"

"She'd have had to be crazy."

"Yeah. I asked her why she came back to the moon. She said she was in a black mood, and the lifelessness of the moon suited her fine. But she only went out that once. Hovestraydt City isn't lifeless at all, and she wasn't staying in her room all that time, either."

"So?"

I didn't have an answer.

Taffy said, "I'll be leaving for Mare Orientale this evening. Marxgrad wants a—"

"Futz!"

"—surgeon with specialty training in the autonomic muscle system. I can learn a lot there. I'm sorry, Gil."

"Futz, I'm just glad you didn't go yesterday. I'll get drunk with Harry."

"Turn over. Do you want to go to sleep? Here?"

"I don't know what I want. I thought I didn't want to talk."

The lights dimmed. I barely noticed. They brightened again half a minute later, and suddenly I was sitting upright, bug-eyed, sweating.

Taffy said, "The linear accelerator?"

"Yes. She's on her way. When Luke Garner was a boy, that flicker would have been the electric chair."

"The what?"

"Skip it."

"Lie down." She went to work on my abdomen. "I don't see why you're quite this shook up. I had the idea she never even slept with you."

"No. Well, once."

"When?"

"About two this morning."

I'd been a little startled when Naomi had raised the subject. "I'd have thought sex would be the last thing on your mind."

"But it's our last chance. Unless you wait six months and then buy the appropriate—" She stopped, horrified.

"*Not* funny," I said.

"No. I'm sorry."

"Maybe you'd rather just be held? Cuddled?"

"No." She was out of her dress in an instant. I plucked it out of the wind on its way to the air circulation unit. Then I turned to look at her. I had never seen her naked before. It took my breath away. I caught myself thinking,

Where were you ten years ago, when I needed you? and was ashamed.

She opened a drawer in the bed table and took out a tube of jell. She was frigid; she was expecting to be frigid; she kept that tube very handy. This was normal for Naomi.

I couldn't bring her to climax. She faked it very nicely . . . and didn't I owe something to the Gil Hamilton of ten years ago? Wouldn't he have given up a testicle for this night? I made myself enjoy it.

I moved from love into massage. Taffy had taught me massage, both sensual and therapeutic. I managed to relax her a little. Naomi was on her back, staring at the ceiling while I worked on her hands, when she said, "I'd love to have another baby."

"But you said—"

"Never mind what I said!" Suddenly she was enraged. I turned her over and went back to work till I had her relaxed again.

We made love, or I did. She couldn't concentrate. I didn't try again. I told her stories from my time in the Belt. She talked about her days in college. She asked about my life as an ARM and cut me off when I spoke the word *organlegger*. And she kept glancing at the clock.

"What time is it?"

"Oh-eight-ten," Taffy said.

"Time to go to the conference."

"You're a basket case. I'll call them and tell them you'll make the afternoon session."

"*Oh*, no. Let me make that call. My reputation." I got up. "Chir—"

"Then put some clothes on, too," she said sharply.

I got Bertha Carmody, worse luck, and told her the situation. I sat down on the bed, and flopped back, and found my head in Taffy's lap.

I half woke when a pillow was substituted for the lap.

Then Taffy's phone was saying, "Time to wake up, Ms. Grimes. It's twelve hundred. Time to wake up."

I called it off, but it wouldn't obey my voice. I swore and rolled off the bed. I should have smashed the phone instead. Or else I should have made the morning session ...

8. THE OTHER CRIME

The morning session that fourth day of the conference was when they started getting specific about lunar laws. Naomi or no Naomi, I should have been there. By the time Carmody called the afternoon session to order, all I could do was listen and learn what the fighting was about.

Item: Death penalties on the moon included murder, attempted murder, manslaughter, rape, armed theft, theft involving betrayal of trust, and assault. A similar ARM list would have included far more minor crimes, but—

What constituted assault? We ran that around for a good hour. Armed theft and rape were covered by other laws. What about a simple brawl? To Belters, a barroom brawl classed as recreation. Corey Metchikov from Mare Moscoviense explained that lunies were more fragile than Belters *or* flatlanders, and their longer reach gave a fighter extra leverage. A brawl among lunies was *likely* to be lethal, he claimed.

Marion Shaeffer expressed doubt that a lunie had the muscle to hurt even a lunie. Bertha Carmody offered to Indian wrestle. Marion accepted. We moved some chairs. They looked ridiculous: Marion wasn't even shoulder high to Bertha. Bertha turned Marion in a complete cartwheel, and it was done purely by leverage.

Stone repeated an earlier demand for a legal definition of rape. That started an uproar. There were statutory penalties to protect minors and the marriage bond, and four outnumbered lunies looked ready for murder or war to preserve them. To Budrys and Shaeffer and Quifting, such laws added up to murder plus invasion of privacy.

I could see their point, but we were *not* here to start a war. I was glad when we got off that subject.

Manslaughter. On the moon that covered a variety of

sins: sabotage, criminal carelessness, arson. "Any act which, by damaging a local life support system," said Marion Shaeffer, "*could* have caused deaths or injuries. Is that right?"

"Essentially correct," Ward said.

"That goes a little far," Marion said. "*We'd* execute someone who botched repairs on an air recycler if someone died from it. But if nobody actually gets hurt, why not just assess him for damages?"

Ward was on his feet by now, towering over the seated goldskin. "You go a little far yourself," he told her. "Twenty years ago the moon became the execution grounds for every planet, moon, and rock in the solar system, barring Earth itself. We allowed that. It was a needed source of income. But we will tolerate only limited meddling in our affairs. Beyond that, you may kill your own or ship them to Earth."

Bertha Carmody broke the angry silence. "We're all here to make that step unnecessary. The last conference left us with a considerable expense in research and construction and maintenance. The holding tanks have cost us well over three billion UN marks to date. We don't *want* to eat the cost. Agreed?"

We looked at each other. At least nobody disagreed.

"Your suggestions, Ms. Shaeffer?"

Marion looked uncomfortable. "I'll make it a motion. Alter the law. Fines for accidental damage to equipment unless the damage causes death or injury. Anyone who ruins something vital when he can't pay the damage gets broken up. We can live with that. And I'll move to table the motion till we work up a proposed program of changes."

That passed.

Jabez Stone had some details on the holding tanks and wanted them read into the record. In particular, there had been a power failure at Copernicus in 2111. Four Belt criminals had had to be broken up at once, and almost half the organs had been lost.

"There are safeguards now," Ward told us. "It couldn't

happen again. Remember, holding tank technology was somewhat primitive twenty years ago. *We* were made responsible for developing it."

"That's reassuring, but it wasn't what I was getting at. Shouldn't those felons have been revived?"

"They were too badly damaged. Only organs could be saved," Ward told him.

"It bothers me," Stone said. "Never a reversal of sentence. Either this is an admirable record—"

"Stone, for God's sake! Should we have convicted some innocent just to satisfy you by reviving him? Can you name one single sentence which *should* have been reversed?"

Stone said, "Case of Hovestraydt City versus Matheson & Co. It's in the city computer memory."

And everybody groaned.

If what I needed was something to take my mind off Naomi, then for four days I got my wish.

Days we spent arguing. We spent a full day on Hovestraydt City versus Matheson & Co., not to mention the night I spent reviewing the case. Allegedly the company's carelessness had contributed to the Blowout of 2107. Two Matheson & Co. employees had gone to the organ banks. Penzler and I got Metchikov to admit in private that they might have been scapegoats, that the case should have been reviewed after the hysteria died down. Publicly, forget it.

Late afternoons I watched the news. Steeping myself in lunar culture was worth a try, but the lunie commentators didn't make it easy. They used unfamiliar slang. They gave excessive detail. They droned.

Evenings I met with Stone and Budrys to discuss policy.

The Belters clearly saw their right, nay, their duty to make the lunar law more humanitarian. The moon didn't see it that way. I made a long phone call to Luke Garner for instructions. All I could get out of him was that the ARM would support any decision I made.

So I backed Budrys and Stone. To us the lunar law had

its peculiarities, but it wasn't unduly harsh. Cultures are entitled to their variety, an attitude you'd expect from a club whose members have been battling with words and weapons and economic pressures for close to two hundred years. The drive that spread mankind through the solar system should have given Belters the same attitude, and I said so during a morning session. It fell flat.

Chris Penzler spoke to me afterward. He wasn't moving like a cripple anymore, and some of the foam had sloughed off his chest, leaving bare pink skin bordered by thick black hair. He was a lot more cheerful now. "Kansas boy, you didn't see variety in the Belt. You saw customs different from *Kansas* customs. What would happen to a Belt woman who wanted to raise her children in free fall? How do Belters treat a miner who neglects his equipment? Or a Naderite?" He patted the crown of his head, where what remained of his Belter crest started. "We all cut our hair the same way. Doesn't that tell you something?"

"It should," I admitted. "We committee members, we're all politicians of a sort, aren't we? Natural meddlers. But what if the UN was meddling with Belt law?"

He laughed. "I don't have to wonder about that."

"Too right you don't. It happened, and you seceded from Earth! How do you feel about ARM law?"

He told me what I already knew: the laws of Earth made us not much better than organleggers. I said, "Why don't you do something about it?"

"How?"

"Yeah. You don't have the power to pressure Earth. But you think you've got the lunar economy by the throat."

"Gil, I push where I think something will give."

"The moon might be stronger than you think, or more determined. You could win a war if it comes to that, but will you like yourselves afterward? And can you keep the UN neutral? Belt ships using asteroids as missiles; we wouldn't like that this close to Earth."

These casual conversations were getting to be more important than the sessions. We took to adjourning in midaf-

ternoon. We formed dinner triads: a lunie, a Belter, and a
flatlander meeting to seek compromise while full bellies
made us mellow. For some of us it worked. Some got in-
digestion.

A nightmare started me off again.

That fourth day, with three hours to go before dinner
with Charles Ward and Hildegarde Quifting, I had gone to
my room and flopped on the bed to watch the news.

I remember this item: Mary de Santa Rita Lisboa, the
Brazilian planetologist, was doing some excavating south of
Tycho. Early that morning she had waded into a dust pool
to place some equipment. Her feet grew cold, then numb.
She grew frightened almost too late. By the time she
reached the edge, her legs were frozen to the knees. Before
help reached her, she had fallen hard enough to break ribs
and rip a pinhole leak in her suit. Ten minutes passed before she recognized the pain in her ears for what it was.
She had slapped a patch on the gash and kept going, on frozen legs, with both ears and one lung ruined by decompression.

A basically interesting tale, yes? But what I remember is
the *patronizing* tone, as if nothing above the level of a
plains ape would have done such a damn-fool thing. The
rest of the news was local and dull. Presently it put me to
sleep.

I shouldn't sleep in the afternoon.

Wandering through a dark, blurred forest, I found Naomi
asleep in an ornate twentieth-century coffin, the kind with
a mattress. I knew just how to wake her. I approached her
coffin/bed, bent, and kissed her. She fell apart. I tried to put
her together with my hands . . .

And woke with questions chasing each other through my
head.

. . . Why would anyone lie herself into the organ banks?
It was her own business, I told myself; she'd made that
clear. But what could she be hiding that would be worth
that?

Another crime?

... She had phoned me my first night on the moon. Why? Not because she was eager to see me again. She knew I was an ARM. Was she checking up on me to see what I suspected?

... She had claimed to be exploring the badlands west of the city. Call that her alibi. Alibi for what? Where could she have gone in four hours on foot?

I was hooked.

In my copious free time, with ten minutes to go before a dinner session with Charles Ward and Hildegarde Quifting, I tried to call Laura Drury. Her phone told me that she was asleep; please call back after 1230 tomorrow. My answer wasn't recorded, I hope.

Late that night I summoned up a map of the city environs and spent some time studying it.

I called Laura again after the next day's morning session. Laura was in uniform, but she hadn't left her room. I said, "I can't stand the suspense anymore. Did Naomi in fact reach a holding tank?"

She blinked. "Of course."

"Is this of your own knowledge?"

"I haven't seen her lying in the tank, no. I'd have heard if there was an escape." She studied my image. "It wasn't just casual sex, was it?"

"I left Earth to mine the asteroids because Naomi married someone else."

"I'm sorry. We tend to think ... I mean ..."

"I know; flatlanders are easy. Have you got a minute to talk?"

"Gil, why don't you stop tormenting yourself?"

"I got to wondering. Naomi was a computer programmer. It was one point against her. The jury assumed she could have got to the message lasers without leaving a record in the computer. Do you believe that?"

"I don't know how good she was. Do you?"

"No. I got to wondering if a computer programmer that good could steal a puffer, again with no records."

She sat down to think. Presently she nodded. "Anyone that good could have stolen a puffer, too. No wonder you didn't find the weapon."

"Okay." Though that wasn't exactly what I was after.

"Hold it. With a puffer she could have reached the Belt Trading Post. She could have taken a ship out. Gil, we'd have found her anyway, but at least she would have had a chance! Why would she come back?"

"Yeah, you're right. It was just a thought. Thanks," I called the phone off, and her puzzled frown vanished. Then I started laughing.

Some alibi! And perfectly genuine, too. Naomi could have been committing an entirely different crime at the Belt Trading Post!

I was going to have to walk softly. I would have to find Chris's failed killer *without* showing the lunie police where Naomi had been.

I was stripping for a bath when Laura called me back that evening. I said, "Chiron, voice only. Hi, Laura. I'm glad you called. Has anything unusual happened lately at the Belt Trading Post?"

"Nothing I've heard about. And there weren't any puffers missing that night."

"What? How sure are you?"

"Mesenchev was on duty. He says there were no puffers checked out and no slots. No computer program could keep him from noticing one empty slot. And is that finally the end of the Naomi Mitchison case?"

"Yes. And if it isn't, I'll at least quit bugging you. I've done too much of that."

She studied me thoughtfully ... no, she must have been studying a blank screen. She'd better, because I was just climbing into the tub. She said, "Did I louse up a voice-only command a few days ago?"

"Eee-yess. I wasn't about to be the one to tell you."

"Well, you're a gentleman," she said, and called off, leaving me bemused. What did lunies consider a gentleman?

No puffers missing. Futz. While water and air bubbles churned around me, I called up the map again and traced the trade road west. Roads branched off to the water and oxygen works, to the abandoned metal mines, to a linear accelerator project that had gone bankrupt.

I was back to assuming that Naomi had been on foot. Could she have met someone somewhere within reach? The air works required sunlight. At night they might be deserted. Or what about the old strip mine?

The screen blinked, and Laura Drury glared out of it. "Now, what are you doing with that map again?"

Watery amoebas left the tub with the force of my flinch. "Hey, are you sure that's your business? And how do you break into a computer display without permission, anyway?"

"I knew how to do that when I was ten. Gil, will you give up on her? Maybe she wasn't out there when Penzler got shot. Maybe she researched it somehow. Gil, if she wasn't shooting at Penzler, she must have been committing an organ bank crime somewhere else!"

"You saw that, huh? I went to the wrong person. Well, if you must know, I can't leave puzzles alone."

Long silence. Then, "Want help?"

"Not from a cop. If you found a crime, you'd have to report it."

She nodded reluctantly.

"Hey, why did you call me a gentleman?"

"Well, you didn't . . . if a lunie saw a, a person naked on his phone screen—" She stopped.

"He'd crawl out of the screen at you, drooling and leering?"

"He'd think it was an invitation." She was blushing darkly.

"Oh. Hahaha! No. If a lady wants to give me an invitation, I expect her to say so. Flatlanders don't hint." I stood up. "Especially on the moon. I was told *never* to make advances to a lunie." I started scraping the half inch of water off me with the edges of my hands. Then I saw her eyes bugging. "Have you got vision?"

She was stricken. *Caught!*

"Serves you right." I reached for a towel. I used it on my hair, concealing my grin, concealing nothing else. Why shouldn't a lunie be curious? And she'd given me the same privilege inadvertently.

"Gil?"

"Yeah."

"It was an invitation."

I looked at her over the towel. Her lids were lowered, and her blush was darker yet.

"Okay, come on up."

"Okay."

It took her forty minutes. She might have been changing her mind over and over again. She arrived still in uniform, carrying a briefcase.

I'd put clothes on in case anyone was in the hall. Even so, she looked everywhere but at me. Nervous. Her eye caught the phone display.

She studied the map. "On foot for four hours. Well, what was she doing for four hours?"

"It's like this," I said. "If Naomi wasn't out there shooting at Chris Penzler, then someone else was. We'd both like to find him, right? Because we're cops. But you're a cop, so I can't tell you what I think Naomi was doing."

She sat down stiffly on the edge of the bed. "Say she met someone. Maybe a man who works at the air works. Married. Would she protect him?"

I had to laugh. Naomi? With her *life*? "No. Anyway, what kind of assignation is that? As soon as they take off their clothes, *poof!* Explosive decompression. Laura, how do I go about relaxing you?"

She smiled flickeringly. "Talk to me. This is unusual for me."

"You can change your mind at any second. Just say the word. The word is *halogens*."

"Thanks."

"Then you have to list them."

A short silence which I had to break. "If she wasn't out there, it makes her useless as a witness, doesn't it? What she swore she didn't see doesn't count. And Chris said there could have been an army out there hiding in the shadows. He wasn't even sure he saw a human being."

She turned to look at me. "That leaves your testimony."

In my mind I flexed my imaginary hand, remembering the feel of miniature moonscape. "There wasn't anyone out there by the time I looked. Laura, what about mirrors? The laser could have been somewhere else, and the killer, too."

"But there wasn't any mirror, either."

"I wasn't looking for one."

"We'd have found it."

It was impossible. I scowled at the map. I wanted to ignore the facts and just start toting up suspects according to motive. What stopped me was my first suspect: *any* lunie angry enough about our meddling in lunar affairs and clever enough to have worked some kind of trickery.

Laura picked up her case and went into the water closet.

I was having trouble keeping my priorities straight. First: I hadn't touched a woman in several days. Second: I didn't want Laura hurt, damaged or embarrassed. Third: my own part in the conference could be endangered. Fourth: I wanted Laura Drury in my bed, and that was part lust, part spirit of adventure. How to reconcile all that? Hold it down to talk for now? Let her list her own priorities on her own time?

She came out wearing a garment the likes of which I'd never seen before. It was sexy and strange: floor length, shoulderless, and not quite opaque. The thin, cream-colored fabric hugged her body by static electricity. It could almost have been a dress, but it looked too fragile—there was a lot of lace—and much too thin to hold heat.

"What is it?"

She laughed. "It's a nightgown!" Quite suddenly she came into my arms. I found myself standing fully upright and nuzzling her throat. The garment was nicely tactile: silky smooth over warm skin. I felt her goose bumps through it.

"What's it for?"

"It's to sleep in. For now, I guess it's to take off."

"Carefully? Or do I rip it off?"

"Jesus! Carefully, Gil; it's expensive."

Lunie customs. Sooner or later they'd get me. A sensible man wouldn't have invited a lunie to his room. I knew it and didn't care.

9. THE TRADING POST

It was amazing how good we felt on a couple of hours' sleep. Laura was glowing. She kept picking me up in her arms, Rhett Butler style. She'd jump when I goosed her, then steady herself with a hand on my head and let me lift her one-handed. I played tricks with my imaginary arm.

We went formal and cautious when it came time to leave. I left first. Desiree Porter and Tom Reinecke were coming down the hall. They hailed me and swept me up and tried to pump me for news on the conference.

I sidestepped. "What have you two been doing all this time, just waiting for one of us to crack?"

Tom said, "There was Penzler. There was the trial. We've been interviewing lunies, too. You know, a lot of them aren't going to be happy no matter *what* you do."

"And we screw a lot," Desiree said.

"That I kind of assumed. Hey, did you two know each other before you got here?"

"Nope. It was just one of those things."

"Lust at first sight. I think it's his legs I like best. Belt men have their muscles mainly in the arms and shoulders."

"So you only love me for my legs, huh?"

"And your mind. Didn't I mention your mind?"

We had reached the elevators. I started to step in, then told them I'd left something in my room, which was true enough.

Now the hall was empty. I called the door open, Laura joined me, and we went down to breakfast. We weren't even holding hands. But our hands brushed sometimes, and Laura kept suppressing a smile, and I wondered just how much we were hiding. For that matter, I'd seen Reinecke's oddly sardonic smile as the elevator doors closed.

At breakfast I told Laura I wanted to check out a puffer. She didn't like it. "Isn't there a committee meeting?"

"I'll skip a day. Hell, this *is* committee business. If the courts have convicted an innocent person—"

She shrugged angrily. "If she didn't try to murder Penzler, then she was doing something else!"

The idea percolated through to me that as a man newly in love, I was supposed to forget old loves entirely. Laura didn't want to hear that I still hoped to save Naomi Mitchison.

I sidestepped again. "I left a case half-solved once," I said, and I told her how Raymond Sinclair's surrealistic death scene was linked to two organleggers found with their faces burned down to the bone. I had nearly reached the morgue in the same condition.

Maybe she bought it. She did help me check out a puffer.

The puffers were racked along one wall of the mirror works. Today there were several gaps. The only difference between the orange city police puffers and the rentals was that the rentals came in all colors.

I chose a police puffer. It was a low-slung motorcycle with a wide padded bucket seat and a cargo framework behind. There were three tanks. The motor had no intake. An exhaust pipe forked to left and right just under the seat. The shock absorbers were huge, and the tires were great fat soft tubes.

Laura showed me how to get it going and tried to tell me

how to run it, how to maneuver, how to steer, where not to steer. "*I* could cross a dust pool," she told me, "like a bat out of hell, and if you slow down you'll turn over, and if the wheel hits a submerged rock you'll be under the dust trying to figure out which way is up. You stay away from dust pools. Don't hit any rocks. If you fall, get your arms over your helmet."

"I'll stick to the road," I said. "That's safe, isn't it?"

"I guess so." She was reluctant to admit that anything was safe.

"Why are there three tanks?"

"Oxygen, hydrogen, water vapor. We don't throw away water, Gil. The exhaust is just a safety valve, and of course it powers the side jets. You shouldn't have to use them, but do it if you think you're falling over."

I climbed on. I could barely feel the vibration. "It isn't puffing," I noticed.

"It's not supposed to. If it starts puffing steam, something's wrong. That's why they're called puffers. If it happens, slow way down and check your air, because you may have to walk home." She insisted on showing me how to bleed oxygen from the puffer tank into my backpack.

"Have you got all that?"

"Yup."

"Keep it slow till you learn how to steer. This is the moon. You'll have to lean farther than you think."

"Okay."

"I don't get off till 2000. Will you be back by then?"

"I'm bound to."

We clinked helmets in lieu of a kiss, and I went.

From the city's east face, the mirror works, the trade road hooked around and aimed straight west. I bounced along at a fair rate for an off-road vehicle. I marked the tilted rock far off to my left and a road that wound uphill to my right, up to the air and water plant. I had seen it from a height, miniaturized in the projection room: mirrors mounted around the rim of a fair-sized recent crater, focusing their light down onto a pressure vessel filled with red-hot lunar rock. Pipes to lead hydrogen in, water vapor out. I was tempted to go up and look at the real thing. Maybe on the way back . . .

To my left was the land Naomi had tried to lead us through and the peak Naomi had tried to climb. I kept going.

The road twisted like an injured snake. A broad road led left toward the strip mines that had made Hovestraydt City rich. When they had played out, the city had turned to mirror making.

Naomi wasn't a native. To meet someone out here, she would need some obvious landmark. The same would hold if someone had simply left a puffer parked somewhere for her. The mines? She couldn't get lost, witnesses were unlikely, and the tailings might fool radar for a small vehicle.

She'd led us a merry chase the day after the attack on Chris Penzler. Alan Watson must have given her what she needed when he showed her the projection room. And she'd danced her way right into the organ banks. To hide what?

Or else the jury was right.

Presently I was bouncing downhill, beyond the region I'd searched with my imaginary hand, beyond anywhere Naomi could have reached on foot. Far ahead was a line of silver: the mass driver built to supply ore for the L-5 project of the 2040s. The company had gone bankrupt, and the mass driver was half-built and long obsolete.

I kept checking my watch.

There was the trading post ahead. Unused to picking out details in moonscape, my eyes had been missing it for some time. I found the shapes of two spacecraft first, then the outline of the spaceport, then the crescent of stone and glass buildings around it. The road became a circle between the buildings and the spaceport. I had made the run in just thirty-five minutes.

* * *

The trading post was strange by anyone's standards.

There was no dome. Oblong buildings were individually pressurized; sometimes they were linked by tunnels. In Selene's Bar and Grill, where I stopped for lunch, I found racks for fishbowl helmets but none for pressure suits. The customers kept their credit coins in outside pockets.

Selene's Bar and Grill, Mare Serenitatis Spa (with a pool and sauna), the Man in the Moon Hotel (he was shown yawning), Aphrodite's: all the place names were moon-related. Half the people I saw were lunies. Aphrodite's rented sexual favors. The waitress at Selene's told me it catered specifically to lunies. I was a little shocked.

The administration building was all the way around the circle. It was big enough to get lost in. The police, licensing, and port administration were scattered through the building. I finally found the goldskin offices.

"ARM business," I told the only clerk in sight.

He was watching a fold-up 3D screen propped in front of him. He didn't look up. "Yah?"

"Last Wednesday someone shot a Belt delegate to the conference on—"

Now he looked up. "We heard about that. Didn't they solve that one? I heard—"

"Look, there's a possibility that our suspect was *here* at the time. That would mean she wasn't shooting at Penzler. We never found the weapon, either. That adds up to a would-be killer with a message laser still hunting a Belt delegate."

"See your point. What do you need?"

"Were there any crimes committed here between 2230 Tuesday and 0130 Wednesday?" Naomi would have had to walk to where someone had left a puffer for her, then drive here. At least half an hour coming and half an hour back. Later I'd have to pace it off on foot.

He set aside his fold-up screen and tapped at a computer keyboard. The screen lit. "Mmm . . . we had a fight at Aphrodite's about that time. A lunie dead, two Belters and a lunie under arrest, all male. But you're looking for something premeditated."

"Right."

"Zip."

"Futz. How about disappearances?"

He summoned up the missing persons records. Nobody had been reported missing since Wednesday. It seemed that Naomi had not been committing a crime of violence.

"How well do you keep track of your puffers?"

"They're licensed. Generally the residents own their own." He was typing as he spoke. The screen filled. "These are rentals."

"*Chili Bird?*" The name rang a bell.

"Two puffers charged to the *Chili Bird* account for two days. Well, that's reasonable. Antsie had passengers."

"Tell me more."

He scowled—I was inventing work for him, and he would have preferred not to—but he typed, and more data appeared. "Antsie de Campo, owner and pilot of *Chili Bird* out of Vesta. Arrived April 10. Left April 13. Passengers, Dr. Raymond Forward and a four-year-old girl, Ruth Hancock Cowles. Cargo . . . he had a light load. Monopoles. He took off with some chicken and turkey embryos; maybe that's why the doctor was along."

April 13 was the day after the attempt on Penzler. "Where are they now?"

"Headed for Confinement Asteroid. Probably because of the little girl." He typed. "I remember her now. She was a doll. Interested in everything. She loved low gravity; she was bouncing around—" The screen responded. "*Chili Bird*'s almost to Confinement now. Is this any use to you?"

"I hope so. Where can I send a message to *Chili Bird*?"

He told me how to find Interplanetary Voice on a peak outside the city circle.

There would have been several minutes' lightspeed delay in conversation. I sent a straight 'gram.

TO: DR RAYMOND FORWARD

NAOMI MITCHISON TRIED AND CONVICTED FOR ATTEMPTED MURDER COMMITTED HOVESTRAYDT CITY 0130 WEDNESDAY APRIL 13. EXECUTION PENDING. IF YOU KNOW OF HER MOVEMENTS DURING RELEVANT TIME, CALL ME HOVESTRAYDT CITY.

GILBERT HAMILTON, ARM

I didn't stop on the way home. I couldn't guess where someone might have left a puffer for Naomi. Maybe I had already wasted time I couldn't afford. I felt time's hot breath on the back of my neck, an unreasonable conviction that Naomi didn't have months but only hours.

McCavity hailed me in the hall. "Hello, Gil. The offer's still open," he said.

"Offer?"

"Someone to get drunk with."

"Oh. I may need it yet. Let me buy you a drink now. I haven't seen a bar—"

"There aren't any. We tend to keep our own supplies and drink in our rooms. Come on, I've got a good stock."

McCavity's quarters were near the bottom level of the city. He didn't have any kind of bartending device; the drinks were going to be simple. He offered me something he called earthshine poured over ice, and I took it.

Smooth.

"Distilling is dirt cheap here," Harry said. "Heat, cold, partial vacuum, they're all just outside the wall. Do you like it?"

"Yeah. It tastes like a good bourbon."

"I got a call from Taffy. She reached Marxgrad okay. She says she left you a message, too."

"Good."

"I gather you got together okay?"

"Yes, thank God. I was a basket case. She reassembled me." I sipped again. "I wish I had the time to get drunk in good company. It might be just what I need. Harry, do you know of a Belt doctor, a Raymond Forward?"

McCavity scratched his head. "Rings a bell. Yeah, he's got some lunie clients. Specialist in fertility problems."

Futz. Naomi didn't suffer from infertility. "He was on the moon for a few days. Maybe he had a lunie client."

"There'd be records. We don't have restrictions on fertility except the natural ones."

"Okay, I can check that out."

"What's it all about?"

"He was here at the right time, and he came in with a light cargo. Maybe there were ulterior motives."

"Right time for what?"

"Naomi. Maybe I'm going at this wrong end around. I should be looking for whoever shot at Chris Penzler. But if Naomi wasn't where she said she was ... well, it's one handle on a puzzle. I can track that down. She could have been meeting someone. Maybe Antsie de Campo, maybe Forward. Could there be two Raymond Forwards?"

"Both Belt doctors? Well, it's possible." He sipped at his own drink. "Was Naomi infertile?"

"She was fertile. She'd also sworn never to have another kid."

"Then *that's* out."

"By another man."

"What?"

"She swore she'd never have children by another man. This Forward, he solves infertility problems?"

"Right. You've got something, don't you?"

"Cloning?"

"If all else fails, he can grow a clone for a patient. It's hellishly expensive."

"Can I borrow your phone?"

"I'll call for you. What number?"

I told him.

Artemus Boone stood frowning in the doorway of his office. "I was just closing up. I can meet you tomorrow at 1000. Unless it's urgent?"

"It feels urgent," I told the phone image. "Do you still regard Naomi Mitchison as your client?"

"Certainly."

"I need to discuss her case confidentially."

He sighed. "Come to my office. I'll wait."

I turned to Harry McCavity. "Thanks for the drink. I'll be pleased to get drunk with you when this is all over, but just now—"

He waved that off. "Will I ever know what this was all about?"

"There's more than one kind of crime," I said cryptically, and left.

Artemus Boone sat behind his ancient, lovingly maintained computer terminal and propped his beard on his folded hands. "Now, what's this all about, Mr. Hamilton?"

"I want a legal opinion on a hypothetical situation."

"Go on."

"A flatlander woman hires a Belt doctor to take a clone from her and grow it to term. The operation takes place on the moon. The woman returns to Earth. The child is raised in the asteroids. Four years later they meet again, on the moon. The woman is still on the moon when it all becomes public knowledge."

Boone stared as if I'd sprouted horns. "Damnation!"

"Sure. Now, the United Nations Fertility Laws would have our hypothetical flatlander woman sterilized if she had an illegal baby. They'd sterilize the baby, too. But this particular woman still has one birthright, so she could have a baby with no problem. But what about a clone?"

Boone shook his head. He was still thunderstruck. "I don't know. My field is lunar law."

"Would the UN try to extradite the woman? Would the moon let them get away with it? Would they try to extradite the baby, too? Or are they both safe because the crime took place off Earth?"

"Again, I don't know. I'd want to research this. In some legal respects the moon is part of the United Nations. Damnation! Why didn't she discuss this with me?"

"She could have been scared to. She never mentioned any such situation?"

He smiled like a man in pain. "Never. Damnation. I'm nearly certain that the baby could not be extradited. If only she'd asked! Hamilton, is our hypothetical baby still on the moon?"

"No."

"Good." He stood up abruptly. "I'll be able to give you a better answer tomorrow. Call me."

I reached my room expecting to spend some time on the phone. Getting Budrys to tell me what went on at the conference could take up to an hour. I wanted to check Dr. Forward's credentials and recent movements. And Taffy's message was waiting . . . I dropped onto the bed and pulled my shoes off and said, "Chiron, messages."

And Laura Drury's image, in full pressure suit, said, "Gil, you'll have to have dinner without me. I'm going out with a search party. I don't know when I'll be back. Chris Penzler's turned up missing."

10. THE TILTED ROCK

I wasted a few seconds cursing. The urgency I'd felt hadn't been for Naomi Mitchison. Naomi was feeling no impatience. Death had been hunting Chris Penzler.

I called Laura's room and got no answer. I called the police and got Jefferson.

"He left about sixteen-twenty this afternoon," the freckled lunie told me. "He checked out a puffer."

I said, "Idiot."

"Right. How well do you know him? Could he think he's playing detective?"

"Why not? Somebody wants him dead, and it bothers him. He's not likely to be out there playing tourist."

"Well, that's what I thought," Jefferson said. "I sent a search party west, to the area where Penzler testified he saw something. Laura Drury's with them, in case you were wondering." A trace of disapproval in his voice. What the futz? "But they haven't found him, and they've been out over an hour."

"Set the area up in the projection room and search that."

"We have *got* to have another Watchbird satellite," Jefferson said. "There used to be three. The replacement keeps getting proxmired in the budget hearings. Hamilton, we've been waiting for the Watchbird One to rise. Why don't you meet me down in the projection room?"

"Good."

Tom Reinecke and Desiree Porter were waiting outside the projection room. They'd heard Chris Penzler was missing. Jefferson wanted to tell them to go to hell until I said, "We can use some extra eyes."

Yet again we waded out into the hologram, knee-deep in miniature moonscape. Jefferson and Reinecke and I fanned out into the choppy lands west of the rim wall and the city. Porter searched the crater itself because nobody else had. Partly to honor her theory, I stopped at the tilted rock.

Jefferson and Tom Reinecke kept going. They glanced back at me, then resumed their search by eye alone, three to four hundred yards from the west wall of the city.

I looked around. The tilted rock was small enough to heft in both arms, except that it wouldn't have moved, of course. I saw tiny orange suits with bubble helmets scattered over the rocks to my west. I called, "What kind of suit would Chris be wearing?"

"Blue, skintight, with a gold and bronze griffin on the chest," Jefferson called back.

There were annoying blank spots in the landscape where the Watchbird's cameras weren't reaching. I tried to feel around in them, but my talent wasn't up to that. I felt nothing.

I found no blue skintight suits, vertical or horizontal. Where Reinecke and Jefferson were searching, bright orange puffers were parked in a ring on flat ground. None in my area.

There was a deep dust pool twenty yards south of the tilted rock. The surface looked roiled. I ran my imaginary hand beneath the surface and flinched violently. Then I made myself touch it again.

I called, "I've found the puffer. It's under the dust."

One and all, they abandoned their own search. Desiree reached me first. They watched (for what?) while I let go of the puffer and searched further. I found it almost at once. I said, "God."

Desiree said, "What? Penzler?"

I closed my hand around it. It felt light and dry, like a dead lizard left in the sun. "Somebody. A suit with somebody inside." I made my imaginary fingertips follow the contours of the thing, though there was nothing I wanted less in the world. "God. His hand is gone."

My hand stopped sending. My talent had quit. Imaginary hand, hell; it's my mind, my unprotected mind, that feels out the textures of what I touch. I can take only so much of that.

"We'll have to check this out," Jefferson said.

"Use your belt phone. Send the search party that way. Tell them we'll join them as soon as we can."

It took almost an hour. I was twitchy with impatience. When we finally set forth, our team included Jefferson, both newstapers, dredging machinery, and a couple of orange-clad operators.

The Earth was a broad crescent, not quite half-full. The sun was well up the sky, leaving fewer shadows, but they were impenetrably black. Our headlamps didn't help. Our bubble helmets had darkened, and our eyes had adjusted to lunar day.

The dozen cops on the original search team were already waiting at the dust pool. Laura Drury bounced up to me. "Do you really think he's down there?"

"I felt him," I said.

She grimaced. "Sorry. Well, we found this. It was just under the dust, just at the edge." She held an elastic strap with a buckle, the kind that locks when you pull it tight. "We use them on puffers to hold small stuff on the frame behind the seat. Does it mean anything to you?"

"Not a thing," I said.

"Maybe the killer dumped the body in the dust," Laura speculated, "and then found the strap. He just stuck it under the dust with his hand."

That would mean he was in a hurry, I thought. It would also mean the strap was evidence of something. Otherwise he'd have just kept it.

Jefferson called Laura, and she waved and went.

I noticed Alan Watson by his height. While the cops were getting the equipment ready, Alan and I adjusted our radios for privacy.

"I've got news," I said. "Maybe good, maybe bad."

"About Naomi?"

"Right. She wasn't here when someone shot Penzler in his bath. She wasn't anywhere near here. She was at the Belt Trading Post."

"Then she's innocent! But why wouldn't she say so?"

"She thought she was committing an organ bank crime."

Alan's face twisted. "That isn't a whole lot of help."

The dredge moved into the dust, sinking. The dust was deep. I'd felt it.

"It could help," I said. "We have to prove that someone else tried to shoot Chris without showing what Naomi was actually doing. Then we could get her revived."

"By God, we could! If that's Penzler down there, then the original assassin got him."

"Maybe not. His methods seem to have turned crude. We'd still want to show how he could fire a laser at Chris Penzler's window from out here and then get back into the city, or wherever he did go, and why I didn't find him in the projection room. And after all, that might not even be Penzler's body. All I know is there's someone down there."

"Um."

"What I'd rather do is show that what Naomi was doing

wasn't an organ bank crime. She should've discussed it
with her lawyer. What I think she—"

The dredge came out of the dust, and I dropped the conversation and loped over.

The corpse wore a blue skintight suit. The right hand had
been sliced off cleanly four inches above the wrist. The
face seemed shrunken, but I would have recognized him
even without the torso painting, the Bonnie Dalzell griffin
clutching Earth in its claw.

I opened my radio band and announced, "It's Chris
Penzler."

Jefferson examined the severed forearm. "Clean cut.
Message laser on high," he said. "The beam must have
sliced right through. If there was rock behind him, we'll
find the marks." He set some of the cops to searching.

We didn't bother to look for bootprints. The search party
had left too many. But they hadn't left puffer tracks. We
found a set of puffer tracks and followed them backward
from the pool until they disappeared on bare rock.

Someone behind us announced that he had found the
hand. Jefferson went back. I didn't. Those tracks could lead
from the general direction of the tilted boulder.

Six nights ago Chris Penzler had glimpsed someone
through his picture window. Only for an instant . . . and afterward he couldn't decide which side of this particular
boulder he'd been looking past. Maybe he'd come out to
see.

The flat side of the rock was in deep shadow. I stepped
close to the rock, out of the sun, and waited for my darkened helmet to clear again and my eyes to adjust. Then I
played my headlamp over the rock.

My yell brought them running. They clustered around me
to look at Chris Penzler's dying message: big, malformed
letters scrawled across the rock, black in the light of the
headlamps.

NAKF

"He must have written it in his own blood," Jefferson said. "In shadow, so the killer wouldn't notice. He must have been jetting blood from the severed artery. But . . . that isn't a name, is it?"

Desiree said, "It isn't anything. I think."

"The strap!" Laura cried in the joyful tones that go with the *Eureka!* sensation. "The strap; he must have used it for a tourniquet! He must have known he was dying—maybe he had to hide from the killer—" Her voice dropped. "It's *awful*, isn't it?"

"Take a scraping of that blood," Jefferson ordered. "At least we'll find out if it was Penzler's. He must have had *something* in mind."

I got back to my room around midnight. I set it up on my phone screen:

NAKF

So here's Chris Penzler out there on the meteor-torn moon, looking for clues. Maybe he remembers something. Maybe he finds something. Maybe not.

But a killer finds him.

A lunie citizen would be more likely to know it when Chris Penzler checked out a puffer. Assume he followed immediately . . . on foot, unless he was an idiot. I'd ask the computer if someone had checked out a puffer right after Chris did. Some killers *are* idiots.

If Chris had recognized his killer, he'd have written a name. I'd get the computer to search the city directory. Offhand I didn't know anyone on the moon whose name started with NAKF. Or with—I started filling in letters. Written in haste in jetting blood, and possibly in darkness, a K could be a ruined R, F could be E, N could be M or W . . .

NARF NAKE NARE MAKF MAKE MARE WAKF WAKE WARE

No names sprang to mind. And Chris wasn't a lunie; here on the moon I knew everyone he did.

NAKF NAOMI

It was a bad fit. And Naomi had one hell of an alibi. I should be able to persuade the lunar law to disgorge her on the strength of Penzler's murder. If there were indeed two killers after Chris's blood—Naomi the clumsy one, somebody else the skillful or lucky or more straightforward one—Naomi could be returned to the holding tank.

I called, "Chiron, phone. Get me Alan Watson." And my nasty suspicious mind gave me:

NAKF   ALAN WATSON   WATS

Alan was out on the moon at the time, in the search party, looking for Chris Penzler himself. So maybe he found him. How much would Alan do for Naomi? Would he murder a stranger who had done her harm if it would buy her life?

Alan's long black-browed face appeared. On the phone screen he was easier to take; his height didn't show. "Hello, Gil."

An N could be a W with the first vertical botched, but an F could not be a botched S, I decided. I said, "I wondered if we can get Naomi out of Copernicus now."

"I've already filed with the court. All we can do now is wait. I expect they'll revive her, but it would help if we could tell them where she actually was. Gil, where was she?"

"I should know that within a few hours." I didn't add that I might not tell him then.

Assume Chris didn't recognize his killer. He couldn't give us a name if all he saw was a pressure suit. Short, medium, or lunie? Inflated or skintight? Chris hadn't bothered to tell us. Could he have had something more specific in mind? Like a torso painting?

Lunch was a long time in the past. I had seen corpses uglier than Chris Penzler's. Maybe I could have done something to save his life ... but I still had no idea what it might be. I phoned down for a chicken and onion sandwich.

Then I put the display back on the phone screen and stared at it.

He must have known he was dying. He'd have kept it short. Unless I was overlooking some significance to NAKF, he had *still* run out of time or blood.

Try NAKE, then. SNAKE? But if I made the F an unfinished E, then he wasn't writing backward. And why should he? So try

NAKF   NAKED

For a torso painting? That wouldn't help much. Naked ladies were very popular as torso paintings . . . in the Belt, at least.

Try something else. Picture a vindictive, dedicated killer tracking Chris across the moon, bare-assed but for his trusty laser . . . taking his vengeance just before internal pressure rips him apart in a gust of cold scarlet fog . . . no? Then how about a vehicle with a transparent bubble cockpit? Park it in shadow with the cockpit lights on, and Chris would see only the killer. But I didn't know of any such vehicle. A custom job? And it would have shown on radar if it flew, would have left tracks if it didn't.

I tried some other words.

My door announcer said, "Gil, are you there? It's Laura."

"Chiron, door open."

She'd showered away the sweat secretions that accumulate on your skin when you're in a pressure suit. I hadn't. Suddenly I felt grimy. She said, "We've made a little progress. I thought you'd want to know."

"What have you got?"

She sat down on the bed beside me, comfortably close. "Nobody checked out a puffer after Penzler did. Not till the search party went out. That puts our killer on foot. It would slow him down."

"Maybe. Maybe he can get a puffer without leaving a

computer record. Wouldn't he have to do that to get at the lasers?"

"Um."

"Or if he was a cop with the search party, that would get him the puffer and the laser, too."

She scowled.

"Skip it. What have you got on the body?"

"Harry McCavity's doing an autopsy outside the mirror works. The condition of the body . . . well, it's freeze-dried. Harry got positively nasty when I wanted a time of death. And the tanks bled empty within half an hour, and his watch didn't conveniently stop, either."

"Laura, can I ask you some questions about lunar customs?"

She looked down at me. "Go ahead."

"I already know that people here are supposed to share a bed only when they're married to each other. What I want to know is, if two unmarried people *did* share a bed, would they be expected to share a bed only with each other?"

Her voice turned brittle, and she sat very straight on the bed. "What started you on this?"

"I've been getting some funny vibrations." I didn't name Jefferson.

"Yes. Well. I haven't been bragging about the short, strong fellow I managed to entrap, if *that's* what you're thinking. I don't know how anyone would know about us."

"Maybe lunies tend to know each other better than flatlanders do. Smaller population. Smaller cities. And there *is* such a thing as telepathy." And Laura had been smiling and sparkling as we had left her apartment that morning. Someone might have noticed.

"What is it you want to know? Should you resume your relationship with Dr. Grimes? Did you think you needed my permission?"

"I think there are five lunies I don't want to offend," I said. "You and four committee delegates from four lunar cities. If you and I are now supposed to be monogamous, I want to know it. I came to the moon largely because Taffy was here. Should I now stop seeing Taffy in private? Or at all? Come on, give me some help. If the committee is too busy fighting to make decisions, everybody loses."

She screwed her eyes almost shut. "This is all new to me. Let me think." Pause. "I want you for myself. Is that immoral?"

"Depends on where you are. Silly but true. I am flattered."

"All right. Stop seeing her in *public*." By now she was on her feet and pacing like a tiger. "Even in the halls. In private, make *sure* it's private. No phone calls. No room service breakfast for two."

"Taffy's gone to Marxgrad."

"What?"

"She's got her own career to pursue. Now she's pursued it to the back of the moon. But I had to know these things for future reference, Laura. Are you angry?"

She looked at me. She turned to the door. I said, "Remember, I'm likely to believe anything you tell me. Call me ignorant. Are you angry? Shall we avoid each other from now on?"

She turned back. "I'm angry. I made the same mistake anyone else would have. I want you back in my bed as soon as I get *over* this!" She swung around to the door and back again. Hesitated. Finally she dropped back on the bed just behind my shoulder.

It wasn't me that had stopped her, I think. It was the display.

```
                        NAKF
NARF  NAKE  NARE  MAKF  MAKE  MARE  WAKF
            WAKE    WARE
              NAKF    NAOMI
              NAKF    WATS
    NAKED  SNAKE    SNARE    WAKEN
```

"See anything?"

"Beware?"

I said, "He'd have to add on at both ends."

"That applies to Ms and Ws, too. Oh, I see. If he missed a stroke right at the beginning—"

"Yeah. Do lunies tend to put nudes in their torso paintings?"

"No."

"Do lunies use any kind of vehicle with a *lot* of glass in it? A full bubble cockpit? Do the Belters at the trading post?"

"I don't think so. Why?"

"NAKED. And now I'm stuck. Futz. Maybe he was trying to describe a torso painting."

Laura said, "He must have got away from the killer. Maybe he ducked into the shadows and tied a tourniquet and kept going. Otherwise it's too easy for the killer. A second swipe with the laser cuts him in half."

"Maybe. What's your point?"

"He knew he'd die when he took the tourniquet off. He would have thought it through in detail before he wrote any message." She studied the screen. She reached past me and typed:

NaKF

"Chemistry. Sodium, potassium, flourine."

"What does it mean? What do you do with those three elements?"

"*I* don't know. Gil—"

The door announcer said, "Room service."

Laura yelped. In an instant she was behind the door, flattened against the wall. I stared. Then I went to the door, called it open, stepped into the hall, took the tray, said, "Thank you. Good night," and closed the door in the bemused waiter's face.

Laura exhaled.

I was trying not to laugh. I took a huge bite out of a sandwich and spoke around it. "I need a bath almost as much as I need food. I'm hoping you'll stay; I'm just telling you."

"I'll do your back," Laura said.

"Good."

11. THE EMPTY ROOM

I was half-awake. My mind, idling in neutral, played word games.

NAKF LAURA DRURY DESK COP NAKF

I couldn't make it fit.

Laura's foot was hooked under mine. When she tried to turn over, I came fully awake. I worked my foot free, and she rolled just to the edge of the bed.

NAKF . . . DRURY . . . what the *hell* was I doing?

Properly horrified, I pushed the whole topic way down to the bottom of my mind and left it there. But I couldn't get back to sleep. I finally moved to the foot of the bed and said, "Chiron, low volume. Chiron, messages."

Taffy looked good, brisk and happy. "I like Marxgrad," she said. "I like the people. I'm brushing up on my medical Russian, but everyone speaks enough English for social purposes. I miss you mostly at night.

"I hope you haven't changed your mind about having children. I can find the time starting a year from now. We do have a problem. Neither of us intends to drop his career, right? And we're both subject to emergency calls. That could be tough on children."

Another complication I hadn't dealt with yet.

"So think it over," the recording said. "We may want to go into a multiple marriage. Think about the people we know. Is there anyone we can both stand to live with for the first, oh, five to ten years? For instance, how do Lila and Jackson Bera feel about children? Do you know? Think it over and then call me. My love to you and Harry," she said, and was gone.

Laura was watching me. She started to say something, but the next message beat her to it.

The picture was fuzzy. Two men and a laughing little blond girl floated in free fall at skew angles. The man holding the little girl's hand was a rotund, cheerful man with thick white hair. The other was short and dark and very round of face, partly or wholly Eskimo, I guessed. I didn't know any of them.

"I am Howard de Campo, called Antsie, citizen of Vesta," the smiling Eskimo said. "You called to be informed of the motions of Mrs. Naomi Mitchison during certain hours. From 2250 Tuesday to 0105 Wednesday the lady in question was in *Chili Bird*, visiting I and my passenger, Dr. Raymond Q. Forward. The purpose of the visit is secret, but we will tell if necessary, of course. If you have to know more, call us at Confinement, please." The picture blinked out.

"By God, you were right," Laura said. "I could probably even guess the crime."

"They haven't admitted anything," I said. But the blond, blue-eyed little girl must have been included deliberately. She was Naomi at age four.

Laura said, " 'Love to you and Harry.' No lunie could ever have said that."

"She meant it."

"Suppose she'd known I was listening?"

"Would you object to my telling her someday?"

"Please don't," Laura said. She controlled it well, but the idea upset her. "Are you thinking of having children by Taffy Grimes?"

"Yes."

"What about us?"

I hadn't thought of that at all. "I wouldn't be here to act like a father. And I'll be sterile for another four months. Anyway, would my genes be right?"

"I didn't mean . . . never mind." She rolled over and came into my arms. The rest of our conversation was non-verbal. But what *had* she meant?

* * *

Shaeffer and Quifting had called Ceres to ask that a third Belter be chosen and sent to the moon as quickly as possible. Meanwhile, the conference would continue without Chris Penzler.

A nervous urgency was apparent while we were still involved with coffee and rolls. Charles Ward tried to assure us, before anyone else had suggested the possibility, that Chris had *not* been murdered by local terrorists bent on disrupting or exterminating the conference. The other lunies were quick to agree. Sure. Where were they getting their data?

Just before 0900 I phoned the mayor's office from the conference room. "You've heard about Chris Penzler?"

"Yes. A very sticky situation, Gil." The mayor was perturbed, and it showed. "We're doing all we can, of course. I imagine this will disrupt the conference."

"We'll see. That might have been the whole idea. Has Naomi Mitchison been released from the holding tanks?"

"No."

"Why not?"

"Releasing a convict from a holding tank isn't done by a wave of the hand. The medical—"

"Mayor, your holding tanks aren't that different from the ones on the slowboats, the interstellar colony ships. Crew members go in and out of the holding tanks a dozen times during any trip."

Hove's eyes flicked past my shoulder. I glanced back and found that I had an audience. Several conference members were following our conversation. That was all to the good, I thought.

Hove was saying, "You know nothing about the medical complexities. Furthermore, Mrs. Mitchison is a convicted criminal. Reversal of her sentence will not be accomplished by a wave of the hand, either."

"In that case, I'm going to raise some hell," I said.

"How do you mean that?"

I said, "The proceedings of the conference have been confidential so far—"

"And should be!" Bertha Carmody barked in my ear.

"Futz, Bertha, this is at the heart of what's been blocking us all along! Mayor, there's some question as to whether your law gives adequate protection to the defendant. Trials are over almost before they begin, and in twenty years not one sentence has been reversed. Naomi Mitchison's trial is the first to be investigated by outsiders. We now have evidence that someone else wanted Chris Penzler dead all along. Your son has filed to obtain Mrs. Mitchison's release. But when a committee member, me, checks with the mayor of Hovestraydt City, it turns out the conviction isn't even under review!"

"Damn it, Gil, the conviction *is* under review, right now!"

"Good. How long would you expect it to take?"

"I have no idea. A reversal may have to wait until the new investigation is over."

"Fine. In the meantime, get her out of the holding tank."

"Why? Chris's death may be unrelated to the first attempt."

"Granted. I won't try to guess the odds. I'll put it to you that Naomi is likely innocent—"

"Likely is too strong a word."

"—*and* a possible witness. Aside from that, the committee may want to call her to testify firsthand on how she's been treated. We've examined exactly two trials under lunar jurisprudence, and the other one . . . ah—"

"Matheson and Company," Stone put in helpfully.

"Yeah. That one looks kind of funny, too. And Naomi is still in a holding tank waiting to be broken up. How will all of this look to the newstapers?"

Bertha roared, "These proceedings are confidential! Hamilton, how can you think of exposing our deliberations to the news media?"

I said, "All right, Bertha. I'll stick to my opinions on the Mitchison case."

"I hope that that will not be necessary," the mayor said. "I intend to order Naomi Mitchison revived at once. She will be returned here under arrest to play her part in the investigation into Chris Penzler's death. Is *that* satisfactory, Mr. Hamilton?"

"Yes. Thank you." I called off the phone, and Bertha called the meeting to order.

When we broke for lunch, I suited up and headed for the mirror works. I found Harry McCavity just outside the air lock, waiting for it to cycle.

"I'm beat," he said. "It's been a long night. Morning, Gil . . . no, let me show you something first, and then I'm for bed."

He led me through the mirror works. "Penzler died from loss of blood," he said. "He was wearing a skintight suit. Cutting his hand off didn't release the pressure on his skin. But the blood must have jetted like a fire hose."

"He used it to write with."

"Drury told me. He'd have had to write *fast*."

Penzler's corpse was outside, in vacuum, under a silvered canopy to keep it cold. The dry remains had been sliced to obtain cross sections. They looked like petrified wood. Penzler's skintight pressure suit was next to it, opened along the back and spread like a pelt. The golden griffin glowed on its chest.

Harry picked up Chris's hand, a withered brown claw with four inches of wrist attached. He held it against the severed forearm. What with the shrinking of the flesh, it was hard to tell whether they belonged together. "Look at the bones," he said.

The ends of the bones were quite smooth and fitted perfectly.

"And here." He picked up the right glove from the pressure suit. "His hand was in it. Now look." He held it against the sliced fabric of the pressure suit's forearm.

There was almost no material missing. The laser had sliced through cleanly, at very high energy density, and no thicker than a fishing leader. Even laser beams spread with distance. "They must have been close together when it happened," I said.

"Too right. Penzler and his killer couldn't have been more than three feet apart."

"Huh." I tried to scratch my head through the helmet. "Harry, I don't know what it means yet."

We went back inside, and Harry headed for his bed. I called Artemus Boone and got him to join me for lunch.

We moved down the buffet table collecting dollops and samples of everything in sight. The food on Boone's plate became a precariously balanced cone with a hard-boiled pigeon's egg at the apex. He lowered it to the table slowly with both hands.

"It's not bad," he told me. "It's only complicated. I could argue either way: that Mrs. Mitchison is subject only to the lunar law or only to United Nations law, whichever she likes."

"So?"

"United Nations law would sterilize her, I think. She is both the father and the mother. One could argue that she has used two birthrights. Sterilization wouldn't stop her from growing another clone, so she might not object. For the same reason, the law might demand the right to execute her, but I think I could block that."

"How sure are you?"

"Not very. UN law isn't my home turf. I'd rather work within lunar law. As for the child, she can't be extradited, but she should never visit Earth."

"What's the position under lunar law?"

"Lunar law includes nothing like your fertility quotas. Women who bear children without previous marriage are on their own unless the father sues for his rights . . . well, that doesn't apply. But de Campo and Mrs. Mitchison *have* violated lunar medical restrictions. I'd think we want to stand trial here, then claim double jeopardy before the UN."

"She'd be safe then?"

"Up to a point." Boone coughed delicately. "The lady's attitude toward men might hamper her popularity with a jury. And there is still the matter of an attempted murder charge."

"Yeah. I need to talk about the murder," I said, "and I've run out of people to talk with. Have you got some free time?"

"Some. You don't propose to solve both crimes yourself this afternoon, do you?"

"Why not?"

Boone smiled. "Why indeed? For my defense of Mrs. Mitchison I needed a suspect other than Mrs. Mitchison. My main obstacle was your testimony."

"I can't change it. There wasn't anyone else out on the moon and no message laser."

"Well?"

"I keep thinking in terms of mirrors. Boone, I wish to hell I could put a mirror out there. That way the killer and the weapon could both be somewhere else."

Boone had been eating, talking between mouthfuls. He had a voracious appetite for so lean a man. He chewed and thought, swallowed, and said, "But the mirror would have to be in place."

"Remember how Chris acted when we asked him what kind of pressure suit the killer was wearing? He sweated. He dithered. He said he might have seen an optical illusion."

"A terrible experience. He might have blocked the memory."

"Sure. Then six days later he left us a dying message. Do you know about that?"

"N A K F. Meaningless."

"I've been assuming he died before he could finish. What was he trying to tell us? NAKED?"

"On the moon?" Boone smiled.

"Naked to vacuum," I said. "Chris stood up in his bath and saw someone out on the moon without a pressure suit. Don't you see? He was looking in a mirror."

"But what was he seeing? Himself?"

"No. He saw the killer. The killer must have been in one of the other apartments. Poor Chris, he must have thought he was going crazy. No wonder he wouldn't talk about it."

Boone ate quietly for a time. Then he said, "Mrs. Mitchison was on the second floor. We tend to put offworlders on the ground floor. Were all the ground floor apartments full? This is something we can check, but you see the implications. The killer is not a native."

That didn't fit my other assumptions, but— "Yeah, check those records. You've got the authority."

"I will." Boone smiled. "Now tell me why the mirror wasn't found by the police when they searched for an abandoned message laser."

"What about a mirror in low orbit? Mirrors don't have to be opaque to radar. A plane mirror with the right rotation might give the killer a couple of minutes to pick his shot. And we *know* he was hurried."

Boone snorted. "Ridiculous. An orbiting mirror would have had to be large enough for the killer to see Penzler and vice versa. It would probably have been in sunlight, since the assault took place just before dawn. *Anyone* could have seen it blazing like a beacon."

"All right, it's a stupid suggestion, but it's the best I've got. If we can put a disappearing mirror out there, we've cleared Naomi, haven't we?"

"Absolutely. I think we have enough to get her out of the holding tank *now* pending a second trial."

"Get together with the mayor," I told him. "I expect he's inclined to be reasonable."

"Good." Boone went back to eating. He had nearly finished that huge plate.

I said, "A mirror can be a thin film stretched on a frame, can't it? If the killer was a lunie cop, he could just pull it apart and stash it. Penzler said three hundred to four hundred meters from his window, but the mirror would be only half that far . . . hey. That tilted rock was 190 meters away. And everyone else would be searching in the wrong place."

"Tilted rock?"

"Futz, yes! There's a big boulder out there 190 meters from his window. Chris thought he was looking past it, but he couldn't say which side. The mirror was probably propped on the rock!"

Boone's deep-set eyes seemed to withdraw further. He ate steadily while he thought. Then, "Very good. Did you have a particular suspect in mind?"

I knew of a policewoman who had been involved in yesterday's search for Chris Penzler. I knew she had a liking for flatlanders. In her love affairs (plural or singular?) she was possessive in a fashion more typical of lunie than flatland custom. She might have involved herself with Chris Penzler, then been rejected by him, at least by her own standards.

She was thoroughly familiar with the Hovestraydt City computer from age ten. If Naomi could have taken a message laser without leaving a record, why not Laura Drury? She could get into an empty apartment the same way.

A lunie cop could have committed the later, successful murder. The moon was swarming with them. The killer could have joined the swarm before or after the murder, given that we didn't have an exact time of death.

But Laura had been at the desk the night Penzler was shot in his bath. Hadn't she? When had she come on duty? Would she have had time to go outside for a folding mirror? The killer had been in a hurry that night . . .

"Hamilton?"

"Sorry. Yeah, I've got suspects, but I still don't have a disappearing mirror."

"This isn't a courtroom."

"I know. Keep thinking about the mirror. I'm not a lunie; I'm handicapped."

I returned to my room after the afternoon session.

Outside my window the dreadful alien light of lunar noon was somewhat softened by filter elements in the window. It was still too bright. I tried commands on the window until I got it dimmed a bit.

By now I could have picked out the tilted rock while

blind drunk. A hundred ninety yards away ... Chris had
seen a human figure three to four hundred meters away,
past the tilted rock. I looked out at the tilted rock and tried
to recall the darkness of a week ago, when Chris Penzler
had glimpsed ... what?

An image in a mirror?

The distances were close enough. One hundred ninety
meters to a mirror on the tilted rock, another hundred
ninety back. Chris had said three to four hundred meters.
More reason to think he'd seen a lunie. A lunie taller than
the Belters Penzler was used to would seem closer.

He'd gone out to look at the tilted rock. Had he found
what he was after before someone had found him? Probably
not; he'd left us only a puzzle written in frozen blood.

Alan Watson and I hadn't found much, either ...

My phone was calling me.

It was Boone. "The court has ordered the lady revived,"
he told me. "She's already out. She'll be returned to
Hovestraydt City around noon tomorrow. I was told she
would need to recuperate overnight in the Copernicus hospital."

Why? But she was out; that was what counted. "Is she
awake now?"

"Yes, I've talked to her."

"Okay, I'll—"

"Please don't call her, Hamilton. She sounded tired. She
wouldn't give me visual."

"Um. Okay. What's the situation with apartments?"

Boone looked cautiously triumphant. "There's some inconsistency in the records. Mrs. Mitchison was given a
room on the second floor because the computer registered
all ground floor rooms as occupied. I got a printout of the
occupants as of that date. The computer does not list room
oh-forty-seven as empty *or* occupied."

"Have you tried to look in oh-forty-seven?"

"Not yet. I'll need a court order."

"No, you won't. Have Naomi ask for that room. If anyone flinches, it may tell us something."

He smirked an un-Lincolnesque smirk. "I like it."

"Okay. Now *tell* somebody about this, will you? Get the judge in charge of reviewing Naomi's conviction and tell him about that disappearing room. Or tell anyone at all."

"Surely you're being overdramatic?"

"You know too much to be safe. We're dealing with someone who can control the lock on your apartment. Look, do it just to make me happy."

"All right, Mr. Hamilton." Smiling, he called off.

I went back to the window.

A mirror would reflect a laser beam for only an instant. No mirror is perfectly reflective, of course. In the first instant of a laser burst the face of a mirror would already be vaporizing, going concave, defocusing the beam . . . and it *had* defocused in midburn!

But where had the mirror gone?

The case was loaded with traditional elements. Locked room, inverted, with the failed murderer locked out on the moon. Cryptic dying message. Now I was looking for mirror tricks. What next? Disappearing daggers of memory plastic, broken clocks giving spurious alibis—

The moonscape blazed at me through the window. I rubbed my fingers together, remembering . . .

Alan was on top of the tilted rock, finding nothing. I'd scraped at the shadowed back of the rock with my gloves. White stuff had come off. I'd watched it disappear from my fingertips.

Frost, of course. Water ice. But on the surface of the moon? It had startled me then. Now, suddenly, it made sense.

And now, suddenly, I had half the puzzle solved.

12. THE TRADITIONAL ELEMENTS

"Phone call, Mr. Hamilton. Phone call, Mr.—"

"Oh, futz."

"—milton. Phone call—"

"Chiron, answer phone." I disengaged the strap across my chest and sat up.

"Hello, Gil." The screen was blank, but the voice was Naomi's. She sounded tired. There was none of the jubilation you'd expect of someone raised from death.

"Hello. You going to give me vision?"

"No."

Something like postoperative depression, maybe. "Where are you calling from?"

"Here. Hovestraydt City. They say I'm still under arrest."

Had she arrived early? But my clock said noon. I'd been a long time falling asleep.

"Have you talked to Boone yet? We still have an attempted murder to deal with. We'd like to pin both murders on someone."

"Go ahead."

"Are you under drugs?"

"No, but nothing seems to matter much. Who got me out of the freezer?"

"Mostly Alan Watson," I said for sweet charity's sake.

"Um."

"Naomi, we know where you were when someone shot Chris Penzler in his bath. Boone and I discussed it over the *chili* at lunch yesterday."

"Over the . . . oh." She thought it out. Clearly I knew and didn't trust the phone system. "All right. Now what?"

"You're still a suspect. We'd like to produce an actual killer. But he wasn't outside after his first try at Penzler. We have to explain why, or else we have to show where *you* were at that time. Boone says that's not as bad as it sounds. You should talk to him."

"All right."

"We'd like to see you in your apartment."

"Gil, I'd rather not see anyone." Bitterly, "I was just getting used to the idea of being dead."

"So you're not dead. Now what?"

"I don't know."

I couldn't tell her why we had to see the apartment. Not

by phone. In her present state, would she take orders? "Call Boone," I said. "Tell him I'll meet him in your apartment. It's oh-forty-seven, isn't it? Tell him to get the police to let us in. Then order us breakfast. Plenty of coffee."

There were several seconds of dead air. Then, for the first time, I heard emotion in her voice. "All right, Gil," she purred, and was gone.

Bitter satisfaction, that was what it sounded like. But why?

The lunie cop guarding room 047 was a stranger. I had to nerve myself to turn my back on him. Paranoia . . .

Naomi ushered me in.

Boone was already there, seated at the breakfast table. I didn't understand why he watched me so intently. I was concentrating on what I had to say, not on what I was seeing.

But it seemed to me that my eyes blurred when I looked at Naomi. She seemed distorted somehow.

She had recovered some of her self-possession, I thought. But she seemed clumsy, and she moved with care. I'd thought she was used to lunar gravity. She said, "Surprise."

And then I saw.

"When you're in the holding tanks, they're not supposed to touch you except in emergencies," she said. "Did you know that?"

I had trouble getting my breath. "I knew it. We've been discussing it in the conference. What do lunies consider an emergency?"

"Aye, there's the rub," Naomi said. "They apologized of course. They did the best they could. Seems a Brazilian planetologist waded into a dust pool near Copernicus. It's a wonder she got out at all with her legs frozen solid. She managed to fall and rip her suit, too. Vacuum ruptured both eardrums and one lung and an eye, and the fall broke two ribs. Guess who happened to have the right rejection spectrum to help her out?"

Her legs weren't bad, but they didn't look quite right.

Her face didn't look quite right, either. And something about her body . . . maybe the way she carried herself . . .

"She's famous, I gather, this Mary de Santa Rita Lisboa. All hell would break loose if she couldn't get adequate medical treatment at Copernicus. Terrible publicity. For God's sake, tell me how I look!"

"Just about the same," I said. It was true. She seemed just faintly distorted. Surgery on her inner ears, twice, had changed the outline of her face. Her eyes weren't quite the same color; how could I have missed that? Her torso seemed twisted. She'd cure that when she learned to walk again. After all, her legs were changed, too. They were too thin . . . not lunie legs, thank God; she'd have looked like a stork. They'd probably come off a Belter.

Somehow the doctors had found parts that matched, almost. That didn't alter the fact that they had raided a holding tank!

"I'll want you to testify before the committee," I told her. "I'm going to raise hell."

"Good," she said venomously.

"Boone, did you explain the legal situation?"

Boone nodded. Naomi said, "I wish I'd known all of this before the trial. I don't much like the thought of going through *two* more trials, you know. One to get me clear of this attempted murder charge, one to nail me for having a clone made."

"Will you do it?"

"I suppose so."

I was fighting the abstract horror of knowing that lunie hospitals had been raiding the holding tanks and a purely personal horror that it could happen to Naomi. Naomi was changed. She wasn't unsightly, just . . . changed. Patchwork girl! This was not the woman whose untouchable beauty had sent me fleeing to the asteroid belt long ago.

"Reversing the judgment against you may be more difficult than you think," Boone said. "No judge enjoys ruling that another judge was wrong. We—"

Which reminded me. "Boone? I've found the disappearing mirror."

"What? How?"

"Water. You pour a big, flat pan full of water. You freeze it. You take it outside, into vacuum and shadow. Out on the moon it'll stay at a hundred degrees below zero or less as long as you keep it in shadow. Now you use the mirror-making facilities to polish it optically flat and silver it. Would it work?"

Boone gaped. It made him look a lot less like Abe Lincoln. He said, "Yes, it'd work. My God, that's why he was in such a hurry! He wanted to kill Penzler just before the sun touched the mirror!"

I smiled. The *eureka* sensation. "But Chris wouldn't cooperate. He liked playing with the water."

"When the sun touched the mirror, it would just disappear!"

"Almost," I said. "When it evaporated, some of the water vapor wound up on the back of the tilted rock, in shadow. I found frost there. It'll be gone by now, but we've got other evidence. Harry McCavity says the beam either spread or constricted during the burn. The ice was vaporizing. That's what really saved Chris's life."

I turned to Naomi, who was looking bewildered. "What all of this means is that the murder attempt happened here in this room. Boone, have you had a chance—"

He shook his head. "Nothing odd here at all. These rooms are kept clean by automatics. I expect we won't find anything. Gil, the problem is that any citizen of Hovestraydt City could use some corner of the mirror works without being noticed. We even let Boy Scout troops run projects there."

"I know. Too many suspects."

"There ought to be some way to narrow it down."

"How am I fixed for lawsuits?"

"Nonsense. You're an ARM trying to solve a murder. I'm a lawyer in conference with my client."

"I'd like to know more about Chris's love life," I said. "Naomi—"

"He made a pass at me. Rather crude," she said.

"Would he want to sleep with a lunie woman?"

"That I don't know. Some men like variety. Itch did."

So did I. Futz. So try the phone—

Laura was busy. I got her by belt phone, voice only. "Gil? I couldn't make it last night. I'm short of sleep now. It was the Penzler case."

"No sweat. I was playing detective. I'm playing detective now. Do you know anything about Chris Penzler's taste in women? Even by hearsay?"

"Mmm. Hearsay, maybe. Do you remember the prosecution attorney from Naomi Mitchison's trial?"

The elf woman. Face of cold perfection. "I remember."

"Caroline's fiancé got drunk with some friends and was going to go looking for Penzler. They had to talk him out of it. That's all I know. It might have nothing to do with Caroline at all. He never said."

"Anything else?"

"Nothing I can think of."

"Thanks. When can I call you back?"

"I'm off duty at noon, with luck. But I need sleep, Gil."

"Sometime this evening?"

"Good."

I called off the phone. I thought hard. Then I called the mayor's office.

"Mr. Hamilton." I wasn't Gil anymore, not since yesterday's power play. "You'll find that Naomi Mitchison is out of the holding tank and has been returned here."

"I'm with her now. She's got a few parts missing; did you know that? Missing and replaced."

"I was told," Hove said. "I won't take responsibility for that. I can guess what your attitude will be. Is that why you called?"

"No. Right now I'm more concerned with keeping her out of the holding tank. Hove, you're a politician; you have to deal with all kinds of people. Do you happen to know if Chris Penzler was attracted to lunie women?"

He stiffened a little. "I presume he wouldn't show it. An offworld diplomat wouldn't jeopardize his position in such a fashion."

Was Hove that naive? "We know damn well he offended *somebody*, Hove, and we've got good reason to think it was a citizen of Hovestraydt City. You were here twenty years ago, weren't you? And so was Penzler. Did you hear any rumors then? Were there complaints that had to be settled quietly? Or . . . yeah. Did he make regular trips to the Belt Trading Post, that stopped suddenly?"

"I know the place you mean," Hove said reluctantly. "Aphrodite's. They don't keep records. I can look up records of puffer rentals from twenty years ago if it's important to you."

"Good. It is."

"Gil, why do you think a local man killed Chris?"

"Nobody else could have made the . . . Mayor, it's too easy to plug into the phone system."

"I'll get you your data," Hove said, and called off.

Boone and Naomi were both looking at me. I said, "If Chris had an affair with a lunie woman, she might be annoyed when he went off with someone else. Lunie customs are funny."

"Flatlander customs are funny," Boone corrected me, "but you may be right. Who?"

"Oh, it's just a possible situation." I got up to pace. I was going to *hate* it if it was Laura. "Here's another. I know a couple of newstapers who might commit a practical joke for kicks and news value. The Belter arrived early; she came to meet our ship. Maybe she had time to make the mirror and place it. She could pass for a lunie. Her torso painting is a naked lady."

"Didn't they actually save Penzler's life?"

"It'd still be a very rough practical joke. Chris might have brought his own enemies from the Belt. Either of the two could know enough programming to steal a message laser."

Boone was nodding. "They're living like a married couple. They must have known each other for some time."

I grinned at him. "They're not lunies, Boone. I just don't know. There are two other Belters on the committee. They could have had something against him . . ."

Naomi had a thoughtful, puzzled look. I assumed she was confused, not following our line of thought. I hardly noticed when she went to the phone.

"This case does have its traditional elements," I said. "What time is it in Los Angeles?"

"I have no idea," Boone said.

"I should call Luke Garner. He's got a tape library of old mysteries. He'd love this. Dying messages, locked rooms, tricks with mirrors."

"We don't *have* to produce a killer, you know. That's for the police. Now that we know how the mirror trick was worked, we can clear Mrs. Mitchison."

"Boone, I get edgy when I've solved two-thirds of a puzzle. That's the time when you can get killed."

Naomi tapped at the keys. Hologram head-and-shoulder portraits appeared in a quartered screen. I stepped behind her for a better look. A woman I'd never seen before . . . and Chris Penzler . . . and Mayor Watson . . .

The door announcer said, "Mayor Watson speaking. I'd like to talk to Mr. Hamilton if he's still there. May I come in?"

"Chiron, door open," Naomi said without looking up. Then, "No—"

I looked around as Hove came in. He came in fast. "Close the door," he told Naomi. He was carrying a police message laser.

I went for my gun. ARMs carry a tiny two-shot hand weapon at all times. It fires a cloud of anesthetic needles. I'd turned it in on arrival, of course. If that first reflexive move hadn't slowed me, maybe I could have done something.

Boone, half reclining in a web chair, hadn't had a chance to move at all. Now he raised his hands. So did I.

Naomi said, "I should have thought. I just . . . futz!"

The mayor told her, "Close the door or I'll kill you."

Naomi called the door closed.

"Good enough," Hove said, and he slumped a little. "I'm not sure what to do next. Perhaps you can help me with my problem. If I kill all of you, what are my chances of getting away with it?"

Boone smiled slowly. "Speaking as your lawyer . . ."

"Please," the mayor said. The little glass lens in the end of the gun wavered about, pointing at us all. He could chop us all up before we could do more than twitch. How had he slipped it past the cop? "If you don't speak, I'll kill you. If I catch you in a lie, I'll kill you. Do you understand?"

Boone said, "Consider the political repercussions of three more murders. You'll destroy Hovestraydt City."

I saw it in Hove's face: that shot drew blood. But he said, "You're in a position to convict the *mayor* of murdering a Belt politician. How would *that* affect the city? I can't allow it. Gil, why did the killer have to be a resident?"

"We're talking about the bathtub attack, remember. Chris saw the killer too close. That makes him tall. It took a resident to borrow the facilities in the mirror works and know how to use them. He also had to futz with the city computer. A lot of residents seem to be good at that." And the mayor, I thought suddenly, would have to be even better.

"So you know about the mirror. Can you tell me how Chris was able to see me? I wasn't fool enough to leave the room lights on while I waited for him to stand up."

"Huh. You weren't?" I thought about it. "Oh. *His* lights were on. You were lighted by the mirror."

He nodded. "That's bothered me ever since. Was it me you suspected?"

"I'm flabbergasted. Hove, *why?*" And then I saw why, out of the corner of my eye, on Naomi's phone screen.

Hove seemed almost disinterested. "Twice he came to the moon to meddle in our internal affairs. First to impose the holding tanks on us, then to criticize the way we use them. Never mind. Can you think of any way in which the police can trace me? Without your help, of course."

"The guard at the door?"

"He didn't see me. He won't see me leave."

I couldn't think of a thing.

Naomi said, "Mayor, do you see where my finger is now?"

It was on the *Return* key for the phone keyboard. I saw that much, and then I stepped between Naomi and the gun. Hove didn't react fast enough to stop me. "You'll have to shoot through me," I said. "You'll never make it."

Naomi said, "One tap of this key and these four faces appear on every phone screen in the city."

"We can negotiate," I said quickly, soothingly, I hoped. Hove's eyes were going desperate. "You tried to kill Chris Penzler for political reasons? Fine, so say we all. You sliced his hand off six days later? Fine. Do you want to tell us how you managed that?"

He'd been about to fire. Perhaps he still was. "When did it happen?" he asked.

"Chris could have died anytime in a five-hour period. You can't possibly have an alibi. You must have posed as a policeman. The computer would have issued you a police skintight suit and lost the records."

"Yes. Certainly."

"And Chris left a dying message that points toward you."

I saw the intensity setting on the laser start to unwind and saw Hove thumb it back to maximum. Hove said, "Did he? Did he really? That's very interesting."

"It points toward you," I said, "but not directly. Chris was only three feet away when the laser sliced his hand off. He must have seen his killer's face and his chest symbol, too. Why didn't he just write T R E E or M A Y O R ? Somebody's bound to wonder. Of course, if you just turn yourself in, the case is solved."

Hove seemed lost in thought. Then, "Gil, do you understand what this affair *could* do to my city?"

"It's bad now. It could get much worse if things run their course."

"Yes. God, yes." He drew himself up and, looking down on us from a great height, said, "Here are my terms. I want an hour to escape. After that you can tell the police *all that we've discussed.* Agreed? Your word of honor?"

"Yes," I said.

"Yes," Boone said.

Naomi hesitated for several nerve-shattering seconds. Her hand was starting to tremble where she held it poised above the *Return* key. She said, "Yes."

"That on the screen goes back into storage."

"Yes," Naomi said.

"Open the door," the mayor said.

The laser was under his coat as he stepped into the hall. Naomi called the door closed. Then she said, "Well?"

I mopped away sweat with a napkin. "*My* word of honor is good."

Boone, faintly smiling, was looking at his watch.

"And so say we all," Naomi said. "The bastard! Where will he go?"

"Someplace where he can't be questioned," I said. "He'll get a puffer and go till he's out of air, then find a dust pool."

"You think so?" She looked at the hologram portraits. Four of them. Chris Penzler, and Mayor Hovestraydt Watson, and Alan Watson, and a very tall, elfishly beautiful young woman with long light brown hair. I could guess who she was from the context. Naomi said, "I wonder how she died."

"You think he killed her? Maybe. It hardly matters now."

"Right." Naomi typed rapidly. The screen cleared.

We waited.

13. PENALTIES

We found the guard snoring outside Naomi's door. Hove had fired a cloud of soluble anesthetic crystals into him from an ARM-issue handgun. It was mine. I'd turned it in on arrival; Hove must have persuaded the computer to release it.

Hove . . . well, we waited it out, more or less grimly. He had checked out a puffer and gone. We searched the projected moonscape while we could; he probably hid until Watchbird Two set. Jefferson's police searched old mines and known cave systems. Nothing. He certainly hadn't reached the Belt Trading Post; the Belters were looking for him, too. Jefferson sent men to search the launch head for the Grimalde mass driver.

Their mistake, I think, was in assuming Hove was desperate to live. Hove's problem was to hide a puffer and a corpse; his own. My own theory is that he blew them both to bits by exploding the puffer's fuel and oxygen.

Alan Watson came in late that night, looking used-up. He came back to life when he saw Naomi. They talked seriously for a while, and then she went off under his long arm. I didn't see them again until the next morning.

By then I had talked to Harry McCavity again.

Alan and Naomi were eating a huge breakfast together on the dining level. I managed to be at the buffet when Alan went for more coffee.

"I have to see you in private," I said.

Coffee sloshed. I startled him, I think. He asked, "Isn't it over yet?"

"Mostly it's about you and your father."

A momentary wariness showed in his face. Then, "All right."

I ate breakfast while I waited. Presently Naomi left, and Alan came to join me. "She told me about yesterday," he said. "He could have killed you all. I wish none of it had happened."

"So do I. Alan, you're leaving the moon."

His mouth opened. He stared. "What?"

"Come on, you're not that surprised. I made some promises to Mayor Hove, but I made them at gunpoint. Be off the moon within a week. Don't ever come back. Or I'll break those promises."

He studied my eyes. No, he wasn't that surprised. "You'll have to spell it out for me."

"I'm not enjoying this," I said. "I'll try to keep it short. Chris Penzler was close enough to get a good look at the man who killed him. We know it was a lunie. Even if Penzler didn't know his name, he could have tried to describe the chest emblem. Instead, he left a reference to the attempt to kill him in his bathtub a week earlier. Why would he protect the man who murdered him?"

"Well?"

"You're his son. Naomi finally saw it, and I should have. You've Hove Watson's height, and I took that for genes, but it isn't. You were raised in lunar gravity. Otherwise you look a lot like Chris Penzler and somewhat like your mother and not at all like Hove Watson."

Alan was looking down into his coffee. He was quite pale. "This is all pure speculation, isn't it?"

"It's the kind of speculation that could finish Hovestraydt City, I think. You're supposed to be the mayor's son, the heir apparent. It's bad enough if Hove killed Penzler for political reasons—"

"I know. You could be right."

"Anyway, I did a little more speculating. Then last night I got Harry McCavity out of bed and made him check a certain pressure suit helmet for traces of dried blood."

Alan looked up. I might have stepped out of a nightmare, the way he looked at me. I said, "What did he do, offer to legitimize you?"

"Offer?" Alan laughed out loud, an ugly sound, then looked quickly around him. Faces had turned. Alan lowered his voice. "He insisted! He was going to name me as his heir and bastard!"

"Did you kill him to get Naomi off the hook?"

"No, no. I wouldn't have hurt him at all if I'd had time to *think*. I could have explained it to him, couldn't I? He just didn't know what he'd be doing to me.

"He said he was my father. He said he was going to *announce* it. He wouldn't listen. And I was holding the laser. I lost my head. It was all over in a thousandth of a second. I sliced his hand off, and he pointed at me and sprayed blood in my face. Blinded me. When I wiped it off the glass, he was gone. I looked for him to get his suit sealed and get him to a hospital. When I found him, he was dead."

"Uh huh."

Alan was very pale. He wasn't seeing me at all. He said, "His wrist was still bubbling."

I said, "You could blame Chris for letting his gonads lead him around. You could blame Hove for trying to kill him. It didn't work, but that's what started Chris thinking about his children. Sure you're bound to blame yourself, but Alan, it wasn't all your fault."

"All right. Now what?"

"If the truth came out, hell wouldn't hold the political repercussions, and you'd be broken up for parts. I don't want that. But I won't have you in a position of political power, and there's no way you can stay on the moon without becoming mayor. Get off the moon within a week or I'll start talking."

"I suppose you left a letter somewhere in case something happens to you?"

"Get stuffed."

He stared. "But you're giving me a week to kill you!"

I got up. "You're not the type. And I meant it. I meant it all," I said, and left.

The rules the committee laid down during the following week included provisions for periodic review of lunar legal practice. None of the delegates were especially happy with the new laws. The lunies liked it least, but how could they object after Naomi's testimony? They compromised.

We were wrapping up the conference the day Alan Watson left for Ceres. I'd have preferred to see him go, but it didn't matter. Given who he was, he got a police escort. He was definitely gone.

Laura told me about it that evening. "Naomi Mitchison went with him," she said.

"Good."

"Do you mean that?"

"Sure. I like to keep things tidy."

Naomi had asked for her Belt citizenship a few days ago, and Hildegarde Quifting was glad to ram it through for her. Naomi would be an embarrassment on Earth or on the moon. Moving her to the Belt let everyone breathe easier.

Including Naomi. Old friends on Earth could remember her as she used to be. She needn't stand trial for illegal cloning. Her little girl would be waiting for her.

She might even be in love with Alan Watson. Futz, I even like the idea. Let it stand.

✳
THE WOMAN IN DEL REY CRATER

We were falling back toward the moon. It's always an uneasy sensation, and in a lemmy I felt frail. A lemmy is a spacecraft but a very small one; it won't even reach lunar orbit.

Lawman Bauer-Stanson set the attitude jets popping. The lemmy rolled belly up to give us a view. "There, Hamilton," she said, waving at the bone-white land above our heads. "With the old VERBOTEN sign across it."

It was four T-days past sunrise, and the shadows were long. Del Rey was well off to the side, six kilometers across, almost edge-on and flattening as we fell. There were dots of dulled silver everywhere inside the crater, clustering near the center. A crudely drawn gouge ran straight across the crater's center, deep and blackly shadowed. That line and the circle of rim formed the VERBOTEN sign.

I asked, "Aren't you going to take us across?"

"No." Lawman Bauer-Stanson floated at her ease while choppy moonscape drifted nearer. "I don't like radiation."

"We're shielded."

"Suuure."

The computer rolled us over and started the main motor. The lunie lawman tapped in a few instructions. The computer was doing all the work, but I let her land us before I spoke. She'd put us a good kilometer south of the crater rim.

I said, "Being cautious, are we?"

Bauer-Stanson looked at me over her shoulder. Narrow shoulders, long neck, pointed chin: she had the lunies' look of a Tolkien elf matriarch. Her bubble helmet cramped her long hair. It was black going white, and she wore it in a feathery crest, modified Belt style.

She said, "This is a scary place, Ubersleuth Hamilton. Damn few people come here on purpose."

"I was invited."

"We're lucky you were available. Ubersleuth Hamilton, the shield on a lemmy will stop a solar storm, the *wildest* solar storm. Thank God for the Shreveshield." The radiation signal pulled at Bauer-Stanson's eyes and mine. No rads were getting through at all. "But Del Rey Crater is way different."

The Earth was a blue-white sickle ten degrees above the horizon. Through either window I could see classic moonscape, craters big and little, and the long rim of Del Rey. Wilderness.

"I'm just asking, but couldn't you have set us down closer to Del Rey? Or else near the processing plant?"

She leaned across me, our helmets brushing. "Look that way, the right edge of the crater. Now lots closer and a bit right. Look for wheel treads and a mound—"

"Ah." A kilometer out from the rim wall: a long low hill of lunar dust and coarser debris with a gaping hole in one end.

"You should know by now, Hamilton. We bury everything. The sky is the enemy here. There's meteors, radiation . . . spacecraft, for that matter."

I was watching the mound, expecting some kind of minitractor to pop out.

She caught me looking. "We turned off the waldo tugs when we found the body. They've been off for twenty hours or so. *You* get to tell *us* when we can turn them on again. Shall we get to it?" Bauer-Stanson's fingers danced over pressure points on the panel. A whine wound down to profound silence as air was sucked from the cabin.

We were dressed alike in skintight pressure suits under leaded armor, borrowed, that didn't fit well. I felt my belly band squeeze tight as vacuum enclosed us. Bauer-Stanson tapped again, and the roof lifted up and sideways.

We moved back into the cargo bay and positioned ourselves at either end of a device built along the lines of a lunar two-wheeled puffer. We lifted it out of the bay and dropped it over the side.

The Mark Twenty-nine's wheels were toroidal birdcages as tall as my shoulders with little motors on the wheel hubs. In lunar gravity wheels don't have to be sturdy, but a vehicle needs a wide stance because weight won't hold it stable. The thing stood upright even without the kickstands. Lowslung between the wheels, a bulky plastic case and a heavy lock hid the works of Shreve Development's experimental radiation shield, power source, sensor devices, and other secrets, too, no doubt. A bucket seat was bolted to the case, with cameras and more sensing devices behind that.

Bauer-Stanson scrambled after it. She pulled it several feet from the lemmy and turned on the shield.

I'd done spot repairs on the Shreveshield in my own ship, years ago when I was a Belt miner. The little version is a flat plate, twelve feet by twelve feet, with rounded corners and a small secured housing at one corner. Fractal scrollwork covers it in frilly curves of superconductor, growing microscopically fine around the edges. You can bend it, but not far. In my old ship it wrapped around the D-T tank, and the shield effect enclosed everything but the motor. In a police lemmy it wraps the tank twice around.

No Shreveshield could have been fitted into the Mark Twenty-nine puffer.

But a halo had formed around it, very like the nearly imperceptible violet glow around the lemmy itself. I'd never seen that glow before. The rad shield normally doesn't have to fight that hard.

Lawman Bauer-Stanson stood within the glow. She waved me over.

I crossed the space between one shield and the other in

two bounces. Vacuum and hard bright stars and alien landscapes and falling don't scare me, but radiation is something else.

I asked, "Lawman, why did we only bring one of these puffers?"

"Ubersleuth Hamilton, there *is* only one." She sighed. "May I call you Gil?"

I'd been getting tired of this myself. "Sure. Hecate?"

"He-ca-*tee*," she said. Three syllables. "Gil, Shreve Development makes active radiation shields. They only make the two kinds, and they're both for spacecraft."

"We use them on Earth, too. Some of the old fusion plants are hotter'n hell. The Shreveshield was big news when I was, oh, eight years old. They used it to make a documentary on South-Central Los Angeles, but what got my attention was the spacecraft."

"*Tell* me about it. Thirty years ago a solar storm would have us marooned, huddling underground. We couldn't launch ships even as far as Earth."

The big shields had come first, I remembered. They were used to protect cities. There was a Shreveshield on the first tremendous slowboat launched toward Alpha Centauri. The little shields, eight years later, were small enough for three-man ships, and that was enough for me. I lofted out to mine the Belt.

"I hope they got rich," I said.

"Yah. When nobody gets rich, they call that a recession," Hecate said. "They spend some of the money on research. They'd like to build a little man-sized shield. They don't talk about the mistakes, but the Mark Twenty-nine is what they've got now."

"You must be persuasive as hell."

"Yonnie Kotani's my cousin's wife. She let us borrow it. Gil, whatever we learn about this is confidential. You are not to open that lock, ARM or no. *Puffer*," she said in fine disgust.

"Sorry."

"Yah. Well, this version works all the time, Yonnie said. It's still too expensive to market."

"Hecate, is it just conceivable," I wondered, "that Shreve would like me to test their Mark Twenty-nine active shield for them?"

She shook her head; the pepper and salt crest swirled inside the helmet. Amused. "Not *you*. A dead flatlander celebrity riding their Mark Twenty-nine Shreveshield? They could watch your death grin in every boob cube in the solar system! Shall I take the first ride?"

"I want a fresh look. I don't want to deal with your tire prints." I boarded the Mark Twenty-nine before she could object.

She made no move to stop me. I said, "Check the reception."

She was into the lemmy's cabin in a lovely graceful leap. She brought up the feed from my helmet camera. "You're on, nice and ... actually the picture's jumping a little. Good enough, though."

"Keep your eye on me. You can coach." I kicked the Mark Twenty-nine into gear and rolled toward the rim.

I'd been wakened from a sound sleep by her call. They keep the same time over the whole moon, so it was the middle of the night for Hecate Bauer-Stanson, too.

Ah, well. I had time to shower and get some breakfast while she landed and refueled, and that's never guaranteed. But it didn't sound like the intruder in Del Rey Crater needed *immediate* justice.

During the flight I'd had a chance to read about Del Rey Crater.

Just before the turn of the millennium, Boeing, then more or less an aircraft company, had done a survey. What kind of customer would pay how much for easy access to orbit?

The answers it got depended heavily on the cost of launch. A hundred thirty years ago those costs were the stuff of fantasy. NASA's weird political spacecraft, the Shuttle, launched for three thousand dollars per pound and up. At that price there would be no customers at all: nothing would fly without tax-financed kickbacks, and nothing did.

At two hundred dollars a pound—then considered marginally possible—the Net could afford to hold gladiatorial contests in orbit.

Intermediate prices would buy High Frontier antiweapons, orbiting solar power, high-end tourism, hazardous waste disposal, funerals . . .

Funerals. For five hundred dollars a pound, an urnful of ashes could be launched frozen in a block of ice for the solar wind to scatter to the stars. They launched from Florida in those days. Florida's funeral lobby must have *owned* the state. Florida passed a state law. No funeral procedure could be licensed in Florida unless grieving relatives could visit the grave . . . via a paved road!

Boeing also considered disposal of hazardous waste from fission plants.

You wouldn't just fire it off. First you'd separate the leftover uranium and/or plutonium, the fuel, to use again. Then you'd take out low-level radioactives and bury them in bricks. The truly noxious remainder, about three percent by mass, you would package to survive an unexpected reentry. Then you'd bomb a crater on the moon with them.

Power plant technology would improve over the decades to come. Our ancestors saw that far. In time that awful goo would once again be fuel. Future stockholders would want to find it.

Boeing had chosen Del Rey Crater with some care.

Del Rey was little but deep, just at the moon's visible rim. Meteors massing 1.1 tonnes, slamming down at two kilometers per second, would raise dust plumes against the limb of the moon. An amateur's telescope could find them. Lowell Observatory could get great pictures for the evening news: effective advertising, and free. The high rim would catch more of the dust . . . not all but most.

My search program had turned up a Lester del Rey with a half-century career in science fiction. The little crater had indeed been named for him. And he'd written an early story about an imaginary fission power plant: "Nerves."

To a man used to moonscapes the view from the crater rim was quite strange. It's not unusual for craters to overlap craters. But they clustered in the center, so that the central peak had been battered flat, and *every crater was the same size*. Yet more twenty-meter craters shaped the line that made Del Rey into one huge FORBIDDEN sign.

Everything around me was covered in pairs of tractor treadmarks a meter apart, often with a middle track as of something being dragged. A kilometer away, the tread marks thinned out and disappeared. There I began to see silvery beads at the center of every crater.

And one a little shinier, the wrong color, off center. I used the zoom feature in my faceplate to expand the view.

A pressure suit lay facedown. It was a hardshell, not a skintight. I was looking at the top of its head.

Corrugated footprints ran away from the body, three and four yards apart. The intruder had been running toward the rim to my right, south-southeast, leaping like a Lunar Olympics runner.

"Still got me, Hecate?"

"Yes, Gil. Your camera's better than the one on the waldo tug, but I can't make out any markings on the suit."

"It's head-on to me. Okay, I'm setting a relay antenna. Now I'll get closer." I started the Mark Twenty-nine rolling into the crater. If the shield around me was glowing, I couldn't see it from inside.

"I think you were wrong. That isn't a flatlander's suit. It's just old."

"Gil, we went to some effort to get the ARM involved. That was *never* a lunie design. It's too square. The helmet's wrong. This fishbowl design we're wearing, we were already using it when we built Luna City!"

"Hecate, how did you find this thing? How long has it been lying here?"

Hesitation. "We don't send sputniki over Del Rey Crater

very often. It's hard on the instruments. Nobody saw anything odd until the waldo tugs went in, and then we got a nice view through a tug's camera."

Even if a few sputniki did cross over Del Rey, the suit wouldn't contrast with the other silver dots around it. How long had it been here? "Hecate, divert a sputnik or a ship with a camera. We need an overhead view. Do you have the authority, or do I have to play dominance games?"

"I'll find out."

"In a minute. These waldo tugs. What are you stockpiling? The moon has helium-three fusion and solar power, too!"

"Those old impact tanks go off to the Helios plants."

"Why?"

Hecate sighed. "Beats the hell out of me. Maybe you can find out. You've got clout."

I saw a canister broken open and steered wide around it. Invisible death. I couldn't see any kind of glow around me: no evil blue Cherenkov radiation and nothing from my own shield, either.

What if my wheels broke down? I might trust the Shreveshield, but how careful had Shreve Development been with something as simple, as off-the-shelf as a pair of power wheels? I couldn't leave the Mark Twenty-nine without frying . . .

Dumb. I'd just carry it out. Hecate and I had picked it up easily. *Why* does radiation make people so nervous?

I stopped a little way from the downed suit. There were no tracks nearby, only the marks under the gloves and boots. The deader had clawed at the dust, leaving finger and toe marks. I ran the Mark Twenty-nine in a half circle, helmet camera running. Then I pulled as close as I could get and lowered the stand.

At this moment I still couldn't testify that that wasn't an empty suit. The only markings were the usual color-coded arrows, instructions for novices. They seemed faded.

I didn't much want to step down. Radioactive dust on my boots would be carried inside the Shreveshield. What I

could do was lean far over, gripping the belly casing of the
Mark Twenty-nine with legs and hands, and reach into the
suit with my imaginary arm.

It's like reaching into water rich with weeds and scum.
My fingers trail through varying texture. Yup, there's someone in there. It seems dehydrated. Corruption isn't obtrusive, and for this I'm grateful. Maybe the suit leaked. The
chest . . . a woman?

I reach around to touch the face lightly. Dry and ancient.
I grimace and reach, trailing phantom fingers through chest
and torso and abdomen.

"Gil, are you all right?"

"Sure, Hecate. I'm using my talent to see what I can feel
out."

"It's just that you didn't say anything for a while. What
talent?"

I never know how someone will react. "Wild talent. I've
got some PK and esper. It amounts to being able to feel
around inside a locked box with an imaginary arm and
hand. I can pick up things, little things. Okay?"

"Okay. What have you got?"

"She was a woman. Hecate, she's shorter than I am."

"Flatlander."

"Likely. No markings on the suit. Corruption isn't advanced, but she's dried out like a mummy. We should
check the suit for a leak." I continued to search as I talked.
"She's covered with medical telltales outside and in. Big,
old-fashioned things. Maybe we can date them. Her face
feels two hundred years old, but that's no sign of anything.
Air tanks are dry, of course. Air pressure's near zero. I
haven't found an injury yet. *Hel*-lo!"

"Gil?"

"Her oxygen flow is twisted right over, all the way up."
No comment.

I said, "Bet on a leak. Even money, a leak got her before
the radiation did."

"But what the hell was she doing there?"

"Funny how that thought occurred to both of us. Hecate, shall I collect the body?"

"I sure don't want it in my cargo hold. Gil, we *don't* want it on the Mark Twenty-nine. If you let me start up the waldo tugs, I can guide one to the body and move it that way."

"Start 'em up."

I rolled past the dead woman. I stayed wide of the line of footprints leading north-northeast, but that was what I was following.

. . . Bounding across a crater that was the most radioactive spot in the solar system, barring the sun itself and maybe Mercury. Frightened out of her mind? Even if there was no leak, it was a sane decision, giving herself maximum oxygen pressure, nothing left for later as she ran for the crater rim like a damned soul escaping hell. But what was she doing *in* the crater?

I stopped. "Hecate?"

"Here. I've started the waldo tugs. Shall I send you one?"

"Yah. Hecate, do you see what I see? The footprints?"

"They just stop."

"In the middle of Del Rey Crater?"

"Well, what do *you* see?"

"They start here in the middle, already running. They get halfway to the rim. The way my rad sensor is losing its lunch, I'd say she made a good run of it."

I trundled back to where I'd left the corpse. There was a signal laser in the service pack on my back. I spent a few minutes cutting an outline in the rock around the corpse.

"Hecate, how fast are those tugs?"

"Not exactly built for speed. It's more important that they don't turn over, but they'll do twenty-five K on the flat. Gil, you'll have your tug in ten minutes. How's your shield holding?"

I looked at the rad counters. Hell raged around me, but almost nothing was getting inside the shield. "Whatever got through, I probably brought it in on my boots. From *outside* Del Rey at that. I'd still like to leave."

"Gil, give me a camera view of the boots."

I wheeled into place and leaned far over the corpse's boots. Without Hecate's mention, I might never have noticed them. They were white. No decoration, no custom touches. Big boots with thick soles for lunar heat and cold, heavy treads for lunar dust. Built for the moon. But of course they would be even if they'd come straight from somewhere on Earth.

"Now the face. The sooner we find out who she was, the better."

"She's lying on her face."

"Don't touch her," Hecate said. "Wait for the tug."

I spent some of my waiting time easing a rope line under the body. Then I just waited.

A pair of arms on tractor treads was bumping toward me. It crossed crater after crater like it was bobbing on waves. It was making me queasy—if that wasn't the radiation—but the counters were quiet. I watched, and it came.

"I'll turn her over first," Hecate told me. Metal arms a little bigger than mine reached out. I lifted the rope. The arms went under and over the pressure suit and rotated.

"Hold that," I said.

"Holding."

Three centimeters from her faceplate I still couldn't see through. Maybe the camera could in one frequency or another. I said, "She's likely still got fingerprints, and we'll get her DNA, but not retina prints."

"Yah." The cargo tug backed and began moving away. "Get a view of where it was lying," Hecate said, but I already was. "Can you get closer? Okay, Gil, move out. You don't have to wait for the tug."

I passed another waldo tug as it was latching on to a canister. A third crawled over the crater rim ahead of me. I followed it over the rim and out.

I said, "I suppose nobody will disturb the scene of the crime? *If* there's a crime."

"We've got cameras on the waldo tugs. I'll set up a watch."

I watched the tug drag its canister toward the hole in the mound.

In my mind's eye, that hill was an ancient British barrow and all the ancient dead were pouring through the portal in its side, into the living world. But on this dead world what crawled out of the factory was only another set of arms riding tractor treads. Still, it was more deadly than any murderous old king's risen army.

Hecate Bauer-Stanson said, "Soon as we reach civilization, you start a search for missing flatlanders who could have wound up on the moon, *and* a search for that model pressure suit. We've already ruled out anything manufactured here. It's got to be flatlander."

"Not Belter?"

"The boots, Gil. No magnets. No *fittings* for magnets."

Well, hell. I'd just lost serious sleuthing points to Lawman Hecate Bauer-Stanson.

"Come on, Gil. We'll let the waldo tug take the body back."

"You can program it?"

"I can get it down from Helios Power One, which is where we're going. It'll be five hours en route. She's waited a long time, Gil; she'll wait a little longer. Come on."

"We taking the Mark Twenty-nine?"

"It could go back by itself . . . no. If anything happened . . . no, I think we bloody have to."

Hecate directed me: we set the Mark Twenty-nine on a rock ridge. I didn't guess why until she went back to the lemmy for an oxygen tank.

I asked, "Can we spare that?"

"Sure, the whole lunar surface is lousy with bound oxygen. I have to get the dust off, don't I?" She pointed the tank and opened the stopcock. Dust flew from the Mark Twenty-nine, and I stepped back.

"I mean, we wouldn't want to run out of breath."

"I packed plenty." She emptied the tank. Then we lifted the Mark Twenty-nine back into the lemmy's cargo hold. Hecate took us up and away.

How hard would she hit? Isaac Newton had it all worked out. I was trying to remember the equation, but it wouldn't come. Postulate a mass driver on the rim wall. Launch her in lunar gravity, three kilometers to the center. Up at forty-five degrees, down the same way, Sir Isaac had that straight, and land running. Keep running. Switch the oxygen to high and *run*, run for the far side of the rim, away from the—*rap rap rap*—mad scientist who had set her flying. "Gil?" *Rap rap rap.*

Knuckles on my helmet, an inch from my eye sockets. "Yah?" I opened my eyes.

We were falling toward a hole in the moon, a vast glittering black patch with fine lines of orange and green scrolling across it. As we dropped—as the lemmy's thrust pulled me into my couch, creating a sudden scary sense of down—I could make out the shape of a rounded hill with a few tiny windows glittering in the black.

Hecate said, "I thought you might freak if thrust started while you were asleep."

The orange and black logo was upside down. Helios Power One was sheathed in Black Power. I was amused, but it made sense: If the fusion plant went down, they'd still want lights, cooling, and the air recycler.

"What were you dreaming? Your legs were kicking."

I'd been dozing. What *had* I been dreaming? "Hecate, she turned the oxygen all the way up. Maybe there was no leak. Maybe it was to run better."

We settled into an orange and green mandala, Helios Power One's landing pad. Hecate eeled out of the cabin, then hustled me out. She said, "We'll see if her suit really has a leak. Anything else?"

"I was thinking a ship landed in the middle of Del Rey and left her there. A little ship, because you'd want the drive flame splashing into a crater, and those are little craters. Your lemmy could do that, couldn't it? And nothing would show—"

"Don't bet on that. It's always amazing what you can see from orbit. Anyway, *I'd* hate to ride *anything* into Del Rey Crater. Gil, I'm feeling a little warm."

"Just your imagination."

"Let's get to decontamination."

Copernicus Dome was three hundred kilometers northeast of Del Rey. Helios Power One was only a hundred, in a different direction, but both would be just a hop in the lemmy.

Copernicus Dome certainly had medical facilities for rad poisoning. Any autodoc off Earth could treat us for that. Radiation treatment must date back to the end of World War II! Nearly two centuries of improved techniques leave it difficult to die of radiation . . . but not impossible.

But *decontamination*, washing the radiation off something you want to live with afterward, is something else again. Only fission and fusion power plants would have decontamination facilities.

So far so good. But Helios Power One used He³ fusion. There's He³ all over the moon, absorbed onto the rocks. The helium-three nucleus includes two protons and a neutron. It fuses nicely with simple deuterium—which has to be imported—giving He⁴ and hydrogen and energy, but only at ungodly temperatures. The wonderful thing about He³ fusion is that it doesn't spit out neutrons. It's not radioactive.

Why would Helios Power One have decontamination rooms? It was another intelligence test, and I hadn't solved it yet. I could ask Hecate . . . eventually.

I have used decontamination procedures to get evidence off a corpse. At Helios Power One they were far more elaborate. There were rad counters everywhere. Still in my suit,

I went through a magnetic tunnel, then air jets. I crawled out of my suit directly into a zippered bag. The suit went somewhere else. Instruments sniffed me. Ten showerheads gave me the first decent shower I'd had since leaving Earth.

Then on to a row of six giant coffins. They were Rydeen MedTek autodocs, built long for lunie height, and I wondered: Why so many? They didn't look used. That was a relief. I lay down in the first and went to sleep.

I woke feeling sluggish and blurred.

Two hours had passed. I'd picked up less than two hundred millirem, but a red blinker on the readout was telling me to drink plenty of liquids and be back in the 'doc in twenty hours. I could picture Rydeen MedTek's funny molecules cruising my arteries, picking up stray radioactive particles, running my kidneys and urogenital system up to warp speed, shutting down half-dead cells that might turn cancerous. Clogging my circulation.

I used a phone to track Hecate Bauer-Stanson to the director's office.

She stood and turned as I came in, graceful as hell. When I try that, my feet always leave the floor. "Nunnally, this is Ubersleuth Gil Hamilton of the Amalgamated Regional Militia on Earth. Gil, Nunnally Sterne's the duty officer."

Sterne was a lunie, long-headed, very dark. When he stood to shake hands, he looked eight feet tall, and maybe he was. "You've done us a great favor, Hamilton," he said. "We didn't like having the waldo tugs shut down. I'm sure Mr. Hodder will want to thank you in person."

"Hodder is—?"

"Everett Hodder is the director. He's home now."

"Is it still nighttime?"

Sterne smiled. "Past noon, officially."

I asked, "Sterne, what do you want with radioactive sludge?"

I'd heard that sigh everywhere on the moon. *Flatlander. Talk slow.* Sterne said, "This isn't exactly a secret. It just wouldn't exactly be popular. The justification for these generators, on Earth and anywhere else, is that helium-three fusion isn't radioactive."

"Uh huh."

"The flatlanders started lobbing these packages into Del Rey in . . . early last century. They—"

"Boeing Corporation, USA, 2003 A.D.," I said. "Supposed to be 2001, but there was some kind of legal bickering. Makes it easy to remember."

"R-right. They kept it up for nearly fifty years. At the end the targeting was more accurate, and that's when they used the packages to paint that VERBOTEN sign across the crater. You must have—"

"We saw it."

"It could just as easily have been COCA-COLA. Well, deuterium-tritium fusion was better than fission, but it wasn't much cleaner. But when we finally got the helium-three plants going, it all turned around.

"We ship He³ to Earth by the ton. When we had enough money, we built four He³ plants on the moon, too. Del Rey Crater was out of business. And that held for another fifty years."

"Sure."

"What's finally knocked the bottom out is this new solar electric paint. Black Power, they call it. It turns sunlight into electricity, just like any solar power converter, but you spray it on. Place your cables and then spray over them. All you need is sunlight and room.

"On Earth they're still buying He³, and we can keep that up until your eighteen billion flatlanders start spraying the tops of their heads for power."

"You use it yourselves?"

"Stet. Black Power is a great invention, but it's so cheap that it's no longer feasible for us to build *new* He³ fusion plants. You see? But running the old ones is still cheaper than the paint."

I nodded. Hecate was pretending she already knew all this.

"So my job is safe. Except that He³ fusion has to be ten times hotter than D-T fusion. The plant is starting to leak heat. Fusion is running slow. We have to inject a catalyst, something to heat up the He³. Something that fissions or fuses at a lower temperature."

Sterne was enjoying himself. "Wouldn't it be nice if there was something already measured out in standard units and uniform proportions, just lying around ready to pick up—"

"Stet. I see it."

"This radioactive goo from Del Rey Crater works fine. It hasn't lost much of its kick. The processor doesn't do much more than pop off the boosters and lift off the dust."

"How?"

"Magnetically. We had to build an injector system, of course, with a neutron reflector chamber. We had to install these decontamination rooms and the autodocs and a human doctor on permanent call. Nothing is simple. But the canisters—we just pop them in and let them heat up until the stuff sprays out. We've been using them for two years. Eventually the waldo tugs moved enough canisters that we noticed the body. Hamilton, who was she?"

"We'll find out. Sterne, when this leaks out—" I saw his theatrical wince. "Sorry—"

"Don't say *leak*."

"Nothing gets attention like a murder. Then the media will all be looking at a fusion plant that was supposed to be radiation-free that you guys have got running radioactive. We can keep that *half*-secret for a day or two while we thrash around and you work on your story. If you'll do the same."

Sterne looked puzzled. "It was all fairly public, but . . . yes. Be glad to."

Hecate said, "We need phones."

We bought water bottles from a dispenser wall in the technicians' lounge. The lounge had a recycler booth, too. Hecate hadn't gotten nearly the dose I had, but we were both taking in water and funny molecules, and we'd be needing the recycler a lot.

There were four phones. We settled ourselves under the eyes of curious techs and turned on privacy dampers. I called the Los Angeles ARM.

A message light was blinking on Hecate's phone. I watched her ignore it while she talked rapid-fire in mime. I waited.

It always takes forever to connect, and you never learn the problem. No satellite in place? Lightning sends its own signals? Someone left a switch point turned off? Muslim Sector is tapping ARM communications, badly? Sometimes a local government tries that.

But a perfect multiracial androgynous image was inviting me to speak my needs.

I tapped in Jackson Bera's code. I got Jackson explaining that he wasn't there.

"Got a locked room for you, Jackson," I told the hologram. "See if Garner has an interest. I need an ancient pressure suit identified. We think it was made on Earth. I can't send the suit itself; it's radioactive as hell." I faxed him the videotape I'd taken in Del Rey Crater, dead woman, footprints, and all.

That should get their attention.

Hecate was still occupied. Given a free moment, I called Taffy in Hovestraydt City. "Hi, love, the lu—"

"I'm off performing surgery," the recording cried wildly. "The villagers say I'm mad, but this day I have created *life*! If you want the *heeheehee* patient to call back, leave your vital stats at the chime."

Bong! I said, "Love, the lunie law has me halfway around the moon looking at something interesting. Sorry about tomorrow. I can't give you a time frame or a number. If the monster wants a mate, I'll look around."

Hecate had been watching me as she talked. Now she rang off, grinning. "You'll get your view of Del Rey," she told me. "None of the sputniki are handy, but I got a Belt miner to do the job for a break in his customs fee. He'll do a low pass over Del Rey. Forty minutes from now."

"Good."

"And I've got another bugful of men coming here. We can send the Mark Twenty-nine back with one of them. Who was that?"

"My highly significant other."

She lifted an eyebrow. "You have others of lesser significance?"

I lied to keep things simple. "No, we're lockstepped."

"Ah. Next?"

"I sent what we've got on the suit to the ARM. If we're lucky, I'll get Luke Garner's attention. He's old enough to recognize that suit. And your message light's doing back flips."

She tapped *acknowledge*. A male head and shoulders spoke to her, then fizzed out. Hecate said, "Shreve Development wants to talk to me. Want in?"

"Is that the guy who loaned us—"

"I expect it's Yonnie's boss." She dialed and got a lunie computer construct who put her straight through.

He was a beanpole lunie, young but balding, his fringe of black hair a tightly coiled ruff. "Lawman Bauer-Stanson? I'm Hector Sanchez. Are you currently in possession of a piece of Shreve Development property?"

Hecate said, "Yes. We arranged the loan through Ms. Kotani, your chief of security, but I'm sure she—"

"Yes, of course, of course. She consulted my office, all most proper, and if I'd been available, I'd have done just what Ms. Kotani—but Mr. *Shreve* is extremely upset. We'd like the device back at once."

This was starting to feel peculiar. Hecate hesitated, looking at me. I opened the conference line and said, "Shall we decontaminate the device first?"

Faced by two talking heads, he became flustered. "Decontaminate? For what?"

"I'm not at liberty—I'm Gil Hamilton, by the way, with the ARM. Happened to be available. I'm not at liberty to discuss details, but let's say that there was a spacecraft involved, and citizens of Earth, and—" I let a stutter develop. "I-if we hadn't had the, the *device*, it would have been an impossible situation. Im*poss*ible. But some r-radioactive material got tracked inside the S-shreveshield— Is that how you pronounce it?"

"Yes, perfect."

"So we need to know, Mr. Sanchez. We sprayed any dust off with an oxygen tank, but n-now what? Shall we run it through decontamination at Helios Power One? Or just return it as is? For that matter, may we turn it off? Or are there neutrons trapped in that field just waiting to be sprayed everywhere?"

Sanchez took a moment to collect himself. Thinking hard. Mr. Shreve—what would *he* want? It seemed their experiment had been used to clean up after a spacecraft accident involving celebrity flatlanders! Just as well that it was being hushed up. Witnesses might still remember a two-wheeled *thing* moving safely through radioactive debris. Meanwhile this ARM, this flatlander seemed scared spitless by the Mark Twenty-nine.

Ultimately Shreve Development would want the tale told. What they didn't want was noses poking into their experimental shield generator for details of construction.

Hector Sanchez said, "Turn it off. *That's* quite safe. We'll do our own decontamination."

"Police lemmy okay?"

"I . . . don't think so. We'll send a vehicle. Where are you?"

Hecate took over. "We'll bring it to Helios Power One. We're a bit busy now, so give us two or three hours to get it there."

She clicked off and looked at me. " 'May we turn it off?' "

"Playing dumb."

"Convincing. The accent helps. Gil, what's on your mind?"

"Standard practice. Hold something back. It lets a perp display guilty knowledge."

"Uh huh. You may find that's harder on the moon. There aren't so many of us, and communications are sacred. You can be dead a thousand ways because someone didn't speak, or didn't listen, or couldn't. But be that as it may, *what's on your mind*? Is this another talent?"

"Hunch, Hecate. Something funny's going on. Sanchez doesn't seem to know what it is. He's just worried. But this Mr. Shreve must be the Shreveshield Shreve, the inventor himself, the way Sanchez is acting. What does *he* want?"

"He's supposed to be retired, Gil. But if there was a radioactive spill somewhere—"

"*That's* what I mean. Something radioactive, he'd want the Mark Twenty-nine, but he'd want it *right now*. He doesn't. He'd want it where the spill happened, but no, he doesn't. He'll come get it at Helios Power One. Maybe it's more a matter of where he *doesn't* want the Mark Twenty-nine."

She mulled it over. "Suppose his man gets here and the Mark Twenty-nine hasn't arrived yet?"

I liked it. "Somebody might get upset."

"I'll fix it. Next?"

I stretched. "It'll be a while before we have anything to look at. Let's see if there's a commissary."

"You scout out dinner," she said. "I'll make their widget vanish, and then I want to check on the corpse."

There was no commissary and no restaurant, either. There was a coin-operated dispenser wall in the lounge. I glanced into the greenhouse: dead of night.

So we bought handmeals from the dispenser and took them into the greenhouse.

An artificial full Earth glowed overhead. The stars weren't flaming, but something about them . . . ah. They were color-coded. Deep red for Mars, brighter red for Aldebaran, violet for Sirius . . .

Lunies try to turn their greenhouses into gardens, and

there are always individual touches. There were fruits and
vegetables to be picked as dark surprises from a hill
sculpted into a shadowy sitting Buddha.

Hecate reported, "The body is en route. John Ling got us
two waldo tugs. The second one is keeping the first in view.
That way there's a camera watching the corpse at all
times." She stopped to spit cherry seeds. "Good man. And
Nunnally Sterne says he's set aside one of the handling
rooms for an autopsy. We'll do it through leaded glass, with
waldos."

I was carving a pear the size of a melon, partly by feel.
"What do you think we'll find?"

"What am I offered?"

"Well, radiation, of course, or a leak. No gunshot or stab
wounds or concussions—I'd have found that."

"Psi powers are notoriously undependable," she said.

I didn't take offense, because of course she was right. I
said, "I can generally count on mine. They've saved my
life more than once. They're just limited."

"Tell me."

So I told her a story, and we ate the pear and the
handmeals, and a quiet descended.

Taffy and I aren't exactly lockstepped. But Taffy and I
and Harry McCavity, her lunie surgeon, and Laura Drury,
my lunie cop, *are* lockstepped, and Taffy and I are affi-
anced to become pregnant someday. I used to like a complicated love life, but I've started to lose that. So the dark
and quiet companionship began to feel ominous, and I said,
just to be saying something, "She could have been poi-
soned."

Hecate laughed.

I persisted. "What if you murder someone, *then* freeze-
dry her, then toss her three kilometers in lunar gravity? You
don't expect anyone'll find her, not in Del Rey, but if
someone did—"

"Tossed how? A little portable mass driver on the rim?"

"Damn."

"Would you have found bruising?"

"Maybe."

"And *then* she made the footprints?"

Double damn. "If we had specs on our mass driver, we'd know how accurate it was. Maybe the footprints were already there and the killer just fired the body at where they ended. Then again, there aren't any portable mass drivers."

Hecate was laughing. "All right, who made the footprints?"

"Your turn."

"She walked in," Hecate said. "Trick was to erase any footprints that led in from the rim."

"Blast from an oxygen tank?"

"A lemmy doesn't carry *that* much oxygen. A serious spacecraft would. A spacecraft could just spray the whole area with the rocket motor, but ... Gil, a ship could just land *in* the crater, push her out, and take off. You said so yourself."

I nodded. "That's starting to look like *it*. Besides, why would anyone walk into Del Rey Crater?"

"What if the killer persuaded her she was wearing a rad-shielded suit?"

Riiight. Still too many possibilities. "What if there was something valuable hidden in there? A bank heist. A dime disk with ARM secret weapons on it."

"A secret map of the vaults under the Face on Mars."

"Down comes a lemmy to pick it up. Back goes a lemmy with the copilot left behind."

"How long ago? If it was forty or fifty years, say, your lemmy wouldn't even have a Shreveshield. It'd be a suicide mission."

Which narrowed the window a little. Hmm ...

"I never tried lockstepped," Hecate Bauer-Stanson said.

"Well, it's easier with four. And we're constantly being moved around, so getting together is a hobby in itself."

"Four?"

I stood. "Hecate, I need the recycler again."

"And I've probably got message lights."

* * *

The phones were signaling messages for both of us. Hecate punched hers up while I used the recycler. When I came out, she was beckoning frantically. I moved to her shoulder.

"This is Lawman Bauer-Stanson," she said.

The construct said, "Please hold for Maxim Shreve."

Maxim Shreve was seated in a diagnostic chair, a reclining traveler with an extended neck rest for his greater length. Old and sick, I judged, holding himself together by little more than will. "Lawman Bauer-Stanson, we need the Mark Twenty-nine back at once. My associates tell me that, it has *not* reached Helios Power One."

"Haven't they—? Will you hold while I try to find out?" Hecate punched *hold* and glared at me. "The Mark Twenty-nine's under a tarp with dirt on it. We can't uncover it because Hector Sanchez has landed a cargo shell in plain view of it. What do I say *now*?"

I said, "It isn't loaded yet. Your man has a lemmy flying around the site looking for more casualties. Tell him that, but don't admit there's been a crash."

She mulled it over for a moment, then put Shreve back on.

The old man was standing, dark and skeletally gaunt: Baron Samedi. Travel chair or no, in lunar gravity he could *loom*. The instant Hecate appeared, he was raging.

"Lawman Bauer-Stanson, Shreve Development has *never* been in trouble with the law. We're not only a *good* corporate citizen, we're one of Luna City's major sources of income! Ms. Kotani cooperated with your office when you expressed a need. I presume that need is over. What must I do to get the Mark Twenty-nine back quickly?"

I'd figured that out, but it wasn't a thing to be broadcast.

Hecate said, "Sir, the device hasn't even been loaded yet. My man on the spot is still searching for casualties, but her police vehicle is too big to get inside the, uh—" Hecate allowed herself a bit of agitation. "—site. Sir, lives may depend on your device. Are lives at stake at your end?"

Shreve seemed to have recovered his aplomb. He floated back into his chair. "Lawman, the device is *experimental*.

We've never put *any* test subject in an experimental Shreveshield without medical monitors, and I include whole herds of minipigs! What if the field hiccoughed with your man in it? Is she even a lunie citizen? Is her suit equipped with medical ports?"

"Yes, I see. I'll call Lawman Cervantes."

"Wait, Lawman. Did it work?"

Hecate frowned.

"Did the shield perform as it should? Is everyone all right? No radiation?"

Hecate said, "The, um, user tracked some radioactive material into the shield, but that certainly wasn't the Shreveshield's fault. It worked fine, far as we can tell."

Maxim Shreve's eyes rolled up in his head, and all his pain wrinkles smoothed out. In that instant it was as if his life had been vindicated. Then he remembered us.

"I wish you could tell me more of the circumstances," he said briskly. "We will *certainly* want recordings if our device resolved a calamity. *Without* frying anyone!"

"We'll have the device back in your hands within hours, and of course we're very grateful," Hecate said. "I expect we'll be able to tell you the complete story within the week, but even then it may be confidential for a time."

"That's all right, then. Good-bye, Lawman, ah, Bauer-Stanson." He was gone.

She didn't turn. "Now what?"

I said, "Tell your men to get the pilot inside."

"Pilots. Sanchez and a new voice heard from. Better if you invite them in, O Prince from a Foreign Land."

"All right."

"Cameras on their vehicle," she said.

"Um . . . stet. Hecate, what have you got to work with?"

"Six of my police. They've been setting up to examine the body. Two Helios personnel. They cooperated when we buried the Mark Twenty-nine, so they'll cooperate when we uncover it. Two police lemmies—"

"Stet. Here's what we do. One lemmy takes off out of sight. Then the other hovers while the first one lands. We only want the dust cloud and a fast shuffle of police lemmies while your men uncover the Mark Twenty-nine."

"This had better be worth the hassle." She got up and reached past me to connect my phone to the lunie cops outside. "Wylie, ARM Ubersleuth Hamilton wants to talk to your visitors. Then get back to me."

I waited.

Sanchez and a woman with short crisp blond hair fitted their heads into camera view. Bubble helmets still reflect light and hide a jawline. Sanchez said, "We came for the Mark Twenty-nine, Hamilton."

The woman edged him out. "Hamilton? I'm Geraldine Randall. We were told we could pick up the Shreveshield here. I hope it hasn't got itself lost."

Randall was in charge, very much so. I said, "No, no, not at all, but things are a bit complicated at present. Come in and wait, won't you."

"I'll be right in," Randall said with a glowing smile.

She was going to leave Sanchez to watch the damn cargo shell. "Both of you, please," I added. "You may have to sit in. I don't know what authority I have here. Probably whatever nobody else wants." Just a touch of bitterness showing.

She frowned, nodded.

I switched off. Hecate was still miming. My own message light was blinking, but I waited. Presently Hecate sat back and blew hair out of her eyes.

I said, "Sanity check. When you gave him details, Shreve *calmed down.* Yes?"

She thought about it. "I guess he did."

"Uh huh. But you didn't tell him anything reassuring. Device hasn't been loaded for return? It's sitting around the site of a disaster? Involving spacecraft and extralunar celebrities? Waiting for someone to use it? *Again?*"

Hecate said, "Maybe his med-chair doped him to stop a stroke. No, dammit, he was *lucid.* And who the hell is Geraldine Randall?"

* * *

"Bauer-Stanson? Hamilton? I'm Geraldine Randall." We stood, and my feet left the floor, and Randall reached up to shake hands with Hecate and down to shake hands with me. She was six feet five and lush, with short curls of buttery blond hair, full lips, and a wide smile. A short lunie in her forties, I judged her, carrying enough weight to round her out. "What news?"

"Cervantes says it's on the way," Hecate said. "Knowing Cervantes, it could mean he's almost ready to launch."

Sanchez looked miserable. Randall was losing her smile. "Hamilton, I hope you're using the device only for the purpose intended. Max Shreve is seriously worried about security."

I said, "Randall, I was pulled out of bed because there was flatlander politics involved, and I'm an ARM with the rank of Ubersleuth. If somebody's been high-handed, he'll have two governments on his tail, not just Shreve Inc."

"Persuasive," she said.

"Ms. Randall, it's all being recorded. Think of the movie rights!"

"Not persuasive. We may not hold those. The disaster didn't take place on our turf. Hamilton, we want the device back."

"Are you with Shreve Inc. or the government?"

"Shreve," she said.

"In what capacity?"

"I'm on the board."

She didn't look that old. "For how long?"

"I was one of the original six."

"Six?"

Hecate was offering coffee. Randall took one and added sugar and cream. She said, "Thirty-five years ago Max Shreve came to five of us with the designs for an active shield against radiation. Everything he told us proved out. He made us rich. There's not a lot I wouldn't do for Max Shreve."

"He sent you? He wants it back that urgently?"

She ran a long-fingered hand through her short curls.

"Max doesn't know I came, but he seemed very upset on the phone. I don't see it as that urgent myself, but I'm starting to wonder. *How many* lunie police have left eye tracks and fingerprints on the Mark Twenty-nine? And what do I have to do to get it back?"

Message light for Hecate. She picked up. I said, "It's probably incoming now. Randall, I suppose I'll sound naive, but I can't believe you're old enough—"

She laughed. "I was twenty-six. I'm sixty-one now. Lunar gravity is kind to human bodies."

"Would you try the same gamble again?"

She thought it over. "Maybe. I'm not sure a con man *could* have put together as good a package as Max had. He was a lunie; we could track him. He did very well at Luna City University. He could talk fast, too. Kandry Li wanted to go for a smaller version of the shield, and we watched Max talk her out of it. He made diagrams, charts, models, all on the spot. He played Kandry's own computer like a pipe organ. I think I could do his damn lecture myself."

"Do it."

She stared at me.

"I was just a kid when the Shreveshield came out. I wanted one just big enough for me. Why can't I have it?"

She laughed, trailed off. "Well. It doesn't scale up. You need a bigger template to retain the hysteresis effect that traps the neutrons. Otherwise the shield effect just fades out on you. That's what the—" She caught herself.

"Right," I said.

Hecate Bauer-Stanson flicked off her privacy. "It's down," she said. "You can collect it any time. Shall I give you some men to load it?"

"I'd be most grateful," Randall said to Hecate. She didn't have to tell Sanchez to see to it, because he was already leaving. To me she said, "We had to reconfigure the circuitry pattern. It's not the same fractal on the Mark Twenty-nine; it's not even related. Well, thank you both," and she was gone, too.

* * *

"Gil, you've got a message light."

Hecate watched over my shoulder as I played the message from the Los Angeles ARM. Split field, a computer composite of the dead woman's suit manifested next to Luke Garner in a travel chair.

Luke at 188 *was* paraplegic, had been for years, but he looked healthier than Maxim Shreve. Happier, too. He spoke rituals of courtesy, then, "We think your suit was customized from one of the pressure suits that came up with the first moon colony. Thing is, those suits were returned to NASA for study. Your deader really did get it from Earth. It's ninety to a hundred years old.

"So right now you're probably wondering, 'Why didn't she just buy a new pressure suit?' And the answer might be *these*." Luke's cursor highlighted points on the old suit. "Medical sensors. Those early suits didn't just keep an astronaut alive. NASA wanted to know what was happening to them. If they died, maybe the next one wouldn't.

"In the early space program the medical probes were invasive. You wince just reading about it. These later suits weren't so bad, but your deader may have upgraded them anyway. What she wanted was the medical ports on the suit. There are suits like that still being made, of course, but they're expensive and the sale would be remembered. Take your choice; she was secretive or cheap.

"Let me know, will you? And remember, criminals don't *like* locked rooms. They're usually accidents."

I watched the empty space where Luke had been. "Hecate, didn't Shreve say that Shreve Development labs have pressure suits with medical ports? We might've guessed that—"

"I bet they're a lot less than a hundred years old, Gil. You want to see them anyway? I'll arrange that."

Four off-duty technicians had been watching our antics. Now they seemed to be losing interest. I didn't blame them. I got up and paced for a bit, wondering if there was anything more I could do.

Hecate said, "I've got your overhead view, Gil."

"Put it on."

A camera was panning slowly across a shrinking moonscape tinted with violet from the fusion drive of a rising Belt trading ship. Del Rey Crater slid into view, shrinking. Little craters all the same size. Bits of silver in the little craters. Three bronze bugs . . . . *four* crawling around near the southern rim. We watched until Del Rey was sliding off the edge of the field, shrunk too small to show detail.

Then Hecate replayed it, slowing it, slower yet. "See it?"

It's amazing what you can see from orbit.

Waldo tugs had made random tracks all across the southern quarter of Del Rey, like the tunnels in an ant farm. Down there they had obscured the flow lines. But from up here . . .

Something on the southern rim had sandblasted Del Rey Crater from the rim as far as the battered central peak.

Down there would be surfaces clean of dust, sharp crater rims slightly rounded, minicraters erased. Down there you would see only details. Close up I had seen nothing of the overall fan-shaped pattern.

I didn't believe that had been done by a spacecraft's oxygen tanks. It was too intense. That smooth wash must have been made by the rocket motor itself.

"The footprints must have been made afterward," I speculated. "Anything earlier was washed out. I'm going to have to apologize to Luke."

"No. He called it," Hecate said. "Nobody sets out to make a locked room mystery. The perp was hiding something else. Now, he fired from the south rim? And prints made afterward lead from the center south-southeast. She ran *toward* the killer?"

"Right toward her only source of escape. And oxygen. And medical help."

"She was hoping for mercy," Hecate said.

I looked over at her. Hecate didn't seem unduly disturbed, only bemused. Whoever had set a woman down in that radioactive hell would not offer mercy.

I said, "She might have begged. Who knows? I know people who would have been gasping curses. She might run to the center to leave a message, then run away from it to distract the killer."

"Did you see a message?"

"No." I wasn't even sure I liked the notion. "That rocket flame had to be erasing *something*. It looks like the killer didn't have the guts to go into the crater, but propping his lemmy right on the rim took *some* nerve. Why? To erase footprints?"

"Gil, only a madman would trudge out into the middle of Del Rey Crater unless he already knew something was there." She caught my smile. "Like you did. But someone *might* peek over an edge. The perp erased the bootprints that led in from the edge. The ones in the center, he left."

"Could have waited and got them all. And any later message."

"Your turn," she said.

The last time I had read a murdered man's dying message, he'd been lying. But at least Chris Penzler hadn't erased it and then made me guess what it said!

"I need a nap," I said. "Give me a call when you know something."

It felt like I'd been asleep for some time. I was on the rug, totally comfortable in lunar gravity. I had a view of Lawman Hecate Bauer-Stanson's back. She was studying a diffuse rainbow glow. I couldn't see the hologram from down here.

I got to my feet.

Hecate had a split screen going. Through one holo window they were carving a woman like a statue of petrified wood. The band saw was running itself. I could see vague human shapes out of focus behind a wall of thick glass.

One of the slices was passing through a second window. The view would zoom in on some detail: arteries and sections through the liver and ribs. Details might fluoresce before the view backed off.

A third window showed the archaic suit.

"The damn trouble," I said, talking to myself because Hecate had her privacy on, "is that there's nobody to pull in. No witnesses, no suspects . . . *millions* of suspects. With a proper leak in her suit she could have died yesterday. With no leak she could have been out there ten years. More."

What if her suit was *new* when she lay down?

No. Even sixty years ago the missiles were still falling in Del Rey Crater. "From ten to sixty years. Even on the moon that's a million suspects, and *nobody* has an alibi to cover a fifty-year span."

A fourth window blinked on, showing a fingerprint—another—another—something unidentified— "Retina," Hecate said without turning. "Completely degraded. But I got fingerprints and partial DNA. Maybe the ARM can match them."

I said, "Boot them over to me."

She did. I called the Los Angeles ARM. I left a message on Bera's personal code, then got through to a duty clerk. He showed signs of interest when he realized I was calling from the moon. I gave him the dead woman to track down.

Hecate was looking at me when I clicked off. I said, "There are short lunies."

She said, "Bet?"

"What odds?"

She considered, and my phone blinked. I picked it up.

Valerie Van Scopp Rhine. Height: 1.66 meters. Born 2038 A.D., Winnetka, North America. Mass: 62 kg. Gene type . . . allergies . . . medical . . . She was forty or so when the picture was taken, a lovely woman with high cheekbones and a delicately shaped skull under a golden crest of hair. *No children. Single. Full partner, Gabriel's Shield, Inc., 2083–2091 A.D. No felony convictions. WANTED on suspicion of 28.81, 9.00, 9.20—*

Hecate was reading over my shoulder.

I said, "The codes mean she's wanted on suspicion of embezzlement, flight to escape arrest, violation of political boundaries, misuse of vital resources, and some other stuff as of thirty-six years ago."

"Interesting. Vital resources?"

"It used to be the custom; you named every possible crime and then trimmed. Boundaries—that's an old law. Here it means they think she escaped to space."

"Interesting. Gil, her suit isn't leaking."

"Isn't it?"

"There was a fair vacuum inside. We got traces of organics, of course, but it would have taken years—*decades* to lose *all* of her air and water."

I said, "Thirty-six years."

"All that time. In Del Rey Crater?"

"Hecate, at a distance her suit looked just like another of the Boeing packages, and nobody was looking, anyway."

"Then we can guess why the body's in such good shape. Radiation," Hecate said. "What's she supposed to have embezzled?"

I scrolled through the file. "Looks like funds from Gabriel's Shield. And Gabriel's Shield turns out to be a research group ... Two partners: Valerie Van Scopp Rhine and Maxim Yeltzin Shreve."

"*Shreve.*"

"Bankrupt in A.D. 2091, when Rhine allegedly disappeared with the funds." I stood up. "Hecate, I've got to go sharpen my skates. You can study this, or you can summon up a dossier on Maxim Shreve."

She stared, then laughed. "I thought I'd heard every possible way to say that. Go. Then drink some more water."

I waited for a woman to step out of the recycler booth, then went in.

Hecate had a display up when I got back.

Maxim Yeltzin Shreve. Height: 2.23 meters. Born 2044 A.D. *Outer Soviet, Moon. Mass: 101 kg. Gene type ... al-*

lergies ... medical ... No felony convictions. Married Juliana Mary Krupp 2061, divorced 2080. Children: none. Single. A videoflat of his graduation, looking like a burly soccer champ, *used with permission.* A holo taken at the launch of the fourth slowboat, the colony ship bound for Tau Ceti, bearing the larger model Shreveshield, in A.D. 2122. He didn't need a medical chair then, but he didn't look good. *Chairman of the board of Shreve Development 2091, retired November 2125.* Two years ago.

When your body gets sick enough, your mind starts to go, too. I could be putting too much weight on any oddities in this man's behavior.

I hit the key that got me the next dossier.

Geraldine Randall. Height: 2.08 meters. Born 2066 A.D., Clavius, Moon. Mass: 89 kg. Gene type ... allergies ... medical ... She'd had a problem carrying a child, corrected by surgery. *No felony convictions. Married Charles Hastings Chan 2080. Children: 1 girl, Marya Jenna.* She'd been at the launch of the fourth slowboat, too. *Member of the board of Shreve Development 2091.*

Over Hecate's shoulder they were still carving the dead woman. I understood why they were so casual about it. The remains of lunar dead become mulch, whatever can't be used as transplants. Hecate was listening to a running commentary, but if they'd found evidence of disease, she'd have told me.

Valerie Rhine hadn't rotted because radiation had fried all the bacteria in her body. She could have lasted a million years, a billion, without my hindrance.

I turned back to Maxim Shreve as he had been when he had registered as Shreve Development, a lunar corporation, thirty-six years ago. He was posing with five others, and one was Geraldine Randall. A younger man, he already looked sick ... or just worn down, working himself to death. It's one way to get rich. Give everything to your dream. Six years later, A.D. 2097 and looking a little better, he and his partners had an active shield up for patent.

Did lunies just get old quicker? I tapped Hecate's shoul-

der. She turned off privacy, and I asked, "How old are you,
Hecate?"

"I'm forty-two."

She met my stare. Older than me by one year and
healthy as a gymnast. The lunie doctor Taffy saw when I
wasn't around is in his sixties. I said, "Shreve must be sick.
He's less than ninety. What's his problem?"

"Doesn't it say?"

"I couldn't find it."

She slid into my spot and began diddling with the virtual
keys. "The file's been edited. Citizens don't have to tell all
their embarrassing secrets, Gil, but . . . he must be crazy.
What if he needed medical help and it wasn't in the records?"

"Crazy or guilty."

"You think he's hiding something?"

I said, "Call him."

"Now, Gil. Maxim Shreve is one of the most powerful
men on the moon, and I wasn't thinking of changing ca-
reers." She studied me, worried. "Are you just harrassing
the man in the hope he'll tell us something?"

I said, "It seems pretty clear what happened, doesn't it?"

"You're thinking he killed her and took the money himself. Set down in Del Rey and pushed her out of the ship,
still alive. But why not kill her first? Then there wouldn't
be any footprints or dying messages."

"Nope, you've only got half of it."

She flapped her arms in exasperation. "Go for it."

"First: Mark Twenty-nine. You said Shreve Development
has been trying to build a little shield ever since they got
the big ones. I believe it. Twenty-nine is a big number.
Maybe a small version is the *first* thing he tried. That's
what told him about the, what she said, hysteresis problem.

"Second: He didn't act like a thief running away with the
money. When he founded Shreve Inc., he acted like a man
who wants to build something and almost knows how. I
think he and Rhine spent all they had on experiments.

"Third: Someone sprayed part of the crater from the rim,

and I think that was Shreve. There's no sign he was in the crater except for Rhine's footprints, and we already know *something* was erased.

"Fourth: Why Del Rey Crater? Why walk around in the most radioactive crater on the moon?"

Hecate was looking blank. I said, "They were testing a prototype Shreveshield. That's why she walked in. I even know what he was hiding when he sprayed the crater."

She said, "I'll call him. Your theory; you talk."

Hecate looked around at me. "Mr. Shreve isn't taking calls. It says he's in physical therapy."

I asked, "Where's the Mark Twenty-nine now?"

"They took off almost an hour ago." It took her only a few seconds. "En route to Copernicus. That's the Shreve Inc. labs. ETA ten minutes."

"Good enough. Luke Garner's travel chair has a sender in it in case he needs a serious autodoc or even a doctor. What do you think? Would a lunie's chair have one, too?"

It took her longer (I got her coffee and a handmeal) to work her way through the lunar medical network. Finally she sighed and looked up and said, "He's in motion. Moving toward Del Rey Crater. I have a number for the phone in his chair, Gil."

"Futz! Always I get it almost right."

"Call him?"

"I'm inclined to wait for him to touch down."

She studied me. "He's going after the body?"

"Seems right. Any bets on what he might do with it?"

"It's a big moon." She turned back. "He's crossing Del Rey. Slowing. Gil, he's going down."

"Phone him."

His phone must have been buzzing during the landing. When he answered, it was by voice, no picture. *"What?"*

I said, "The thing about poetic justice is that it requires a poet. I'm Ubersleuth Gil Hamilton, with the ARM, Mr. Shreve. On the moon by coincidence."

"I'm a *lunie* citizen, Hamilton."

"Valerie Rhine was of Earth."

"Hamilton, I'm supposed to run now. Let me set my headphones and get on the track."

I laughed. "You do that. Shall I tell you a story?"

I heard irregular puffing, less like a sick man running on an exercise track in low gravity than like the same man climbing out of a spacecraft. No sound of fiddling with headphones: they'd be already in place inside his bubble helmet.

Fair's fair. I said, "I'm perched on the rim of Del Rey Crater, safely protected by my Shreveshield, vidding you through a telescopic lens."

Hecate covered her face, muffling laughter.

"I don't have time for this," Shreve said.

"Sure you do. With the radiation you'll be facing in the next few minutes, you're already dead. That is, if you intend to go somewhere with a body. Do you have a portable Shreveshield? A Mark Twenty-eight or Twenty-seven? An experiment that almost worked? I admit I thought you'd wait for the Twenty-nine."

The puffing continued.

"If you checked out an early experimental Shreveshield, we can track that. They were handy before you retired, but now you'd have to go through someone and get some men to load it, too."

Puffing. Regular exercise: a man on a track or the same man pulling a heavy cart across a bumpy craterscape. He was going to bluff it out.

"Retiring took you out of the system, Shreve. You weren't on top of things when Helios Power One started sending waldo tugs into Del Rey, and when Lawman Bauer-Stanson asked your Ms. Kotani if she could borrow your new prototype, you didn't know it for hours."

He said, "Where is she?"

Hecate spoke. "We've already dissected it, Mr. Shreve."

The puffing became much faster.

I said, "Shreve, I know you're not afraid of the organ

banks. The hospitals wouldn't take anything you've got. Come in and tell your story."

"No. But I'll—tell *you* a story, Ubersleuth. Lawman.

"It's about two brilliant experimenters. One didn't have any money sense, so the other had to keep track of expenses when he'd rather have been working on the project. We were in love, but we were in love with an idea, too."

His breathing had become easier. "We developed the theory together. I *understood* the theory, but the prototypes kept burning out and blowing up. And every time something happened, Valerie knew exactly what went wrong and how to fix it. Warble the power source. More precision in the circuitry. I couldn't keep up. All I knew was that we were running out of money.

"Then one day we had it. It worked. She *swore* it worked. We already had all the instruments we needed. I spent our last few marks on videotape. Camera. *Stacks* of batteries. The—we called it the Maxival Shield—it ate power like there was no tomorrow.

"We went out to Del Rey Crater. Valerie's idea. Test the device and film the tests. Anyone who saw Valerie dance around in Del Rey Crater would throw funding at us with both hands."

"Gil, he's taking off."

Too fast. I suddenly realized why his breathing had eased. He'd left his Mark Twenty-odd sitting in the dust. Maybe it had quit working; maybe he had stopped caring.

I asked, "Shreve, what went wrong?"

"She went out into Del Rey with the prototype. Just walking, turning to cross in front of the camera, then some gymnastics, staying within the shield effect, and all with that glow around her and her face shining in the bubble helmet. She was beautiful. Then she looked at the instruments and started screaming. I could see it on my own dials; the field was just gradually dying out.

"She was screaming, 'Oh, my God, the shield's breaking down!' And she started running. 'I think I can get to the rim. Call Copernicus General Hospital.' "

"Running with the shield? Wasn't it too heavy?"

"How did you know that?"

Hecate said, "Gil, he's just cruising along the crater rim. Hovering."

I nodded to her. I told Shreve, "That was our biggest problem. What were you erasing when you sprayed rocket flame across the crater? I figure your shield generator was big. You had it on some sort of cart that Rhine could pull. She pulled a superconducting cable. She left her power source with you."

"That's right, and then she ran away and left it. If a hospital got her, every cop on the moon would want to look into our alleged radiation shield. The doctors would have to know exactly what she was exposed to. We didn't have a tenthmark left. Nobody would believe we had anything, what with Valerie glowing in the dark, and if anyone did, he could get the designs on the four o'clock news."

"So you pulled it back."

"Hand over hand. Was I supposed to leave it sitting out on the moon? But she saw me doing it. She—I don't know what she was thinking—she ran away, toward the center of the crater. I'd already had more radiation than I wanted, but those tracks . . . not just the footprints but—"

"The tracks of the cable," I said. "All over the dust like a rattlesnake convention."

"Anyone could see them just by looking over the rim! So I moved the lemmy up onto the crater wall and turned it on its side and used the rocket. I don't know what Valerie was thinking by then. Did she write some kind of last message?"

Hecate said, "No."

"Even if she did, who would see it? But I picked up too much radiation. It's nearly killed me."

"Well, it kind of did," I said. "Rad sickness retired you early. It was part of what tipped me off."

"Hamilton, where are you?"

"Wait, Hecate! Shreve, it wouldn't be prudent to answer."

Hecate said edgily, "Gil, he's accelerating straight up. What was *that* all about?"

"Last gestures. Right, Shreve?"

"Right," he said, and turned off his phone.

I told Hecate, "When his Mark Twenty-odd shut down, he had nothing left. He went looking for me. Spray my ship with rocket flame. I lied about being on the rim of Del Rey, but we don't know what he's flying, Hecate, and I don't want him to know where we are. Even a lemmy could do severe damage if you dropped it on Helios Power One at maximum thrust. What's he doing now?"

"Coasting. I think . . . I think he's out of fuel. He burned up a lot, hovering."

"We should keep watching."

Two hours later Hecate said, "His travel chair just quit sending."

"Where did he come down?"

"Del Rey, near the center. I want to look at it before I assume anything."

"It could have been very messy. He was a hero, after all." I yawned and stretched. I could be back in Hovestraydt City by tomorrow morning.

✳

AFTERWORD

SCIENCE/MYSTERY FICTION

I have always gotten too involved with my characters.

I certainly did while finishing "Death by Ecstasy."

Even now, I don't generally write of purely black-hearted villains. Loren the organlegger was my first. I finished the first draft of that story at six o'clock one morning . . . went to bed . . . stared at the ceiling . . . gave up at about ten and went looking for company.

I finished rewriting that scene a week or two later, at six in the morning. I gave up trying to sleep at around eight. Stopping Loren's heart with my imaginary hand was a rough experience. It may not shake you, but it shook me.

That was the first of the tales of Gil Hamilton of the Amalgamated Regional Militia, the police force of the United Nations. The second story bubbled in my head for a long time before I wrote down anything but notes.

Bouchercon is a gathering of mystery fans held annually in memory of Anthony Boucher, for many years the editor of *Ellery Queen's Mystery Magazine* and of *Fantasy and Science Fiction*, and the author of the classic "Nine-Finger Jack." At the first Bouchercon, I already had in mind a most unusual crime with a most unusual motive. I outlined that crime to an audience during a panel discussion. "Death by Ecstasy" just sort of grew, but "The Defenseless Dead" was meticulously plotted in advance, and it didn't hit me

353

nearly as hard. Maybe it should have. The story and the assumptions behind it are terrifying, and uncomfortably real.

Gil the Arm is one of my favorite characters. Riiight. Thirty years of writing, and still there are only these five stories! If I like him so freezing much, why not write more stories?

Because following two sets of rules is hard work, that's why.

A detective story is a puzzle. In principle the reader can know what crime was committed, by whom, and how and where and why, before the story hits him in the face with it. He must have enough data to make this obviously true, and there must be only one answer possible.

Science fiction is an exercise in imagination. The more interesting an idea, the less justification it needs. A science-fiction story will be judged on its internal consistency and the reach of the author's imagination. Strange backgrounds, odd societies following odd laws, and unfamiliar values and ways of thinking are the rule. Alfred Bester overdid it, but see his classic *The Demolished Man.*

Now, how can the reader anticipate the detective if all the rules are strange?

If science fiction recognizes no limits, then . . . maybe the victim was death-wished from outside a locked room, or stabbed through a keyhole by a psychic killer who ESPed where he was standing. Walls may be transparent to a laser outside the visible band. Perhaps the alien killer's motive really is beyond comprehension. Can the reader really rule out time travel? Invisible killers? Some new device tinkered together by a homicidal genius?

More to the point, how can I give you a fair puzzle?

With great difficulty, that's how. There's nothing impossible about it. You can trust John Dickson Carr, and me, not to bring a secret passageway into a locked-room mystery. If there's an X-ray laser involved, I'll show it to you. If I haven't shown you an invisible man, there isn't one. If the ethics of Belt and lunie societies are important, I'll go into detail on the subject.

Detective and science fiction (and fantasy and police procedurals) do have a lot in common. Internal consistency. Readers. All these genres attract readers who like a challenge, a puzzle. Whether it's the odd disappearance of a weapon (a glass dagger hidden in a flower vase full of water) or the incomprehensibly violent behavior of a visiting alien (he needs a rest room, bad), the question is, What's going on? The reader is entitled to his chance to out-think the author.

Much detective fiction, and most science fiction, is also sociological fiction. See Asimov's *The Caves of Steel* and *The Naked Sun*, and Brunner's *Puzzle on Tantalus*. Bester's *The Demolished Man* is that, and is also an involuted psychological study, a subject well suited to its society of telepaths. Psychological studies are common in crime fiction, too. So are puzzles in basic science, like Asimov's Wendell Urth stories. Garrett's Lord Darcy operates in the world of working magic, but the stories are puzzles in internal consistency. Ellery Queen would feel at home with them.

Mystery/sf needed defending once upon a time, back when Hal Clement took up John W. Campbell's challenge (*Needle*, with an intelligent parasite/symbiote as detective), but you're not really in doubt, are you? We could shape a sizable library from detective science fiction. *Needle* is half a century old, and there are older yet if we include Poe's "The Murders in the Rue Morgue." (His murderous ape was more fiction than animal research). Detectives seem to live beyond their stories: Asimov's Dr. Wendell Urth and Lije Bailey, Randall Garrett's Lord Darcy (fantasy/detective fiction!), and scores of pastiches (particularly stories by Poul Anderson and Gene Wolfe) in which Sherlock Holmes's niche is taken by aliens, mutants, downloads, artificial intelligences, or robots.

In the mixed marriage of mystery and science fiction there are pitfalls. A 1950s novel of matter duplicators, *Double Jeopardy*, suffered from internal inconsistency: a coin reversed except for the lettering, a crucial error in multiplication. Edward Hoch writes good tight puzzles, but his near-future mystery *The Transvection Machine* twisted human nature far beyond credibility, merely to make a tighter puzzle.

And me?

I was working on "ARM," which becomes the third story in this volume, before I ever sold a story. Frederick Pohl (*Galaxy*) turned down that primitive version. So did John W. Campbell (*Analog*). What came of that was two letters telling me why mystery/sf is so difficult to write, and what was wrong with "ARM" in particular.

"ARM" needed help. There were too many characters. There were holes in the science, the sociology, the logic. The puzzle grew far too complex.

So I put it away until I could learn more about my craft.

Most of my stories are puzzle stories. Naturally a lot of them become crime and detective stories.

"The Hole Man" involves murder committed with a weapon no normal jury could be expected to understand. "The Meddler" showed a Mike Hammer clone trying to operate with an alien sociologist at his elbow. "The Tale of the Genie and the Sisters" showed Scheherazade in a detective role. "All the Myriad Ways" was a crime story about quantum mechanics. "The Deadlier Weapon" and "$16,940.00" are straight crime stories.

These aside, I generally write more than one story within any imaginary world. It isn't laziness. Honest! It's just that, having designed a detailed, believable, even probable future, I often find that I have more to say about it than will fit in a story.

So it comes about that Gil the ARM lives and works in the 2120s of the "known space" line of history, whose story bulks at a million words as of this writing, including stories by other authors (within the Man-Kzin Wars volumes) and a half-written novel, *The Ringworld Throne*. Most of these novels and short stories take place in human space, thirty light-years across, but lines of development include the Ringworld (200 light-years galactic north) and the galactic core (33,000 light-years toward Sagitarius.) For crime stories set later in "known space," see the Beowulf Shaeffer stories in *Crashlander.*

Five sociological stories that are also crime stories took place along another timeline, the world of JumpShift, Inc., and "Flash Crowd." The assumption is that teleportation was perfected in the 1980s, and by the 1990s a network of instant-transportation booths has spread across the world. Alibis disappear, and a new kind of killer appears. He's the guy who would otherwise have moved away by now. Instead he finds himself living next door (effectively) to his boss and his business rival and his ex-spouse and the guy who has owed him thirty bucks for six years and denies it. Where can he go? So he kills.

Footfall, written with Jerry Pournelle, includes a murder puzzle among the alien invaders of Earth, though the Herdmaster's Advisor isn't even dead until a hundred thousand words into the book. By then you should know the *fithp* well enough to guess who, and how, and why.

Ten years after my first try, with several crime/sf stories in print, I was ready to have another look at "ARM."

"ARM" looked bad. I had to rewrite from scratch. I saved what I could: some nice descriptions, including the surreal murder scene, a couple of characters, and the strongest bones in the plot skeleton. I took out some verbal thrashing about in bizarre restaurants. Gil the ARM replaced Lucas Garner onstage. I took out an irrelevant nightmare, and a coin-operated surgeon device capable of implanting the bud of a new organ: wrong era, and it made things too easy for the killer. I took out the FyreStop device, which killed by suppressing chemical reactions: a fun thing, but unnecessary, and it complicated the bejeesus out of the plot. Losing that cost me three or four suspects, and good riddance.

(But look for excellent handling of the FyreStop idea in

The D.A.G.G.E.R. Affair, an old Man from U.N.C.L.E. story by David McDaniel.)

When I showed the result to Jerry Pournelle, he made me rewrite it. He also showed me where the organleggers came in.

In general, then, I corrected the flaws John Campbell and Frederick Pohl had pointed out. I wish Campbell had lived to see "ARM."

How likely is Gil Hamilton's future?

I don't see how we can avoid the crowding or the rigid, dictatorial population control without the blessing of a major war or plague. As for the conquest of the solar system, one can hope. And as for the UN organ banks . . .

One of my oldest stories, "The Jigsaw Man" laid out the basis of the organ bank problem. If Jeffrey Dahmer had been executed in a hospital, disassembled like a jigsaw puzzle, he could have saved as many lives as he took. So can any adult who has committed a capital crime. Or any child whose crime is deemed to be adultlike . . . and hey, kids are committing a lot of murders these days, and wouldn't you rather have a fifteen-year-old's organs than an elderly Charles Manson's? If that approach still leaves the Red Cross needing whole blood and patients crying for eyes and kidneys, then Rush Limbaugh and John Bobbitt are constantly violating principles of political correctness. And what about the guy who thinks he can ruin a wetlands just because he paid for the land?

Where do we stop?

Ever since publication of "The Jigsaw Man," letters have been flowing in. They come with clippings and photocopies of newspapers stories. An army of readers (the Reluctant Donor Irregulars?) seems ready to alert me to developments regarding transplants and organ banks.

One tells of an interschool debating competition. The question: Shall condemned criminals be executed by dismantling, the parts to be reserved for organ transplants?

The reader who informed me was horrified: the majority voted yes.

You can watch the future fanning out in three directions. Transplanted organs succeed more often and the patients live longer, but prosthetic devices seem to be improving even faster. You don't need a knee transplant; the artificial version is better. Your artificial heart could survive you.

The third choice isn't generating news, but it's important. Clone and grow your own replacement organs! Rejection wouldn't be a problem. You would have to grow what you need before it's urgent, and if you didn't prepare ... then your need for a new liver is no act of God, but your own damned fault. *Now* whom shall we break up?

One evening last month, I got a phone call from George Scithers. He followed up with newspaper clippings. India has been disassembling condemned criminals for transplants since 1964.

The practice is informal. Donor has been condemned to death. Method: bullet in the neck. Afterward the doctors can have him. But the executioner shoots badly, so the organs are taken while Donor still lives.

Transplants are usually rejected because the Indian doctors don't bother much with matching types. But, by God, they're fresh. And you can't blame Larry Niven for pointing out the possibilities.

They're doing it in China, too. A photocopied page in my mail tells me how to get a brochure on the subject from Human Rights Watch, Publicity Department. "Discusses evidence demonstrating that China's heavy reliance on executed prisoners as a source of transplant organs entails a wide range of human rights and medical ethics violations."

Organlegging in our own cities is today's news: unwilling donors found bleeding in the streets, kidneys and hearts missing.

Meanwhile, Bill Rotsler's quadruple-bypass operation moved veins from his legs into his heart. No rejection problem. My own knee is healing nicely from an operation that didn't involve scalpels, just a laser to burn out a torn meniscus. The woman undergoing physical therapy on the stationary bike next to me is doing fine as her flesh heals around a fully artificial knee. Stay tuned. We're shaping the future now.

EXPLORE THE WORLDS OF DEL REY AND SPECTRA.

Get the news about your favorite authors.
Read excerpts from hot new titles.
Follow our author and editor blogs.
Connect and chat with other readers.

Visit us on the Web:
www.Suvudu.com

Like us on Facebook:
Facebook.com/delreyspectra

twitter
Follow us on Twitter:
@delreyspectra

DEL REY • SPECTRA